Praise for

Once Persuaded, Twice Shy

"Smart, swoony, and hilarious, *Once Persuaded, Twice Shy* was the *Persuasion* retelling I didn't know I needed. I fell in love with the brilliant Anne on page one and never looked back. Utterly charming!"

—Lynn Painter, *New York Times* bestselling author of
The Love Wager

"Jane Austen's *Persuasion* is beloved for its capable, introspective heroine and the quiet romantic who's been carrying a torch for her all these years . . . and Melodie Edwards delivers the same in her pitch-perfect modern retelling. *Once Persuaded, Twice Shy* will have you rooting for Anne to learn to live her own life, reading *everything* into the tiniest interaction with the one-who-got-away Ben Wentworth, and cackling at the antics of a certain theater-loving goose. I loved it!"

—Alicia Thompson, bestselling author of
Love in the Time of Serial Killers

"Melodie Edwards charmed me from start to finish with this fresh and original take on a classic tale. . . . [The] small-town high jinks are delightful, and the tension filled, slow-burn second chance romance made me swoon. Readers will root for smart and selfless Anne to find her way back to Ben, the one who got away, and will cheer as she learns to draw boundaries with her family and take back her life."

—Meredith Schorr, author of *As Seen on TV*
and *Someone Just Like You*

"Jane Austen meets *Parks and Rec* in this delightful second chance romance overflowing with heart and small-town charm. With its wonderfully quirky cast of supporting characters, Melodie Edwards's enchanting reimagining will have readers rooting for Anne to find herself as much as find her way back to Ben—and likely wanting to plan a trip to Niagara-on-the-Lake! The perfect read to cozy up and fall in love with."

—Holly James, author of *The Déjà Glitch*

"With hilarious supporting characters and satisfying depth . . . Edwards remains true to the classic while deftly modernizing it, and I loved falling into this fresh, fun story about what happens when you regret letting The One get away."

—Sierra Godfrey, author of *The Second Chance Hotel*

Praise for

Jane & Edward

"Instantly captivating and utterly charming. I found myself smiling (sometimes through tears) from start to finish. This sexy, funny, razor-sharp rom-com is one of the best books I've read all year. Melodie Edwards delivers a first-rate, modern take on the classic *Jane Eyre*, so deliciously romantic that Charlotte Brontë herself would be dazzled."

—Lori Nelson Spielman, *New York Times* bestselling author of
The Star-Crossed Sisters of Tuscany

"Razor sharp, wickedly funny, and touchingly poignant, I was thoroughly beguiled by Melodie Edwards's debut novel, *Jane*

& Edward. Rarely have I been so thoroughly invested in a novel's outcome. This is an absolute must-read!"

—Jenn McKinlay, *New York Times* bestselling author of *Summer Reading*

"Melodie Edwards' witty reimagining of *Jane Eyre* gives us a pitch-perfect protagonist who's somehow even more endearing than the original. . . . This book is brimming with heart; characters that stick with you; and smart, timeless insights about life and love."

—Ashley Winstead, author of *The Boyfriend Candidate*

"Truly a masterpiece that will set the bar impossibly high for other future retellings. . . . A beautifully heartwarming and enchanting story destined to be a comfort read for countless bookworms."

—The NerdDaily

"A jaunty homage to the beloved classic novel."

—Danielle Jackson, author of *The Accidental Pinup*

"Delivers the Jane that we've all been dying for—a thoroughly modern, pragmatic, and droll heroine we can all adore. Set in the savagely funny ecosystem of a storied Toronto law firm, *Jane & Edward* is a sophisticated, sexy, and hilarious retelling that nails the intricacies and idiosyncrasies of workplace relationships and forging your own path in the world." —Jessica Martin, author of *For the Love of the Bard*

"Edwards's debut is a retelling that will please both diehard Brontë devotees and contemporary romance readers."

—*Library Journal*

Once Persuaded, Twice Shy

A Modern Reimagining of Persuasion

MELODIE EDWARDS

BERKLEY ROMANCE
NEW YORK

BERKLEY ROMANCE
Published by Berkley
An imprint of Penguin Random House LLC
penguinrandomhouse.com

Library of Congress Cataloging-in-Publication Data

Names: Edwards, Melodie, author.
Title: Once persuaded, twice shy : a modern reimagining of
Persuasion / Melodie Edwards.
Description: First edition. | New York : Berkley Romance, 2024.
Identifiers: LCCN 2023016609 (print) | LCCN 2023016610 (ebook) |
ISBN 9780593440797 (trade paperback) | ISBN 9780593440803 (ebook)
Subjects: LCSH: Austen, Jane, 1775-1817--Parodies, imitations, etc. |
LCGFT: Romance fiction. | Novels. | Derivative works.
Classification: LCC PR9199.4.E356 O53 2024 (print) |
LCC PR9199.4.E356 (ebook) | DDC 813/.6—dc23/eng/20230720
LC record available at https://lccn.loc.gov/2023016609
LC ebook record available at https://lccn.loc.gov/2023016610

First Edition: February 2024

Printed in the United States of America
1st Printing

Book design by Kristin del Rosario
Interior art: Leaves © Tatyana Pavlovets/Shutterstock.com

With love to Mum,
who made the bookshelves and the books
the architecture of our home

Dear Reader,

". . . her convenience was always to give way—she was only Anne."

That dismissive "only Anne" is the way we're introduced to heroine Anne Elliot in the 1817 novel *Persuasion*; and it's how Anne's family and much of the book's cast treat her—like forgettable wallpaper.

Quite a discouraging opening for one of Jane Austen's most intelligent and sophisticated heroines. But when I reread the novel for the umpteenth time, planning for this reimagining, I looked past the compliant, suppressed, old-before-her-time Anne, to the incredibly competent woman underneath. In the original novel, it's Anne who actually draws up what would be an effective budget in response to her family's debt, Anne who tends to the servants and tenants on the Kellynch estate before leaving, Anne who looks after her injured nephew and sends for the doctor, Anne who diplomatically soothes the grievances of Mary and others, and Anne who triages, acts, and directs everyone when they are frozen in the critical moments after Louisa Musgrove's accident.

". . . no one so proper, so capable as Anne!" is what Captain

Wentworth says, by the time we are halfway through the novel—and *that* is perhaps the most accurate assessment of our heroine.

It was this version of Anne that I wanted to bring forward in my novel; this version of Anne that could avail herself of the opportunities afforded to a modern woman and emerge as Anne Elliot, executive director of the Elysium Theatre Festival, town councilor, mentor, and boss. She is powerful and yet still powerless, because despite all this she retains that fatal flaw—she is defined and valued only by her ability to be of use to others, now as burdened by her professional responsibilities as by her familial ones. What does it look like, to get out from under that mantle of responsibility? How can she retain the work and the relationships worth saving, while taking back some of her control, choices, and boundaries?

These are the issues I wanted to explore in writing *Once Persuaded, Twice Shy*, issues that are as relevant to women now as they were in the nineteenth century, along with questions like: Was Anne right to turn down Wentworth the first time, and let them both grow up? How can you balance the heart and the head in evaluating a relationship? Can anyone really understand a relationship from the outside . . . enough to give life-altering advice?

And perhaps most critically for all us Austenites—which film adaptation of *Persuasion* is the best?

What proved more difficult to translate to modern times was the choreography of this romance—how could I keep Wentworth and Anne always in close proximity but still divided? How could I translate Wentworth's little acts of quiet care and empathy from the original novel—placing Anne in a carriage, rescuing her from a misbehaving nephew, supporting her leadership after the accident—into modern parlance? Without the constraints of the regency era, how does a romance plot function when your two leads can barely make eye contact, let alone talk to each other? So, I threw in a pumpkin festival, a Taylor Swift playlist, a mad assistant, an even madder goose, and just about anything else I could think of to keep Anne and Wentworth dancing around the point, until finally, Anne Elliot gets her long-deserved happy ending.

Reader, I hope you enjoy.

Melodie Edwards

P.S. My vote for the best movie adaptation is the ITV 2007 version, in case anyone was wondering.

P.P.S. My production editor (in reviewing this manuscript) has made an excellent counter argument, which is: Ciarán Hinds.

Once Persuaded, Twice Shy

One

S he should have kept her flats on.

Anne had made a hard rule for herself several years ago, when she thought striding around in her high heels would give her authority and also maybe calf definition. It did neither. It gave her aching feet and ruined her designer pumps.

Louboutins should never be treated liked that.

So, she made a rule. Flat shoes during the day, when she needed to get from her office to the box office, to backstage, to the lobby, in a hurry. Flat shoes in the evening right before the performance when the whirlwind of last-minute panics, missing props, drunk VIP guests, and ancient ushers losing their hearing aids down a seat back kept her running.

And only *after* that, maybe sometime around the third act, would she nip back to her office, touch up her makeup, slip into her cocktail dress, and swap her flats for heels. Then she'd be poised and ready in the lobby by last curtain call, ready to greet patrons and ready to make her speech as executive director of the Elysium Theatre Festival, while champagne flutes circulated.

This evening she had been lulled into a false sense of security. Everything had been running so smoothly.

And now—and she really could not believe she was dealing with this shit—she was walk/running from her office to backstage, her narrow-skirted dress and high heels cutting short each stride, while her assistant, Emmie, rushed along beside her—talking a mile a minute, trying to explain why their lead actress was suddenly convinced her dressing room was haunted—barely breaking a sweat in her ballet flats. Smart girl.

". . . and then after last night's ghost tour they took her to the Angel Inn for lunch, and you know how they like to take tourists down into the cellar and show them the original old beams with the musket-ball scars and talk about the ghost of Captain Butler who died there, and after that they took her to Fort George, where they were doing historical battle reenactments for the afternoon . . ."

Anne grimaced. "Two reports of upset school trips at the fort and now this. No one freaks out when they go to Colonial Williamsburg; why can't we make that our model?"

The town of Niagara-on-the-Lake, of which the Elysium Theatre Festival was the centerpiece, sat wedged between the shores of Lake Ontario and the mouth of the Niagara River, and downstream from the famous Niagara Falls. Its character was a confusing mix of year-round small-town life and seasonal leisure playground; it boasted several spas, a golf course, boutique shopping, romantic hotels, and endless hectares of surrounding wineries. It was also home to multigenerational farmers and small-business owners, a tractor festival, a beloved main street preserved from the last century, and miles and miles of hiking trails frequented by the locals. It had been an early site for European pioneers settling in the new world and had many confusing remnants from its journey through the eighteenth, nineteenth, and twentieth centuries, not cleared away as they are in modern cities, but still standing as the local pub or courthouse or military graveyard. The town was nestled up as close as possible to the American border and had been the site of the infamous and bloody War of 1812: both Fort Niagara on the American side and Fort George on the Canadian side, once manned by the British, still stood—stone and wood and grass edifices forever peering tiredly across the river at their old adversaries.

That the historical society wanted to use this living history to enliven the town was commendable. That they were terrifying tourists and visiting actors was less than lovely. It was just like their idea two years ago—equally ill-conceived, in Anne's opinion—to reintroduce Canadian geese to the pond in the theater gardens. And now they had that one lunatic goose who kept dive-bombing the glass theater doors like it was his primordial purpose. He'd managed to get in once, squawked straight for the bar, and ended up flapping around madly with a martini shaker stuck on his head so that Emmie named him Double-Oh-Goose. The historical society was mysteriously absent when Anne had called them to come deal with *that* situation.

She smothered her frustration with them now. "Make a note for tomorrow: call Professor Davis at the historical society and . . ."

"Tell him his ass is fired and he'll never work in this town again!" Emmie cut in with relish.

"Absolutely do *not* do that; we are not firing anybody." She enjoyed mentoring Emmie, truly, but the girl's bloodlust was beyond comprehension. *What were they doing in business school these days—just watching* House of Cards *on a loop?*

"Please *politely* ask Professor Davis to tone it way, way down. And he if starts talking about his PhD and verisimilitude, you may *politely* remind him that I'm also a town councilor, and terrifying the tourists will be considered a detractor when we negotiate his annual funding. Never threaten someone you need to work with, Emmie; only gently remind them where their best interests lie."

They pushed through the heavy double doors that separated the office suites from the labyrinth of backstage areas, Anne treading carefully as they crossed over a steel-grate walkway just looking for a dainty stiletto to snap, and wound through several twisting hallways, the walls carpeted to baffle sound. A panel was starting to peel in one corner; Anne made a mental note for the production crew.

Quiet and dark enveloped them before they emerged into an antechamber that connected the senior dressing rooms, and there they found half the cast of *Macbeth* assembled watching a stellar diva performance.

"I want to talk to my manager!" Michelle Cranston, lead actress, her hands newly dipped in streaky red paint in preparation for the "Out, damned spot!" monologue, was wailing. "I can't work like this!"

"But we can fire *her*, right?" Emmie asked under her breath.

If only, Anne thought.

Choi, the artistic director, was standing beside a case of

prop swords wringing her hands like she was the one meant to be Lady Macbeth, looking sick and pale. Several of the trees of Birnam Wood were shivering nearby as the stage hands holding them sniggered.

Macduff, Duncan, and Malcolm looked irritated, while Macbeth himself was trying ineffectively to shush Michelle and usher her to her starting spot at stage left. Various other Scottish warriors were watching with avid interest; one had pulled a cell phone out of his kilt and was texting. *Ensemble cast should know better than to have their cell phone with them onstage*; Anne made a mental note for the stage manager.

Right. This was clearly a disaster about to spiral out of control. She straightened her shoulders and waded in.

"Michelle, I'd like you to take a moment and calm down." Anne's tone was firm but soothing.

"Ms. Elliot!" She made a sweeping gesture of relief, like Anne had come to be her savior instead of coming to kick her back onstage. "I was just in my dressing room, and there was this terrible creaking and groaning sound, and a loud bang . . ."

Anne took a subtle step back as Michelle waved her painty hands, her cocktail dress narrowly escaping a gruesome red-streaked fate.

"Michelle, those noises were the pipes. Our matinee production this season is *Singin' in the Rain*. We installed a sprinkler system and the pipes were threaded down behind the dressing room walls. The pressure occasionally omits a bang. You already know this."

"It was a ghost."

"It was not a ghost."

"You weren't there. It was a ghost."

"Michelle . . ."

"It *was* a ghost, because there were details. He's an infantryman, and he's haunting my dressing room probably because some delinquent ancestor of mine killed him on the battlefield. It's xenophobic—he's haunting me because America won the Battle of Niagara."

"Hold up," said Banquo, crossing his arms over his leather chest plate. "Where do you get off thinking you won the Battle of Niagara? Canadians won Niagara in the War of 1812— that's why we have the better view of the falls."

"Canadians didn't win, and the Battle of Niagara was in 1814, you clown," said Arman. His stagehand all-black outfit was covered in red finger streaks. He had been first on the scene when Michelle had come out of her dressing room screeching about ghosts and thrown herself into the arms of the nearest handsome young man, as was her custom. "We weren't even Canadians then. England and France battled it out and France lost. That's why Quebec's still angry."

"Trying to push France out of Niagara was a totally different battle in 1759!"

"What bloody history book did you read?!"

"You know what?" Anne interjected, using her most reasonable voice. "It doesn't matter. It doesn't matter who won, or who lost, or who was what country. You know why? Because it was over two hundred years ago. We are not concerned with a battle that happened over two hundred years ago, and there is no ghost-soldier in your dressing room."

"Infantryman."

"There is no ghost-*infantryman* in your dressing room. There *is*, however, an audience of five hundred people waiting for Michelle Cranston, star of the hit TV show *Law and Wait-*

ing, to deliver her finest performance as Lady Macbeth and show them that Juilliard training never fades."

Michelle preened.

"That's not what's faded," the understudy Macduff sniggered.

Michelle blanched.

Distantly Anne heard the lobby chimes; the backstage lights flickered. One minute to curtain rise.

No more time to play nice.

Anne turned to face Macduff and gave him her sweetest, sincerest smile. "Would you like to contribute meaningfully to this conversation? You've played the corpse on those CSI shows so often, I'm sure you understand the pressure Michelle is feeling moving from television to the stage."

He blushed but quickly folded. "No, Ms. Elliot."

"And, Michelle"—she turned back to Lady Macbeth, still using her mildest tones—"we can, of course, get your manager on the phone, and you can tell him all about the ghost in your dressing room. But I'll need a moment of his time after that, because unfortunately we will have to discuss this breach of contract and how that might affect the advance you were paid for the remainder of the season."

"Hit 'em in the paycheck," Emmie hissed. Anne briefly closed her eyes and exhaled through her nose. *Another conversation about diplomacy tomorrow*—she made a mental note.

Michelle quavered and then sniffed and raised her chin. "I'm a professional; I've never bailed on a performance."

"I'm so very glad to hear it," Anne said mildly. "Now, everyone take your places, please, before your director keels over from stress."

The cast scattered just as the lights dimmed. Anne moved to put an arm around Choi's shoulders.

"Just breathe in, and out. Deep breaths. Everything is fine; there's only the second half to go. You've had standing ovations all this week, and you'll have another one tonight, and then you'll come join me in the lounge, and you'll drink lots and lots of wine, okay?"

Choi gave a weak smile. "Thanks, Anne. I'm sorry I had to call Emmie to get you. I know I should manage . . ."

Anne shooed away her apologies. "Don't even worry about it. I hired you for your talent. *I'm* here to problem solve. I've been the executive director of the Elysium Theatre, all three stages, and all adjacent programming for four years now." She took a step back, ready to head to the lobby now that the crisis was averted. The tip of a discarded plastic sword scraped down the side of her shoe, leaving a laddered leather scratch in its wake. She did her best not to wince.

"This is what I do."

Two

There was a standing ovation, just as she'd predicted. Anne stood behind the closed doors, ensconced in the velvety cocoon of the quiet lobby, with only the soft tinkle of the waiters filling glasses nearby. The noise of enthusiastic applause reached her as a softly muffled wave that rose and fell before the ushers opened up the doors and the evening's theater patrons began to filter out.

This was Anne's showtime.

"Mr. and Mrs. Lightbourne, so lovely to see you this evening. Did you enjoy the performance?"

"Delia, it's wonderful to see you back again this year. We were so sorry to hear about your husband's passing last summer . . . Oh you *did* receive the flowers, I'm glad."

"Sir Phillip, did you enjoy the performance? Yes, our new artistic director, Choi Young, such an incredible talent. We were so lucky to get her after her last Broadway run. I must introduce you later."

"Jason, nice to see you again. And this is your, er, companion? Yes, our staff are circulating with champagne, but of course the bar is open and our very talented bartender will be sure to fix you that drink . . . Pardon? No, your ex-wife declined using her ticket this evening."

"Lilian, so lovely to see you, and your dress is gorgeous! Don't tell me it's couture again—it'll break my heart to know I can never own one like it."

A gentle touch to the elbow here, a gracious smile there, the picture of elegance and poise, with not a drop of her earlier haste, Anne wove her way among the attendees with all the grace of a well-choreographed dancer on full charm offensive. She greeted circulating patrons, delicately made introductions, and subtly signaled waiters when a drink refill was needed or should be neglected based on the sobriety of the guest.

When Anne's mother passed away four years ago and the role of executive director of the festival was left open, the board of directors had tutted and fussed over giving the position to Anne. That an Elliot had always run the festival, for as many years as it had been around, was inescapable. That the Elliots were considered a first family of Niagara-on-the-Lake, and used to own much of the town's property, was undisputed. That Anne's qualifications were excellent, an MBA and a bachelor of commerce degree from a first-rate university with a minor in arts management, was unquestionable. That she had been twenty-eight, delicate looking and soft-spoken, did not drink, and did not play golf was somehow—as Anne would come to realize—an insurmountable series of faults.

The five board members had sat around the conference table that June, their patronizing smug smiles never wavering as they told her.

Anne had come to the meeting prepared to prove that she did not expect to be awarded the job based on tradition or nepotism. She had her résumé, her notes on the theaters' finances, and her business proposals neatly laid out for how to capture a wider market, and she would not mention that she'd been handling more and more of her mother's day-to-day tasks since the cancer diagnosis and that she had de facto now been doing the job herself for some time.

She expected some opposition. She did not expect a diatribe about how if she didn't golf and didn't drink, how could she possibly glad-hand the elite gray-haired patrons whose platinum-level donations and season ticket purchases helped keep the festival running?

Anne really could not fathom losing the job for anything so put-your-hand-in-a-blender stupid as that. So, she politely fought them. She courteously fought them. She "with all due respect, *gentlemen*" fought them.

Eventually they concluded that letting her have the job and fail in it was probably less effort than telling her no.

Which almost felt like winning, so whatever. Close enough.

And she refused to fail. Even when the festival was flourishing, and new talent filled the stage, and newer audiences filled the seats, she never forgot the ways in which she could be found disappointing. She tucked her long hair into a sleek professional bun. She bought conservative cocktail dresses, wore her mother's pearl and diamond earrings (Holly Golightly might think diamonds before forty was tacky, but then her goal wasn't to look staid and older like Anne's was) for receptions, learned the terms for golf, hid the fact that she never drank, and restricted her one bit of flash to the red soles of her Louboutins.

And even now, four years later, at age thirty-two, she was here for the VIP guest evening for a traditional rendition of *Macbeth*, instead of down the street at the Elysium's smaller Court Theatre, where they were performing an experimental new comedy imagining the *Odyssey's* sirens as real housewives, which she had championed. Tweets about it had gone viral and they had been sold out for the summer.

But this was important, too, she reminded herself, as she waited patiently for Sir Phillip to show her photos of his grandchildren on his phone, and then took over once all he succeeded in showing her was his calendarized medication schedule. This was their VIP performance and reception for platinum-level and corporate sponsors and legacy arts patrons. Blue-blood night, the cast usually called it. Jackie Kennedy was what they called her when they thought she couldn't hear them. She told herself the nickname was a good thing.

". . . And my lawyer got me most of the property portfolio, and I hear the bank is looking to forcibly retire him . . ." Anne nodded and discreetly checked her watch as Marcia Demasque detailed the proceedings of her third divorce.

Emmie circled behind Marcia, catching Anne's eye. Anne gave her a subtle nod and Emmie took her cue.

"Ms. Demasque, I'm so sorry to interrupt, but it's time for Anne's speech. Can I refresh your champagne for you?"

"Perfect timing," Anne said as they carried away Ms. Demasque's empty champagne flute.

"She fleeced another husband, then?" Emmie grinned.

"If you want to hone your already Machiavellian impulses,

go learn from her. She's a brilliant strategist . . . That was a joke, Emmie!" Anne said as she saw the thoughtful gleam in the young woman's eyes.

"I know!"

Anne sighed and stepped onto the riser at the far side of the room. The floor-to-ceiling windows behind it showcased the beautiful rolling lawns and flower gardens artfully lit for the evening. One of the bulbs by the lilac bushes was burned out; she made a mental note for the landscaping staff.

Turning to face the crowd, she raised her champagne flute and tapped her ringed index finger lightly against it. The clear ringing sound drew everyone's attention as the murmur died down.

Shoulders back, breathe in, and project your voice.

"Good evening, everyone. Thank you for joining us for tonight's production of *Macbeth*. This year marks our fifty-eighth season." She waited for the polite smattering of applause. "The Elysium Theatre Festival began as a summer festival with a run of eight performances of *Candide*. Today, it is a Canadian cultural icon, with three theaters and ten productions running year-round, and audiences of over two hundred and fifty thousand. But the business of running the arts, no matter how successful, could not be achieved without the support of arts patrons like yourselves. The people here tonight are a critical part of the Elysium Festival's success. Your continued involvement will ensure that the legacy of the festival will continue for many generations to come. On behalf of the Elysium Festival, we thank you. We'll be opening up the doors to the patio momentarily, where several members of our orchestra from this season's musical production will be playing for us. Please enjoy your evening."

Another smattering of polite applause and Anne stepped down. Another hour or two to circulate while the music played, and then they could call it a night—the benefit of a seniors-dominant crowd was the relatively early bedtime. The *Odyssey* drama opening party went into the wee hours of the morning . . . or so she'd been told.

"Ah, Anne, let me introduce you to the Fairchilds—they've specifically asked to meet you." The head of marketing, Naomi, seized her by the elbow as she plowed across the room, Anne eddying in her wake. "They're new money," she hissed in her ear, "just retired and bought that gorgeous winery up on the escarpment."

A very ordinary-looking couple: mid-sixties perhaps, nicely dressed, but perhaps a little underdressed in comparison to the rest of the crowd. The wife looked like she was aware of it, from the way she straightened her silver necklace and tipped up her chin just a bit when Ms. Demasque passed by in her glittering diamonds and scanned the couple up and down.

"Mr. and Mrs. Fairchild, let me introduce you to Anne Elliot, our executive director."

Anne shook hands with Mrs. Fairchild and then, noticing that Mr. Fairchild's right sleeve was pinned neatly down over the wrist, quickly switched to her left hand to shake with him.

"Lovely to meet you both. I hope you enjoyed this evening's performance."

"We did; it was wonderful," Mrs. Fairchild replied, a little formally. "The costumes were stunning."

"Speaking of which, your dress is stunning; that's such a lovely color," Anne countered, wanting to soothe the sting of Ms. Demasque's appraisal. Mrs. Fairchild regarded her warily for a moment, weighing her sincerity, and then relaxed and dropped the formal tone.

"Thank you! But who would look at my dress with all those kilts filled with strapping young men on the stage." She laughed, and her husband turned and smiled at her fondly before launching into the conversation with Anne as if he'd been waiting for an opening. "So, you're in charge of this whole operation! You're awfully young for a job like that. It's very impressive; I bet you have to be pretty fierce keeping all this running smoothly. I'm sure your parents are proud." Here his wife elbowed him slightly. "Well, when you're old like me you start to think of everyone as someone's kid," he defended himself with a rueful grin.

"Ms. Elliot, we wanted to say we've bought the old Kellynch Winery. We were told it used to belong to your family, and when we got the invitation to come tonight, we just thought we'd say a friendly hello."

Naomi flicked her eyes to Anne, chagrined. Clearly, she'd forgotten about the estate's previous owner. Mrs. Fairchild caught the look, and her own eyebrows flicked up in sudden worry. "We just wanted to tell you how beautiful the property is and how much we love it, but I hope we haven't misstepped . . ."

"Not at all," Anne cut in smoothly. "And please, call me Anne. My family sold the property many years ago and it's gone through a number of hands since then. It is a beautiful place and I'm glad it has appreciative new owners. Do you have any connection to the area or . . . ?"

"Decades ago, when we were newly married, we were honeymooning in Niagara Falls, but we ended up driving down here and—"

Here Mr. Fairchild was interrupted by a distant muffled squawking and a dull thud.

"Double-Oh-Goose is back! I've got it!" Emmie went careening off, still so enviously speedy in her ballet flats. *Tomorrow, a conversation about diplomacy* and *a conversation about discretion*, Anne reminded herself as a headache began to squeeze at her temples.

"Er . . ." Mr. Fairchild began, sliding into an irrepressible grin.

"Everything's fine," Anne said smoothly, professional face still completely intact, and she stepped slightly to the right to block his view of the lobby entrance. "You were saying you honeymooned here?"

"Well, we always joked our retirement would be some winery nearby," Mrs. Fairchild supplied.

"And Ben approved. Said it was a good growth area and a good business opportunity," her husband added, as though Ben's approval was the final word on the matter.

"Benjamin's our favorite nephew," Mrs. Fairchild explained. "He came down from Toronto to look at the place and help us with the purchase."

Anne took a quick breath.

A favorite nephew. Named Benjamin.

. . . And then she whisked the reminder from her mind like it had never been there at all. Deft, like a cat flicking its tail. Involuntary but habitual.

"Well, I'm so happy for you both that your dream has become a reality. If you'll excuse . . ."

Naomi put a hand on her arm, halting her polite exit. There was something she wanted from this couple and their new winery, then—Naomi always had an angle—and their latching on to Anne was her way in.

Anne suppressed a sigh and continued the conversation. She liked the couple instinctively and would be happy to roll out the welcome wagon for them, but maybe tomorrow, when she hadn't been on her feet for hours, and Emmie wasn't somewhere battling waterfowl, and she should really check on Choi again . . .

"And will your nephew be helping you with the business?" she asked, mustering her energy. She sensed he was a point of pride for them, like Sir Phillip with his phone full of blurry grandchildren, like they'd assumed about Anne's own parents.

"Oh no, he's far too important to spend his time faffing about with grapes with us." Mr. Fairchild chuckled.

Bingo. Now they'd carry the conversation for her.

"Ben Wentworth, he's a banker and . . ."

Anne's breath stuttered; her pulse roared in her ears. *Ben Wentworth.* She hadn't heard that name in years. Hadn't even thought it in the privacy of her own mind for years. He'd been here, he'd been in her town, at her winery; she might have bumped into him in a shop or on the road or anywhere . . . She tasted bitterness on her tongue and knew it was adrenaline, a useless and delayed reaction to the near miss. Her balance felt off in her heels; the floor and ceiling swooped.

I should just be practical and wear my flats all the time . . .

*. . . was her last thought before it all went black.

Three

If passing out was mortifying, then waking back up was so much worse that Anne would have opted to pass right out again just to avoid it.

Except then I'd just have to wake up a second time. Embarrassing and inefficient.

A small semicircle of people hovered around her, Naomi and the Fairchilds among them, and she could hear from the worried murmuring that had replaced the previous happy-party sounds that she had become a scene that extended beyond their circle.

Surprisingly it was the genial Mr. Fairchild who seemed to be in charge of the situation, his expression now serious, demeanor surprisingly firm and commanding, though his voice stayed calm. His left hand gently but expertly pressed against the pulse in her neck.

"All right, Ms. Elliot, if you feel able to, you can sit up slowly, but take it easy." He moved his hand from her neck to her back, supporting her movement. "Now, do you have any existing medical conditions? Diabetes, pregnancy, or a heart condition?"

Anne shook her head. Mr. Fairchild's face relaxed into a smile. "All right, then, I'd say you just had a bit of a faint. I bet you've been on your feet all day, stressful job getting this event together, probably skipped a meal, then the champagne goes to your head. It could happen to anyone."

Anne didn't bother to correct him about the drink, pathetically grateful for the excuse. (Annoyingly, he was right about the skipped meal.)

"Well, based on the way you're blushing, looks like your blood pressure's coming back up again. No need to be embarrassed. I've seen full-blooded soldiers faint for nothing more than their pack being strapped on too tight."

"Soldiers?" Naomi queried, sounding confused. The only live soldiers in town were the historical reenactors at Fort George, their weapons as fake as the plastic blade that had scratched Anne's shoe.

"My husband was in the military," Mrs. Fairchild explained.

But Anne already knew that. Ben's uncle had been a colonel in the Royal Canadian Air Force ten years ago; the Fairchilds were the aunt and uncle he loved better than his own parents, the ones she was supposed to meet. She never got the chance to learn their names.

She saw his handless arm as he moved back to give her space, now that she was sitting on her own. Something had happened; he must have been forcibly retired because of his injury. She felt a terrible wave of sorrow that the man Ben told such happy stories about, thought so highly of, should have undergone something so traumatic. And she could say and do nothing because she was a stranger to him, a stranger who had been trying to shake him and his wife off moments ago because she was tired and there were more guests to see. She felt ashamed.

"No need to be embarrassed, Ms. Elliot," he repeated, mistaking her silence. "Now, what you need is a bite to eat and a good night's sleep, and some peace and quiet."

"She has a town council meeting coming up; that's, like, basically the opposite of peace and quiet." Emmie had returned, surfacing from the crowd, eyes huge as she took in the scene. "Should I cancel for you?"

"No, don't cancel—"

"But it's basically like the Red Wedding every time. I could take over for you . . ."

Ah, Game of Thrones, *then*, *not* House of Cards, Anne thought nonsensically.

"No, I'll be fine. Please, no one needs to fuss. He's right, I just went too long without eating and got a little light-headed. Thank you, Colonel Fairchild. I'm feeling fine now." She got slowly to her feet, concentrating on Emmie and the town council meeting as a point of focus, like a dancer coming out of a spin. She flicked the nauseating lurch of her feelings away again.

"Did the string quartet stop playing? I need to speak with—"

"Anne," Naomi interrupted her, uncharacteristically kind, "you need to go home and lie down. Emmie and I can take care of closing down the evening. People are only going to linger for another half hour or so. You don't need to be here."

She *did* need to be there. She was the linchpin, holding everything together, sometimes by the skin of her teeth, but she did it, she made sure it held; she would not fail, would not let *any* of them see her fail. Anne was about to say something, something appropriately demurring and polite that would convey some small measure of this, of why she had to stay, but Colonel Fairchild was still standing there and she couldn't take that kind, concerned look from him for one more second. It looked, with its family resemblance, too much like how someone else's caring face once looked, back when he still cared for her.

"Okay, I'm just going to grab a snack in my office and then head home."

"Is there no one who can come pick you up?" Colonel Fairchild asked.

Anne smiled and shook her head. "I'll take a taxi. I'm only a few minutes from home."

Back in her well-worn flats, Anne passed the taxi stand in favor of walking; she didn't want to chat, and every taxi driver in Niagara knew her by name.

She grimaced at the green goose poop on the driveway, narrowly avoiding ruining her second set of shoes for the night.

The air was tepid, but the heat-soaked pavement still emanated warmth from the day, like a cooling oven. Blue-blood night was the Thursday before Labor Day weekend every year, to mark the close of the summer season. The same shows would continue until November, when they switched to their holiday-themed performances, but the crowds and the vacationing tourists would lessen, the wine tours at the surrounding wineries would start to dry up, and the bike rental shops and patios would begin to shutter. Their audiences would become less international and more of the nearby Toronto crowd or New Yorkers crossing the border for a long weekend, along with matinees for school trips. Understudies would be allowed to take over more performances as lead actors began to leave for other gigs.

Nearing midnight, as it was now, things were simply quiet and peaceful, and she could see her town in all its beauty as she walked down the main street. The glow of the ancient streetlamps, the twinkling fairy lights of the patios, the brightly lit awning of the Elysium's Royal Theatre, where a production of *Blithe Spirit* was still ongoing, the antique storefronts, and the clock tower. There was the old apothecary shop, left as a living museum, a bakery with pictures of Queen Victoria in the window, hanging right over their gleaming cappuccino machine and the bone china serving platter that during the day would showcase fresh-baked scones and empire biscuits. There was the old Irish pub, the costume hat shop, the art gallery, and the wrought-iron balustrades that twined like ivy up the stone front of old city hall, which was now the Court Theatre. The white pillars and flower boxes that dotted the veranda of the Prince of Wales Hotel, its painted sign lovingly recopied in the same whorls and curlicue gold lettering that it had first displayed in 1901, when the Duke of York had visited. The touches of modernity were softened at night, the tourists and cars gone, the kitschy T-shirts in the boutique windows half-hidden by shadow. The remaining disparate pieces of past centuries blurred and blended together harmoniously. The past stood brighter in relief.

The town that time forgot.

In her more maudlin moments—nights when she stood back from her life and saw the crumbling of so many of her earlier hopes—in moments like that she felt a melancholy kinship with the town. Both trapped, flattened at a point in time like petals pressed into a book. An image of something that was—other people could come and go, other people visit and move on. But Anne and the town stayed, and stayed, and stayed.

And then usually she would shake it off. She was Anne Elliot; the Elliots had always lived here. She loved her quaint little town. She loved living in a vacation destination twelve months of the year. She loved the townspeople and all their quirks, and though she might want to tear her hair out with frustration sometimes, she loved the challenges of her job. What would she exchange this for? Life in a nine-to-five office, staring at spreadsheets all day? Would that really be better than the spontaneity of madcap actors or knowing that the picturesque geese, instead of staying on the picturesque pond, had made a mad dash for the theater again? Would she trade a full house, on their feet in a third curtain call of applause after a three-hundred-year-old play made fresh, to what, teach history to a sea of students more interested in their phones?

No. Given the choice, this is always where she would want to be.

But sometimes, maybe it would be nice to feel her own life had some progress. Something to break up the summers of *Macbeth*s and Oscar Wildes, some way to mark the passage of time that was more than calendar years passing by.

And tonight, brushing up against the path not taken . . . He was a banker? That didn't sound right. Was he married? Did he have children? How long had he been in Toronto? Her hand lightly touched the phone in her purse. There was an easy way to find out.

No.

She'd worked to overcome that habit a year or so after they'd broken up. It wasn't healthy. And what would be the point? Any answer would be painful.

Her phone chose that moment to buzz against her fingertips, and she jumped—but it was her sister texting.

> Ur assistant left me vm. You pass out Wtf?
> Dad at golf dinner, I'm out w the girls. Be
> home late. Lv porch light on.

Emmie shouldn't have called Liz, but that was sweet. Her ferocious young assistant really could be strangely sweet sometimes.

Anne turned right on King Street, seeing the pink-and-white veranda of the home she shared with her father and Liz. Like much of the main street, it had been meticulously preserved in its turn-of-the-century state, its scalloped edges like a gingerbread house in the dim light. It had once belonged to a famous painter, Trisha Romance, who had possibly been responsible for the pink paint job, before the Elliots moved in after the Kellynch Winery was sold. Some folk still called it Trisha's House, just like they called Kellynch the old Elliot place.

Will he come back to visit Kellynch Winery, now that his aunt and uncle are settled there?

She left the porch light on, as Liz had requested, and made her way through the massive silent house to her room, where she opened the windows to hear the soothing sounds of Lake Ontario lapping nearby and tumbled gratefully into bed.

He won't come back here again. They'll visit him in Toronto. He has no reason to come back. I'm perfectly safe. Everything will look better in the morning.

Four

Nothing looked better in the morning.

She now faced the dual humiliation of passing out the night before and a day full of meetings where everybody probably already knew she'd passed out the night before.

As if on cue, her phone buzzed with a text from her friend Vidya.

> Grapevine says u conked out @ blueblood
> night. U doing ok? If in the office 2day, stop
> by my workshop. Bring coffee.

A moment later it buzzed again.

> Did u get my grapevine joke? Winery
> owners? 😊

Anne sighed. No escaping that upcoming interrogation.

She picked out business-casual attire for the day, slim-fitting tailored black pants and a silky blouse in a soft butter yellow with pintucking down the front. She added pearl earrings and slipped her phone and wallet into her leather tote.

Downstairs Liz and Dad were sitting in the grand dining room in dull silence. Sunlight filtered weakly through the small stained-glass panels that topped the rounded bay windows at the end of the room.

Her father was sipping coffee and reading his newspaper. Liz was sipping coffee and scrolling through Instagram. A carton of eggs sat on the table between them.

"Have you seen this?" Liz waved her phone at her father. "Microneedling is the best way to treat crow's-feet now."

Her father peered over the top of his newspaper. "I thought it was lasering."

"It was, but now they're saying microneedling. Less recovery time." She peered at her phone. "Results are pretty good too." She flicked over a photo and snickered. "Nothing's going to treat that set; they're in deep."

"I wonder if either of the spas in town offers it. It would be good to know, for when the time comes."

"Yes, but not now. I don't think it's time yet." Liz touched the smooth skin next to her own eye tentatively, as if fine lines might have sprouted up overnight.

"No, no, of course not." He smirked. "You and I are blessed genetically that way; the antioxidant, anti-aging creams are more than keeping up the job for now. And a little preventative Botox never hurt anyone. But these, what are they again, tweakments? It's good to know the technology is making such rapid advances. For when it's time."

They'd been having a variation of this conversation for the last five years, always concluding it "wasn't time yet" for either of them. Her father was sixty-five. When exactly it *was* going to be time was a mystery, and Anne sometimes had a macabre worry he'd be expecting her to arrange his "tweakments" when he was at the undertaker's getting prepped for an open coffin—but that was silly; her father never acknowledged he was going to die one day. Death and aging were things that happened to *other* people.

Liz looked up from her phone at Anne's entrance. "You look like a bumblebee," she noted dryly, taking in the yellow top and black pants. Anne sighed. She was sighing a lot this morning.

Her father wasn't wrong that Liz needed no beauty assistance. Anne had always been described as "pretty" by those who knew her—she had a smooth curtain of brown hair, large eyes, and delicate features—but next to Liz's stunning, movie-star-worthy good looks, Anne's prettiness faded to something ordinary, the variety of prettiness most women can enjoy when they're simply young and smiling. And what was worse, Liz at thirty-nine seemed to be getting even better-looking. The apple-cheeked flesh of her youth had receded, but it'd left the striking architecture of her face in brighter relief. Her high cheekbones and almond-shaped eyes, the pout of her upper lip and the clean line of her jaw, all combined with her height and slender figure, turned heads wherever she went. The stress of their mother's long hospice stay had prematurely aged Anne. Now her delicate features were often described as wan. Liz somehow remained immaculate. It was hard not to resent her for that.

"We were thinking poached eggs this morning," her sister said casually.

Anne looked at the untouched carton on the table. "And I see thinking about it was as far as you got."

Liz sometimes left out various food items and then suggested a meal that might be nice, like a feint that she might do it herself but actually more of a hope that Anne would do it. Anne had learned long ago not to take the bait. The housekeeper had been lost with the winery.

"I'm going into the office early. I'm getting a bite to eat on the way."

"Oh." Her father roused himself a little. "How was blueblood night?"

"It went well."

"Good, good. My old friend Sir Phillip, was he there? I saw him last spring on the golf course; he had hair coming out his ears and none left on his head! And he was getting that old-man stoop." He gestured with one hand in a dramatic swoop over his own upright and square shoulders. "I felt sorry for him. He'll have to give up the game soon if he keeps falling to pieces."

"Sir Phillip was there, and he seemed very happy and healthy, telling me all about his grandchildren."

"Oh well, it's good he focuses on the positives of his situation, poor man. Although grandchildren will make him look even older." His attention returned to his paper. "Were you going to make eggs?"

Anne left the two of them alone in the cavernous house, counting their acquaintances' wrinkles and waiting, no doubt, for the eggs to make themselves.

B alzac's coffee shop, the only coffee shop in town, really, was a cheerful yellow cottage around the corner from the main street. There, she got a latte for herself and one topped with every sweet syrup possible for Vidya. While she stood in line her phone chimed with an incoming email. It was from Emmie to say the Fairchilds had called and would she please call them back. Of course they would call, Anne told herself, convinced the swoop in her stomach was only from watching Lucy behind the counter pour another nauseating pump of sweet syrup on Vidya's drink. They were decent, caring people and she blacked out on them at a swanky reception. *They're just calling to check that I've recovered, totally normal courtesy.*

She made her way back to the Maxwell Theatre, seeing the smudged glass and stray feathers from Double-Oh-Goose's latest attempt now made visible by daylight, passed through the lobby—the scene of last night's embarrassment—and wound her way into the backstage area and then deeper into the building, where the workshops and corporate offices lay, and into the costume department.

Vidya was a costumier and brilliant seamstress with a shock of purple hair and an athletic figure. Anne had been passing through her workshop once, talking to the head of wardrobe, when Vidya had tugged her aside and told her that with her fabulous legs her skirt ought to be at least an inch shorter. Secretly Anne agreed, so she stepped up on a box in front of a tri-mirror while Vidya pinned up the guilty skirt for hemming, all the while chatting to her about her designer pumps and the cost-benefit analysis of sewing corsets with plastic boning instead of metal. As an MBA graduate, Anne could appreciate the numbers aspect of the latter topic.

Anne's adolescence in an elite girls' boarding school, where female friendships were conducted like a cold war, had left her wary. Liz was more about having fans than family, and so long as Anne mildly declined joining her girl squad, nothing like friendship could ever exist between them. Really, her mother had been her only friend, which would still be a depressing fact even if her mother had lived.

So, she was embarrassingly grateful for this friendship strangely thrust upon her. She liked Vidya, she liked her warmth and her care and her counsel, incomprehensible as it sometimes was, but she never could figure out what Vidya got out of the arrangement.

"Christ! Anne, you fainted?"

Anne handed over the second coffee. "I just got a little woozy."

"Woozy? You? Miss Anne 'competence is my middle name' Elliot. Two years ago, when that guy accidentally cut off the tip of his finger with the oyster knife at that reception, you scooped it up, popped it in your purse with ice from the champagne bucket, and got him to the hospital while everyone else was still screaming in shock at the blood."

"They managed to save the finger."

"But not your purse," Vidya said sadly.

"Priorities, Vidya. Human welfare over fashion, remember?" Anne joked.

"Speaking of priorities, I heard it was a military man who took charge last night as you swooned."

"I didn't swoon," Anne said sharply. "And Colonel Fairchild had nothing to do with my faint. I was just overtired."

"Overtired, Miss Anne 'competence is my middle name' Elliot . . ."

"Oh for god's . . . My middle name is Maria."

"Speaking of competence," Vidya continued, ignoring Anne's interjection and changing tacks at light speed, "I hear you rocked some big energy last night to put Michelle in her place and keep the show on track."

"I did not. I very simply reminded her how she gets her paychecks that we all know are so important for keeping her flush with vodka and vapes. Except I didn't say that last part. Obviously."

"Obviously," Vidya echoed. "So, it sounds like you were in your usual kick-ass fine form last night, no weariness at all, and then bam, outta nowhere you went down like a politician with a horrifying Twitter history."

Thrown, but also a little impressed by her U-turn back onto the topic, Anne sat down heavily on a bolt of fabric and felt her false cheerfulness drain away. Vidya and her workshop had that effect on her, of getting her to drop her guard. In the gaudy room, where sequins, feathers, strips of leather, spools of colorful thread, and half-mashed flower crowns lay strewn about, where dressmaker dummies in varying states of disarray stood in a headless gossipy circle by the window, and where random tufts of wool wafted by, blown by the stand fan in the corner, there was no place for careful diplomacy or polite formality. This was a fairy bower and a mad hatter's tea party all in one, a safe cocoon where rules did not apply, and Vidya with her bizarre jokes never judged.

"I was in this relationship," she started haltingly, staring down at her cooling coffee, trying to remember the pat answers she used to give people for why it ended. It felt so long ago.

"A serious one?"

Anne scoffed. "As serious as anyone is at that age." Vidya silently raised an eyebrow; she stood up and began adjusting a drape of fabric on one of the headless dummies, pulling pins from her ever-present tool belt, knowing it was easier for Anne to talk without eyes on her.

"It was serious to me. Very serious. I think . . . I'm pretty sure it was serious to him too."

"Since you're here now and single, I'm guessing it didn't work out. Why?"

"It didn't work out because it wasn't ever *going* to work out." Anne sighed.

"You'll have to explain that one to me."

"He wasn't . . . I wasn't . . . We were just very different people. We were so obviously going to go down different roads. I mean, I'm *me*. He was . . . He was fearless. He loved bouldering and white-water rafting. He was bold. He absolutely didn't give a shit about what other people thought. He didn't plan ahead. He just *went* for things, you know? He wanted to go backpacking after university to New Zealand and travel until his money ran out. I would have still been planning the itinerary at home and budgeting while he was halfway around the world. I was in grad school finishing my MBA; he was two years older than me and still trying to finish his undergraduate degree because he'd switched majors five times."

"Sounds like he was just young, no crime in that. Some

of that sounds like Anne Elliot's reasoning, and some of that sounds like your mother," Vidya said gently. She had joined the festival and worked for Laura Elliot for two years before Laura's illness.

"Mom didn't like him," Anne agreed. "I mean, Dad and Liz didn't like him, but I wouldn't have listened to them. But Mom . . . You know what my father is like. She didn't want that kind of relationship for me."

"You just said he didn't care what people thought," Vidya interjected with exasperation, her mouth full of pins, "and she thought he was like *your* father? Your father would never go out and have adventures; he'd never leave his precious throne at the golf club." She whipped up a ribbon tape measure and checked the width of a fold before looping the tape around her neck and starting to unpin and repin everything again.

"Yeah," Ann said shakily, and then before she could help herself: "But she hit the roof when I told her about all his majors and no graduation in sight, and the travel-till-the-funds-dry-up plan, and maybe he *was* a bit directionless, but he was . . . god, he was so great." Anne stopped herself there, feeling disloyal to a mother whose every concern had been for Anne's happiness, however she might have misjudged it, and not wanting to remember and dwell on the merits of a man lost to her. At twenty-four those merits had paled next to her mother's fears, her own uncertainty about the future. With the wisdom and hindsight of thirty-two, she saw things differently.

"So, when you say it wouldn't have worked out, what you mean is people got in your head, and a relationship that made you happy was stopped dead in its tracks. Why didn't you call him up and try again when you figured it out? Boomerang yourself."

"He was so hurt when I ended it. So pissed off when I tried to explain why. All he heard was that he wasn't good enough. If you knew him, you'd understand there was no walking it back after that."

"Damn, Elliot, you're a heartbreaker," Vidya teased, snapping her tape measure ribbon at Anne playfully like a towel, lightening the atmosphere.

Anne snorted in spite of herself. "Oh please, it's almost eight years ago now. For all I know he got over it and can barely remember my name. 'Uh, what was that girl's name, the stuck-up one? Amy, Alice, uh, Anne?' Anyway, he's the Fairchilds' nephew; he helped them purchase Kellynch Winery. When they mentioned him at blue-blood night it just threw me for a loop, that's all. End of story." She gulped the last of her cold coffee.

"Please tell me you at least cyberstalked him after the breakup, like a normal person. What's he up to now?"

"I stopped doing that a year after we broke up and I've never done it since."

"Ugh, you're so self-disciplined it makes me sick." Vidya rolled her eyes and spun the dressmaker model at the same time, creating a dizzying effect. "Why can't you handle a breakup as well as I did with mine?"

"You did *not* handle your breakup well," Anne cried loudly. "You bought forty houseplants and wore an animal onesie for a week!"

"Exactly. Classic bottoming-out behavior. Like a normal person. And then when I was done with that, I shipped all forty houseplants to my ex's house. And some of them had mites."

"That is passive aggression writ large, is what that is."

"You, on the other hand, have got a serious case of suppression. You're like an overstuffed seam just waiting to pop its stitches and rip, when instead we could have unpicked you with some healthy coping mechanisms and made you into a very nice new hem."

"Sewing analogies?"

"I live for my trade. Now, while you've been telling me your sad story, which is a healthy first step, I might add, I have been finishing this prototype for next season's leading lady. What do you think?" She wheeled the dressmaker dummy over to Anne with a flourish.

"I think with a neckline that low, Juliet is really tarting it up for a fourteenth-century bride."

"This is for the Tennessee Williams production."

"In that case Maggie the Cat has discovered a newfound sense of modesty."

Vidya stood back from her creation, eyeing it critically. "Maybe we could dye it red . . ."

The buzzing of her tote bag pulled Anne's attention away—emails no doubt piling up. She felt a little dazed, having given Vidya more information about that time in her life than anyone before. Time to shake it off and get back to work. "Shall I leave you here with Maggie, then?" she teased, shouldering her bag and dropping the empty coffee cups in the bin.

"Yes, you go do your kick-ass thing"—Vidya gestured distractedly—"but don't think you're fooling me. You fainted. You've avoided even saying his name. It was clearly heartbreak, or . . . wait, what's the present tense—you're heartbroke!"

"Actually, I think heartbroke is an adjective . . ."

"DEFCON Taylor Swift level of heartbroke."

"Not everything can be solved with a Taylor Swift soundtrack," Anne protested.

"Wow. I know you're stressed out about it, so I'm going to pretend you didn't just say that."

"Vidya . . ."

"T Swift is the zeitgeist of female feelings. She is *our* Shakespeare. She is—"

"Okay, okay, just, y'know, send me the songs and I'll ignore it like I always do," Anne relented.

"On it!" Vidya whipped her phone out of a tool-belt pocket, thumbs flying across the screen, and Anne felt a corresponding buzz against her hip.

"Just out of curiosity," Anne said, on her way out the door, "why Swift and not Adele for a breakup? Isn't Adele the queen of heartbreak?"

Vidya looked uncharacteristically solemn for a moment. "Adele is pain, but Taylor Swift is perspective."

In her office Emmie was waiting with large, worried eyes and an even larger muffin.

"Emmie the Terrible, did you bring me a muffin?"

"They said you fainted because you skipped meals yesterday—not happening again on my watch."

"That's very sweet, thank you."

She moved to put the muffin on the desk. Emmie glared and crossed her arms. Anne dutifully took a large bite instead, and Emmie nodded in approval.

She's going to start force-feeding me if I so much as wobble, isn't she?

"Right," Anne managed around a mouthful of what had to

be the driest muffin to ever come out of an oven. "Any messages? What's on for this morning?"

"Just the message from the Fairchilds hoping you're feeling better and if you could call them back when you have a free moment, and I rescheduled all your meetings so you can have a nice, quiet day."

"That's . . . wonderful, thank you." She felt vaguely queasy at the prospect of empty hours, giving time for her errant mind to dwell, but she fought down the feeling as she looked at Emmie's self-satisfied expression at having taken the initiative.

Right, well, just because she emptied the schedule doesn't mean you can't fill the time. Anne pulled up her mental list of notes from last night; there had been the landscaping staff, the production crew, the stage manager, and Professor Davis for the reappearance of Double-Oh-Goose, but she would see him this afternoon.

"Emmie, who's on shift today for the landscaping team?"

A productive morning helped buoy her mood up from where it had plummeted the night before, and it made the ground more solid under her feet after that dangerous conversation with Vidya, where skimming the surface of her memories had threatened to nearly plunge her in.

It felt good to get so many of those in-house chores done. It felt better to throw the rest of the bran muffin in the trash when Emmie wasn't looking.

Five

She didn't call the Fairchilds back that day, even though it pricked at her conscience. It pricked at her sense of professionalism, too, but still she let the sticky note with their message linger on her desk where Emmie had left it. The week after she had done her ridiculous faint, she was on Main Street grabbing a quick lunch to take back to the office when she saw them, across the street and one block over. They were puttering about in front of a window display, obviously pleased and amused by whatever it was they saw there, chatting happily with each other; one of those golden older couples you sometimes see, happy as honeymooners but with the easy familiarity, warmth, and contentment of decades passed in perfect harmony with each other.

It made Anne's chest ache.

But still it was a strategic opportunity to be seized. Stepping into a recessed shop doorway to half conceal herself, she pulled out her cell and dialed their number, praying that her assumptions were correct and they'd be the type to own a landline and still use it as their main number. The phone rang in her ear. Neither the colonel nor Mrs. Fairchild so much as twitched a hand to a pocket. A voicemail flicked to life on the line, the colonel's kindly voice relaying the outgoing message. *Perfect.*

"Hello, Colonel and Mrs. Fairchild, this is Anne Elliot from the Elysium Theatre Festival returning your call. I'm sorry to have missed you . . ." She watched as down the street they strolled on to the next shop. "It was so kind of you to call and check up on me; I'm feeling quite recovered. I hope my little episode didn't disrupt your enjoyment of the show and the gala. If you have any questions about tickets or programming, my assistant, Emmie, would be very happy to help you." She watched as the colonel tugged on his wife's hand, gesturing delightedly with his shortened arm to the confectionary shop opposite them, where long pulls of taffy rotated in the window, his ecstatic grin as bright as those of the small children pressed up against the glass. Ben had adored them, no small wonder why. She could have adored them too. "Congratulations again on purchasing Kellynch. I'm sure you'll be very happy here in Niagara-on-the-Lake. Bye, now."

The first song of Vidya's Taylor Swift custom heartbroke playlist—and really, Anne figured, she should probably be grateful it was only a playlist and not a custom animal onesie or a starter plant—was called "right where you left me." Halfway through the song she clicked it off.

September's heat was extinguishing quicker than usual, and the farmers agreed it would be a long, cool autumn followed by a snowy, brutal winter this year. Anne paid more attention to their predictions and their faithful farmer's almanac than she did the TV weatherman. A long, cool autumn meant brighter fall colors for more weeks, which meant more tourists and more theater tickets sold.

The Fairchilds were clearly putting down roots in the community. In the time since Anne had seen them, they had joined a church, gotten involved with several local charities and donated to several more, joined the small-business owners' association and the winery owners' association, and become regular ticket holders to all the festival's shows.

Was it reasonable to think she could dodge them forever? No. Was she going to try? Yes.

Healthy coping mechanisms, healthy coping mechanisms, Anne chanted internally as she goaded herself to go say hello but then ducked behind the box office counter instead, as the couple passed her in the lobby for a matinee of *Singin' in the Rain.*

Clearly, she was not as self-disciplined as Vidya gave her credit for.

She knew her luck would run out. It was a matter of when, not if. She did risk assessments all the time for work, and this was a no-brainer.

But if there was anything to truly resent about the whole situation, it was this: after years of mental discipline, decidedly *not* thinking about him, he was now, once again, all she could think about.

After their breakup, there had been this period of time when she was still half-convinced she was doing the right thing. Yes, it hurt like hell. Yes, she missed him. Yes, she thought of him. Constantly. He had this terrible habit of scribbling notes and reminders on whatever scrap of paper was closest at hand, sometimes mixing them up. Anne came to look forward to finding crumpled receipts or restaurant napkins tucked into her schoolbag, "I love you. Apples, eggs, cereal" scrawled on the back, or "see you later sweetheart," along with maybe a reminder to himself about a dentist appointment the previous week. He'd once accidentally handed in an essay with an appreciative note in the margins about how she'd looked in a particular dress the night before; the professor had not been amused. God, she loved that quirk of his, disastrous as it sometimes was. That, and the adorable furrow he got between his brows that she liked to smooth over with her hand . . . So yes, she missed him. But the logic and persuasion that breaking up had been the right thing to do was still there. And she was young, someone else would come along, her mother reassured her, and then Ben Wentworth would be forgotten.

A few others did come along. He was not forgotten.

Which really, *really* sucked.

In fact, those other nice, handsome, unobjectionable young men that came along only served to vividly demonstrate to Anne just what she had lost. She found them all rather flat after Ben. She told herself that she was being too spoiled, too picky, as one by one her friends started to move in with, get engaged to, get married to, their significant others. She told herself that of course first loves made a big impression, and a more settled, mature relationship wouldn't compare.

But really, had her relationship with Ben been as immature as all that? His moments of impetuosity, his independent spirit, his shaggy hair and beat-up jeep that had alarmed her mother—they softened in remembrance, and instead Anne circled the sensation of being the nexus of his world. And his warm, protective nature, that devil-may-care attitude that only hid his determination to take everything on the chin and keep going, his dry sense of humor and occasional terrible dad jokes. The contentment of lying her head on his shoulder, the way she could always look up in a crowded room and find his eyes on her. He knew who he was, and he knew who Anne was, so thoroughly, and that knowledge had made the ephemeral tie of loving each other feel solid and grounding in a way no other romantic relationship she experienced afterward could replicate.

And she had cut that bond, taken a straight razor to it with clinical cruelty, believing it a kindness to them both.

It didn't take long for regret to sink in. Ben Wentworth was the one that got away.

She stopped stalking him on social media (most of his presence was behind private accounts anyway) and began to methodically weed out thoughts of him until they were as faint and far between as possible. It was healthier. She would move forward. Dating was disappointing, yes, but another guy might still be out there that she would want to have, even if it would never be like being with Ben.

And then her mother's diagnosis wiped everything else out.

And now she was right back in it like the breakup was eight weeks instead of nearly eight years ago, and every little thing was reminding her of Ben.

It was distracting and depressing.

So, it was almost a relief when Naomi strode into her office one morning, with the grace and force of a slightly aggressive swan, and declared she had a project proposal.

"I want us to take a meeting with the Fairchilds."

It was such short-lived relief.

"The Fairchilds . . ." Anne repeated slowly, as if searching her memory, stalling.

"Yes, you met them the night you passed out, new owners of Kellynch Winery."

"Oh yes, I remember." Anne feigned sudden recognition. "They seemed nice."

"Yes, nice. They took a liking to you." She shifted in her seat as she said it, poorly masking her irritation at this preference. Naomi was attractive and, in Anne's estimation, quite talented at her job, but there was something hard-edged about her, some calculating quality that no amount of elegant skirt suits and softly waved hair could disguise. People were instinctively wary of Naomi.

Anne privately thought her colleague might be happier in a more fast-paced environment where business wasn't mingled with small-town ways, perhaps in Toronto or New York, but she wasn't close with the marketing director and so kept her thoughts to herself.

"I'm sure they were just concerned for me. What's the meeting for? Are they interested in becoming corporate sponsors? They can't have got the winery up and running that fast."

"I want to approach them about buying their field."

Anne blinked. "Do we need a field?"

Emmie chose that moment to knock on her open office door. Anne waved her in and then sighed when Emmie deposited yet another bran muffin on her desk.

Do we even sell bran muffins at the refreshments counter? Where is she getting these?

"Why do you wanna buy a field? Aren't there, like, fields everywhere around here? That winery is outside the town," Emmie said bluntly.

Now it was Naomi's turn to sigh. "During the pandemic, when indoor theater was banned, how did we stay afloat? We rented a field and a marquee and did outdoor theater."

"I thought we stayed afloat because Paranoid Paul is our CFO and bought pandemic insurance," Emmie interjected.

"Emmie, don't call him that . . ."

"What did you call him . . . ?"

Emmie looked between the two women and shrugged. "Paranoid Paul, the Pandemic Prophet. That's what *everyone* calls him."

"Well, they shouldn't. It's disrespectful and we are not making light of the pandemic," Anne said sternly as Naomi's mouth twisted up in a repressed sort of grin. "And it's a grotesque amount of alliteration."

"Also inaccurate." Naomi smirked. "Can you call him paranoid if he was right? He should be Justified Paul, and—"

"Prescient Paul!" Emmie exclaimed.

"We must have been the only theater this side of the Atlantic with a specific insurance policy for business disruption due to 'communicable diseases,'" Naomi acknowledged. "Everyone else went to court with their provider to try to get coverage; we got a straight payout."

"Which kept five hundred people on the payroll instead of massive layoffs," Anne added firmly, "so we should be grateful to Paranoid . . . *shit*, grateful to Paul." Emmie laughed and

Anne considered throwing the bran muffin at her. "We're getting off topic, Naomi . . ."

Naomi picked up the thread again. "Yes, the insurance payout got us through the first year, but the revenue from ticket sales from the outdoor theater—even with seats spaced out—gave us a needed boost and kept us going as well. Even without another pandemic, why not set up something more permanent, with low-budget whatever-in-the-park-style productions? The cost of a semipermanent marquee or a band shell, maybe heaters through the fall . . . We could run until the snow fell each year. We could have a killer profit margin on this."

Anne leaned back in her office chair and thought it through. *It has potential . . .*

"Would it cannibalize our regular ticket sales? People choosing the tent instead of our more expensive indoor productions?" she asked.

"I'm sure with the right programming we could sufficiently differentiate the shows and go after a completely new demographic in sales. I've got target figures I can email you. I'm thinking of families with babies and picnic baskets, maybe we try out different styles of entertainment, singers doing Broadway medleys, radio play readings . . ."

Anne nodded slowly and Naomi huffed, clearly irritated with this lackluster reaction.

"I'm not saying no. It's a good idea and I like it, but I'd need to see the figures first." Then she remembered why this conversation had made her queasy in the first place.

Right, the Fairchilds.

"Why a field from the Fairchilds? They're outside of town."

"Precisely my point." Naomi leaned forward and tapped one manicured nail on the desk in emphasis. "The town limits are on the brink of stretching, everyone's buying on the outskirts, and there's a whole new set of wineries setting up between here and the town of Grimsby. The Kellynch Winery is smack in the middle of it all, not far from the new highway turnoff they're putting in. We could establish a new epicenter and expand our reach, and that would also help keep the venue distinct from the in-town festival."

She'd clearly spent time planning and thinking this through, which meant . . .

"You've already talked to the Fairchilds, haven't you?"

"Yes. It's not a full green light yet, but they're interested in discussing it."

"Okay," Anne said slowly, trying to think of a way to have these discussions that would minimize her own involvement, "so these discussions . . ."

"They're calling you in ten minutes." Naomi checked her watch. "Actually, this conversation took nine minutes longer than I expected. They'll be calling you now."

"What!" Anne said sharply. "Why did you—"

"Emmie has been guarding your schedule lately like you're on your last legs." Naomi shot Emmie a look that Emmie returned with venom. "You're not ill, are you? I mean, you look tired but that's not new. I figured shoehorning them in was the best way to make this phone call happen."

Anne stared at her, unsure if she needed to exert some authority here or if she was overreacting because it was the Fairchilds. She didn't have long to ponder—thirty seconds to be exact—before the phone started ringing. **Kellynch Winery** flashed across the display screen.

Get it together, Anne, she told herself, and hit speaker on her phone.

"Hello, Anne Elliot speaking."

"Ms. Elliot, how are you!" The colonel's usual genial enthusiasm radiated through the tiny speaker. "We got your message—oh, my wife is on the line, too, by the way, say hi; oh, Jenny, no, it's on speaker; I don't think we need the second handset in the living room—to say you were feeling better, but are you feeling better? That was a bit of a tumble you took, m'dear."

Anne saw Naomi stifle her sigh at these rambling pleasantries. Her own heart rate was going double time.

"I'm quite recovered. It was nothing more than a little low blood sugar, but thank you for inquiring and thank you for helping me up that evening. How are you both?"

"Oh, we're settling in nicely, and we've been seeing all the shows. The winery is . . . Well, the previous owners left it in a bit of a state, but once we get our sleeves rolled up, I'm sure we'll have it humming in no time. It's such a beautiful property—so beautiful, in fact, I hear you'd like a slice of it!" He chuckled.

"Yes, my colleague Naomi is sitting here with me, and I understand she has approached you with a business proposition. There's absolutely no pressure, of course, you've only just taken possession, and we're still in the stage of exploring the concept itself, but if you are interested, we'd love to discuss it further with you."

"We are interested." That was Mrs. Fairchild's voice chiming in. "It sounds like a wonderful opportunity to work with the festival and bring visitor traffic to the winery."

"Dinner party, tell them about the dinner party," Colonel Fairchild prompted his wife in a whisper, clearly unaware that the speaker was still picking him up.

"Shush, they can still hear you," she chided him back. "Ms. Elliot . . ."

"Anne," Anne interjected.

"Anne," she corrected herself, "we're having some guests over Friday evening, just some new friends we've met in the community. It's nothing fancy, just dinner and drinks on the patio—we thought we'd take advantage before the weather got too chilly, but we do have some space heaters—and we'd love it if you would come . . ."

Naomi gave a little cough.

". . . You and Naomi, of course, and then perhaps after dinner we could chat about this idea."

"We'd absolutely love to come, Jenny," Naomi cut in decisively, before Anne could even arrange her thoughts. "What time should we be there?"

"Oh wonderful. People will start arriving at six, but really whatever time works for you. I'm sure your workdays sometimes stretch long."

Out of the corner of her eye, Anne could already see Emmie using her phone to put it Anne's calendar. This was happening so fast. But Mrs. Fairchild wasn't done.

"And then you'll be able to meet our nephew, Ben. He's coming down from Toronto for a few weeks, to help us sort out the business and paperwork—he's aces at these sorts of things—and he can hear the proposal from you directly."

"Wonderful, we look forward to meeting him. We'll see you Friday at six," Naomi said briskly, and then immediately reached over the desk and hit the button to end the call.

Fuck, fuck, fuck! Anne sat there stunned.

Naomi got to her feet and checked her watch again, clearly already mentally moving on to her next task. "We can take separate cars if you want, Anne, but I'm happy to carpool. Let me know." And she walked out the door, completely unaware of the bombshell she'd detonated in her wake.

Anne felt the blood drain from her face. In two days, she would be seeing Ben again—no, in two days' time she would be forced to have a prolonged conversation with Ben again, in which they would have to discuss a business deal in front of his relatives and Anne's colleague, while no one knew what they had been to each other, and probably pretending that they didn't know each other . . .

She felt dizzy and light-headed and a sob was rising in her chest. "What the hell? I mean, really, what the hell?" Anne wailed plaintively and dropped her head on her desk with a thump. "Oh god, this is horrible," she moaned to herself.

"Anne?" Emmie prodded nervously; she had her thumbs poised above the keyboard on her phone.

"Just kill me." Anne was past caring that her assistant was still in the room, a slightly hysterical feeling taking over. She pushed out of her chair, thinking she would go after Naomi and cancel this, cancel the whole idea. "Emmie, call Naomi, get her back here, we need to . . ." But she couldn't, could she? "No, no, don't call her, never mind." Anne stopped midstride across her office and spun back around to her desk. Emmie, who had moved to follow her, jumped out of her path. "Emmie, get the Fairchilds back on the line. We have to tell them I'm unwell, I can't . . . Crap, no." Anne slammed a hand down on her desk instead, and Emmie jumped again. "No, don't. Call them, just tell them—No, I can't say, oh shit. Shit. Shit. Shit!" Anne shrieked, and Emmie leapt backward, like she'd been electrified.

"Okay," Emmie said. "Okay, okay, okay—"

"Why do you keep saying 'okay'?" Anne cried.

"I don't know!" Emmie was flapping her hands and bouncing on the spot now, looking panicky. "I've never seen *you* freak out before and it's freaking *me* out! Even when that usher ruptured his ulcer during *The Music Man* and sprayed half the third row with blood you were like super calm! You did first aid and called the ambulance and your Dior dress looked like a horror show and now you're like, *losing* it because you have to meet with old people and I don't understand what's happening and . . . Do you need another muffin?"

Anne stared. Then she couldn't help it; she started to laugh.

At that moment Vidya skidded around the corner, ricocheted off the office door with a bang, loose pins and tape measure flying from her apron, and came to a breathless halt in front of Anne's desk. "Emmie texted me, said it was an emergency." Her eyes snapped back and forth from Emmie's panicked confusion to Anne's teary laughter. "What the hell did I miss?"

Anne collapsed back into her office chair. "I have to meet with the Fairchilds and their nephew to discuss a business venture on behalf of the festival."

"Oh . . . *Oh!*" Vidya's eyes widened as the implication sunk in. "And your response was to go into hysterics and have me run up three flights of stairs when I was in the middle of a fitting? Have you not been listening to the playlist I made you?"

Anne tipped her head back and laughed some more.

It took Anne only a few minutes to pull herself together again. She calmed Emmie, thanked her for texting Vidya, reassured her that one muffin a day was more than enough, and sent her for an early lunch.

She then helped Vidya tidy the trail of pins and threads she had left down the hall in her mad flight, let her use her office phone to reschedule the fitting, made her a coffee, and split the bran muffin with her. Vidya ate her half happily, while Anne crumbled hers into pieces absent-mindedly.

"I can't let Naomi go alone, she doesn't have the authority to negotiate this deal, and you know she's . . ."

"She's Naomi," Vidya finished. "That woman would strip-mine the winery if she thought she'd get an extra buck or a promotion out of it. You can't send a falcon to negotiate with turtledoves."

"Turtledoves?"

"I've seen them in town. They're cute."

Anne sighed. "Maybe I could send Paul. This would be a financial deal in the end, and he'd need to sign off . . ."

"Paranoid Paul? You can't let him talk to actual people—"

"Don't call him that."

"—he'll want to audit their books before the canapés are served, and his small talk will be the rising cases of wine-label fraud—he'll convince everyone they're being served antifreeze in stemware before the night is out."

"I know, I know!"

Vidya dusted her hands off from the last of her muffin and then snagged what remained intact of Anne's portion and popped it in her mouth. "Anne, do you think this proposal is a good idea?"

Anne reached for her usual analytical calm business focus and turned Naomi's reasoning over in her head for a moment. "Yes," she said emphatically. "I need to see some of the target research, but it's an excellent idea. I should have thought of it myself."

"And if this were any other business deal or partnership in the community, would you send someone else or go yourself?"

"I would go myself," she admitted. It was like pronouncing her own doom.

"Okay, then. If they're living here, chances are you're going to bump into him sooner or later. Do it now, while it's on your own terms and you're braced for it. Look fabulous and rip that Band-Aid off." She drained the last of her coffee and then helped herself to Anne's before getting up to leave. "Maybe dye some of those grays."

Six

The party was in two days.

In that time Anne vacillated wildly between wanting to take Vidya's advice—namely, to look great—and telling herself that any kind of extra preparation would only make her feel colossally stupid in the long run.

She went to events like this all the time. So much of the tourist trade was shared by the local small-business community, including wineries like the Fairchilds', that Anne, in her roles as executive director, town councilor, and "one of the Elliots," often felt she was on a constant tour of vineyard openings, weddings, dinner engagements, and small parties, where people mingled business with pleasure. The way the Fairchilds were working to become part of that community, in the ordinary course of things, Anne would have expected an invitation long before this, only she had been so skillfully avoiding them.

And in the course of attending those events, she would never go to any extra lengths to look any different than she normally did. So, if she went out now and bought a new dress and got a facial, and dyed her hair . . . well, that would be for him, wouldn't it? And what would be the point? Either he would have nearly forgotten her—mortifying—or he would still hate her. How would a new dress and hairstyle fix either of those outcomes?

God, what if he has a wedding ring on? And pictures of a few gorgeous toddlers on his phone.

Anne had stopped walking in the middle of the street at that thought. A passerby cast her a concerned look. Her face must look positively ill, because that's how she felt. It was a possibility; she'd always known it was a possibility, but she never before thought she was going to have to *witness* it, and see him in person and know that he'd built a life with someone else. It was why she was so strict on her social media stalking ban. Knowing a thing was possible and having it confirmed were two very different things.

How would she keep a neutral face and carry on with the evening when she saw that flash of gold on his finger?

If she got gussied up, Anne decided as she washed her hair in the shower, a few hours before the party began, it would mean that deep in her heart she was entertaining a third option, a foolish, ridiculous, moronic option, a hope that somehow he'd be single and see that she was single, and . . .

Don't be an idiot.

Getting that hope up would be the biggest humiliation of all, even if no one would know but her.

You are the executive director of Elysium, the revenue from which is indirectly responsible for two-thirds of this town's income. This is an opportunity to build relations with new community members and broker a deal that could prove not only highly lucrative, but an exciting avenue to further expansion and growth. Your responsibility and focus should be clear. You are not a contestant on The Bachelor. *Stop mooning and pull it together!*

Satisfied with this pep talk, Anne surveyed herself in the full-length mirror in her room, ignoring the fact that her stomach was already trying to climb its way up her throat with nerves.

Her hair was in its standard pinned-up sweep, the usual threads of gray curling behind one ear; a navy Peter Pan–collared sweater dress and pearl earrings toed the line between professional and dinner-party social. Low-heeled, knee-high black suede boots were her concession to the creeping chill in the air, and they were sleek and discreet and would pair well with her black knee-length coat.

God, she looked like someone's maidenly aunt at a funeral.

At that moment Liz passed by the open bedroom door, glanced at Anne, and snickered. "Going as Pollyanna Grows Up for Halloween? Bit early, isn't it?" Having delivered that sisterly comfort—her thumb hadn't even paused scrolling on the phone in her hand—she continued to her own room.

"For Christ's sake," Anne moaned, and began immediately undressing.

Two outfits and twenty minutes later, perilously close to being late, she was finally out the door, unhappy and uncomfortable with the final choice—a beige sweater and matching skirt—and wishing she'd stayed in the first outfit, which had at least been reassuring in its familiarity.

Driving to Kellynch should have been lovely. It was a beautiful, crisp evening, the sky just beginning to darken and smudge. The town fell away as she turned the car onto the single-lane country highway that spooled through farmers' fields and more vineyards, a long, flat stretch of driving that always made Anne feel alone and free with land stretching out all around her; she could be heading to the horizon, she could be heading anywhere. The delicious smell of smoke and damp leaves drifted in through the window, and she breathed deeply, finding her calm as she deftly sped the car through the deepening dusk.

Anne Elliot does not lose control, she reminded herself.

Thirty minutes later she hooked a left at the roundabout and started driving up the massive hill, the first rise on the Niagara escarpment—on which Kellynch perched. The angle brought her in view of the last burst of sunset, brilliant fiery reds pushing against the rapidly purpling sky, rolling green fields filled with meticulously straight rows of twisting dark vines, and the far-off perimeter edged with lush trees just beginning to burnish into their autumn colors, the same fiery hues as the sunset. There above it all sat the house, a nineteenth-century farmhouse, expanded and refurbished to stand proudly like an emperor on its throne, owning all it surveyed. Anne knew from experience that from the front door you could see all the way to Lake Ontario and the glimmering lights of the cities beyond.

Approaching the house, no matter the season or time of day, never failed to take her breath away.

Her mother had loved Kellynch. When Anne was young, she remembered how her mother used to joke that seeing Kellynch was what made her fall in love with Anne's father. Kellynch had been his family's property for four generations.

"It's like Elizabeth Bennet seeing Pemberley and deciding Mr. Darcy might be a good man after all!" She would flirt with Mr. Elliot, who would smile at her indulgently.

Those jokes stopped the day a bank put a "For Sale" sign on the lawn.

The driveway finally leveled out at the pinnacle of the rise and, with a wide berth, curved around the main house. Behind it lay several smaller buildings, one of brick that was the restaurant, tasting room, and wine store; and two that were wooden barns, the larger one an event rental space. The smaller one had usually been used for farm equipment when her family lived here. She left her car in the small parking lot behind the restaurant and followed the cobblestone path that swirled and curled among the three buildings—elaborate gardens bordering every side of the path—until she reached the massive square patio adjacent to the back of the house. Fairy lights wrapped about the nearby trellises and snaked along the wooden railings that ringed the patio; between the twinkle of the lights and the glare of the setting sun, Anne could only make out the silhouettes of the dozen or so people, mingling and chatting, as she approached.

Which meant no opportunity to scope out who was there and whom she might encounter first as she made her entrance.

It was good that she had so vigorously steeled herself for this meeting, good that she consciously clapped on her Jackie Kennedy professional persona with iron-clad determination, as if she were going to face the board of directors . . . or a firing squad.

It meant she didn't flinch when the moment came, didn't double take. Anne passed under the garden arbor that marked the entrance and stepped onto the glossy wooden planks of the patio. An autumn breeze lifted her hair slightly and made her shiver. A tall, dark-suited man turned.

She betrayed herself with nothing more than a sharp inhalation of breath.

There was a moment of double vision, a twenty-six-year-old Ben superimposed over this imposing stranger, and then the two visions aligned and she saw Ben Wentworth again, after nearly eight years, standing, chatting with a small semicircle of people.

There was a moment of confusion. Anne felt half-blinded, like there were too many people on the patio, too much noise, and he was both too close and too far away.

Then he laughed quietly at something someone said, and the sound curled down her spine, warm and familiar even now, and she fought the urge to flee.

"Ah, Anne, we're so pleased you made it!" Colonel Fairchild's beaming face was suddenly in front of her. She saw Ben's eyes shoot over to them at the sound of his uncle's voice saying her name—a flicker, nothing more—and then immediately his full concentration was back on the guests in front of him, his expression of polite interest never wavering. Anyone else would have missed it.

"Colonel Fairchild, thank you so much for the invite," Anne said, grateful when her voice didn't quaver. She returned the colonel's warm handshake. "Only I feel as if I shouldn't be intruding with business matters, on such a lovely party . . ."

"Not at all, not at all!" he said dismissively. "I imagine you already know everyone here."

Anne scanned the guests, now that she could see them properly. There was Naomi chatting with Dr. Kovalenko, who had a dentistry practice in town, Councilor Singh, a few local business owners, a few actors from the festival company, a farmer Anne knew by sight but not by name . . . "Yes, I think I probably know most of them," she replied. There seemed no rhyme or reason to the guest list, and she imagined the dinner party guests truly were whomever the Fairchilds had met as they settled into the community.

"Excellent," the colonel replied, "then I'll introduce you to the one exception, although not an exception," he corrected himself, "because I think he said you were already acquainted . . ."

Anne's heart flipped over in her chest. *Already acquainted? There's no way he told them . . . they wouldn't be welcoming me into their home if . . .*

"Ben! Come and meet Anne Elliot. She's the festival director extraordinaire, and one of the town councilors."

She had been prepared for seeing him again, but not prepared for what he had become.

He was standing with Councilor Singh, a drink in one hand, nodding along seriously to whatever was being said to him.

Still six feet tall, still broad, but leaner now, in a way that fitted the long lines of his suit. He was clean-shaven—had she ever seen him without a beard or at least two days' worth of stubble?—his hair cropped neatly short—god, how her mother had hated his shaggy long locks; he'd always worn them tied up in a man bun when they went hiking. His hair was still chestnut colored—she remembered it gleamed with a rusty-red tint in the sun or when it was wet—and his eyes still dark navy blue.

He'd always been good-looking, but now his features were even more sharp and handsome, the new, faint beginnings of crow's-feet around his eyes adding charm. He was like Liz, then; aging only made them better. Anne couldn't even spot a thread of gray or a half inch of recession in his hairline. *Jerk*.

"This is my nephew Ben Wentworth," the colonel was saying, and Anne automatically reached out for a handshake. Ben's larger fingers wrapped around her hand loosely, without pressure or a meeting of palms. They both let go quickly. His eyes landed on hers and he held her gaze for just a moment . . .

And she had her answer. No, he hadn't forgotten her, nor had he forgiven her. His gaze was cool and guarded, giving nothing away. Indifference, not hate, was the opposite of love, and Anne felt his indifference all the way down to her bones.

But was it really indifference if it was so pointed?

"Ben is a banker," the colonel said, beaming with pride at his nephew.

With uncle and nephew standing side by side, the resemblance Anne had glimpsed the night she had fainted and first met the colonel was much more pronounced; so much so that she wondered how she hadn't spotted it instantly. They had the same navy-blue eyes under a strong brow, the same wide mouth; the colonel's hair was salt-and-pepper now, but it had probably been a similar color in his youth. Ben was a few inches taller than his uncle, and when he looked away from Anne and down at the older man, his neutral expression vanished into loving warmth.

"A venture capitalist," he gently corrected his uncle.

"Just about the same thing." The colonel laughed. "I suppose Anne would know all about it. You were at the same university, right? That's how you know each other?"

"We know each other slightly, yes. It was a big university." Ben said it with a certain firmness and Anne gave a nod. This was the story he had decided on, then, rather than pretend to be total strangers and risk awkward questions about their alma mater. She accepted it.

"I understand from your uncle you're working in Toronto . . ." She grasped for the kind of small talk one might have with a professional and slight acquaintance and tried to ignore the fact that he knew the location of every freckle on her body. "Do you work for a particular firm in the city?"

"Yes, my own."

"Oh," said Anne, thrown by this information. How had he created his own firm so young? And a venture capitalist? She would have never guessed that future for her Ben.

"I was with a bank for a number of years—"

"See? Banker!" His uncle laughed again.

"—and did quite well. A few colleagues of mine and I decided to form our own firm three years ago, and now that's doing quite well. Turns out I wasn't quite as directionless as people thought I was, back in my twenties."

Anne barely hid her flinch. His tone was polite, neutral, but it didn't matter.

"Well, that sounds wonderful. Congratulations," Anne managed. "I understand you're staying with your aunt and uncle for a few weeks and will be helping with the winery business."

"Yes. The previous owners weren't very professional, but in a few weeks we'll have some new accounting software installed, inventory records, and perhaps reconsider some of the suppliers and contractors."

"It's a retirement project, Ben. It doesn't need to run like IBM," his uncle said wryly, but he nudged his nephew's arm affectionately.

"I just want to ensure things are running smoothly for you and Aunt Jenny, that's all."

"And we appreciate it, and I'm sure we'll appreciate your help on this field business, but let's save that for after dinner. You entertain this lovely lady while I get her a drink."

"She doesn't drink," Ben said.

He and Anne both froze.

But the colonel simply waved a hand and said he'd get her a sparkling water, oblivious that anything was amiss.

Now came the living nightmare—stuck alone in a farce of a conversation until the colonel came back. Anne strained for a topic.

"I'm glad they've purchased the property. I hope they'll be very happy here."

"Yes, they're very excited about it," Ben answered.

Silence.

Don't panic. How long does it take to get a water?

Ben cleared his throat. "Is your husband here this evening?"

Anne gave a start; she glanced down at her left hand for one wild moment as if a ring might have magically appeared there. He glanced down, too, and something, some slight emotion, passed over his face, too faint and quick to discern. It might have been surprise.

"I'm . . . I'm not married," Anne said calmly, while her mind sputtered. Was this a joke at her expense? Blatantly marking out her single status because he wanted some sick proof that her love life was a shambles after she had broken up with him?

But he didn't look gloating; his cheeks had a tinge of color. Embarrassment. "Oh, my mistake. I must have confused you with another town councilor my aunt mentioned." And then, faintly dismissive: "There's so many of you for such a small town."

"Here you are." The colonel was back and handing Anne a flute of sparkling water, and she could have melted in relief. "I think Jenny is just about to bring out dinner. Why don't I seat you down here toward this end of the table . . ."

Seven

With a gentle hand on the small of her back, the colonel led her to one side of the patio where two long tables had been set up. They were beautifully decorated with a deep cream tablecloth, simple place settings, and two large centerpieces composed of fiery maple leaves and golden yarrow. Under the twinkle of the fairy lights, the darkening indigo blue of the evening sky, and the surrounding greens and golds of the vineyards and woods, it was a setting worthy of a photo shoot. Anne wished she could enjoy it, instead of feeling every moment tense and mortified.

Naomi slid into the seat beside her with a huff. "Jesus, how long do we have to play happy guests before we can talk business?" she groused, oblivious to the care the Fairchilds had put into the evening for their guests. "Who's that?" she asked Anne with a jerk of her chin. Anne looked at the guest in question, seated two chairs down from them.

"He's the receptionist at the veterinary clinic out by Harrow Road."

"So, what—they just invited whoever to this thing?"

"I think they invited people they've met and liked, since arriving."

Naomi rolled her eyes. "When they said come to dinner and talk business, I thought this was a strategic dinner with the players. If this is just to play at being Norman Rockwell characters, you could have come alone."

Anne bit her tongue rather than point out that Naomi had engineered this meeting along with her own invitation.

Councilor Singh soon sat down across from Anne and quickly absorbed her into conversation about the latest town hall meeting, for which she was grateful, and soon dinner started in earnest, when Mrs. Fairchild and two local waitresses, who had clearly been hired to assist, came out bearing massive old-fashioned silver tureens and baskets of fresh bread, which they placed along the table. When the covers were removed, the tureens turned out to be holding a first course of butternut squash soup, warmed with a helping of ginger and decorated with a dollop of sour cream that melted into faint creamy swirls as it was ladled into each bowl. The next course, again brought out by the assistants and Mrs. Fairchild—who seemed to be doubling as hostess and server, so often was she jumping up from her seat to tend to things in the kitchen, all the while keeping up a running chatter with her guests—was sliced pork tenderloin stuffed with wild mushrooms and sage.

The food was excellent and the guests seemed to naturally quiet a little as each savored their meal. Anne's stomach was still slightly in knots despite the delicious smells. She managed some bites and then surreptitiously clocked the rest of the table.

Naomi was eating one-handed, the other hand discreetly texting on her phone in her lap. Dr. Kovalenko was chatting with the vet's assistant and drawing Councilor Singh into the conversation. The Fairchilds were laughing with the farmer, who was clearly a neighbor . . .

Ben was sitting in the middle of the table but was solely focused on the dining companion to his right, a young actress named Sabrina. They were laughing at something together.

Anne immediately looked down at her plate.

Sabrina, she knew, was one of the actors from the festival's company, an understudy for the *Macbeth* witches, though she couldn't be further from something witchy. She was about twenty-four, newly graduated from her drama program, with a peaches-and-cream complexion, long strawberry-blond hair, and a round, dimpled face. There was a vague memory of chatting with her at a rehearsal, and something about her being from Newfoundland. Anne had liked her and found her very sweet, if a little trivial. Choi, the director, had mentioned she thought Sabrina had the right look for Juliet for next season but wasn't sure if she was fully up to handling the text. Anne and Choi had left her name on the short list and promised to return to the discussion if Sabrina showed improvement.

Well, she's certainly captivating a would-be Romeo now, Anne thought, and then immediately chided herself for being unkind. *I have absolutely no right to anything concerning him, other than a professional business interaction when we discuss the field.*

But still she couldn't untrain her ears from picking up his voice, smoother and surer than it had been eight years ago, but still with the same deep timbre. He was trying to explain, to the fascinated Sabrina, how a venture capitalist was different from a banker.

God, was this really the man she used to spend hours with on some barely discernable trail in the woods? Whose idea of a long weekend away was sleeping in a camping tent patched over with electrical tape, the night sky full of stars?

"Banks invest money in businesses that are already well established and look like they'll keep doing well in the future. They like a sure thing. Venture capitalists, we get in on the action early and invest when companies are still new and their future uncertain. It's a bigger risk, but there's a bigger reward too."

"Oh, I get it now!" Sabrina exclaimed. "That's so much better—what kind of a person only invests if something is a sure thing?"

"Someone with an ounce of economic or financial knowledge," Naomi muttered under her breath, eyes still on her phone.

"Not everyone is comfortable with taking a risk," Ben said to Sabrina, but he was smiling at her enthusiasm.

"Not everyone is brave," Sabrina countered playfully. "I didn't become an actress because I thought it was a steady profession or a sure thing. Auditions are nothing but risk and rejection and sometimes a win, but I do it because I love acting, I love making art, and when you love something, you have to be brave about it. If these entrepreneurs and new businesses are passionate about what they're doing, then of course you should invest in it! That way you're being brave, too, and you're on the journey together."

"I think that's a beautiful life philosophy," Ben said, his

smile softer, more intimate now. And Anne could swear she heard her own heart crack. If a person was already heartbroke, as Vidya called it, shouldn't there be a moratorium on incurring further breaks?

Sabrina's every word felt like an indictment against Anne's own past behavior.

"Anne, I've been meaning to get your opinion," Councilor Singh said, unaware that she was interrupting Anne's eavesdropping. "These new bylaws we're proposing to stop some of those awful condo developments, do you think they're strong enough?"

D essert was—of course—Canadian butter tarts, both the classic version and the ones with various toppings. The Fairchilds were clearly still in the process of discovering the contents of Kellynch's preexisting wine cellar, as bottles of Cabernet Franc ice wine, merlot, rosé, riesling, and sparkling riesling all adorned the table in a sort of Bacchanalian jumble.

Colonel Fairchild had clearly passed on the information that Anne didn't drink, as Mrs. Fairchild made a point of offering Anne a cup of coffee instead, which Anne gratefully accepted.

"Why don't you come with me into the house—you and Naomi—and we can have that chat with Ben while I make it. My husband will keep an eye on the guests out here," Mrs. Fairchild said.

The two women obediently followed their hostess through the double-wide back door and down a long hallway—one that Anne could remember playing in as a child—past a dining room where the sound of the two hired servers enjoying their own meal and giggling could be heard, and into the kitchen. There lay a veritable tsunami of cooking pots, dirty plates, and cloth napkins that had been pushed unceremoniously onto a long kitchen table in a bid to clear up some counter space. Mrs. Fairchild immediately set to work rehoming leftovers in order to get access to the coffee machine, while dodging the extra serving platters and bottles of wine that stood tall among the food debris.

And there, somehow still looking impeccable and professional even amid this homey clutter, was Ben, leaning casually against a counter and enjoying a beer.

Anne could only hope being perpetually surprised by his presence would wear off soon.

"We buy a whole winery and you only want beer," Mrs. Fairchild chided him playfully, reaching up to flick his ear. He grinned at her and gave a one-shouldered shrug, moving quickly to put down his beer and lift a heavier tray out of his aunt's path, but when his eyes turned back to Anne and Naomi, his gaze was cool and assessing. He stood tall in his sharp suit, sure and confident and without a whiff of his earlier embarrassment. This was a man accustomed to doing business.

"It's my understanding that your festival would like to annex one of Kellynch's fields," he said smoothly, by way of an opening. "I don't know how far you've gotten in the agreement, but I'll be the liaison for my aunt and uncle on this matter from here on."

Annex? We're a theater company, not an authoritarian state.

In the face of this slightly aggressive opening, Anne's diplomacy and gracious manners, so well honed over the years as executive director, rose to her aid.

"Thank you for taking the time to speak with us this evening. We don't want to detain your aunt too long from her guests, but why don't we take a step back and start at the beginning. This is my colleague Naomi, our director of marketing," Anne said, and Ben and Naomi shook hands. "This proposal, in its very early stages, was her idea, and we think it has a lot of potential. Naomi previously discussed it with your aunt and uncle to learn if they were open to it, but we haven't entered into any formal discussions, nor would we until they were indeed properly represented. I have no doubt that your aunt and uncle are lucky to have your professional eye on this matter, and with careful consideration I hope we can come to an arrangement that is amenable to everyone."

"And what is this amenable proposal?" Ben asked.

"We want to buy Kellynch Winery's north field and use it for a semipermanent outdoor theater venue," Naomi said, direct and to the point. "It'll increase traffic to the winery for them, and expand our reach."

"Why do you need an outdoor theater venue?" Ben asked. "You already have three indoor venues, one with a seating capacity of over three hundred; your own customer traffic isn't in excess of that."

Clearly, he'd been reading up on the festival. Anne immediately realized he'd have gotten what information he could on their finances, future planning, corporate governance, and the cost of real estate in the area. Naomi was mistaken if she thought she could push this over on the Fairchilds as a quick deal—they weren't dealing with the turtledoves, as Vidya called them; they were dealing with a Bay Street shark intent on protecting his kin. *Good.*

Naomi seemed to have gotten the memo, too, and Anne watched her mentally marshal her arguments. This was going to be way too combative for Mrs. Fairchild's kitchen; it was just meant to be a preliminary discussion. A full negotiation like this would need to be moved to a boardroom ASAP.

"We had some learnings from the pandemic," Anne cut in smoothly, before Naomi could speak. "We were very fortunate in our insurance policy, but many other theaters were not. Outdoor theater wasn't a necessity for us, but it was a contributing factor to how we stayed afloat. We're now considering how to properly diversify our venues, as well as our entertainment offerings, as both a future source of income and an operational work-around—hopefully we'll never need it for the same reason as COVID. We've reviewed a few locations"—*a lie but oh well*—"but the north field would be ideal for a number of reasons we can enter into later. We think this proposal could enhance the Kellynch Winery as well as our own business."

"Tourists could take in a show at our venue and follow it up with a drink on your patio, a tasting or vineyard tour, or a browse through your wine shop," Naomi added. "Increased signage from the highway, increased traffic for everyone."

Mrs. Fairchild had gotten the coffee machine up and running at this point, and its quiet gurgling filled the silence. Like in a poker stalemate, everyone kept their face neutral, except Mrs. Fairchild, who gave Ben a pointed look. He glanced at her and then nodded at Naomi and Anne.

"My aunt and uncle are interested, but if they're going to be neighbors with your shows, they want a say in the programming, how it's advertised, and what marketing deals we might work up for all-inclusive packages for visitors. Any arrangement we made would have to have provisions for their involvement, nonnegotiable."

Mrs. Fairchild gave an exasperated sigh, and Anne surmised that Ben had conveyed what she wanted said, but not in the manner she wanted to say it.

Naomi looked mulish at the request, but Anne ultimately had control of programming and so it was up to her.

"That would certainly be . . . unusual," Anne said carefully, "but not necessarily a deal-breaker for us. Unless there are any other caveats, are we agreed, then, that we can in good faith try to broker a deal?"

Ben eyed Naomi as if daring her to voice her objections, but Naomi thankfully must have been biting her tongue, and so he gave one short, sharp nod and the thing was done and begun.

They would be negotiating with Ben for the next few weeks.

"Wonderful," Anne said. "My assistant will email you a draft of an initial proposal—it'll be a very rough outline, but it will give you something to react to—and we can go from there." *And now I have to get out of this kitchen before someone snaps, possibly me.*

"Wonderful," Mrs. Fairchild echoed briskly, seeming to feel some of the same tension that was clawing at Anne. "And your coffee is ready just in time. Cream or sugar?"

For a glance of a second Anne wondered if Ben would accidently come out with her coffee order like he had her teetotal status, but he didn't so much as flicker, still busy staring down Naomi.

Clearly that slipup would not be happening again.

———————

The dinner party wound down and Anne drove home.

Back down the driveway of her family's former homestead, back past the fields of perfectly straight creeping vines, back around the roundabout, and back onto the long stretch of country highway, now completely empty at this late hour.

She listened to "my tears ricochet" from Vidya's playlist. She prided herself on not crying.

Eight

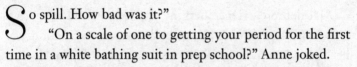

"So spill. How bad was it?"

"On a scale of one to getting your period for the first time in a white bathing suit in prep school?" Anne joked.

"Well, we're absolutely circling back to that story one day— it was way too specific to be fiction—but also . . . that bad?"

Anne groaned and burrowed down into her blazer and angora sweater, even as she tipped her chin up to catch the warmth of the sun on her face.

She'd gone into work that Monday morning doing her level best to shake off Friday night. The first order of business had been to read over Naomi's target numbers and research for the outdoor venue; the second was to start on a proposal for Ben and the Fairchilds. Okay, so maybe the proposal had actually been the third thing on her list, because the second thing on her list turned out to be googling Ben's firm. Turnabout was fair play, she told herself; he obviously knew all about the festival, and why wouldn't he if he was going to strike a deal with them? So really, she would be remiss if she didn't similarly brief herself on his background and dealings.

That was when Vidya had found her and declared she needed an update on the "Anne Drama," as if this was one of their shows that had resumed after intermission. They'd grabbed two to-go cups of coffee from the shuttered lobby concession and taken them into the landscaped lawns behind the theater. Their bench overlooked the man-made pond that Double-Oh-Goose had declared his home for the morning, as the landscaping crew tried to persuade him otherwise, and Professor Davis not-so-silently fretted nearby.

"How bad was it?" Vidya asked again.

Anne closed her eyes and tried to think how to articulate what Ben's behavior had been like.

"He definitely remembers me, and it's not fond memories. I wouldn't say he hates me, or he'd show more emotion, but he . . . he's just so scrupulously neutral and professional when he has to interact with me. He told his uncle that we knew each other *slightly* from university."

"Ouch," Vidya said sympathetically. "That's definitely enforcing distance."

"Once or twice, he said something that seemed sort of pointed, but honestly that could just be my own brain interpreting it that way."

"Did no one else pick up a vibe from you two?"

"There was no vibe to pick up," Anne said, ignoring the way Ben had frozen after letting it slip that he knew Anne didn't drink.

Vidya sighed and took a sip of her coffee. Both women were silent for a while as they watched the landscapers with their long-poled pool skimmers try to circle the far end of the pond. Professor Davis stood nearby, wringing his hands and looking like he might leap in and intervene lest one feather be ruffled. Double-Oh-Goose was serenely observing the proceedings, paddling leisurely around in the dead center of the water, just out of reach.

"Do you ever get the impression that bird is secretly laughing at us?" Anne asked.

"He's managed to score three martinis in one season—if I got that many free drinks from a bar, I'd be laughing too," Vidya replied. "But back to Wentworth . . ."

"He's made it so we can't be openly exes, and I agree with him on that at least; it would be so difficult and embarrassing to explain. We're not friends—we can't ever *be* friends now. So, what are we? We are what we appear: professionals interacting on a business venture." Anne's mood soured further at her own pronouncement as the truth of it hit her. "It's small talk for forever, it's banal questions about the weather, and awkward handshakes, and pretending that I don't know there are a thousand more things going through his head than what he's saying, and pretending I don't want to know what those thousand more thoughts are. It's bloodless, it's perpetual estrangement, it's all my doing, and now I know for certain it can't be undone."

She should have already known that, though.

Anne had lied to Vidya when she said she never contacted him again. A year after the breakup she'd sent him an email—not trusting that he hadn't changed his phone number. It was brief but friendly, a sort of "How are you?" A gentle approach, Anne had thought, to reestablishing contact. Just a hopeful first step. He never replied, and that was answer enough. She never tried again.

He would never forgive her because he wouldn't, couldn't, understand why she had broken them up in the first place. An army brat brought up without roots, without the ties to place or people like she had—no siblings, distant parents, only a beloved aunt and uncle constantly being redeployed—his love for Anne had the permanency and significance of a duck imprinting for the first time. Anne was both partner and home to him. So what did it matter if they were backpacking in New Zealand or doing the trails in Whistler or staying in Niagara? So long as they were together, that was all the stability and planning he needed. That it hadn't been enough for her was incomprehensible to him. He knew Anne wasn't so free-spirited, but until that horrible day, he hadn't known that her fear of the future could supersede their relationship.

So what if he was freshly breaking her heart now? It was only fair—she'd broken his first.

Why had she hoped the dinner party might go any other way?

"Hope is the thing with feathers," Anne quoted quietly.

"The thing with feathers is what's taking out your landscaping crew," Vidya said dryly, gesturing with her coffee cup.

"No! No! Don't touch him. We're just trying to *encourage* him to move!" Professor Davis was shrieking at one of the younger staff who had leaned out over the pond's edge, his pool net nearly touching Double-Oh-Goose, paddling tantalizingly closer.

"If I can scoop him up . . ."

"Scoop him up? Scoop him up?! He's a magnificent Canada goose, you dimwit! You don't scoop him up like a rogue pool float!"

"We're doing our best here, Professor Davis . . ."

"Your best isn't good enough! Your best is a slight on Canadian wildlife! Your best is ham-fisted blundering about with ill-advised equipment!"

"Well, what is the proper equipment?!" roared Wilson, the head of the crew, who was wearing his full fishing waders and was trying to trudge through the shallow reeds.

"NOT A POOL SKIMMER, THAT'S FOR DAMN SURE!" Professor Davis bellowed back, and grabbed the coat back of a second crew member, who was trying to triangulate his skimmer with his colleague's. The motion overbalanced all three men and, in a cacophony of noise and cartwheeling arms, toppled them into the pond with an almighty splash.

Double-Oh-Goose gave a derisive honk and began to preen the feathers of his back end in what could only be bird language for *Catch* me? *My ass, you will.*

Wilson gave a grunt of frustration and waded over to disentangle the flailing, soggy ball of men in the shallow water.

"What's going on out there!?" Disturbed by the noise, Paul, the CFO, had poked his head out a window on the second story, where his office was located. Naomi, when she first joined the festival, had wanted that office for the beautiful view overlooking the gardens. Paul had insisted on having it for its proximity to a fire escape.

"I'm sorry, Paul, they've just been trying to move the goose again," Anne said apologetically.

"Is that a euphemism?" Paul asked, and Vidya sniggered. He glared down at her and Anne both. "I am just trying to enjoy my morning coffee and a good risk-benefit analysis, but all I hear is waterworks and shrieking! Is this a place of work or one of those E. coli–infested water parks?!"

"We are relocating an endangered creature." Professor

Davis had finally extracted himself from the pond with Wilson's help and was now standing dripping on shore. "I am trying to protect this creature and these buffoons are fouling it up!"

"No 'fowl' puns, Vidya, I beg of you," Anne said. Vidya closed her mouth.

"Canadian geese are not endangered," Paul shot back at the professor. "They multiply like rabbits. Their conservation status is literally 'least concern' . . ."

"I beg your pardon, but that is an incredibly ill-informed . . ." Professor Davis was now standing directly beneath Paul's window.

"Okay, this is my cue to leave." Vidya snickered. "Before Romeo and Juliet here finish their angry balcony scene." She tipped her coffee cup to Anne in a salute and left to go back inside.

It was another twenty minutes before Anne managed to calm Paul, calm Professor Davis, soothe the soggy landscaping crew, and assure everyone that—Double-Oh-Goose having clearly gotten bored and flown off—a more effective and more humane strategy for dealing with his next appearance would be found.

Carrying the cold dregs of her coffee, Anne finally headed back inside, only to run into Sabrina in the lobby.

"Oh, Ms. Elliot! Good morning!" She looked fresh and sporty in a pair of brightly colored leggings and a crossover sweater, her vivid hair in a long, shiny ponytail. She looked like the lead in a rom-com.

"Hi, Sabrina, and 'Anne' is fine, really."

Sabrina blushed a little. "Right, Anne, I always forget. Did you enjoy dinner Friday night? Wasn't that winery totally gorgeous?"

"It was and I did," Anne said, smiling gently at her. "You're at the theater awfully early. I thought call time wasn't until noon for the matinees."

"Oh, it is! I came in early to use the warm-up room. I wanted to practice my barre work. I'm going out for brunch so I might be a little bit late for call time, and I wanted to limber up. Choi said she didn't mind!" She said the last part worriedly, though Anne hadn't reacted. She wondered if Choi was simply too distracted trying to manage Michelle to notice what her other actors were up to. She made a mental note to check in with the director.

"Well, brunch sounds lovely; have a wonderful time."

"Thanks, I will," Sabrina responded, but she was already looking past Anne and out the lobby doors, her whole face lit up.

Anne turned at the sound of a motor pulling into the driveway. It was the truck Anne often saw the Fairchilds driving into town. Behind the wheel sat Ben.

Of course.

Despite Sabrina's cute but informal attire, Ben was—from what Anne could see—in another beautiful suit, this time in charcoal gray. It should have looked incongruous with the truck, just like he should have looked incongruous with Sabrina in her yoga wear, but when she skipped past Anne to climb into the passenger seat, it all made a charming picture.

The truck rumbled off. Anne stood in her empty lobby, clutching her cold coffee.

Nine

As the Fairchilds had invited her to dinner, it was only proper etiquette to return the favor. She would have avoided it at all costs, but such was the price of doing business in a small town. Her mother would have been disappointed to think Anne was anything but a gracious hostess within the community or on behalf of the theater. Her conscience demanded it, though she dreaded the prospect.

But where could she host them? Her own home was off-limits—she wouldn't subject them to her father and sister by inviting them to the pink-painted house on King Street, nor could she bear the idea that Ben might come along and have to encounter her family again, watch them snub him again, if they even remembered him . . . No.

In the end, she sent them a quick email inquiring if they'd be at the next town hall, and if so, that she'd love to host them for a drink at the Pillar and Post afterward. She cc'd Ben so that he couldn't accuse her of trying to circumvent him when he'd been so adamant that all business matters were to go through him, but she worded her email carefully so that he'd understand this was purely a social reciprocity. She also extended the invitation to Naomi, who, upon hearing the "purely social" part, flatly declined.

The Fairchilds wrote back accepting immediately and delightedly and added in a postscript that they hoped to see her for another visit at Kellynch before too long. Anne winced when she read that part. She didn't want to turn this into an ongoing thing.

They didn't cc Ben on their return email. She took that part as a good sign he wouldn't come.

H e came. *Because of course.*

Town hall meetings were meant to happen once a season, but truthfully they took place far more often than that. Anytime something of even mild note happened in the community, someone called for a meeting, and invariably someone would second that, which meant, according to the town charter, a meeting had to be held. Anne had a long-standing mental note for someone to revisit and update that charter.

There was that town hall called because someone had put a fish in the Simcoe Park fountain last year, and that time the military costumes for the live reenactors went missing. Then there was the great debate of 2015 over whether a waffle breakfast or a pancake breakfast should be served at the Canada Day Fete in July. After two hours of discussion, they ended up serving both.

Luckily, this was the predetermined and planned annual

autumn town hall, to cover normal(ish) things, but Anne still could have done without his presence.

The courtyard outside the Pillar and Post Hotel and Spa had been chosen for this particular meeting, a rectangular yard hemmed in by wooden fencing. In the winter this would become an outdoor skating rink for guests, but for now it served as a reception area when the hotel had large weddings. Strings of Chinese lantern plants looped over the fences, and massive clay planters with chrysanthemums in riots of red, orange, and yellow rimmed the perimeter. The rest of the area had been cleared and set up with folding chairs for the attendees, with a few stand heaters scattered here and there. A lectern was placed at the front of the chairs, where Anne and the seven other councilors would do their speaking—or shouting—from.

The first twenty minutes had been Councilor Singh instructing attendees what were and weren't off-leash areas of the parks. When she went hoarse, Anne took over.

"Second order of business," Anne said firmly, when everyone had finally quieted down about the merits of golden retrievers versus collies and Anne had gotten them back on track. "This year's upcoming Santa Claus parade. Our events committee would like me to remind you that applications to host a float are now available, and that it cannot be larger or heavier than what a tractor can reasonably pull. In regards to who will get to play Santa Claus . . ."

There was a collective indrawn breath from the crowd.

". . . they'll be drawing lots. So, if you'd like to be Santa this year, just put your name in . . ."

They exhaled with disappointment.

"What?! Why we hafta do it that way? I wanted to—"

"*Because* . . ." Anne said pointedly, eyeing the speaker until they were quelled and sat back down, "last year there were some miscommunications about who was selected"—she deliberately avoided eye contact with the parade committee head in the second row—"and we didn't want to hurt anyone's feelings, but I think we can all agree that seven Santa Clauses in one parade is a bit much, no? A draw is fair and impartial and we will all abide by the outcome, yes?" There were scattered, noncommittal grumblings. "We will *all* respect the outcome, yes?"

"Yessssssssss," the crowd intoned, like sullen students forced to accept their homework.

"Excellent," Anne continued briskly. "Next item on the agenda. The town has received an application"—she paused, dreading the next bit—"for a building development . . ."

The room erupted.

"Those goddamned eyesores . . ."

"Why hasn't the whole town been designated as a heritage . . ."

"Please, everyone, if I could just get through this. They will of course have to go through the same process as any other development company . . ." Anne said, raising her voice. "Gui Samye, sit down this instant. This is not a call for a *Les Misérables*–style uprising!"

The young man who wrote highly incendiary political pieces for the town paper that no one read grudgingly climbed down from standing on his chair and turned off his cell phone, which had started up the barricade song on its tinny speaker.

"As I was saying, they will have to go through the same process as anyone else. I don't have many details yet," Anne continued quickly, desperately trying to keep control of the room. "Town council will be meeting with the developer soon to learn about the application. I will now take questions . . ."

The room erupted again.

"We should run them out of town!"

"Not a question," Anne clarified.

"Is it true their CEO is super handsome?"

"*Relevant* questions," Anne clarified.

"Is the CN Tower still the tallest building in the world?"

"Relevant questions *that I can answer*," Anne clarified.

"Not since 2009."

"Relevant questions that I can . . . what?"

Anne looked around at the non sequitur. There was Ben, moving quickly down an aisle away from the last row of seats, where the Fairchilds were sitting. He looked like he was equally surprised he had spoken, but he continued on his mission, gently but firmly removing the cell phone from the hand of Gui Samye, who was up again and trying to start another protest song.

"The CN Tower hasn't been the tallest tower since 2009. The kid in the third row doing homework asked," Ben clarified, and, with a firm hand on the reporter's shoulder, sat him back down. "Go on, Councilor Elliot."

The rest of the meeting passed in a haze.

Ten

Y ou survived your first town hall, and that calls for congratulations," Anne said, approaching the colonel and Jenny as people began to trickle away. Ben was standing a foot behind them, seemingly engrossed in his cell phone, as if he hadn't just waded into the thick of the meeting at all and was merely a bored bystander.

Jenny laughed. "What fun! Are they always like that?"

"Not *always* . . ."

"Yes, totally, one hundred percent," Emmie chimed in, popping up at Anne's side.

"Yes, thank you, Emmie. I think you both met my assistant, Emmie, that first night at the gala after *Macbeth*," Anne said, as Emmie grinned at them and shook hands.

"Yes, the lovely voice at the other end of the phone when we call your office. Hello, dear," Colonel Fairchild said, grinning right back at her. "And I'm not sure Emmie's met *our* sort-of assistant, Ben . . . Ben!" he boomed at his nephew, who reluctantly tucked his phone away and joined their group.

"Ben, this is Anne's assistant, Emmie."

"Yes, nice to meet you. We've emailed to set up a meeting for Ms. Elliot and myself," Ben replied.

"I googled your LinkedIn profile," Emmie said unashamedly. "You're like a business Jedi, right?"

Ben fought down a smile. "May the force of finance be with you," he replied seriously, and Emmie cackled with delight.

He still makes those terrible dad jokes, Anne marveled.

"Yes, such a business Jedi he's straight back to Kellynch this evening for some work calls. Sure you won't join us for a drink with Anne?" the colonel asked his nephew.

"I'm afraid not. My apologies, but I need to catch up on a few things."

"If you need to go back to Toronto . . ." the colonel started to say, but Ben cut him off gently and firmly; this was clearly a conversation they'd had a few times before.

"Uncle Grant, I'm staying until you and Aunt Jenny have the business up and running. Toronto is only a two-hour drive away. I can go back for a day if I need to, but I can just as easily work remotely. I've taken the time off. I just need to make a few calls this evening to check in on things."

Anne wondered if his urgency to get away this evening was as much about work as about a strong desire to avoid being forced into an intimate group setting with her.

"Well, at least you didn't miss town hall!" Emmie said. "Hey, if you guys liked this, you should totally check out the Pumpkin Festival!"

"The what?"

"The Pumpkin Festival," Anne said patiently. *Please, please stop inviting him to things!*

"There's actually a . . . Pumpkin Festival," he said slowly.

She couldn't tell if he was disdainful, confused, or amused. It was amazing how he could be warm and joking with Emmie, and immediately microshutter his expression when he addressed her.

"Yes, there's a pumpkin-judging contest, a scarecrow-making contest, food tents, a lot of apple cider and pies . . ."

"How do you *judge* a pumpkin?" Jenny asked.

"Snub it if it came from the poorer patch, maybe check its vines and see if it's well-connected," Ben joked to his aunt; Anne was left to ponder this time if the double meaning and subsequent sting of the joke were intentional or not.

"Prizes are usually awarded to the largest and heaviest pumpkins," Anne said, as seriously as if they'd asked in earnest. "You'll find we have quite a lot of festivals throughout the colder months; it helps to draw the tourists as the weather gets bitter. Our biggest event is the Ice Wine Festival in February. The hotels sell out and people often book months in advance. The Pumpkin Festival is not nearly as popular, but it's very enjoyable."

"It's totally awesome!" Emmie chimed in. "Last year this guy tried to cheat. He hollowed out his pumpkin ahead of time and then put weights inside and glued the lid back on, so it was super heavy, but he got caught because then they decided to use it as a jack-o'-lantern at city hall, and soon as they tried to carve into it, it was, like, game over . . ."

"It was an unfortunate—" Anne started, but Emmie had warmed to her theme.

"And then the year before that, someone was trying to get

the biggest pumpkin so they let it grow and grow until it rotted so it was all soft and squishy, but they still tried to compete, so they left it on the judging table, and Mr. Williams, who owns the golf course, tripped and fell into it and landed headfirst in the pumpkin and was covered in pumpkin guts!"

"Thank you, Emmie," Anne said. "I have been assured that the town events committee will thoroughly check all the pumpkins this year to ensure they're structurally sound and not tampered with."

"Sounds wonderful! We'll all go," Jenny said.

Anne was beginning to be quite impressed with how she kept her face and voice steady when these sorts of slings and arrows appeared, but in this third encounter with Ben, perhaps she was just getting so much opportunity for practice.

"I'm sure you'll all have a lovely time. If your nephew needs to get back, we'd best let him go, and we can go grab that drink if you're still up for it, and maybe some dessert. They have a lovely tiramisu here."

"All right, then, you heard the lady, off you trot. We're in good hands with Anne here." Jenny flapped her hand at Ben. He nodded at Anne and Emmie, kissed his aunt on the cheek, and took off, already back on his cell phone.

Emmie left soon after, with Anne reassuring her that she could take a late start at the office the next day.

And she was left alone with the Fairchilds. She took a deep breath.

"Shall we?" Anne asked, and conducted them into the hotel lounge.

Anne dreaded that the evening's conversation would be spent with the doting aunt and uncle telling her about Ben. That she would have to smile and nod through stories she'd heard before from the source. That they would want to tell her about Ben's parents, both military doctors who had divorced and then taken deployments, so that Ben had come to routinely live with his aunt and uncle on his holidays from boarding school, and how they had practically raised him.

And then Anne would have to try to block the memory of Ben telling her the same things while they were entwined one morning in bed.

"In a way I think I'm pretty lucky," he said, turning over onto his stomach to burrow farther into the pillows, and creating something like a tidal wave for Anne resting against him. He reached out one long arm to snuggle her firmly back into his side from where he had accidentally displaced her, with a mollifying kiss to the cluster of freckles on her shoulder. "Uncle Grant and Aunt Jenny are amazing, better parents than most people get, even if they're not usually home. Even if there isn't really a home."

She didn't have a response for that, but she smoothed his hair back and kissed him, and soon the talk meandered to other things, before turning into a playful debate about staying in bed or venturing out for a late breakfast. When his large hands encircled her ankles and dragged her back under the covers, she shrieked with laughter and gladly allowed herself to be rolled beneath him once more. She didn't really want waffles right then anyway.

Anne pushed away the memory. Shrieking with laughter and warm bodies on a Saturday morning were not things she did anymore.

"I don't want you to think we're . . . pushing our way in

here," Mrs. Fairchild was saying hesitantly. The colonel had stepped across the room to say hi to someone, and the two women were temporarily alone. Anne tried to dial back into the conversation. "Pushing your way in?" Anne tilted her head in curiosity, unsure what the other woman meant.

Mrs. Fairchild—Jenny—was looking across the room at her husband, a combination of affection and well-worn worry on her kind face.

"I told you it was our dream to retire to Niagara-on-the-Lake, and that's true, but it wasn't meant to happen for another ten years."

At Anne's encouraging look, she continued, haltingly.

"Grant was too old for active duty, but he's not the type for a military desk job, so he became an instructor back with the force. That's how he lost his hand two years ago; a training exercise went wrong." Here she sighed and shook her head. "Two tours of Afghanistan and it's on home base that he's injured. It was hard at first . . . very hard." Jenny swallowed, and in that short, sanitized description Anne read two years of loss, trauma, grief, and slow rehabilitation.

"But the hardest part," Jenny continued, "after . . . after it all, was that he was *bored*. The man has had a lifetime of action. His service kept us traveling, kept us meeting new people. We've lived on military bases where everyone knew everyone—Grant's an extrovert, in case you haven't noticed." She smiled wryly. "He's used to being responsible for things, being busy, being important to so many people. What are you supposed to do after a lifetime of that and retirement comes too soon—golf all day long?"

She shook her head ruefully, and Anne was uncomfortably

aware that her father, whole and fit and younger than the colonel, did in fact spend his days eating out and golfing.

"It was Ben that figured out the problem, said we needed a project and a community again. So here we are. Embarking on this business of the winery is good—that's the project—but the community? That's why we're joining every committee or charity that will let us. And that's why, when we sell you this field, we'd like to be a partner in the outdoor venue you're setting up."

Jenny looked down at the wine in her hand with a self-conscious laugh. "My goodness, that was a very long-winded explanation for what I was trying to say. Sorry about that! All I'm *trying* to say is this: that I know you and your family have long been a hub of this town and this community, and I hope you don't think as newcomers we're barging our way into the party uninvited or trying to take over. It's just that Grant—that both of us—want to be involved."

The plea resonated with Anne. The pandemic had given so many people a taste of isolation and inactivity. It wasn't as hard as it might once have been to empathize with the Fairchilds' plight.

"I think," Anne said slowly, putting a hand on her shoulder, "that the more people who care, who work to *take care* of this town and this community, the better. It's everyone's home."

And she meant it.

Eleven

The day Ben was meant to come to the office dawned bright and breezy. From her window Anne could see leaves beginning to tremble and fall—soon there would be an equal amount on the ground as on the trees. That was Anne's favorite part of fall—when everything was carpeted and draped in swirls of gold and red and amber. But today she woke up and felt like telling the beautiful weather to fuck off.

She dressed with her usual care for her professional agenda—only this time it felt a bit more like suiting up for battle. She put on a navy-blue tailored trouser suit over a light blue polo-neck cashmere sweater. She decided to forgo her usual neat bun in favor of a chignon and left off most of her jewelry, except for a pair of small silver stud earrings. The days were getting colder, so she threw a warmly lined trench coat over her arm to take with her, along with her trusty tote.

The kitchen was devoid of her family for a change—no

food suggestions lying about. But there was a note on the table from Liz.

My car towed last night, borrowed yours.
Dad @ sailing club.

Anne let out a noise of exasperation. She usually walked to work but today she was planning to drive to keep her hairstyle intact, out of the strong wind. That'd teach her to leave her spare keys at the front door where Liz could grab them.

"If you would stop parking in the goddamned tow-away zones . . ." she muttered to herself, getting out her phone. She was planning to give Liz a piece of her mind—*how do you live here your whole life and* not *know what is a parking spot and what is not?*—but was halted by the sight of a text message from her father. He rarely texted; he was terrified looking down at the phone would give him tech-neck and jowls.

Anne, down at sailing club, forgot wallet.
Please drop off on your way to work.

This time Anne let out a full growl.

It was only a ten-minute walk to the sailing club, but by the time she got there, her careful chignon had been nearly pulled apart by the strong wind, and she had to take it down and let the wind do what it would with her hair.

Her father was not on any of the boats or the dock but was sitting in the clubhouse, a fancy coffee in front of him that would no doubt become an expensive scotch as soon as the day progressed enough, holding court with several wealthy retirees who were in Niagara for the tail end of the boating season. A few of them Anne knew were snowbirds and would be taking off for their warm second homes in Florida, enjoying the boating and golfing there and waiting out the Canadian winter.

"Ah, Anne!" her father called, waving her over. "Gentlemen, you know my other daughter, Anne."

"Nice to see you all. Dad, here's your wallet." She handed it over. "I've really got to run . . ."

"Ah, sweetheart, give me a hug before you dash off."

Anne hid her wince and complied, already knowing what was coming.

"Listen, Anne, we've just had the loveliest breakfast," he whispered in her ear under the guise of their embrace. "The things their staff can do with egg whites! And it's my turn to pick up the tab for the fellows, but I appear to be a bit cash-strapped at the moment . . ."

"So, I wasn't really bringing your wallet, was I? I am the wallet."

"Anne, let's not make a fuss . . ."

Anne could see that her father's entourage and the wait-staff of the sailing club were within earshot.

As discreetly as possible she reached into her tote to flick open her own wallet and slid her father her credit card. "Breakfast and no more, Dad, I mean it."

"Of course, of course, have a wonderful day at work. By the way, your hair looks much nicer like that, all down and wind tousled. Much more youthful than those severe updos you always have. You look more like your sister."

This is the thanks I get.

Anne left the club making a mental note to use her banking app, freeze her account by midafternoon, and cut him off.

She took a deep breath of the chilly air, turning her face toward the sparkling water and the fresh wind, walking a little way along the dock and trying to center herself. She needed to shake off the impositions of Liz and her father and be wholly self-possessed to face down Ben in exactly one hour.

In the summer this harbor was always filled with sailing boats and speedboats of all sizes, the water crisscrossed with traffic. Now in autumn many had been removed from their docks, stored under tarps in a nearby yard for the winter, creating a sadly empty effect. Still, there were a few boaters left, out taking advantage of the autumn sun and strong wind. One midsized sailboat was just coming in from the open water, maneuvering expertly as it approached a pier, the sailor finished with the day's jaunt. It was a beautiful, classic Bermuda sloop with wood paneling and cream sails, and for a while Anne just watched it glide through the water, fantasizing about getting on board and sailing away from this awful day.

As the boat finally docked, Anne realized that while she'd been admiring the boat, the man on board looked like he was admiring her—or more likely he'd mistaken her ogling his boat for ogling him and was preening under the attention. He certainly looked handsome and accustomed to female attention, with his thick knit sweater and dark windswept hair.

Like a Ralph Lauren ad, Anne thought.

"Hi there," the man called.

Anne nodded. "That's a beautiful boat; she moves like she's certainly yar."

"Thank you," the man responded. "I worked on her myself."

"Bit late in the season to still be out, isn't it?" Anne asked.

"Oh, I can keep her out to the last possible moment—either

until the harbors shut down at the end of October or until the first early freeze. I like to live a little dangerously."

Oh boy, Anne thought, in response to this clearly self-aggrandizing claim, but outwardly she only replied lightly with a "Well, good luck with that," before turning to retrace her steps back down the pier and to head to work.

The man gave her an animated salute before busying himself with mooring his vessel.

There was no point in fantasizing about boats and rugged sailors taking her away. She had a meeting to grit her way through.

Hurrying into the office with only a few minutes to spare, Anne whipped into the ladies' room to try to frantically comb her hair back into some semblance of her usual plain bun and put her clothes to rights; they had been pulled askew by her hasty walk. She looked in the mirror. Her cheeks were flushed, but her eyes looked tired. She splashed her face with cold water to both perk herself up and cool her face down. With her wet hands she slicked back her flyaways until she looked more professional.

It was important, she told herself, because she was going up against a very professional adversary.

She'd stuck to her rule about not social media stalking Ben—what was the point? He was clearly dating Sabrina now, so it wasn't like she needed to check his relationship or marital status. The proof had been right there when he met Sabrina for brunch outside her lobby—but she had allowed herself to finish her research on his career and qualifications.

He had finished his undergrad in engineering after all,

and then had gotten his MBA at the University of Toronto while working for a big bank in the city. His stint at the bank lasted for about five years, and after that he began his new firm, which had been running for three. That pretty much accounted for their full eight years apart, so if he'd taken that trip to New Zealand, it must have been brief. When did he abandon his plan to simply backpack, hike, and travel until he ran out of money? Or did he run out of money that fast?

She'd combed through his organization's website, telling herself it was no more than the reconnaissance she'd do before negotiating with anyone on a business venture. His firm was nascent but impressive; the "About" page featured a brief video of Ben giving a keynote at a conference six months ago—she had watched it several times through. She thought she'd understood his full transformation as he stood there radiating confidence and control in the Kellynch Winery kitchen, but at the conference? It was another level.

Ben had adamantly refused to follow his father, mother, and uncle into the military, but he'd been run through the cadets as a teen and couldn't quite shake off the military bearing. He'd certainly tried: his long hair, beard, and old flannel shirts from when Anne had known him—which, along with appalling her mother, had appalled certain professors, already unimpressed with his wandering studies and the crumpled essays, scrawled across with notes, they were used to receiving from him—had done much to cover it. But deeply buried he still had that physical and mental discipline, that sharp control of himself and awareness of his surroundings, that spoke of a man trained for more. It reminded Anne a little now of the genial Colonel Fairchild, switching into commander mode when she had fainted at the gala. But before, when Ben was that shaggy-haired boy with a lazy grin, the power had only flicked out when he needed it, like a switchblade, from innocuous to dangerous in the breadth of a second.

But now?

She barely recognized this man, who wore his power so prominently. Everything about him was sharp and commanding, from the cut of his suit to the knife-edge of his smile. This was a man who could command a room.

It made her edgy even going into the meeting.

B en had come alone, in another one of his impeccable suits and without the Fairchilds, and Anne felt self-conscious that she was walking into the meeting with both Paul and Naomi like she needed support, but perhaps that was still preferable to a one-on-one with just her and Ben.

In the end it was really a nonevent.

The meeting lasted less than thirty minutes. Ben held his side of the table like he was born to broker deals. He had been through their proposal, which Anne, having had her conversation with Jenny after the town hall about being more involved, knew would be inadequate. Ben clearly thought he was bringing new information to them, that this wouldn't just be a property sale, but rather a partnership. Anne enjoyed, just a little, having the upper hand there, by saying she'd already discussed the matter internally and the festival would be delighted to enter into such an arrangement, and could they perhaps have a little time to create a new proposal? She sketched out a few ideas—a committee composed of the festival and the Fairchilds to determine programming, with the festival maintaining final veto power, an exclusive arrangement for Kellynch Winery to provide refreshments, an opportunity for the Fairchilds to approve the design of the band shell and stage and seating they planned to erect.

"The seating would be made by favoring natural materials, so as not to disrupt the pastoral view, of course. We're thinking of the stone-and-turf sort of design they have at the outdoor High Park theater in Toronto, but of course we can discuss all that further down the road," Anne said.

No need to ask him if he'd seen the High Park theater— they'd had a date there once.

"I would need to be involved in the selection of your contractor and the planner who would be carrying out the work. I won't have my aunt and uncle inconvenienced by prolonged months of construction and incompetence."

"Contractors are notoriously hit-or-miss. You think you have the magic touch to find the right one, be our guest," Naomi said, her tone polite but not quite polite enough.

His undergraduate degree is in engineering. He'll know better than us.

"My undergraduate degree is in engineering. I'll take my chances using my own judgment," Ben said firmly.

"Of course," Anne said quickly, trying to defuse the beginning of tension in the room. "Our point is, these are just a few ways that we've brainstormed for Kellynch Winery and the Fairchilds to be involved in the short and long term. If we're on the right track, then we'll draw up a new proposal for you and your family to review."

"What state is the field in?" Paul piped up suddenly. He'd been mostly quiet through the meeting.

For the first time Ben looked perplexed. "It's a field . . . I haven't actually gone to look at it." He addressed his next remark to Anne, though he kept his eyes on the paperwork in front of him, thumbing through it carelessly rather than look at her. "I understand your family owned Kellynch previously. Do you know anything about the condition of the field?"

Anne shook her head. "We never used it. My father shut down the winery as a business and only used one or two small fields for creating his personal wine collection. Any number of fields on the property were left to grow over."

"I'm uncomfortable with the unknown," Paul voiced, and Anne restrained a sigh.

They adjourned shortly after that, Ben exited the building, and Anne was left to try to shake out her nerves.

Paul followed her to her office.

"We didn't discuss price," he said immediately, hovering by her desk. Paul was tall, taller even than Ben, and exceptionally thin. He had sharp classical features and a shock of white hair. Despite his eccentricities Anne was rather fond of him, though he wasn't the easiest person to work with.

"No, we didn't. I think we want to scope out the project first, before we start negotiating price," Anne replied.

"Real estate around here has gone through the roof in the last three years. You know how much that field is worth?"

Anne named a figure.

Paul nodded. "That's what my estimate is as well. We're still building up our financial reserves again after the pandemic. We'd have to finance the purchase. That's risky."

Anne sat back in her seat and gave Paul her full attention. "Are you changing your mind on the plan? When I ran it by you and you crunched the numbers you seemed okay with it. I know there are probably slightly cheaper fields, but Naomi took full responsibility for the research on this. No other property is as ideal."

"I am . . . in support of the plan," Paul said slowly, "but the Fairchilds being involved complicates things. If we finance buying the field, we go into debt for it and we need to pay it off within a certain time frame or we won't be able to manage it. If we can get the venue up and running by next summer, even assuming a conservative return on ticket prices, then, yes, it's feasible to pay it off. However, these Fairchilds— Fairchildren?"

"Not children, Paul, just the two, and their last name is Fairchild," Anne said, not wanting him to get off track.

"Well, if they're going to be involved in every decision, they could slow down the process considerably, and then how long before we get to start turning a profit on this investment, and how long are we holding the debt for the purchase price? And this couple—who are they? What's their angle? Where did they come from? Why do they want to be involved? And why have they sent this Ben character? Is he really their nephew?"

"Whoa, whoa, whoa, okay, let's slow it down," Anne said. "Paul, they're a nice older couple. He's a veteran, had to take an early retirement, and they want to be part of the community and this project. Naomi came up with the plan and found the field, but I've checked out the Fairchilds. They're perfectly lovely and very reasonable, easygoing people, and I don't think they're going to slow us down."

Paul nodded, but after a moment's consideration added, "This Wentworth character, he was nervous. Why?"

Anne looked at him in surprise. "He didn't seem nervous to me, quite the opposite. What makes you say that?"

"He has an excellent poker face, but I saw the pulse in his throat and I timed it by my watch, and for a man of his age and apparent fitness level, I've calculated that it was above baseline."

Anne took a moment to digest that. "Hey, Paul, remember we talked about not using interrogation tactics on our guests?"

"I didn't *ask* to take someone's pulse this time, I merely *observed*," he said defensively.

Anne held up her hands in surrender. "Okay, we'll call that a compromise. Listen, thank you for flagging the financials. You know I appreciate your diligence on these things, especially when we have to get the board to sign off, but leave the Fairchilds to me. We'll buy the field for the price range we agreed on, no more, no less, and we'll get it up and running by summer. This project is under control."

Paul nodded and breathed out, appeased for now. It had taken a long time for Paul to trust Anne the way he had trusted her mother, and Anne appreciated it in moments like this, when she was able to get through his fears and communicate.

"Red meat will slowly kill you," he said, eyeing the roast beef sandwich on her desk, left there no doubt by Emmie.

Okay, getting through some *of his fears.*

After he left, Emmie poked her head into Anne's office.

"Is he gone?"

"Yes, Paul is gone. How many this time?"

"He asked nine questions in under three minutes. New record!"

A nne spent the rest of the week putting together the new proposal, meeting with Choi and the other directors to plan next year's opening season, and talking Vidya down from buying her own loom to make her fabrics from scratch after she found a certain cotton to be substandard. She spent a few late nights going over Paul's budget numbers in painstaking detail; in case he had further objections, she wanted to be well apprised of the information. Paul was right; things were tight. His pandemic coverage and those outdoor theater sales had pulled them through it, but the cost of shutting down for so many months had still been high. She reviewed Naomi's initial project plan and research again and reassured herself that this was going to work.

One night she fell asleep at her desk, listening quietly to music alone in her office and reviewing the numbers. She dreamed about Ben, a little bit of memory she thought she'd forgotten surfacing again.

"What do you mean you forgot your cell phone?" Anne asked incredulously.

"I mean what I said. I forgot it." Ben grinned at her from behind his thick beard. "C'mon, Annie, we're just walking over to the restaurant for dinner. What do I need a cell for? The person I want to talk to is right here." He leaned down to kiss her.

"One day you'll be tied to a desk, there will be budgets and spreadsheets and having your phone on you all the time. Live a little now."

"And while I'm tied to a desk, what will you be doing?"

"I'll be tied to you."

When she woke up, she realized she was twisted up in her earphones, and Vidya's heartbroke playlist was playing on repeat.

Twelve

With the start of October it was like true autumn had erupted overnight. Trees had abandoned their gentle, slow makeover and were now blazing with color as if a fire had run riot through their tops, the famed Canadian maples a particularly vivid red, lighting up the ridge of the escarpment like a sunset in Anne's periphery every time she drove into or out of town.

The day of the Pumpkin Festival she woke up early, saw that the sun was shining in a blue and cloudless sky and that a crisp, cold breeze was fluttering through her curtains, and felt buoyed in a way she hadn't experienced since Ben came to town. She relished the reprieve from her low mood as much as she relished the gorgeous autumn weather.

It was a perfect day to spend outdoors.

Trekking around a farmer's field while still acting as a respectable town councilor called for chinos, loafers, and a dark purple sweater set. She arranged her hair into a neat bun—detangling straw from your hair after a hayride or from the corn maze was always a nightmare—packed her trusty tote, throwing a warm cashmere scarf in for later, and was out the door.

The festival was held in the grounds surrounding Fort George, not only because it had the space and also brought in visitors to the fort itself, but mainly because it had the parking facilities. The fort itself was like a swelling from the ground, with grassy ramparts sloping up to its wood-and-stone lookouts. Inside the barricaded gates was a clearing the size of two football fields with small reconstructed barracks where officers would have dwelt now serving as living museums. Outside the fort, the lake with its view of the American shore stood to one side, a small patch of woods led to the adjacent parking lot, and the rest was acres and acres of open grass.

It was here in the open grass, cozied up against a sloping exterior fort wall, that they had set up the festival. A marquee tent was the central attraction, food stalls and other small booths dotted around it, and then a massive corn maze erected with hay bales and corn stalks from the local farmers bracketed the area.

"Anne, you're here early!" One of the festival organizers waved to her.

"Hi, Arva. Wouldn't miss a minute of it. Besides, all the good food is always gone so quick!"

"Well, get yourself to the cider booth; there's a hot first batch."

She did indeed get to the cider booth for a cup of hot apple cider and an apple-cinnamon twist pastry. Another stand selling Thanksgiving decorations caught her eye, and she impulsively purchased a bouquet of bright Autumn Beauty sunflowers, thinking how lovely they would look on the dining room table at home; their shades of golden yellow, rust red, and brown winked out of their paper wrapping, peeping over the side of her tote.

Anne breathed in the green of the grass and crisp note of autumn and munched on her treats, watching the festival fill up.

"Liz!" she called in surprise, seeing her sister nearby. "What are you doing here? You don't usually come to Pumpkin Fest."

"Balzac's is supplying the coffee for this thing, so they've shut down the shop in town. Had to come to get my latte," Liz said, holding up her paper cup, and then moved to walk on to the parking lot.

"Hey, Liz, wait," Anne said, her happy feeling extending to her sister and making her nostalgic. "I know it's not your kind of thing, but why don't you stay for a bit? We could get a few treats and walk around. Remember when we were little and Mom used to bring us here every year? We used to love the corn maze and eat all the slices of pumpkin pie we could get away with."

"Sunlight," Liz said succinctly, pointing up and then pointing at her skin. "Potential sun damage. Pass. And I don't do carbs," she said, eyeing Anne's pastry with disdain. "By the way, Professor Davis is looking for you. I'd leave now if I were you."

She exited with her coffee, and Anne was left to wander around the stalls alone with her happy memories, smiling at the kids queuing up for the face-painting stop, where Professor Davis soon found her. He was in full historical costume as a British redcoat from the War of 1812, including the heavy wool uniform, the white crisscrossing stripes across his chest, the tall hat—he looked exactly like a toy soldier.

"What does this look like to you?"

"Hello, Professor Davis. Isn't it a lovely day for a festival?" Anne said, and then, at his stony look, she obligingly looked at the object being thrust at her. "It looks like a rifle."

"Exactly!" he exclaimed.

"Okay, so you have a rifle . . . ?"

"It should have been a musket!"

Don't ask, don't ask . . . dammit. "And the difference is . . . ?"

"Anne, are you serious? I am clearly a foot soldier, not someone from a rifleman regiment. The most common weapon for the foot soldier was the musket; calling it a rifle is like calling a bicycle a motorcycle! Rifles were a more advanced technology with a series of long grooves in the barrel that gave the bullet, or ball, a spin that allowed for greater accuracy, but the reload time was nearly twice as long! The musket has a bayonet attachment and a quick reload. Rifles wouldn't have been wasted in field combat with foot soldiers in 1812! Your props department has clearly messed this up!"

Anne replied with the most soothing tone she could muster in the face of this crisis of authenticity. "Professor Davis, you asked if we had any spare equipment in the props department to help with your reenactment today since you were missing some pieces. This is a historically accurate weapon; I cannot control how many we have of either muskets or rifles. They look the same to me. I'm sure they will look the same to the festival-goers."

This was clearly not the response he wanted. Professor Davis straightened to his full height, righted his tall hat, which had been slipping, and with great dignity said, "This conversation has been most unhelpful. I bid you good day"; saluted her, did an about-face as if he were on military parade; and marched away.

Anne sighed and went in search of pumpkin pie.

She was enjoying a slice of pie and ice cream while admiring the early results of the daylong scarecrow-building competition, when Vidya found her.

"He's dating Sabrina?" was Vidya's opening line, a plated slice of pie in her own hand. Hers was adorned with three scoops of ice cream sprinkled over with cinnamon and caramel.

"Hello, Vidya. Isn't it a lovely day for a festival?" Anne said with forced cheer.

Vidya just raised her eyebrows and shoveled some pie in her mouth. No use for Anne to pretend she didn't know what Vidya was talking about.

"Yes, it would appear they are seeing each other," Anne replied.

"The redhead from Newfoundland with the body of a limber cheerleader is dating your magnificent ex. Somethin' you want to share with the class?" Vidya asked. "You knew, didn't you?"

"Yes."

"And you're okay with this?" Vidya looked puzzled.

"I don't have a right to not be okay. He and I were eight years ago, so, yes, I think I can be reasonable about that fact that he's moved on," Anne replied with sarcasm.

"Okay, I'm not going to push on the wound," Vidya said with her free hand raised in a defensive motion, though Anne only raised a skeptical eyebrow in reply.

"It's just . . ." Vidya said, and then trailed off, the puzzled look back on her face.

"What?" Anne asked.

"Well, that's kinda a big swing, to go from an Anne Elliot to a Sabrina."

"Sabrina is lovely," Anne replied, feeling compelled to be honest. She focused her attention on one half-built scarecrow that was clearly being dressed to match the reenactment soldiers, weaponry included. She had a sneaking suspicion she knew where Professor Davis's missing equipment had gone.

"Oh, she's a very nice girl, I know that, but I mean . . . well, if you're attracted to an Anne, you're probably not going to be satisfied with a Sabrina. I mean, those are two very different types of women. Yeah, Sabrina's sweet . . . But what else? Sweet and . . . ? I mean, whereas you—"

"Whereas I broke up with him and left him reeling. Maybe sweet and straightforward suits him now," Anne countered.

"I guess . . . but I mean, like, I would never sew the same style of dress for a Marilyn Monroe that I would for an Audrey Hepburn. I mean, both style icons sure, but a pink corseted number is very different than a black sheath dress, and they appeal to very different tastes."

"Is that like your seamstress fantasy? To create a dress for Audrey Hepburn?" Anne asked.

"Wrong Hepburn. In my fantasy I would have wanted to do Katherine Hepburn's pant suits. The tailoring on those things was a masterpiece."

"Vidya, is this why you keep suggesting we do *The Philadelphia Story* for our Elysium summer season?

Vidya laughed and shoved more pie in her mouth. "Maybe.

Anyway, I think I've made my point about people having a type."

Anne wasn't really sure that she had, but let it slide. Vidya finished the last bite on her plate with satisfaction. "One slice of apple pie down, one slice of pumpkin pie down, one slice of pecan pie to go. When is the pie-judging contest?"

J ust as Anne was contemplating a walk through the corn maze on her own, she bumped into Mrs. Fairchild.

"I see we have similar taste in florals!" She laughed, gesturing at Anne's tote with the peeking sunflowers. Jenny's own arms were filled with four or five of that same bouquet, a riot of color reflecting back on her smiling face. "I'm going to decorate Kellynch with them for Thanksgiving."

Anne had a moment of deep longing—Thanksgiving at Kellynch. Canadian Thanksgiving used to mean her mother taking time off (whereas November's American Thanksgiving meant her and the town were rushed with cross-border visitors eager for a long weekend away). It used to mean her mother taking over the kitchen to put on a big turkey dinner, wreaths of pine cones and flowers on the doors, and a thick throw blanket on the couch to snuggle under when everyone had eaten their fill of a table so laden it groaned.

She had tried to keep the tradition up herself for a few years afterward. But neither her sister nor her father liked to eat carbs, and rather than let it be a family event, her father had taken to bringing the worst of his golf buddies home, so long as Anne was cooking for everyone. Anne was starting to wonder just how many of her "family" memories were really just her and her mom.

"Do you have plans for Thanksgiving?" Jenny asked, and then before Anne could reply she laughed at her own question and went on. "Well, of course you do, I was just going to ask if you wanted to come round, but what was I thinking? I'm sure you have loads of people coming. Anyway, Anne, I'm glad I caught you."

She shifted the flowers to lean a little closer. "I know Ben has been emailing back and forth with your office on the proposal, and I think we might be getting close. He won't promise me a time line, but do you think the transaction will be done soon? Don't tell Ben, I know he wants us to put the sale money back into the business, but I was thinking Grant and I could splurge a little and go do a tour of Europe in the spring, just for a week or two."

Anne tried to focus, still caught in Thanksgivings past. "What do you mean? Surely you could do both, once the sale goes through."

"Do you think there will be that much?" Jenny said, uncertain. "I was planning to tell Ben to offer . . ." She named a figure that was in keeping with real estate prices from before the pandemic. Since then the area had seen a massive spike as people who had fled the city started paying city prices for country homes. It would have been a fair offer a few years ago, but not now.

"Jenny, that's nowhere near . . ." Anne started to say, but at that moment they were interrupted by several apparent friends of Mrs. Fairchild's who, loudly exclaiming, insisted on carrying her off to another booth.

"Oh, I'm sorry. I've got to run, Anne, and I know I'm supposed to leave the haggling to Ben, but let's chat soon."

Feeling uneasy now, Anne watched her go. Surely Ben

would correct that number when Jenny discussed it with him, right? But what if Jenny told someone else, like Naomi? Naomi would insist on taking it as a legitimate price point. It would weaken the Fairchilds' negotiating position, for the festival to have known they were willing to start with a price so low. Anne resolved to talk to Ben at the next opportunity, to simply let him know that the suggestion had and should stay between Jenny and her, no one else, and they could still set an appropriate price.

Feeling not much better, Anne continued to browse among the stalls before spotting her assistant on the sloping ramparts.

"Emmie, what on earth are you doing?"

Emmie had a massive pair of binoculars hanging from her neck, the weight of which looked like it could nearly pull her down.

"When the organizers were setting up last night, Double-Oh-Goose apparently was squawking around, flying down and trying to eat some of the pies, so I'm keeping an eye on the skies. I can call out an early warning if he decides to dive-bomb the festival like he does our glass windows."

"Where'd you get the binoculars?"

"Colonel Fairchild! I told him about Double-Oh-Goose when I bumped into him in town a few days ago, and he offered to loan them to me. He said they were from his equipment he took on his last tour," she said delightedly.

Anne made a mental note to talk to Colonel Fairchild about loaning Emmie anything that was military grade.

"What happens if you spot him? They hide the pies?"

"Better than that! Check it out. FIRE IN THE HOLE!" Emmie bellowed, making Anne jump, and then jump again when a reenactment soldier who had been lounging on the grassy hill nearby, sweating in his red wool uniform, suddenly sprang to his feet and fired his musket at the sky. The noise cracked across the field and people shrieked and ducked, looking around wildly for the source of the gunshot.

Anne put a hand to her chest, waiting for her heart to slow down.

Emmie flapped her hand at the young soldier, who, after discharging his weapon, had turned to her for instruction, a small plume of smoked curling from the tip of his barrel.

"No worries, Peter, that was just a test run. Stand down."

He grinned crookedly at her, clearly besotted, before resuming his position on the grass, lying back and enjoying the sun.

"Emmie! You cannot shoot Double-Oh-Goose! What am I saying? You cannot shoot *anything*, this is a festival, there are children here . . ."

"We're not going to shoot him! Peter isn't actually packing—it's just the pop-its they use for the reenactment demonstrations. It'll frighten Double-Oh-Goose away. It's like those noisemakers some of the farmers have instead of scarecrows in their fields. It mimics the sounds of a gunshot and the birds take off, but there's no actual shot. Also scares the shit out of trespassers, according to Mr. O'Clannery. He inspired my idea." She waved to an elderly gentleman over by the cider stand. Anne recognized him as the owner of O'Clannery Farms—and the only person who hadn't jumped at the gunshot, incidentally. He waved cheerily back and gave Emmie a double thumbs-up.

Anne let her head fall back and stared at the cloudless blue sky, mentally counting to ten.

"Would Councilor Elliot please report to the judges' tent? That's Anne Elliot to the judges' tent." The loudspeaker crackled.

"Right, I have to go, but, Emmie, as your mentor, please know that I encourage and applaud your creative problem solving, but I am, as always, horrified by the solutions you arrive at. Let's work on that together."

Emmie just grinned.

A nne made her way to the judges' tent, where a crowd had gathered. Just like she had on blue-blood night, she made her way onto the raised dais and accepted the microphone from a volunteer. Arranged neatly on a tarp-draped table were three large pumpkins, a placard number in front of each.

"Hello, everyone, and I hope you're having a wonderful time at this year's Pumpkin Festival!"

The crowd clapped and cheered.

"I see a lot of families in the crowd today. If you're not from around here and this is your first time at the festival, make sure you take the kids to the yellow pavilion, where our lovely volunteers are doing face painting."

A number of children made excited noises, and Anne smiled. This was such a fun part of her job.

"All right, now, let's get down to business. We've had a few mishaps in the past with judging the pumpkins by size and weight, so this year we're going a more traditional route with a beauty contest. We're looking for shapeliness, firmness"— *yikes, this sounds like I'm judging breasts; make a mental note to find out who wrote these criteria*—"color, and most likely to be an excellent jack-o'-lantern. The pumpkins are numbered, so

I have no way of knowing who submitted what. These three have been deemed the best of the lot by our festival organizers. So, let's get started!"

Anne approached the pumpkins, microphone still in one hand. The president of the farmers' association had walked her through the finer points of pumpkin judging last year, and Anne hoped she remembered the terms correctly. Pumpkin judging really was no joke. Farmers could make an incredible amount of money selling pumpkins for jack-o'-lanterns to tourists and locals alike, and a winning festival pumpkin was great advertising.

"Well, it has a beautifully colored rind, good deep ribs, perfect shape, the peduncle is very healthy and strong . . ." She made the mistake of looking up at her audience for a moment.

There were Ben and Sabrina, at the back of the tent, watching the festivities, his arm around her shoulders.

She was looking like a Hallmark autumn-themed dream, in a beautiful cream-colored sweater and cute denim jacket, her hair as bright as the fall leaves in a swingy ponytail. Ben hadn't quite fully relaxed his dress code for the occasion, in chinos and a dark button-down, but still both looked like a picture-perfect couple having fun at the festival. Anne couldn't help it; her mind immediately flashed forward a few years and saw a toddler at their feet, with Ben's eyes and Sabrina's hair, excited about the face painting. The festival would become their first-date story and turn into a family tradition, like it had once been in her own family, and then they would all sit down to Thanksgiving dinner in a beautifully decorated Kellynch. Was she overimagining or just prescient?

Did it matter?

The pain was still acute.

She swallowed hard and focused on pumpkin number two.

"Right, pumpkin number two also has excellent ribs, a unique curl to the stem . . ."

There was a murmuring from the back of the crowd, a growing swell, distracting her. From far outside the tent came distant shouting and several loud bangs; she could just make out Emmie's voice . . .

Oh no! NO!

"FIRE IN THE HOLE! FIRE IN THE HOLE! PETER, STAY ON IT! LOOK OUT, IT'S MAKING HIM ANGRY!"

There were gunshots and squawking, and people near the tent entrance started to shriek. Anne looked to her right, the best of the pumpkin pies laid out beautifully on a table, next up for judging. Contestants who participated last year clocked the look, heard the sound of wings flapping, and panicked.

"Not the pies! My pie is going to be the blue-ribbon winner this year!" cried Macy, the local high school English teacher. She had come in second last year to her archnemesis, Catherine the chemistry teacher. Both had witnessed the Double-Oh-Goose debacle.

"Not if a bird shits in it!" shouted Catherine from the first row. "And not if he doesn't either! You stole my recipe this year!"

"Did not!"

"Did too!"

"Ladies, if we could just—"

"Anne, the pies! We have to protect the pies! What do we do?" cried Councilor Singh.

"If we can just keep everyone calm . . . Everybody, this is fine, it's a . . . bird problem," Anne said to the crowd, as people started to jump out of their seats, pushing and shoving to get away like the tent was about to be set on fire.

"FIRE IN THE HOLE! DOUBLE-OH-GOOSE IS HEADED FOR THE PIES!" shrieked Emmie, running full tilt into the tent, the massive binoculars bouncing ludicrously around her neck.

Right behind her was Double-Oh-Goose, no longer airborne, but waddling along at an incredible speed, wings outstretched broadly, spitting and hissing and craning his serpentine neck at the remaining people, who quickly leapt out of his way.

Right behind Double-Oh-Goose was Professor Davis, still in his reenactment gear and waving his rifle about. "DON'T HURT HIM! DON'T HURT HIM! THAT GOOSE IS ENDANGERED!"

"My PIE is ENDANGERED," shrieked Macy.

"YOU'RE about to be ENDANGERED if you don't admit you took my recipe!" said Catherine, charging at Macy.

Abandoning his chase of Emmie, Double-Oh-Goose made a hard turn and dove straight into the nearest pie.

"Nooooo!" cried Councilor Singh.

"Watch out for the tent!" someone else shouted.

In the pandemonium and crush of people leaving, and rifles being swung about, and birds attacking pie, and two high school teachers rolling about locked in mortal combat, the large marquee tent had come unmoored from its aluminum frame and pinnings, and with a *ziiiiip* and a *snap*, massive flaps of white glossy canvas were starting to collapse, each fold pulling down another. It would blanket everyone.

Anne sprang into action and started issuing orders. "Singh,

grab the teachers, pull them apart, and get them out before their students witness this. Emmie, you and Professor Davis get the last of the people out. Abandon the pies, and . . ." Anne ducked as a tent strap went whizzing by her head and braced for the heavy blanket of canvas to knock her down.

It didn't come. She turned around. There was Ben.

He hadn't fled with the rest, although Sabrina clearly had. Instead, he was gamely grabbing hold of one side of the escaped tent material, pulling with all his strength, trying to keep a portion of it temporarily aloft; his dark button-down was straining across his biceps, his body stretched to its full length, and his jaw clenched tightly.

Anne stared at him in a daze of astonishment and badly timed lust.

"What do you need?" he asked, his voice slightly strained with his efforts.

"What?" she asked.

"What do you need me to do?" he asked, serious and intent.

Anne pulled herself together. "Keep using your height—act like a tent pole while I get them out."

Emmie and Davis had done as she told them, but Singh had abandoned the teachers, grabbed the one untouched pie, and gone.

Typical.

Anne immediately waded into the Macy/Catherine fighting blob and shoved them apart. The tent was collapsed on three sides now, and she was starting to sweat. "Break it up! For Christ's sake, go now, or I'm having words with your principal! And you . . ." She rounded on Double-Oh-Goose enjoying his spoils, carving into the decorative pumpkins and pumpkin pies alike.

Like King Henry VIII at a goddamned banquet. The goose paused and hissed at her, like it could hear her thoughts.

"You know what, bird? You're on your own." Anne turned back to Ben, ready for them to make their escape as he released the final side of the tent.

Double-Oh-Goose squawked and suddenly took flight, escaping out the remaining opening into the fresh air, but not before dropping a chunk of mushy, half-digested pumpkin filling on Anne's head.

Thirteen

Anne emerged blinking into the gloriously cool, fresh-smelling air as pumpkin innards dripped down her neck and onto her sweater. The tent gave a final shudder and fully collapsed behind her.

The hubbub and chaos of the crowd outside were worse than she imagined, with everyone upset and shouting, even those who had been nowhere near the tent.

Ben, who had been a warm presence at her back a moment ago, had melted into the crowd and disappeared. No doubt gone to find his wayward date. The high of his rushing to her aid, of working with her, asking her what she needed—like he used to do—withered quickly.

A member of the festival staff was shouting fruitlessly into a bullhorn, trying to calm everyone. Arva, one of the organizers who had greeted Anne at the beginning of this oh-so-promising event, came running toward her, a plea in her eyes that Anne could already hear.

"Yes, yes, of course I'll help," Anne agreed, before Arva could say a word. "Grab the staff, and stop that fellow shouting into his silly horn. We'll offer discount theater tickets to anyone affected. No one was hurt, and the rest of the festival is still intact. It was just the main tent and the pie and pumpkin competitions. We can salvage this."

It took the better part of two hours to settle everything. Most of the festivalgoers did resume their day, once the excitement had died down, but others had to be soothed and cajoled into realizing that a collapsed tent and a few smashed pies were not the catastrophe they had believed in the moment. There were strong words for Councilor Singh.

Anne also had to try to quiet the many complaints that Double-Oh-Goose was surely mad and rabid and dangerous wildlife that needed to be dealt with. And the many concerns that he had attacked the pies because surely he must be starving and it was animal cruelty to chase him off. It was difficult to explain without sounding ludicrous that having contended with his antics for more than a year now, Anne could definitely say he really was just an asshole.

It was late afternoon when she finally got a moment's peace to herself. She stunk of sweat and pumpkin and was exhausted and cranky, but there was one last thing to do before she could head home and wash this terrible day off of her. She never left the Pumpkin Festival without doing the corn maze at least once. It was an annual tradition.

When Arva finally called their work done, Anne slipped away to the start of the maze before gratefully plunging into the cool and quiet. Most people had started to head home, so there were no crowds of giggling children here. The stacks of hay and stalks of corn that made up the maze's walls stretched well above her head, making her feel secluded, and she walked deeper into the labyrinth, turning left and right at random to ensure she got at least a little bit lost. The sticky pumpkin guts were picking up every bit of dirt and hay she brushed against, but Anne was past caring what she looked like right now.

When she was nearly at the center, and considering turning around to wend her way back out, she paused a moment to breathe in the silence.

And heard giggling instead.

Some randy teenagers no doubt, taking advantage of the privacy of the maze to make out. She remembered Liz used to have frequent rendezvous in here when she was a teenager.

The giggling grew a little louder, followed by what sounded like kissing. It was coming from the other side of a particularly thick corn wall, and the amorous couple was obscured.

"You were like Superman! I can't believe you stayed to try and hold up that tent," said a high, feminine voice. There followed a low male chuckle.

Anne froze. She knew that chuckle. It was Sabrina and Ben, no more than an arm's length from her, and completely unaware she could hear them.

She should leave, head for the exit now. Some perverse masochism kept her rooted instead.

"I had to try. People might have gotten hurt," Ben was saying lightly, as if it was a given. Like just the sight of him, gorgeous and steadfast and rescuing her, hadn't made Anne reconsider everything in that moment—his cold manner toward her, whether her pride was really worth more than asking for a second chance, the existence of Sabrina—in favor of just throwing herself at him.

Thank god I didn't.

He hadn't been helping *her*; he'd been helping the festival. They'd worked together in that moment for convenience, nothing more.

"You're so brave." Sabrina was sighing, and if Anne hadn't had the same thought not two hours ago, she would have rolled her eyes at the fawning.

"Nah, they would have been fine without me," Ben was saying with charming self-deprecation. "We even got to enjoy the rest of the festival."

"Don't you know, when Anne Elliot's in charge, the show *must* go on." Sabrina laughed, and Anne jolted guiltily to hear herself mentioned. There was a rustle—Sabrina was probably throwing her arms around his neck and cuddling up to him for another kiss. It made Anne feel ill. She remembered the physical sensation of doing just that like a phantom limb, stretching on her toes to reach him, and the way he would dip his head down.

But Ben spoke again, his voice a little off. "Do you . . . like working for Elliot?"

"I mean, I mostly work with the director . . . Anne is kinda intimidating. Like, everyone is in awe of her, but she's also kind of terrifying, in a good way, I guess? She totally lives for the festival and has, like, *no* life."

"Really?" Ben sounded surprised.

"Yeah, I mean I love my job, but not like *that*. I don't want to end up where I'm forty-five and alone and basically living in my office."

Ben coughed, amused. "I don't think she's forty-five."

"Oh really?" Sabrina didn't sound snarky, just genuinely surprised, which was even worse. "Well, whatever age she is. I just mean, like, she comes to visit rehearsal sometimes and everything has to be *just so*. I don't think she understands us creative types. We need to get messy."

There was more giggling and a shiver of movement from the cornstalks, like they'd brushed up against them. Anne imagined Sabrina playfully messing up his hair as she said the last sentence, both of them smiling at each other.

"Messy and fun. I like it. The festival company would be an idiot not to give you the Juliet role."

"Thanks," Sabrina said shyly. "Anyway, my friend Dani, she plays *Macbeth* witch number two, always says she just needs to get laid, then she wouldn't be so prim and anal about stuff. God, isn't that awful?" Sabrina said in a laughing "aren't I naughty" voice.

"Who needs to get laid?" Ben asked, confused, but Anne was already covered in a thousand hot sears of mortification, a lead weight pressing on her chest. She was more used to Sabrina's flips back and forth between topics. She knew "who."

"Ms. Elliot, of course! I mean Anne."

"Oh. Does she . . . um, not have any . . ."

Whatever Ben had been about to ask, Anne would never know, because at that moment a group of shrieking young women ran in the far side of the maze, their noise carrying above the high walls. When it quieted down again, as they turned a corner, the voices of Ben and Sabrina were gone.

Fourteen

Anne wasn't driving home. She wasn't driving back to her office. That open stretch of empty country highway that was always her escape was tainted now. It led back to him, to Kellynch, to her family's losses and her own. So not that road anymore.

Her sensible sweater set covered in pumpkin guts, straw in her hair, and the cruel—*cruel but accurate*, she reminded herself—words of Sabrina and Ben ringing in her ears, she drove on, blinking desperately to clear her vision as her eyes swam with tears.

Where the hell am I going? she asked herself, except really, she knew where.

She was driving in the opposite direction, past the south border of town, following the winding S-shaped turns of the road. On her right, inland, the way was dotted with stately homes, public gardens, and long stretches of green grass. On her left the gently sloped embankment became a perilous drop to a gorge below, and the placid lake narrowed and picked up speed, becoming a rushing river as it got closer and closer to being downstream of the falls. The trees grew deceptively thicker, shielding the dangerous ledge from view, until Niagara Glen area appeared. It was a jut of land that hung out over the river, the trees cleared and a lookout established to take in the sweeping view.

A gangway connected hikers from the lookout to the wild trails cut into the rock face below, sandwiched between the cliff and the river.

Anne drove past, but slower now, scanning the left side of the road—there! A little parking lot, just a few spots by the trees and next to a nearly hidden entrance to a certain hiking path, if you knew where to look. The Devil's Whirlpool, it was called. A wild route. Only for experienced hikers.

She'd brought Ben here that ill-fated weekend he'd come home with her to meet her parents. She'd promised him some real bouldering on the paths of the Niagara Glen, but first she had wanted to show him this, her favorite place. She hadn't been so *prim* back then.

There was no sanitized gangway here, only rough-cut logs acting as crude steps, shoved into the mud, and descending through thick forest until arriving at a clearing that coincided with a bend in the river, where a rocky shore overlooked gentle eddies of water beneath towering rock formations and the most breathtaking view . . . It used to be her favorite place, a place to go on those occasions when the town had just felt too small, or her father and sister just too much. It was a place she felt happy and untethered.

Anne wanted that view now; she wanted to stand in that

clearing and have that feeling of awe and wonder; she wanted to feel free with the soaring rock walls, rushing water, swirling gusts of wind; she wanted her problems and her hurt to feel small by comparison, and her office and her job and her hurt to feel far away. She wanted to be in her favorite place, the place she never went back to after that weekend—not after taking Ben there, losing Ben, and everything that followed. She wanted it like her next breath of air.

She threw the car into park, haphazardly stretched across two parking spaces, and nearly fell out, finally letting her tears fall. She stumbled toward the hiking path, her watery vision so obscured that the gold leaves above on the branches, and the gold of the leaves fallen and underfoot, blurred together into one hazy halo, a cyclone of gold, a shining tunnel downward, the sound of the water just beyond. She took the first step . . .

. . . and sunk straight into mud. Her sensible loafer sunk four inches deep. Moisture was already seeping through the thin leather, between her toes, chillingly cold.

Anne burst into sobs.

If the door to Narnia had been slammed shut, she couldn't be more bereft and lost than she felt now. She didn't have the footwear for this, not for this or for hiking or any of it. She had her designer pumps and her sensible flats, but her hiking boots were gone. Once upon a time they had been lovingly broken in and always handy in her car trunk, but they had been disposed of years ago.

Anne cried and cried, listening to the rushing water just beyond her reach, a memory that could still be real if she could get there. She was so filled with longing for that path so long forgotten.

Late afternoon sunk slowly into early twilight, and the chilly breeze—and having finally run out of tears—brought Anne to her senses. This wasn't happening today.

With a squelch she pulled her foot up out of the mud and turned back to her car—she'd left the driver's-side door open and the interior lights on; she'd be lucky if her battery wasn't dead—to go home.

Except Anne didn't drive home that night. She couldn't—*wouldn't*—face that cavernous, cold house, another conversation about Botox and another suggestion of what she might cook for dinner, and the mild, lukewarm interest in her day, which she would still have to lie about and put a best face on. She couldn't face any of it the way she was feeling, hollow and pissed off, hurt and trapped.

She drove instead toward the Niagara business center, where a bland, impersonal chain hotel stood, and checked herself in. She bought a tacky oversized tourist T-shirt to sleep in, sent her muddy, pumpkin-guts-spattered clothes for in-house laundering, and went to sleep.

Fifteen

Things did not look better in the morning. Anne ordered room service and stayed in bed, watching pay-per-view movies and listening to Vidya's playlist.

Late that afternoon she called Vidya.

"What is wrong with me?" she moaned to her friend, in lieu of "hello."

"Is this . . . Anne?" Vidya replied hesitantly.

"What, like you don't have caller ID? Of course it's Anne; I'm calling you from my cell phone!"

"Okay there, snarky, calm down. I've never had a crazy call from you before. Where are you, what's happened?"

Anne relayed the events of yesterday, the Pumpkin Festival, Ben coming with Sabrina, the overheard conversation, the disaster with Double-Oh-Goose, and her own meltdown and subsequent hotel slobbery.

"Oh honey, there's nothing wrong with you. You had a shitty day, and you had a breakup."

"Eight years ago! Eight fucking years ago I had a breakup!" Anne wailed in reply.

"Yeah, and you just kept on being Anne. You had your mother to take care of, the festival, the town, one thing and the next. You never actually sat down and dealt with the emotional fallout of that breakup, and now it's been festering for years, and he's moving on right in front of you. Honey, welcome to rock bottom. We've been expecting you."

Anne laughed, though she half wanted to cry again. "So, what do I do?"

Vidya's sigh gusted through the phone. "You accept that you can't fix this with your impeccable management skills, you accept that it's broken, you eat your weight in ice cream . . ."

"I ordered ten lava cakes from room service and I just ate the fudgy center out of each of them," Anne admitted, looking at the wreckage of plates and hollowed-out cake around her.

See, she mentally hissed at Sabrina, *I can do messy.*

"Good, that was a really good first step," Vidya praised her. "Stay in bed, watch sad movies, hide from your life for a little bit. Resist the urge to get a haircut—I really can't stress that one enough, breakup haircuts are just the worst—and, Anne, so help me god, if you're taking notes right now . . ." Anne put down the hotel stationery and cheap pen. "And then when you've finished that process, you tell me when you're ready for the best-friend hard truths and pick-me-up speech."

"Can I get that speech now? Please?"

Vidya sighed. "Fine." She took a deep breath. "Well, first of all, Little Miss Understudy, Miss I've Been in the Real World for Five Minutes, Miss I'm Blowing My Shot at Being

Juliet Because I Can't Be Bothered to Learn Shakespeare, is totally wrong. *I* am a creative type, and you don't kill my vibe at all. You understand and respect my work but also keep me on track. Second, there's nothing wrong with being forty-five; she clearly thinks anything over thirty is the Crypt Keeper."

"There's nothing wrong with being forty-five except I'm thirty-two!" Anne whined. "And this is it, this is my life, I live in the office and I'm on the shelf."

"Anne, for god's sake, if you're on the shelf, it's because *you've* put *yourself* on the shelf!" Vidya huffed in aggravation and then took a moment before she resumed in a much gentler tone.

"Look, I was working here when your mother passed, and I haven't lost a parent so I won't pretend to know what's it like or the weird ways you react to that grief, but from where I'm sitting, your mother died and it's like you got lost. Or maybe it's because after you lost Ben you didn't have time to find your feet again, your mom got sick and you threw yourself into taking care of her, but now she's gone *and you can't stop.* You can't stop trying to—I don't know—pick up where she left off. But for fuck's sake, Anne, she was twenty-six years older than you! You're wailing that you're thirty-two, so act your own age."

Anne buried her face in her pillow and groaned.

"Anne, it's okay," Vidya soothed. "It was probably too soon for the truth talk. Forget it. You've had a shit kicking, it's okay to just be flattened for a little while."

After a little more conversation, and a promise to call if she needed anything, they hung up. After an hour of stewing on things, Anne took stock of herself.

Vidya's advice to keep hiding from her life for a little while longer was tempting, but while she'd enjoyed the reprieve and the privacy to wallow for twenty-four hours, this wasn't really her. There were cake smears everywhere. *Gross.*

She *liked* getting on top of things, being active, and doing—it gave her a feeling of agency. Screw Sabrina, Anne *liked* her job, it was just that . . . yesterday's disasters—well, on top of her heartbreak—just compounded the feeling that her life, the Pumpkin Festival, everything had spiraled out of her control. She didn't want to sit and wallow and eat more cake centers. She wanted to be *doing*. But what?

She looked down at her half-aborted notes from her call with Vidya.

Haircut.

Now, that was an *excellent* idea.

The hotel had a salon, which was perfect. She didn't want her usual quaint place in town where Barbara had been cutting her hair since she was twelve.

She walked in with her tacky oversized tourist T-shirt tucked into her now-clean but still visibly stained pants, looking like a hot mess no doubt, but thoroughly enjoying the novelty of not caring. There were three hairdressers free, all youngish women in professional smocks looking edgy and glam, with impressively long nails. Anne picked out the one who looked the fiercest—extreme winged eyeliner and a bright red lip, both immaculately applied—and approached.

"Are you free? I want a haircut, like, immediately."

The woman must have read something in her face, because she stopped scrolling through her phone and became serious and businesslike at once.

"Do you know what you want?"

"Not this." Anne said, gesturing to her sensible, no-nonsense hair.

The eyeliner queen nodded. "A breakup?"

"Yes."

"Jen," she called to one of the women standing around. "Prep a chair ASAP, we're gonna need a cut and color. It's a breakup."

As if they were an ER that just got a code red, the women flew into motion with terrifying efficiency. Anne found herself wrapped in a cape and seated in a chair facing a mirror, half a dozen fashion magazines dumped in her lap, while the eyeliner goddess ran her hands through her patient's hair, familiarizing herself with its texture.

"Now, take a look at those magazines while we do the wash, let me know if you see anything you like. Tell me whether you suffer split ends, humidity frizz, how short you might want to go, if your ex was tall, and how long you were together."

I have never felt so understood. The woman's professionalism was soothing. It was like her own when a budget dipped into the red.

"No splits, no frizz, my career is corporate so not too far off the deep end, but I don't want to look like a character from that ladies-who-lunch Sondheim song anymore, we were together over a year, and he's six feet tall."

She nodded, cool and in control. "You did the right thing coming in. When did it happen?"

"Eight years ago."

Well, that made her double take.

After a scalp massage and a wash—they were still pulling out bits of pumpkin tendon—Anne was feeling better than she had in the last forty-eight hours. Her hair did not belong to the board of directors, or the town, or her carefully crafted image. Her hair was her own.

"This one," she told the beautician, pointing to a picture in one of the magazines she'd been given. It was a long bob, stopped maybe an inch or so above the shoulders, with layers and heavy fringe bangs that swept down and to the side a little. The model wore it tousled and piecey with a blond ombre dye job.

The eyeliner queen nodded. "Good choice, sexy, fresh, a little modern punk rock. It'll give you some definition on your cheekbones. You can straighten it for work if you want to look sleeker, and wear it bed-head-style the rest of the time. You want the blond ombre?"

Anne thought of Sabrina's strawberry-blond swinging ponytail. "No. And keep the patch of grays by my ear." At the hairdresser's look Anne added, "I'm not trying to be twenty-two again, I just want to look thirty-two and myself and I like the gray."

The woman nodded. "How about a few lowlights, just to bring out the definition of the tousle?"

Anne agreed to it.

An hour and a half later the cape was whipped off, and Anne swiveled around to face the mirror. She raised her eyes from the reflection of the tacky T-shirt and saw . . .

The woman staring back at her was not the prim director of blue-blood night. She wasn't the woman who looked faded and wan next to her older sister, or funereally serious next to Sabrina's fun and young vibe. Her new haircut looked . . .

"Professional meets a little punk rock," the hairdresser said, watching Anne examine herself.

That's it.

The emphasized color brought out her eyes and her cheek-bones, as promised, and gave her gray hairs a steely silvery glint. The shorter length would look good above the collar of a blazer. The jagged layers and fringe gave it an edgy vibe. This was the haircut of a woman who wasn't afraid, who could tackle anything.

"It's perfect."

Anne paid the bill and tipped well. The woman thanked her and then gave her one last rejoinder.

"You go shopping next, get something new to go with the new look."

"Oh, I'm definitely going shopping."

This probably wasn't what the eyeliner queen meant.

Anne pulled into the industrial-type plaza, parking her car in front of the shop signed "Hiker's Haven." A canoe and a jumble of wooden oars were propped haphazardly beside the door.

It had taken her nearly two hours to get here from her Niagara Falls hotel, operating mostly on memory, but it was still here. The best hiking equipment specialty shop in Southern Ontario.

The inside looked just the same, only instead of an older woman with a cat, a man with a massive Bernese mountain dog at his feet manned the checkout island in the center of the store. It was a bare-bones sort of place, no flashy displays or fake greenery to mimic the outdoors, just rows and rows of every bit of equipment and clothing you could need if you were serious about the outdoors. Anne headed straight to the alcove at the back where shelves tacked up on the walls displayed their range of footwear, from light sneakers to heavy hiking boots.

"Can I help you?" The Bernese mountain dog had come over and nudged her knee, nearly knocking her over with his weight, and for one wild moment Anne thought the dog had asked the question. "Are you looking for something in particular?" It was the man from the counter; the dog returned to him to sit obediently at his feet. He didn't clock Anne's bizarre attire at all, nor her excessively determined manner, which was out of proportion with simply buying a pair of shoes; clearly, he'd seen some things.

"Yes, hiking boots. Something good enough for multiday hikes, rough trails, all terrain. I need good grip, and none of those shoe-sized ones. I want the proper ones that lace up over the ankle, and waterproof." Anne named the brand she used to purchase regularly.

"Well, we have that brand for sure," he pointed to the wall on the far left, "but they're not really top-tier."

"What are you talking about, they're the number one recommended," Anne said in disbelief.

He patted his giant dog unconcernedly. "Yeah, maybe like seven years ago, but then they had all those recalls and y'know . . ." No, Anne didn't know.

He pointed with his other hand to the opposing wall. "Can I tell you about the best brand you've never heard about? Oboz."

"Beg pardon?" Anne asked.

"Oboz," he repeated, "named for the Bozeman valley they come from. Small company, couple of people who spent their lives in footwear, then quit and started their own company.

Small operation, environmentally conscious, and the best boots out there; they've got crazy traction, and all the grip you could want."

Anne let him lace her into a solid-looking brown pair. She paced around the small area.

"Check the grip," the salesman said, dragging over a small knee-high ramp that had rocks and stones glued to it. "Walk up and down this thing for a minute." Feeling slightly ridiculous, as the dog and his owner watched, Anne climbed up on the simulated terrain.

They were in fact the most comfortable, well-built boots she'd ever been in. It was like coming home.

"Sold," Anne said decisively. The dog wagged his tail.

She threw a couple of pairs of thick wool socks in with her purchase, and a merino long-sleeved shirt for a base layer.

By the time she left the shop it was nearly evening. As Anne drove home she realized she'd been MIA for nearly forty-eight hours over the Thanksgiving weekend. Neither her father nor her sister had noticed.

Sixteen

Anne walked into work Tuesday morning, still feeling a little grim from the long weekend, but also somehow . . . looser? Like some pressure that she hadn't known was there had been relieved, just a little. That morning she had opened her closet and surveyed the carefully arranged tailored suits, the corresponding ladylike blouses and matching sweaters, all color-coordinated in soothing neutrals, and yanked them off their hangers.

She had thrown them on the bed, mixing instead of matching, and when that had proved insufficient, she'd raided Liz's wardrobe. In the end she'd walked out the door wearing a striped Breton sweater in maroon under a plaid wool blazer, and her most flattering black dress pants. She'd tousled her new hair, added her usual pearl earrings, and thrown her favorite sky-high stilettos in her tote. The end result in the mirror had made her smile. The hiking boots in the trunk of her car made her smile more.

"Whoa, Anne, breakup haircuts are usually regret-cuts, which is why I specifically told you *not* to, but damn that looks good!" Vidya said with a whistle.

"Thanks," Anne said. "I brought you a coffee." She passed the second to-go cup in her hand to Vidya, who took it gratefully while surveying Anne's outfit.

"Stripes and plaid? Pattern explosion, I approve."

Anne didn't answer but nodded at one of Vidya's dress dummies. "Looks like Juliet's costume is coming along."

Vidya turned and eyed it critically. "Yes, but the fabric is pretty delicate, so I can only alter it so many times. I need to know the actress's measurements sooner rather than later on this one. Is it . . . going to be Sabrina?" she asked carefully.

Anne shrugged one shoulder. "I'm leaving it up to Choi; it's her production. Let me know when you've got your budget needs finalized for *Cat on a Hot Tin Roof*; we can go over them."

Emmie was waiting in her office with . . . not a bran muffin, but a chocolate chip muffin, and a trembling lower lip.

"Anne, I'm so, so sorry . . ."

"Emmie . . ." Anne tried to stop her, but Emmie was clearly worked up.

"No, I'm really, really sorry. I know how much work goes into the Pumpkin Festival, and how important it is, and I know you give me, like, a lot of leeway with some of my ideas, and sometimes I go too far, and I don't think it through and I super look up to you and . . ."

"Emmie, sit, breathe." She pushed her assistant into a desk chair, broke off some of the chocolate chip muffin, and made the young woman eat it while she calmed down.

And for once it's a muffin I would have actually eaten myself.

"Listen," Anne said slowly, sitting down across from her and choosing her words carefully. "What happened wasn't anyone's fault. We could blame you for the shooting, or blame Professor Davis for bringing Double-Oh-Goose into our lives, or Double-Oh-Goose for being a nuisance. But you were trying to help, Davis is trying to save the wildlife, and Double-Oh-Goose . . . well, we're not sure what goes through his head, but he's a bird, so probably nothing beyond what to eat and where to poop."

Emmie laughed a little at that.

"My point is," Anne continued, "there's a small nucleus of things we can control, and then a whole big landscape of things we can't. We can't control other people, we can't control the weather or animals, we can't control the future—we can't even control the outcomes of our own decisions sometimes. And I know I'm probably the poster child for thinking I *can* control all these things, and the absolute worst person to try and give you this lesson, but running a company, or an event, or a project, sometimes you just have to take the hand you're dealt and do the best you can."

"But you always have things under control, like that time the fire alarm went off—"

"I've had many years of practice," Anne cut in, "but I don't always have it under control, not by a long shot. And that's okay. The Pumpkin Festival was a very memorable disaster, for a whole lot of reasons, but years from now you'll be telling people what happened as a funny story, trust me. You are an amazing assistant, you go above and beyond, you're enthusiastic about every project, and you learn so fast I'm amazed. And you're much braver and bolder than I was at this stage of my career, and I admire you for that."

Emmie was shyly beaming at the praise, her teary expression evaporating.

"But," Anne continued, "I think as your mentor maybe I need to be more honest about the hard part of trying to keep it together."

"Like when you fainted at blue-blood night because you skipped meals," Emmie supplied, and Anne nodded. "Well, I still think you're a badass boss, and I'm still sorry about the gunfire at the Pumpkin Festival, but thanks for making me feel better. And I'm sorry I ate your muffin."

Anne laughed. "Don't worry about it. Let's make a deal: whoever is having a crappier day gets to have the muffin."

"Deal," Emmie said firmly.

"All right, now that we've got that sorted, what do I have on for today?" Anne asked, and watched her assistant immediately flip into high-efficiency mode.

Atta girl. Back on the horse.

"Okay, so you've got a call with Production at ten, a meeting with both Finance and Operations at eleven—oh, and did you know that hottie from Kellynch is here? Is he supposed to meet you? I don't have him down in your schedule."

"Wentworth is here?" Anne asked.

"Yeah, I saw him hanging around down in the lobby," her assistant answered.

No doubt here to see Sabrina. "No, he's not in my books, but you know what?" Anne said, feeling a kind of rip-the-Band-Aid-off mood overtake her. "I do need to speak with him about something. I'll see if I can catch him in the lobby; it'll just take a minute and I'll be back for my call at ten."

"Okay," Emmie said brightly. "He was down by the concession, I think. Oh, by the way, you look kinda awesome today."

That would have to boost up her confidence.

B en was indeed down in the concession area, sitting at one of the small tables, back in his impeccable suit and combed hair, whatever little casualness he had displayed at the festival clearly having been exorcized out of him by the fact that it was once again a workday.

Seriously? He's not even at an office, or here on business. Does he go on all his dates in suits?

"The concession won't be open until this afternoon's matinee performance," Anne said briskly by way of an opening.

In response Ben held up the to-go coffee cup he'd brought.

"Right," Anne said, aware that he was clocking her altered hair and attire, his brow slightly furrowed, that adorable line between his brows she used to like to smooth away . . . No matter. She reassured herself that there was no way for him to know she'd eavesdropped on his conversation with Sabrina, or that their remarks had landed hard.

"I'm waiting for Sabrina, but if you'd rather I wait outside the theater . . ." he said, and Anne read between the lines. He wasn't so mindful of their past that he would tiptoe around the fact that he was seeing another woman—*and after eight years why would he?* Anne thought—but he was acknowledging that the theater was Anne's territory, and he would respect that and keep his distance if she wanted. Because even though he thought so little of her, he was still respectful of boundaries.

"No, it's perfectly fine," Anne said with a wave of her hand, though really, she would have liked him far, far away from here. She was still raw from this weekend; it was an effort to appear nonchalant. "Emmie said you were down here and I'm glad I caught you because I want to say very quickly and off the record that you need to increase the sale price and set it before Jenny talks to anyone."

"What?"

"You need to increase the sale price ASAP." *And you need to understand what I'm saying so this conversation isn't prolonged.*

Ben was looking at her with that neutral mask she was getting rather used to seeing. Anne tried to compose her face to do the same.

"Your aunt has intimated to me a certain ballpark number. I assume she hadn't discussed it with you as their business advisor, but it's risky for her to be telling anyone from the festival, because then that's how low they'll start the negotiations. I am telling you it needs to be at least three hundred grand higher. She wants to price that field way too cheap."

His neutral face was tinged with suspicion now.

"No, she hadn't discussed a price with me yet, and that's an oversight I'll rectify; however, I'm not sure how to tell you this, Ms. Elliot, but *you* are the buyer; *you* are supposed to dicker the price down to make it cheaper. Not drive it up higher."

Anne bit down on her frustration and the urge to snap at his slightly condescending tone. *Professional, be professional.* "Yes, thank you, Mr. Wentworth, having an MBA and a business to run, I am, as you know, exceedingly stupid about business negotiations."

His eyebrows rose, and Anne took a shallow breath to compose herself and tried again.

"Look, I can pretend I didn't hear her, but others won't. If anyone else from my team hears that price, I have to take it to my board of directors—I am professionally bound to get that field at the cheapest option—but it's *worth* more than that price. A developer would give them nearly twice that much, and I know they want sell it to us and be part of the project, but you need to put the price three hundred grand higher and submit it quick, so I can dicker it down a little and get everyone a fair sale."

Ben smoothed his tie down and stared at a point over her head, not making eye contact. "And you're telling me this out of the goodness of your heart for a pair of old people you've practically just met?" The sarcasm and suspicion were lightly pronounced, but they were still there.

Wow. And here I thought I was past being hurt by him.

His treatment of her since resurfacing in her life had hurt at first, of course it had, but it was understandable. She had treated him badly and rejected him; she wasn't going to begrudge him acting with cold indifference now. That he thought she was plain and spinstery—or rather his girlfriend did and he hadn't corrected her, and why would he be expected to defend his ex anyway?—was fine, really.

But she hadn't thought that his opinion of her was sunk so low as to be suspicious of her motives, of believing her capable of underhanded moves. She thought he knew her better than that.

Anne reached deep and summoned the persona she used with the board of directors: forceful, direct, efficient, eminently professional. She stood tall and channeled the power of her new haircut and killer heels.

"I'm not familiar with the business practices of Toronto

and New York bankers and traders and venture capitalists, and based on this conversation I have no wish to be. Clearly you expect lying and plotting and someone willing to take advantage of a veteran and his wife who are endeavoring to give back to the community. That is not how I conduct business, nor will it be so long as I am executive director of the Elysium Festival. Raise the price."

She didn't wait to interpret his expression. She turned and walked away.

If that was the kind of person Ben Wentworth was, maybe she hadn't known him very well either.

That night she hit play on Vidya's playlist and listened to "Mr. Perfectly Fine" through twice.

When the paperwork came through two days later, the sale price was listed as . . . Anne nodded in sharp satisfaction.

She forwarded the email to Naomi and then rang her on the phone.

"I just sent you the initial offer; they've set the price about where you'd expect. I think we can get them to knock it down by about fifty grand or so."

At least he'd listened.

Seventeen

Anne received quite a few remarks on her altered look. Paul frantically asked her if it was because she was interviewing for another job and leaving the festival. Naomi had blinked at her and asked if she was dating someone. One of the blue-blood patrons who passed her in a coffee shop said she looked "energized" but couldn't put his finger on why. Liz's only comment was to insist that if Anne was going to kick up a fuss about Liz borrowing her car, then Anne certainly wasn't allowed to borrow from Liz's closet. Which was somewhat fair, so Anne took a long lunch the next day and picked up a few new things for herself.

"The point is not to do a total makeover–personality switch," she told Vidya, who had tutted that her new clothes haul had not been extensive enough. "I like who I am, I like my job, and I do need to look professional, but I'm trying to look more like me and less like someone doing my job twenty-six years older than me and possibly in the 1950s."

The new hiking boots were still the purchase Anne was most excited about, and one morning she woke up early enough that she thought she'd try them out.

There was no tidy bun or sleek ponytail with this new haircut. She gathered the longer layers into a messy clip and let the shorter pieces fall where they may. A pair of soft, worn leggings, an old university hoodie under a canvas jacket with enough pockets for a water flask, keys, and cell phone, and Anne was out the door.

At 7:30 a.m. the sun was still rising, a glow of soft yellow peeking over the canopy of trees along the river, but it was a losing battle as gray clouds rolled in. It wasn't a good day for a hike; that much was obvious. It was going to rain soon, Anne could smell it on the air, the slight damp bleeding into a sharper cold than the day before. The leaves rustling uneasily as the strong breeze toyed with transforming into a sharper gust. But she had her boots, and she wouldn't be thwarted again. She wouldn't have time for the full hike before work, but she would get to the whirlpool and enjoy that breathtaking view fired with color. It wouldn't be long before a cold snap dulled the leaves to rusty brown and the full effect would be lost. She would get in as many hikes until then as she could. She had lost time to make up for.

Anne parked her car in the same little lot, calmer and within the lines this time, and set out. The wood-and-mud steps were already a little damp, a hint of early morning frost. She descended deeply, until the path back to the car was obscured by leaves and she was enveloped in the quiet calm of the forest.

Halfway down, the steps ended, and a muddy, narrow trail continued the path with a zigzag descent. Anne stepped carefully over the roots and mossy rocks and patches of slippery mud. The man at the store had known what he was about, and the sturdy treads of her new boots carried her safely down the path. She could feel the cold like a thick carpet underfoot, but the new socks kept both the damp and the chill out.

She paused at the halfway point, looked around at the steeply rising walls of gold and green, and breathed in the air with deep satisfaction.

After about twenty minutes, the path leveled out, the trees began to thin, and Anne heard the rushing water.

She ducked under the last set of branches and—there!— the mud underfoot had turned into a rock beach, the feeling of being closed in by woods and valleys disappeared, and soaring openness took its place.

She stood on the shore before the Niagara whirlpool, a mass of turbulent rushing water, deafening and frothy and foaming and giving off an arctic chill. An erosion more than four thousand years old, 365 meters wide, 125 feet deep, swirling counterclockwise to the direction of the river that fed into it. Soaring rock cliffs of red and tan loomed overhead, bordering an air field of shrieking seagulls that hovered en masse high in the air, waiting for any disoriented fish that might stream out the other end.

Anne crunched across the beach, grateful for the tight lacing of the boots, which kept her from turning an ankle on the shifting rocks. She walked the perimeter of the water, careful to keep her distance, knowing how deceptive even the shallow-looking shoreline could be, until she could climb up on the massive flat boulders that jutted over the water like Pride Rock.

Here. Here she stood in the center of it all—the water rushing beneath her, the screams of the circling gulls overhead, the rising wind, the rolling gray skies stretching endlessly upwards, the flare of autumn color blazing in her periphery and over the tops of the soaring rocky cliffs.

Anne closed her eyes, stretched out her arms, and felt . . . free.

It might have been ten minutes, it might have been fifteen, but it was the best therapy she could think of. She committed the view to memory—had it really been eight years since she'd hiked this trail?—and leapt lightly down from the boulders back onto the shore, feeling calm, relaxed, invigorated, and ready to head back to her workday and her life.

She reached the mouth of the woods again, looked back over her shoulder for one last view of the water, turned back around to plunge into the trees, and . . .

Ben.

Because of course.

He looked equally stunned, standing there on the trail, silhouetted between two trees.

They stared at each other, neither moving, Anne with her back to the rushing water, Ben with his back to the trees, immovably in each other's path.

Anne came to her senses first. There was nothing for it but to walk toward him. It was a narrow path; they would have to acknowledge each other, need to step aside to pass by.

He wasn't in the hiking clothes he used to wear, she noted. His outdoors clothes back then had usually consisted of plain T-shirts, flannel, sweatshirts, and canvas jackets like her own, worn and a little frayed around the edges. But present-day Ben was in what looked like expensive gear, some kind of high-tech material for the pants, a Ralph Lauren pullover, Ray-Ban sunglasses hooked in the front—*sunglasses*, Anne scoffed internally, *he's that committed to the look that he has sunglasses when it's overcast and likely to rain*—and hiking boots.

When she was within speaking distance, he seemed to have recovered some composure, though perhaps not enough, because instead of his usual impassive expression he was looking slightly over her shoulder rather than at her directly.

Anne planned—in the split seconds she had available to plan—to walk by with nothing more than a curt nod. A rumble of thunder changed that. He wasn't from around here; he wouldn't know.

"It's not safe to stay down here if it's going to rain. It's too unpredictable, and the trail turns quickly to mud and becomes impassable."

He looked up at the gray skies, like he might argue about that rain, but at that moment the wind suddenly changed direction, and the air pressure shifted. The first few fat drops of water fell on his impeccable pullover.

Told you so.

Anne stepped around him, careful on the narrow trail, and plunged back into the shelter of the trees. If she hustled, she could make it back to the car before the downpour she felt coming would start. Ben would probably ignore her and hang around down . . . No, Ben was an experienced hiker. He'd give her fifteen minutes to get ahead and then head back to the parking lot himself. They'd be within shouting distance on the climb, but at least they'd have some distance.

A crack of lightning sounded farther off. Anne stopped and

counted mentally, dividing by five when the boom of thunder followed. Only a few minutes away. Best to pick up the pace.

There was cursing and the snap of twigs behind her. Anne turned—Ben. He had calculated as well, then; no time to give her that fifteen-minute grace period.

His long legs ate up the distance between them quickly until he was right behind her.

"The storm," he said.

"Yes," Anne said.

"Three minutes?"

"Three," Anne agreed.

It was all they needed by way of communication. They'd done similar calculations together enough times in the past. It served as explanation, maybe a bit of an apology on his part, for the excruciating task before them: two people who could barely speak to each other, with an arduous twenty-minute climb on a narrow path, all the way back to the parking lot, trying to outrun a storm.

Vidya would have either a joke about the tension or a Taylor Swift song for this.

But he could power ahead, easily overtake her on the path, get to the parking lot first, and leave her in peace . . .

Instead, she heard his heavy footsteps steadily following on her heels. *Why? Just pass me.*

She slowed down her gait deliberately.

So did he.

She sped up.

So did he.

A minute passed, then two; he stayed just a step be- hind, matching her pace. She could hear his slightly labored breathing.

Their three minutes' reprieve was up. A boom of thunder shook the air and then the rain came down in earnest, solid sheets of water. The trees provided a little shelter, but not much. A trench-like crevasse ran the length of the steep slope of ground they climbed, a steady trickle of a stream running down it. It hugged the path they followed, but it meant that while trees grew all around, none created a canopy overhead to umbrella them.

The path turned to mud, thick and slippery, just as Anne had predicted. The deep treads of her new boots, although still excellent, were not intended for ankle-deep mud. They grew heavy, caked with the stuff, and her pace slowed down in earnest as she kept her gaze trained down, carefully placing each step, as her thigh muscles started to ache with the slog. It was fast becoming difficult not to stumble and grow sloppy. Her waxed canvas jacket helped slough off some of the rain, but it was starting to give up under the deluge, and the frigid autumn downpour was beginning to permeate and chill her all the way through, her fingertips turning slightly numb, her new bangs dripping into her eyes.

She wondered how Ben was faring in his fashionable pullover. He used to always run hot, no matter the circumstances; he probably wasn't even shivering. She refused to turn around and look.

They were at the worst part of the path's steep ascent, nearly straight up, littered with rocks and roots. The rough wooden steps lay just beyond; they would be easier to manage.

Anne forced herself to pick up a bit of speed, hoping the momentum would carry her up part of the way. Her teeth were starting to chatter.

She managed the first few steps, but then she placed her

right foot on a deceptively deep patch of mud and her foot began to slide back down the slope. Frantically she tried to dig in her heel and grabbed at a rock's edge, the weight of her own body pulling against her efforts.

Every second the mud was deepening, and the stream was widening, becoming more than just a steady trickle; it was coming perilously close to the path, worsening her predicament.

The rock anchoring her hand came loose. *Shit, shit.* She tried to take another step, find more solid ground.

A strong arm wrapped around her waist from behind, immediately halting her backward progress.

Ben.

With his height he'd managed to grab a low-hanging tree branch to steady them both, his heavier weight helping him dig in his feet where she couldn't.

Of course. *Of course.* An experienced hiker. He knew this path would turn dangerous in seconds. He wasn't going to overtake her, leave her behind for the benefit of their cold war. He'd stayed just a step behind her to make sure she was safe, to make sure she made it to her car, a silent sentinel.

She felt sure he all but hated her; he certainly hadn't forgiven her, but he wouldn't let her suffer or be unsafe. Because despite the clean-shaven face and upscale clothes and hurtful words overheard in mazes, he was still Ben. And Ben Wentworth was a good man.

Like Lot's wife, she gave in to temptation and craned her neck to look back over her shoulder at him.

His immaculate hairstyle was gone, the sodden strands plastered to his head. Rusty red when wet, just like she remembered. Water droplets clung to his eyelashes and ran off his chin. She could feel his chest rise and fall against her back as they stared at each other, his arm like a band of steel around her, his head tipped down until they were nearly nose to nose, the close proximity giving them no quarter to avoid direct eye contact. Like Lot's wife Anne froze, turning to a pillar of salt.

"I'm going to brace you."

Anne blinked through the water, still mesmerized by being so close. *What? Did "brace" sound like "kiss"?*

"I'm going to brace you," he said again. If his mouth hadn't been nearly next to her ear, she wouldn't have been able to hear him over the storm. "Dig your foot into that mossy patch to your right—it shouldn't give way—and then I'll brace you from behind. You try and scramble up to that flat rock."

Oh. Right.

Anne wrenched herself back around, back into the here and now. Rain was now dripping from her hair down her neck, making her shudder unpleasantly. The arm that had been wrapped around her waist pulled back, and he moved to rest one large hand on the small of her back, pushing with a steady, gentle pressure, while his other hand kept hold of the tree branch. With considerable effort, using hiking muscles she hadn't used in a long time, Anne managed to gain the flat rock he'd pointed out. Ben followed, using his tree branch handhold for leverage, though Anne was gratified to see that he, too, was straining just a little not to slide in the mud.

Standing on the rock, he let go of her and wiped the rain out of his eyes, still keeping the front of his torso flat along her back as a steadying anchor. With a series of rasped instructions in her ear, he pointed out their next series of steps, trying to find things to grab on to and rough patches of ground where they could get traction.

By the time they made it to the stairs, they were both soaked through and Anne's teeth were chattering. Her lips must be going blue. Ben had immediately let go of her once the trickiest part of the path was over, and she missed the slight warmth his proximity emitted.

When they finally finished the last flight and gained the parking lot, the worst of the storm along with the thunder and lightning had passed over and was heading upstream to the falls. A gentle but steady patter of rain remained.

Anne was thoroughly worn-out and reached for her car keys with shaking fingers, peeling back the sodden flap of her canvas coat pocket to get them.

She sat in her front seat, uncaring of how she must be soaking the leather upholstery, and just let herself decompress, just for a moment.

A moment was all she got.

The passenger-side door opened and Ben dropped heavily into the seat beside her. Anne looked at him in amazement—wasn't this enforced-proximity game over yet?—but he didn't return her gaze, just reached across the console to pluck the keys from her hand, started the car, and with efficient, sure movements turned the heaters on, including her seat heater, directing the gloriously warm vents at her full blast.

Anne sighed with relief and held her numbed fingers out gratefully. Ben said nothing, just stared straight ahead at the rivulets covering the windshield. She could see the colonel's truck he must have borrowed parked a few spots over, but he made no move to leave and drive away. Five minutes or more passed; Anne was beginning to feel warm-blooded again. A glance in the rearview mirror told her that her new hair was starting to wave as it dried in its softer "tousled" style.

Ben's hair was starting to curl at the nape of his neck, his clothes steaming a little, but he didn't press toward the vents like Anne, or even move one of them to direct any heat his way.

"I'm sorry," he spoke at last, his voice low but oh so loud in the small, quiet space of the car, muffled by the gentle patter of rain on the roof above their heads. The windows were starting to steam up. Anne held her breath, like his next words might be vital. "I'm sorry that I thought . . . that I accused you of manipulating the price, or manipulating my uncle and aunt. I know that you're always up-front and do the right thing. Whether it's good news or bad, you always tell people the truth."

She let the breath out, slow and measured. Was he truly just thinking of the price of that field, in the here and now? Or was he thinking—that eight years ago she had plainly told him to his face that they were over instead of using gentler, evasive tactics. Ben had always preferred honesty, she knew that, even when that honesty had turned on him like a knife.

"Thank you. I have great respect for your aunt and uncle."

He nodded, still facing the window.

"What were you doing out here?" Anne asked.

Ben shrugged. "Hiking. I wanted to remem . . . I thought I'd take in the view again, while I'm here visiting."

Remember? Remember what? Our last weekend together, hiking this path, eight years ago?

He glanced at her hands, which had stopped shaking. She dropped them from the vents into her lap.

"You're good to drive now." Not quite a question, but Anne nodded. He leveraged himself out of the seat and out the door without another word, back into the rain. Anne watched him jog over the few spots to the truck. Had he recognized her car when he parked? Did he guess she was on the path when he set out for his hike?

She watched him pull out and drive away, heading back in the direction of Kellynch. Anne scraped her muddy feet against the mat of her car—*god, that's going to be a pain to clean out*—before putting her own foot on the gas and moving her car into reverse, turning on her system to dictate a text to Emmie letting her know she'd be late for work. After she finished, the stereo automatically flicked on, synced to her phone.

She drove home in the rain, listening to Taylor Swift's "cardigan," and wondering what the heck had just happened.

Eighteen

Anne continued to enjoy the small feeling of exuberance her new look brought her, and the regained feeling of freedom her hiking boots brought her. Now it was no longer a choice simply between her professional black heels and her dainty flats. She bought chunky pumps in bright green, English-style oxfords in caramel-colored leather, knee-high boots that could have made Julia Roberts's pretty woman blush. She enjoyed the change-up, the choices each morning, and then wrenching off the footwear at the end of each day to pull on her Oboz and hit another trail. The days were getting shorter, dark Canadian nights showing up earlier each evening, but she was determined to max out the gorgeous fall before the snow fell and she'd need ice spikes over her boots.

The purchase of the field and venue agreement with the Fairchilds were nearing completion. Anne was excited to start the real fun—planning the venue, meeting with contractors, looking at designs for the band shell format they'd agreed on. The board members hadn't put up much fuss with the progress of the plan—they disliked incurring the debt but did like the prospect of expansion and future income. Paul had been a true ally, running over the financial projections with a thoroughness that practically had the men sprinting for the door to get away. Anne took it as a win.

Vidya's Juliet costume remained unfinished, as Choi was still uncertain about Sabrina and Anne refused to weigh in, especially now that she knew she couldn't be impartial about Sabrina, but Choi soon came to her with a bigger concern, which was . . .

"What?!" Anne said, flabbergasted.

Choi repeated herself. "Michelle Cranston would like to be considered for the Juliet part, when she's finished with the Lady Macbeth run."

"Absolutely not! No! Choi, I don't care if you have to hold open auditions, or spoon-feed Sabrina her lines, or if we have to spring to install an autocue for her—because god help me I will find the money for it—but we are not suffering through another season of Michelle Cranston!"

Okay, so maybe there really were worse things than watching Sabrina parade around as a fetching Juliet. It was good to have perspective.

Emmie truly had bounced back after the Pumpkin Festival. Her effervescence never dimmed for long, but she had a new sort of thoughtfulness when she took on tasks; she was as hyperverbal as ever, as colorful in her stories and her feelings, but Anne noticed she was taking the time to plan and think things through rather than plunge in as quickly. She was growing, and it was time to give her more responsibility in her work; the time would come soon—much sooner than she would like—when Emmie would need to move on to the next stage in her career.

But for now, despite the new responsibilities Anne was slowly transferring to her, Emmie's number one priority still seemed to be Anne's welfare, guarding her schedule, her office door, and her forced consumption of muffins.

Which is how Anne came to overhear her assistant outside her office door berating Ben Wentworth for showing up without an appointment.

The encounter with Ben in the gorge had been itching at the back of her mind. Would they pretend the conversation in her car had never happened? Turned out she didn't have long to wait. Anne quickly fixed her bangs and reapplied her lipstick as she listened.

"She's a very busy woman. Do you know how long it takes me to tessellate all her meetings just so that she has time to even eat!?" Emmie was saying.

"All right, I'm very sorry, only she asked me to review a few of the design proposals, and I was down the street and thought I'd stop in," Ben replied, and Anne wondered if he had really been visiting Sabrina down in rehearsals, and why he hadn't just sent an email. "I promise," Ben continued, "I will faithfully abide by your schedule and won't show up unannounced ever again."

"Good, see that you do," her faithful assistant said sternly.

She heard Ben's low chuckle.

"You're a fierce keeper of the gates, aren't you? How long have you worked at the festival?"

"I was a co-op student for two summers in a row when I

was doing my degree. When I graduated last June, Anne offered me a job as her executive assistant."

"Do you like working here?"

"Are you kidding? I'm learning so much; Anne is fucking awesome! Spreadsheets, bam! Budget meetings, bam! Shareholders, stakeholders, sponsors, bam, bam, bam! Crazy actresses, bam! You should see her take on the board of directors. I'm pretty sure this town would fall to pieces without her. And she always answers my questions and lets me listen in on meetings and stuff."

Behind the safety of her office door, Anne put her hands to her blushing cheeks, deeply touched to hear her ferocious young assistant speak so admiringly of her. Emmie's flattering assessment soothed the still-lingering sting of Sabrina's words at the Pumpkin Festival.

Ben didn't respond to Emmie's "Anne tribute," but after a moment he asked, "I heard this used to be her mother's position. Did Anne take it on as soon as her mother retired?"

"Oh, Mrs. Elliot didn't retire," Emmie said, suddenly subdued. "She died."

Unwilling to listen to the story, Anne chose that moment to open her door and make her presence known.

Emmie immediately busied herself at her desk, but Ben looked intensely at Anne. She pretended not to notice.

"Mr. Wentworth, I wasn't expecting you, but I have a few minutes free. Please come in."

He followed her into her office and sat down. There was a moment's silence; she waited for him to mention the design proposals for the band shell and seating.

"I didn't . . . I didn't know your mother passed away. How did it happen?"

"Cancer," Anne said succinctly.

Ben regarded her steadily, his face open for once, instead of the usual neutral or stony expression he habitually turned on her. Anne felt the tug to tell him more, like a muscle memory of past emotions, when she could tell him things, confide in him, and receive comfort and care in return. She steeled herself against it, grounded herself in the present, the press of the leather chair at her back. This was her office now, not her mother's, and the man sitting opposite a near stranger, not her boyfriend.

But in the silence she couldn't help expanding: "It wasn't drawn-out. They tell you that's a mercy with terminal. Is it? I still don't know. They tell you a lot of things that are just cold comfort. We got the diagnosis, I moved back into my parents' home—well, not Kellynch, that was already sold, but the place on King Street—to help care for her, and then I was already working at the festival, so . . . Well, anyway, here I am." She took a breath, embarrassed to have said so much.

"When was she diagnosed?" Ben asked softly.

Anne named the year and watched him do the mental math, knew when he frowned a little and looked away that he had calculated just how soon after their breakup it had occurred. Had things gone differently between them, had Anne not taken that fateful step, he might have been there to hold her hand. To drive her home from the hospital for a change of clothes after another sleepless night at her mother's bedside. At the time Anne hadn't allowed herself to think of that, to imagine that comfort and support. She told herself it would have been too deep, too scary, too involved for him, that he would have run or tried to ignore it like her father. She knew now, now that it was too late, that he wouldn't have done either of those things.

"I know," Ben said hesitantly, "I know that she wasn't my biggest fan, or vice versa, but I am sorry for your loss. I know you were close to your mother."

"Yes, I was," Anne agreed.

"I know she meant a lot to you, and this festival, and this town, and I'm sorry we never saw eye to eye."

Anne nodded. "And I was sorry to learn about your uncle's accident. I know you care for them both deeply. Your aunt told me a little of how difficult it's been for them, these past few years. I'm glad you've been able to help them, that you're helping them now, here, with this. It's such a good thing you're doing for them."

Ben shifted in his chair, always uncomfortable with direct praise. She'd nearly forgotten that about him.

In the time since Ben had arrived in Niagara-on-the-Lake, it was the closest either of them had come to acknowledging their real history. It should have made things more awkward, but instead Anne felt the habitual tension between them relax just a fraction. A thawing of the ice.

When he left her office, she clamped down on a wish that he would stay a little longer.

Nineteen

Anne worked late that night. The visit with Ben had distracted her, and she wanted the quiet and calm of the darkened building for the evening, so she was still sitting at her desk when she got the call to come and collect her father.

Mr. Elliot wasn't what one might call an alcoholic, or at least not in the traditional sense. He didn't hoard drinks, didn't lie about his drinking, didn't drink alone at home. Really, he only drank socially—if there was no company he could do just fine without—and he didn't drink to excess, per se. He didn't drink and become violent or belligerent, or even sloppy, because his vanity would never allow him to appear anything other than immaculately arranged and because he once read a tweet about an article that said too much drinking could lead to premature aging and bloodshot eyes.

He just drank to the point of betraying all of his absolute very worst character traits. Loudly, and in public. He drank to the point that he would say and do things that made Anne absolutely mortified and he would become deaf to her hissed whispers. And he drank to the point that he often outstayed his welcome and sometimes his ability to pay his bill.

While the legacy of the Elliot name still commanded respect, and while Mr. Elliot with his preening and posturing and old-fashioned magnanimous ways still had many of the Niagara community in awe of him, the owners of the fine dining and wining establishments in town had a very different view.

It was not long after her mother died that Anne first caught wind of his behavior. The owner of the Winchester Arms had called her at work one morning, his own embarrassment at the situation making his words awkward and stilted.

"And I'm really sorry to call like this, Anne; I haven't wanted to disturb you so soon after your family's loss. Your mother was a great lady and a wonderful woman, and this town owes so much to her, and it's because of her that I even thought to call you, you're so much like her and . . ."

Until Anne managed to finally extract the bumbling truth from him. Before her illness, Mrs. Elliot used to more often than not accompany her husband out for dinner or for his banquets at the golf club, or bring him along on the rota of social occasions that was now Anne's lot, and by some miracle manage to curb the worst of his appetites and behaviors. When she could not, and he went out on his own, proprietors had learned that a quick call to Mrs. Elliot at the Elysium Festival was the best hope of having an overdue tab paid, or a recalcitrant husband collected, or at least she would apologize and soothe and smooth over whatever embarrassments her husband had dished out.

Since her mother's illness first began, more and more of these little truths had washed up on Anne's shore, until she was rather numb to it all and only listened to Dev of the Winchester Arms resignedly.

Well, she was nothing if not efficient. She had a few quiet words with these proprietors. She would not be accompanying her father, she was not his babysitter, she had a line in the sand, but bills would be paid and taxi fare, too, if they could persuade him into a cab and send him home. It was worth the hassle, Anne had reasoned to herself, to protect her professional standing and that of the Elliot name.

It had been her mother's name, too, after all. She wouldn't leave it unprotected for her father to clumsily damage.

So, it wasn't such a surprise when she got the call from the manager at the Churchill Bar & Lounge, attached to the Prince of Wales, the decadent nineteenth-century hotel on the main strip in town. What was a surprise was the absence of his usually affable tone.

"Sorry, Anne, but we've been run off our feet all night. There's a wedding in the ballroom next door, the bride is losing her shit because the entrees were mixed up, and the kitchen is short-staffed doing the dining room, the ballroom, and the lounge," said Toby, sounding breathless and ticked off. "I haven't got time to deal with your fucking father, so come and get him, *now*."

It took her only a few minutes to get there, but another ten to find parking, every lot overflowing with what were probably the wedding guests' cars. It was near eleven when she finally walked through the doors of the hotel's main lobby.

This hotel, like the festival, was widely considered a centerpiece of the town. But unlike the busy, hustling festival that Anne had worked to modernize, this hotel was a relic of a more luxurious, relaxed past. Walking in, guests were immediately encased in warm tones, ornately patterned carpets, paintings framed with scrollwork, molded cream ceilings, and softly glowing chandeliers shaded by frosted glass. Classical piano tinkled from speakers hidden discreetly behind the glossy wooden canopy that adorned the concierge desk, and French doors annexed the lobby from the other parts of the hotel.

Under normal circumstances Anne loved visiting the hotel. It was peace and tranquility and order. One of her happy places in the town.

Now it just felt like a mockery of the stress and embarrassment squeezing at her temples. Only a few times before had she actually had to come collect her father.

Each one stood out vividly in her memory.

She waved to the young man at the concierge desk and then hooked a right, away from the lovely lobby and into the even lovelier dining rooms, with floor-to-ceiling glass letting diners look out onto the twinkling lamplights and elaborate flower arrangements adorning the white balustrade of the hotel's exterior.

She passed through the rooms until she reached the end and stepped into the Churchill Lounge. Here the airy feminine graces of the dining room decor gave way to deeper hues. The lounge was dimmer, cozier, but no less luxurious. Dark wood covered the walls and ceiling, crisscrossing in elaborate patterns. High-backed leather armchairs sat grouped around tables, away from narrow windows offering a limited view of the street. A roaring fire in a massive fireplace took up the far wall, and a long wraparound bar jutted out from the back of the room, like a small peninsula, multifaceted fine whiskey decanters shimmering in muted golds and reds in the firelight.

Low jazz played in this room, muffled and sultry along with the occasional indistinct murmurs of the few patrons in their seats.

In the late fall evening it should have been inviting. But all Anne felt was disquiet.

She approached the bar, where a young man—*was it Nate, maybe?*—was pouring out a drink.

"Hi . . ." She checked his name badge and relaxed just a fraction. "Hi, Nate, right? You're Nancy's son, home from college? I think your older sister interned with my costume department last year . . ."

"Ms. Elliot, hi, yeah, wow, like, you've got a super-good memory."

"I do my best. Listen, I got a call from Toby, and it sounds like my father has been here having just a little too much fun . . ." She tried to smile conspiratorially, a little ruefully, as if her father was being indulgently silly. In her mind she heard echoes of her mother, laughing off the sale of Kellynch—"Oh, who needs *that* old place, what a hassle to run"—to her friends even as she wept in private, and Anne internally cringed. "And I just thought I'd nip in and give him a lift home. Is he around?"

"Uh, well, he was in the ballroom earlier, he was giving a speech, but, like, I don't think he knew the wedding party? So, they weren't super happy, although, *dude*, it was, like, a *really* good speech . . ."

Anne just resisted face-palming. "Yes, he's very eloquent, but where is he now?"

"Anne!" her father's voice rang out. A grim-faced man in a suit was escorting her father—holding him forcibly by the arm—into the lounge from a door that joined the lounge to a long hallway, at the opposite end of which was the ballroom.

"This is my daughter Anne," Mr. Elliot announced loudly to his escort, as if they were chums. "She's my younger daughter, older than your Samra, though. When my other daughter Elizabeth's time to get married comes, I'll be father of the bride too—maybe you could give me some tips then, eh? I'll give you my card, come and join me at my golf club next Saturday, I'll spot you a round."

"This your father?" the man asked Anne, quiet and dignified. She nodded. He let go of Mr. Elliot's arm with an aggressive shove, pushing him in Anne's direction. "Keep him away from my daughter. I will not see her crying on her wedding day. My wife and I paid a lot of money for this wedding, and if I see him in the party again, I'll call security, and I will take this matter to the management of the hotel."

Patrons in the lounge were starting to stare; Anne could feel their eyes on her from every direction. Nate the bartender was openly and avidly watching.

"Yes, of course, I'm so sorry, really, I'm so terribly sorry," Anne fumbled, her usual smooth courteousness deserting her. "He means well, but of course, I apologize completely, I'll take him home at once."

"Well, if I'm not welcome, you needn't be so ugly about it. I can take a hint. I was only chatting with some of the guests." Her father had straightened to his full height and was looking down his nose at the man he had obviously now realized was not, in fact, his friend. "Really, old fellow, I was only stopping in to congratulate the happy couple. I hardly need to spend my evening with your little party. And if I may give you a piece of advice, it's rather tacky to dither over the price of a momentous family occasion. If you can't afford the wedding, then, good god, man, just send the girl to city hall."

The father of the bride angrily swore, using several particular curse words that made their watching audience murmur and Nate the bartender's eyes widen further, before storming off, back to his daughter's wedding.

"What a rude man. There's no manners anymore. What happened to being a gentleman?" her father said loudly to the room.

"Dad," Anne hissed, "Dad, let's go, we're going home." She tried to direct him to the door, anything but standing center stage like this while everyone openly gawked.

"Anne, if you get married—I know that's not likely—but I want you to know that no expense would be spared for your wedding. Although I hope you have taste enough to know you can't pull off the fairy-tale-princess look. We'd get you a more modern dress, something classic . . ."

With both hands clutched around his arm now, Anne tried to discreetly propel her father to the door, while he loudly planned her "unlikely" wedding. She could feel her face flaming redder and redder, and tears of mortification pricked at her eyes.

"Uh, Ms. Elliot? Your father's card was declined . . ." Nate called, before they could gain the door. "He's been running a tab all evening, and he has an outstanding tab from last week."

"Yes, of course, I'm so sorry, I'll clear both tabs now." Anne pivoted back to the bar, trying to keep one hand on her father while the other rooted in her tote looking for her wallet. Mr. Elliot was clumsily trying to shake her off, no doubt having spotted another "friend" by the fireplace he wanted to talk to, but Anne kept him firmly tethered with her nails dug into the sleeve of his suit jacket while Nate the bartender stood there waiting. Anne urgently tried to dig one-handed for her wallet—*why is my wallet always at the very bottom?*—the tote straps slipping off her shoulder and down to her elbow while she tried to pull against her father's larger frame.

"I can take care of the bill," said a low, sure voice.

Of course, Ben.

Anne closed her eyes for a moment in complete and utter mortification.

He was smoothly withdrawing his credit card from his wallet and handing it over to Nate. Anne looked over to the high-backed group of chairs he had come from—they were facing the street, so she'd overlooked them when she'd walked in—and saw a few members of the winery owners' association sitting there, trying to pretend they, too, hadn't seen and heard everything. The group sometimes convened at the Churchill Lounge; Ben must have been meeting with them on behalf of his aunt and uncle.

"No, no," Anne said, and heard her own voice wobble with tears. "I'm fine, I have this." She'd finally managed to extricate her own credit card. Ben proffered his again, but Anne firmly thrusted her card over the counter in poor Nate's face, and Ben, seeing her distress, quietly put his away.

Mr. Elliot was looking at Ben curiously, and Anne prayed her father wouldn't recognize him as that boy she brought home eight years ago. But why would he? The shaggy boy was someone he'd easily forgotten. The grown man in the suit leaning confidently at the bar, willing to pick up a tab, would be someone her father would like and respect.

"You're not related to Thom Winslow by any chance, are you? He's a dear friend of mine, you have the look of him . . ." her father began, but Ben cut him off.

"I'm not from around here."

"Okay, here's your receipt," said Nate, handing it over. "Uh, Ms. Elliot?" he asked before Anne could get away. She bit back her tears and tried to ignore her flaming cheeks and summon her last reserve of patience.

"Yes, Nate?"

"My sister really enjoyed her internship at your festival, and she's graduated and applying for work now, and I was wondering if you'd give her a reference? I mean, she's getting one from a prof, but, like, I think it would really help her if she had one from you. I didn't think you'd remember her, but since you do . . ."

"Of course, Nate, your sister was a wonderful intern and very promising. Have her contact my office, and I'll see that we get something arranged."

"Awesome!"

And with that, Anne shoved her father out the door, through a back hallway, and into the parking lot behind the hotel where she'd left her car.

Except this hellish night wasn't done with her, because her car was gone.

"Did you walk here?" her father asked.

"No, I drove, I . . ." Anne said, looking around frantically.

"Ms. Elliot?" A man in a hotel valet uniform was standing nearby, having a cigarette break. He butted his cigarette and came over.

"Yes?"

"Yeah, I'm real sorry. They came and towed your car."

"What? Why?" Anne asked. "Why would they tow it? It's a parking lot, I parked in a parking lot!"

"They said you had unpaid parking tickets."

"What? No, I . . . Goddammit, Liz!" Anne cried, realizing that on one of her sister's many jaunts while borrowing Anne's car—before Anne started hiding her spare keys—she must have racked up tickets and left them unpaid.

"Ah," said her father, "yes, Liz did mention that she might have had some trouble a few weeks back. But you can hardly hold your sister responsible, I mean, the parking in this town is so atrocious . . ."

"Where's your car, Dad? Did you drive here?"

"No, I had a luncheon with Sir Phillip and then we came here for a few after-drinks—he drove. Then he left for a dinner with his wife, and I stayed on to chat with a few friends who happened to be in the dining room. Did you know that Mark Patel just turned fifty the other week? I would have thought he was nearly twice that. I had trouble keeping my composure when he mentioned it and . . ."

Anne ignored her father. Home was close enough to walk, it was really just down the street, but it was nearly midnight now, it was absolutely freezing, and her father didn't walk anywhere except the golf greens, even when he was sober. She pulled out her phone to call a cab.

"I can give you a lift."

Ben had quietly followed them outside, his keys in his hand. Anne could see the jeep just a few rows over.

"Thank you, but we're fine. I'll just call a cab and . . ."

No, she wouldn't, because at that moment her phone battery died.

Shit, shit, shit!

Usually, she topped up her phone charge before leaving work for the day, but the phone call about her father had distracted her.

Ben stood there waiting patiently until Anne came to the inevitable conclusion.

"Yes, thank you, we will take a ride."

He nodded once and then put a hand on her father's shoulder. "This way, Mr. Elliot, I'm driving you home."

"Good man."

The cold air and warming alcohol had made her father sleepy and blessedly compliant. He merely yawned, made a casual observation on the quality of Ben's classic Jaeger-LeCoultre watch, and let himself be led to the jeep and deposited in the back seat.

Anne walked to the passenger-side door and discovered one last dilemma. Getting into the jeep required a massive step up onto the running board and then into her seat. Her skirt and high-heeled boots were incompatible with taking that massive leg up with any kind of grace. For once in her life, Anne could have really wished to be wearing the correct footwear, and she thought longingly of her hiking boots in the trunk of her car now, no doubt sitting in some god forsaken impound lot.

"Here." Ben was back around to her side of the jeep and, with the lightest possible touch, turned her around, and then, grasping her by the waist, he lifted her up and into the seat; he was so quick and efficient he was back around to the driver's side before Anne had even processed what happened. There was a flattened empty gum box sticking out the side of the glove compartment in front of her, a reminder in Ben's handwriting scrawled on it that Aunt Jenny had asked him to pick up some pies tomorrow, with the address of a bakery circled underneath. So, he still had that quirk.

"What's the address?" he asked, and Anne quietly directed him to their pink-and-white house on King Street.

Ben maneuvered the clunky vehicle into the driveway with ease and cut the engine. He made no move to let Anne out. He sat there staring through the windshield, a look on his face like he was working something out.

Her father snored quietly in the back seat.

"When we . . ." Ben began, then stopped, and Anne's heart beat faster at what he might say. He tried again. "I've been through a lot of the old paperwork for Kellynch. I know the bank took it."

Ah.

So, her humiliation was complete.

On some level Anne was aware that their financial woes were still a very privileged problem. Their family had begun with more wealth than most could dream of. Even in reduced circumstances, her own salary was still well above average income, she had designer clothes and her mother's jewels, and the Elliots still had property and resources.

It was the shame of the decline, of having been born to such privilege and wealth, and instead of putting it to use, frittering much of it away through sheer stupidity and laziness and her father's wild financial deals. It was leaving unpaid tabs all over town and parking wherever they wanted, entitled and useless. The dwindling wealth—and it was dwindling, faster and faster—was just a consequence, a proof for the world to see, of the feckless, entitled behavior of her family. It was that which shamed Anne. And now Ben knew it too.

She cleared her throat. "Yes, my father gave it to the bank

to relieve some other debts. It wasn't making any money, so it was easier to give that one up, in order to keep the properties and investments that were still generating income. The winery business was too much work; he wound it down so it was only a family home after all. But," she said, trying to inject some false cheer into her voice, "the colonel and Jenny will find it a very good business. It had lots of potential; it only wanted proper management."

Ben didn't respond to her reassurance; he still had that thoughtful expression, his eyes moving back and forth, like pennies were dropping.

"When we broke up . . ." he said, and Anne's heart just about stopped to hear him talk about their relationship. It was the first time either of them had verbally acknowledged their entwined past.

"When we broke up . . ." he repeated, "this is *why*, isn't it? This is what your mother foresaw, for you . . . if you stayed . . . with me." He was still staring ahead, not looking at Anne. "I didn't have a plan and I wasn't thinking about the future. She thought I was irresponsible, and directionless, and no substance. And she thought you would have nothing but burdens in exchange."

"Yes," Anne whispered.

And then because she owed him more, more than that bungled explanation she gave him eight years ago, she went on.

"It was her life for as long as I could remember, though I didn't always fully understand how it . . . how it shaped what she saw, how she saw you, and the future of us. She judged you, the way you dressed and spoke, but it was your free-spiritedness, to her it just seemed like . . . to both of us, because once she persuaded me to make the comparison I couldn't unsee it and it looked so much like . . . Well, I know now that she was wrong. I'm *glad* that she was wrong, and you've done so well for yourself. But her fears had become mine and . . ."

Anne wanted to say more; she had some deep-buried family instinct to defend her father, to say he was basically harmless, just vain, and pompous, and attention-seeking, just living for the moment and not acknowledging that things could go wrong, and now that he was older, he was all the time increasingly foolish until you couldn't help but pity him. But the consequences of those harmless little personality defects were not so harmless after all. She didn't say any of this, just finished weakly with: "She was terrified I'd end up like her."

"But you did anyway," Ben said.

"What?"

Ben turned, and for the first time since she got in the car he faced Anne dead on, his dark navy-colored eyes serious and intent under his furrowed brow.

"She didn't want your life dragged around because you were chained to a useless partner, picking up after him and being pulled down by him. So, what the hell are you doing chasing around after your father and sister? Isn't it nearly the same thing? Only you're being burdened by your mother's partner instead of your own."

Anne stared at him, mind blank. She could only take in his beseeching expression, like he was willing her to understand something that she couldn't wrap her head around.

She'd had so many moments of something nearing despair this evening, and then his stepping in, his witnessing it and helping her and physically putting her in the car to drive home, picking her up like he used to do so playfully when they were together and now all she had was this phantom version of it, and she was so emotionally exhausted that some part of her was simply screaming that she really could not take in one more thing.

But Anne was the queen of rising to the task—she could always mentally take in one more excruciating thing.

Her father chose that moment to wake up with a sleepy snort. "Oh, have we arrived? Anne, tip the man, would you?"

With some assistance from Ben, Anne got Mr. Elliot inside the house, and then under his own steam her father was able to make it up the stairs; they watched his swaying gait from below as he disappeared.

The front hallway was shadowy and still, just the two of them standing there, so much space and yet not nearly enough space between them. The door was open, ready for Ben's departure, the night air sharp and pitch-black at his back, little breezes curling around his tall form, slithering into the stale air of the house.

He would leave now, any moment, and yet he lingered, half in and half out of the doorway. She couldn't look at him, not directly, her gaze no higher than his chest, watching the rise and fall, rise and fall, and then a deeper inhale like he would say something, and it trembled in the air, but it never came, and the hall was silent, just the far-off muffled ticking of a grandfather clock.

"Good night," Anne said softly, into the quiet of the dark.

"Good night," Ben replied finally, his voice gentle and low, and then he was gone.

Anne watched the headlights of the truck retreat back down the driveway as Ben drove off, back to Kellynch.

She made herself a strong cup of coffee, sat down at the kitchen table, and opened up the windows to hear the waves on the lake, made rough by the autumn winds.

She sat, and she thought about what Ben had said in the car.

When did she slide down into this pit of responsibility? Why were all these people and all these burdens hers to bear? When had it begun? When her mother was ill? Was that it? Her mother had been the one to curb her father and soften her sister and support the town and smooth the path of the festival—why was Anne her natural successor?

Anne cast her mind back to those horrible days of slow decay and the endless, ceaseless rot of cancer. It must have begun then, moving home to care for Mom and seeing the burdens tumble down as her mother ebbed away, picking them up, one by one, like strapping heavy packs to herself, thinking *just for now, I'll carry this one just for now*, and one more, and one more, *I'll shrug them off when this horrible thing is done, when she's gone and she doesn't have to see it fail, I'll carry them just until then* . . . It was to give her mother comfort, not wanting her to look up on those fewer and fewer lucid days, when her eyes were clear and present, and see the crumbling of everything around her. Not the loss of another home, and the indifference of her sister or the delusions of her father, who would not, could not, face the fact that his wife was dying, always talking about "these marvelous new treatments, cancer research has come *so far* these days," always sure it would work out somehow, shaking the doctor's hand with authority each hospital visit before escaping to the cafeteria. Anne didn't want her to see the festival handed to some other executive who wouldn't love it in the same way, care for it in the same way. All the people and the committees and the little cares of the town that had depended on Mrs. Elliot—Anne did not want her mother to look up and see their needs unanswered, hear them cry out for what she could no longer provide, the way Anne wished she could cry out in fear and dread of the approaching cold void where her mother's love for her would once have been. Because then who would comfort Mom? Anne loved her mother, she wanted her to live, but if she could not live, then she wanted her to die in peace and in comfort knowing everything was taken care of.

But after? Anne thought.

Why did she never put those burdens down again, like she promised herself she would?

Her mother didn't want her to be alone, and her mother didn't want her looking after a man like her father.

And where was she? Alone. Looking after—not a man *like* her father, but actually her feckless father, and her sister as well, who seemed to feel none of Anne's pull to give care and take responsibility. Clearly such things weren't expected of Liz, but they had somehow been expected of Anne.

Really, it was so horribly ironically funny she could just cry.

The weight of every decision seemed to press down on her at once, the weight of her world, as claustrophobic as it had become. She was tired, so tired she could have gratefully sunk to the floor and not gotten up again.

Vidya had accused her, after the Pumpkin Festival fiasco and hotel meltdown, of dressing like her mother, trying too hard to fill her shoes. Anne hadn't realized just how deep the problem went.

Twenty

The next morning Anne woke up with her head on the kitchen table, a cold cup of coffee and her laptop in front of her, still in yesterday's wrinkled, stale clothing. She'd fallen asleep googling apartments for rent. Tinny sound was coming from her earbuds, stuck in her phone, charging from her laptop; she'd been listening to Vidya's playlist on repeat. She hadn't understood the inclusion of the song "Mine" a week ago when she'd first listened to it, paying too much attention to the verses. Now she understood, it was the chorus that was relevant.

It pissed her off.

The effects of her revelation were as bad as a hangover. She was grumpy, she was tired, she had a crick in her back and her neck, she had no car until she could find time to fish it out of the impound lot, and she had a full workday ahead, while her father slept off his late-night escapade.

Anne groaned and dragged herself into a hot shower and a change of clothes for work, with a promise to herself of getting an extra-large coffee. Today was a councilors' meeting.

It sometimes happened that Anne's job as town councilor did in fact require more involvement and gravitas than mediating boisterous town hall meetings and arbitrating disastrous festivals—or so she would have liked to tell Ben.

The intersection of tourism, agriculture, seasonal workers and visitors, and all the little bylaws that made up their concerns was an extensive network that required deft handling. While sometimes the solution was simple—yes, if your Airbnb guests trashed the golf course, then you as the owner of the house would have to pay to clean it up—other times it was more complicated. The biggest ongoing headache was the aggressive attempts of real estate developers to encroach upon the town. Whenever a classic town building went up for sale, there were half a dozen developers trying buy it, bulldoze it, and put up an eyesore monstrous-sized building. Sometimes it was a farmer's field or a parcel of land with rich soil or an orchard; they drained natural ponds and razed hundred-year-old trees and then would want to put up a shopping mall, or rows and rows of identical prefab housing.

Anne knew that some modernity and progress was good, but she, like many of the local inhabitants and business owners, felt that these aggressive, highly commercialized attempts at development would ruin the old-fashioned, quaint ways of the town, which would ruin the very thing that made it wonderful. To this end, they had started bringing in bylaws—

designations to protect heritage buildings, rules about how many stories high a new building could be—and rigorous application processes; any hopeful developer would need to show that they were building with the community's best interests at heart, with a respect for the town's aesthetic, and receive approval from the town councilors. Only a few applicants made it through the process.

Many simply gave up at the first hurdle.

But it seemed they had another brave contender at their gates, because Anne had been asked to join the other town councilors that afternoon in hearing a development proposal. It was always a wrench to have to book time off during her workday, although Emmie could now manage things on her own for a few hours while Anne slipped out.

In her current mood she would have liked to save everyone's time and just tell this latest fool tilting at a windmill to piss off.

In the spare, squat room they used in city hall, Anne joined her fellow councilors at the semicircular table and looked for the usual fleet of suited city men that would sit opposite, with their reams of PowerPoints and small-scale models.

There was none.

One lone man sat across from them, completely at his ease. It was the man from the sailboat, that late-season sailor Anne had exchanged a few words with in the harbor.

Up close she could see he was handsome . . . very handsome, with dark hair and striking light eyes. What her mother used to call the Elizabeth Taylor complexion. He wasn't wearing a suit, but a collared shirt under a well-fitted sweater, and a pair of dress pants. He sat in the chair like he'd been invited to lunch, instead of to give a presentation. Anne looked around. In addition to not having a team, he also had no visual aids, no leather-bound folders or important papers to shuffle.

He gave a small smile when he saw Anne, and she saw that a slight scar on his upper lip pulled his smile slightly off-kilter. It marred his magazine-level good looks but improved his appeal—it made him interesting.

"This is Councilor Anne Elliot," Councilor Singh introduced her, as Anne shook the stranger's hand before taking her seat. His handsomeness was making her self-conscious about whether the bags under her eyes were still showing, despite painstaking concealer application. "This is Anthony Harbringer, of Harbringer Developments."

"A pleasure to meet you, Councilor. I think I might have seen you at the sailing club in passing."

"Yes, that was me," Anne confirmed. "I was admiring your gorgeous sloop."

"Thank you, I do the work on her myself. I sailed her down from Toronto, but I'm afraid she'll have to be towed back, the weather has turned so quickly. I'm putting her away for the season."

"Perhaps you'll have a reason to be back here in the spring and enjoy the harbor again," Singh said.

Not likely, Anne thought dryly. No one was going to fast-track his proposal just because he was handsome. Also, at least three of the council had aging eyesight and were unlikely to be able to see his handsomeness, so there was also that factor.

With much shuffling and chair scraping—only a few of them made any appearance of being attentive—the meeting was called to order, and Mr. Harbringer of Harbringer Developments was given the floor.

"You're rather famous in the development community," he began in a relaxed, conversational tone. "With land and real estate prices so high, most everyone wants to sell out—pardon me, sell *up*," he said, and Anne knew the slip had been deliberate. "But," he continued, "not this town. You have incredible appeal, a thriving local economy, a glut of tourists, stunning surrounding nature, but you're an Alamo. I submitted a proposal for development five years ago; I was with another company back then. It was a forty-story residential-and-retail-mix building, with a six-story, four-block concrete parking structure. It got shot down before we even made it this far to meet all of you. So, I went away, I worked on other sites, I started my own company, and I learned my lesson. I am interested, *very* interested, in investing in this town and realizing a development here, but I understand it has to be on your terms. I've brought no proposal, no plan, today. I thought perhaps instead, *you* could tell *me* what it is you're looking for."

There was stunned silence from the councilors.

"Excuse me, what *we're* looking for?" Councilor Singh was visibly puzzled, as were most of the councilors.

The handsome stranger—Anthony Harbringer—shrugged. "If I'm asking you to dance, I figure I better ask what type of music you're into first."

Anne held in a laugh.

"This is . . . very unusual." Councilor Rait, superintendent of the local school board, was looking over her glasses at Anthony, clearly unsure what to make of him. Anne herself was a little puzzled and intrigued by the contradiction of his gentle, polite tones and cavalier body language. "You might have made this request in an email," Rait continued, "before we all took time out of our busy day to meet with you, but I do applaud this novel approach. I think myself and the other councilors would like time to discuss and determine perhaps if there is an opportunity for . . . a developer."

Anne could hear the effort it took her to try to say "developer" without it sounding like "delinquent."

"Well, I am sorry if you feel I've wasted your time, but I appreciate that you'll consider the matter. I'll be in town for a few weeks. Please do get in contact with me. I'll give you all my card."

He rose and withdrew from his pants pocket a slender silver card case, removed a few cards—Anne could see they were cream colored, embossed, and expensive looking—and left them on the table in front of Rait.

"You might consider," Anne said, and Anthony looked up—those light eyes were quite piercing—"you might consider some low-rise condo buildings, for rent or to own." The idea had come to her as a result of last night's Google apartment hunt. "We're a very established community; many homes are multi-generational. We have lots of young people who are in the renting stage of their life—but their choices are limited to mostly basement apartments, a few over-the-store units on the main strip, or downsizing retirement-community condos. Your forty-story concrete creation was never going to get through, *but* a few reasonable, low-rise buildings in brick, with the right aesthetic, perhaps repurposing a few of the older plazas that have gotten run-down for being too far from the main strip . . . I can think of one or two that the owners might be happy for a good price and an early retirement . . . but I can't imagine you'd be interested in something so small-scale as that."

"On the contrary, Councilor Elliot, that sounds like an intriguing starting point." He gave her his slightly crooked smile, and Anne was surprised to find herself feeling a little flustered.

"This is something we'll want to discuss in private, Councilor Elliot," Rait said chidingly.

Anne gave her a bland smile. "It was more of a thought bubble than a formal suggestion, to give him an idea of the limitations of what we might suggest. After all, we don't want to waste his time either."

Anthony brought up a hand to scratch his jaw, but Anne saw it was really to cover his laughing smile.

Councilor Rait gave a haughty sniff and snapped her briefcase shut. "Well, we'll discuss at our next meeting, and I'm calling your assistant, Emmie, to schedule some time for us next month to talk about the school trip to the festival."

"Lovely, I'll give Emmie a heads-up you'll be calling. I look forward to chatting," Anne said. *I do not look forward to chatting.*

Councilor Rait made her exit, and Anne was about to pick up her tote and do the same when Anthony stepped a little toward her.

"So, you're *the* Anne Elliot, the one who runs the Elysium and pretty much everything else in this town."

"I don't know if there's a 'the' in front of my name, but yes, I'm the executive director at Elysium."

"I saw your production of the reimagining of the *Odyssey*; it was amazing . . ."

And Anne found herself drawn into a lively conversation about updating classics in theater, which Anthony then likened to modernizing classic buildings in need of repair and they went round and round for at least half an hour. She was sure the town council room had never seen such lively or interesting conversation before.

It was interrupted only by the repeated buzzing of Anne's tote, as no doubt work began to pile up.

Anthony ducked his head as her bag buzzed for the fifth time. "I'm sorry I'm talking your ear off, and I'm sure you've got to get back. Which is too bad," he said with his crooked grin, "because I was going to ask if you were interested in joining me for a drink. My ego loves to talk to people who admire my boat."

Anne hesitated for just a moment, her mind rapidly flicking through possibilities of what this invitation was—professional, personal, flirtatious, just chatting?

But in her moment of hesitation, Anthony politely slid the invitation into something easier. "I'm heading back that way— I'm staying at the Prince of Wales Hotel—perhaps I can walk you back instead? I don't want to keep you from your day."

To this Anne easily acquiesced.

They took a leisurely pace as Anne pointed out highlights of the town and gave him some local history. He liked the ghost stories and was thrilled to hear that there were guided ghost tours in the evening. He stopped and looked with childish wonder at the massive taffy-pulling device in the window of the candy store, just as the colonel had done.

"I'm definitely coming back here tomorrow and stocking up on treats. I'll just shovel them into my hotel room like I'm a kid at camp." He laughed.

"How long are you planning to stay in town?" Anne asked. "With boating season over, and the meeting with us over, I thought you'd head back to Toronto."

He gave her an easy smile. "Nah, I'm staying here for a few weeks. I'm calling it a working vacation. I wasn't kidding: getting a development in this town would catapult my company to the next level—practically no one gets to develop here, and you have such a high profile—and I really do *fully* appreciate how sensitive this town is to any change. So, I thought, while I wait for the council to ponder my request, I would actually spend some time here, y'know, visit the local businesses, take in a winery, do the ghost walk. I hear I missed the Pumpkin Festival, but maybe there'll be some other event soon. And this has got to be the most relaxing, enjoyable reconnaissance project ever." He laughed.

As he stood there in the bright autumn day, handsome and roguish with his dark hair and long dark wool coat—looking around her town with such genuine appreciation and enjoyment, Anne found her interest and attraction piqued.

But then, Ben, the gorge, the festival, their unfinished conversation . . . No! She shut that door in favor of the handsome interested man in front of her. *Too late.*

Ben was with Sabrina. What did it matter? Even though things had been easing between her and Ben, after last night's display . . . She'd been telling herself for eight years that he was lost to her. Now that she got to witness him with another woman, up close and personal, you'd think the lesson would somehow finally stick.

A handsome man was smiling at her—maybe he was available, maybe not; maybe he was interested in her, maybe not—

but how often had she passed on "maybes" like this? And for what?

They made it to the theater—Anthony passing his hotel without a word, in favor of accompanying her the entire walk, and certainly that hinted at least a little interest, right?—where to Anne's further annoyance, Vidya and Emmie were waiting outside, no doubt with a list of problems for her to solve.

She was fatigued from her father the night before, the humiliation and the exhaustion of her emotional revelation and sleepless night, the fact that Ben had witnessed her lowest moment, and now she couldn't even have a good moment with another man without the intrusion of either Ben or responsibility. It made her uncharacteristically angry and short-tempered, though she tried to rein it in.

"That was a short councilors meeting," Vidya called out by way of a greeting. "Did Superintendent Rait finally combust from frigid uptightness?"

For fuck's sake, Vidya, right off the bat?

"This is Vidya, the festival costumier, and Emmie, my assistant," Anne said with utmost decorum, ignoring Vidya's query. "This is Anthony; he's staying in town for a few weeks. He's a developer."

Anthony shook hands with them both.

"A developer? And they didn't try to melt you with holy water?" Vidya asked, unsmiling and with raised eyebrows.

Anne cursed internally. Yes, developers were pariahs in this town, but couldn't Vidya be polite just this once?!

But Anthony only laughed, still as relaxed as he'd been in the councilors' meeting. "No holy water today, but thanks for the heads-up. I'll bring my umbrella next time."

"Anthony hasn't put forward a proposal yet; he wants to learn more about the town first," Anne said.

"You should totally talk with Professor Davis!" Emmie chimed in.

"Nope, no, let's not do that," Anne cut off that idea. "What are you both doing out here anyway?"

Both women immediately spoke at once.

"I ordered linen, but they sent me leather . . ."

"Paranoid Paul wants to know if we can start using military time for scheduled meetings . . ."

". . . and the invoice wasn't even *for* leather, it was for a bolt of satin . . ."

". . . and Choi wants to know if it's okay to cancel the casting announcement; she isn't ready yet . . ."

". . . and I am not sewing red sequins to animal skin like we're a freaking house of horrors . . ."

Anne held up both hands, a silent command for them to stop. She could feel her cheeks turning hot with embarrassment and irritation.

"It looks like you've got your afternoon cut out for you," Anthony said lightly, in the glorious seconds of silence that followed. "I'll leave you to it. It was very nice meeting you, Ms. Elliot, ladies." He shot another smile at them all and then sauntered away.

Great, another man who gets to view me as just a bucket for responsibilities and screwballs.

"He's hot," Emmie said, once he was out of earshot.

"Emmie," Anne said sharply, "back to your desk, please." Emmie, wide-eyed, scampered back into the building.

Anne tried to count to ten in her head.

Vidya was unfazed. She, too, was giving Anthony a lingering appraisal as he made his way down the street. "You should tap that," she said. "He's into you."

"Stop," Anne snapped, "just stop."

"What? Ben's got his cheerleader. Get over one guy by getting under the next . . ."

And although Anne had just been pondering something along those lines on her walk with Anthony, hearing it played back to her so crudely after Vidya and Emmie had scared him off, so that she probably wouldn't even *have* the opportunity to . . . the tenuous hold on her temper finally cracked.

"Christ, Vidya, give it a rest! You've been after me about Ben since the beginning, asking for the backstory, making me playlists, and now you're pushing me at this guy—"

"I'm not *pushing* you, I'm trying to help—"

"Help? Help with what? In exchange for what? Why are you so invested? What are you getting out of this? Because this is way past professional."

"Wow, just wow," Vidya said, rearing back. "This is a professional relationship now? When I had my breakup, who came with me to get my stuff from my ex's place? *You*. When I had the flu last year, who brought me groceries and hot soup? *You*. In my first year at the festival when I screwed up that purchase order and bought way too many Viking hats, who calmed me down? *You*. And you barely even knew me then. What I am getting out of this? Friendship! A really good friend who's there for me, always there for me, and now you're going through a tough time for once, and so I'm trying to be there for *you*, and I'm sorry if I don't always get it right, but I'm trying because I want to see you happy. This is what's called a reciprocal relationship, where we care about each other. Outside of me—

and maybe Emmie—who else in your life do you have that with?"

Anne felt an immediate wave of hot shame. She was so used to people taking, people needing her. She'd always been confused by Vidya's overtures of friendship. When was the last time she'd had unconditional support? Ben. Her mother.

But Vidya had already taken off, back into the building, the door slamming shut behind her.

Well, not really. It was a heavy steel door with a slow close that the ushers usually propped open when it was showtime, so it wasn't really possible to slam it, but Vidya's body language left no doubt that a slam would have happened, had such a thing been possible.

You had one friend, and you've kicked her away. You had one serious ex, and you were humiliated in front of him. You have exactly one possible flirtation with another man, and you're freaking out like you're fourteen. Where's all your diplomacy now, Anne Elliot?

Twenty-One

E mmie forgave her instantly for snapping, was tactful enough not to mention muffins or low blood sugar, and promised not to knock on Anne's office door for the next few hours.

Once behind the privacy of that closed office door, Anne slumped into her plush chair and sighed deeply. She felt nearly as low as she had in that hotel room eating lava cake centers and crying to Vidya on the phone, hurt after overhearing Sabrina's cutting remarks in the corn maze.

Ben's remarks in her driveway last night hadn't been cutting, or even cruel. Just honest.

Anne could admit to herself that there was a pattern here: she didn't respond well to being shown harsh realities about her life. Ben's return had frothed up so many truths that Anne had happily turned a blind eye to by immersing herself in her work and the town and her family, and now she was being bowled over by them one by one.

Vidya was the one to talk her through the last hit. But now Vidya was hurt too. Anne needed to talk herself through this one.

You didn't like your hair, you cut it. You don't like the strings on your every move, cut them, too, she told herself. Could it really be that simple? Last night's halfhearted Google search for an apartment while listening to Taylor Swift's "Mine" wasn't enough, any more than eating ten lava cakes was. *Make a list, and execute it.*

Anne texted Emmie to clear her afternoon schedule—surely she'd given enough to this company that she could take an afternoon to look after her own affairs—drew a fresh blank pad of paper toward her, and made a list to carry out.

First was a phone call to a real estate agent.

Next were calls to the Elliot family lawyer, accountant, and bank manager.

Then a call to the impound lot where her car was being held.

Finally, calls to her sister and father—predictably they both went to voice mail.

Last on the list was *Apologize to Vidya,* which was underscored several times.

Anne nearly added "Come up with an excuse to call cute developer" but lost the nerve and left it off.

So, it was very surprising when **Harbringer Developments** flashed across her phone display a few hours later, when Anne was nearly through her list. For one wild moment she thought she'd dialed him herself, and then realized the line had been patched through from Emmie.

"So, I know it's only been a few hours . . ." Anthony's playful, lilting tone opened as if in midconversation, and Anne found herself already smiling.

"But I figure a few hours isn't too soon to call the theater front office, ask to be directed to your assistant, and then persuade your assistant to put me through, even though you apparently are very busy and important and don't wish to be disturbed."

"You could have called me directly," Anne replied.

"I could have, if you'd given me your business card, but you didn't. I gave you mine, but somehow I didn't think you were going to use it, although you should. I'm a developer on the loose in your town—maybe you should keep tabs on me and my plans. Maybe you should have dinner with me to discuss it."

Anne laughed, but his flirtatious sallies—although enjoyable—were too polished for her to decipher. She decided to approach it head on: "Mr. Harbringer, you're very charming, but you know that you don't have to flirt with me in order to discuss your development proposal, right? That *is* part of my job."

"My dear Ms. Elliot—has it ever occurred to you that I might be using my development proposal so I can flirt with you?"

Anne raised a skeptical eyebrow, and even though Anthony couldn't see it he must have felt it, because he laughed at her. "So suspicious! All right, if you won't buy that, maybe I can at least convince you that both prospects are equally appealing to me. I just happen to be lucky enough that my interests coincide that way."

"Lucky man," Anne agreed, blushing.

There was silence for a moment, and then, in a slightly more gentle and serious tone, he resumed. "You kind of hedged when I asked you for a drink this afternoon. I hope I'm not pushing it with a dinner invite."

"I hedged only because of the schedule I had lined up for this afternoon."

"Ah yes, your team did seem wildly anxious for your return." He laughed, sounding relieved at her answer.

"I am sorry about them—" Anne began, but he cut her off with reassurances.

"No, don't be sorry. I liked them, quirky and unique, just like this town. It's fantastic."

Flattered by his enthusiasm for the town—weirdly more flattered by that than by his flattery of herself—Anne found herself agreeing to dinner Friday night and exchanging contact information.

After hanging up she looked down at the mostly completed to-do list.

Apologize to Vidya.

Vidya was in her workshop, heavy classic rock music blaring. That was never a good sign.

It was difficult to know how to proceed. Anne and her mother had rarely fought. Liz and Mr. Elliot never paid attention long enough to realize anyone disagreed with them. So, not a lot of apologizing and making-up experience to go on.

In the end Anne simply walked in, muted the stereo, and wordlessly handed Vidya the heavy wrapped bundle she'd been storing in a desk drawer.

"What's this?" Vidya asked as she began to untie the packaging.

"An 'I'm sorry' gift. I was saving it to give to you for Christmas, but I think since I was such a colossal jerk, I should probably give it to you now, along with my apology." She took a deep breath. "I'm sorry, Vidya, truly. We are friends, and I've never had very many of those—not real ones anyway—so I'm not very practiced at it, but I'm so glad I have you. I would have been totally lost this fall without you."

Vidya had finished unwrapping her gift and was now delightedly shaking out several lengths of fabric: a dark red paisley, a mossy deep green with an intricate art deco print, another one that had a cream-colored background overlaid with twisting wildflowers. The last one was Anne's favorite. They slid through Vidya's hands like silk.

"Liberty prints on their famous tana lawn fabric! I ranted about these for an hour last year, but I didn't think anyone was actually listening. Anne, these are so expensive, can you even get them in Canada?"

"I ordered them straight from the Liberty store in London, England. I hope I picked out ones you like."

"There are no bad Liberty prints, don't be ridiculous"—Vidya laughed—"and these are gorgeous."

"Good, I'm glad you like them. They're not for work, they're for whatever you want to use them for. And I am truly sorry, Vidya, for snapping at you . . ."

But Vidya had already pulled her into an impromptu hug, the fabrics wrinkling between them. "You didn't need to get me a gift—not that I'm giving them back, they're mine now—but I'd have forgiven you anyway, 'cause we're friends, idiot. And one day you'll admit you love my playlists."

Anne laughed and tentatively hugged her back, feeling like maybe some things in her life were going right after all.

Later, when they were ensconced in a cozy nook of the lobby having a coffee from the refreshments counter, just opening up for the matinee performances, Anne filled her friend in on the debacle with her father, Ben's rescue, Anthony's proposal for the town council, and his recent phone call.

"I knew that Harbringer guy was into you, even if the interactions are quasi-professional. That man can wear the hell out of a sweater," Vidya said with an appreciative whistle.

"That is very true," Anne agreed, for there was certainly no arguing with that fact. "But doesn't he strike you as just a little too . . . I don't know, smooth? Like, too well practiced and polished in everything he says." The initial elation over his invitation was a little subdued now, and doubts were creeping in.

But Vidya only laughed a little. "I hate to say it, Anne, but that's sort of what you're like when you're in professional mode. You should see yourself at blue-blood night; it's a marvel, and it's part of why you're so good at your job. Maybe the reason he sets off your spidey senses is because he's too much like you. Might be spooky looking in a mirror."

"Maybe," said Anne. She wondered if she was being paranoid simply because he was a developer, and if that was fair or unfair.

"Listen, you said the first time he flirted with you was at the docks, right? How could he have known you were a councilor or whatever? He clearly just liked what he saw. Go have dinner, have fun, see what it is. You're spiraling: if it's a date, if it's not a date, if he's a good guy, not a good guy. But there's no way to know any of this unless you actually go out with him. But first, deal with your family."

Anne nodded grimly.

————————

The evening light had faded into the heavy black of night before both Liz and her father were home. Anne sat waiting at the kitchen table, a plate of cinnamon buns in front of her as the easiest way to lure them both to the table for a talk. She tried to shake off her guilt that the buns were like laying down cheese on a mousetrap.

I have to do this. It's way overdue.

"Anne, are you still up?" Her father wafted through the doorway, smelling of cigars but mercifully no alcohol tonight.

"Have a seat, Dad, I want to talk to you and Liz about something. Liz!" Anne shouted, and a moment later Liz came down the stairs, blowing on wet nail polish she'd clearly just applied. Her face was fully made up and Anne surmised she'd only come home for an outfit change and was heading back out again.

"What? Are those store buns or bakery buns? If they're bakery, can you cut one up and put it on a plate for me? I can't mess up my nails, or my lipstick, but it's carb cheat day."

"Liz, sit down," Anne said, ignoring her sister's demands. "We need to talk." She took a deep breath. "Look, when I moved home, it was supposed to be temporary while Mom was sick."

"Anne, really, you have to bring up your mother's illness and upset us all when I'm just heading off to bed and your sister has that party . . ." her father interjected, already pushing back from the table to leave.

"Dad, this will just take a minute. I really need you to hear this," Anne said firmly, and he sat down again with a huff.

"When Mom got sick, I moved home, and I kind of got stuck. Maybe we all did after we lost her. I want to move on, and I want to move out. I love you both, very much—you're my family—but I can't do this arrangement anymore. I've contacted a real estate agent and I'll be looking for my own place." Both her family members looked a little nonplussed, but Anne plowed on. "Dad, I've also contacted Bill Pereskin."

Her father perked up at that. "Our lawyer?" Bill Pereskin Sr. had been one of her father's drinking buddies, and his negligence had equaled her father's own back when things first started going downhill. His son, Bill Pereskin Jr., had taken over the firm five years ago and was a man cut from a very different cloth. He'd promised Anne to do his level best to keep things on track without her.

"Yes, I contacted Pereskin Jr. and some other people. I'm not going to manage the Elliot trust and estate anymore, or pay the utility bills for the house, or check that we have groceries. I've made you an appointment at Pereskin and I would suggest you take Liz with you. They're going to walk you through the budget I've set up for you and the systems we've put in place to manage what's left of the trust and the properties."

"Anne, really, this seems very dramatic. Is this about that other night at the Churchill Lounge?" her father asked.

That night and the million nights just like it that came before, and will keeping coming in the future, if I don't get out of this situation, Anne thought sadly, but out loud she only said, "That night was a catalyst that made me realize a lot of things about my life I didn't like, Dad. I can't do this anymore, and I shouldn't have to."

"Wow, I didn't realize you'd been such a martyr for us," Liz said sarcastically, but Anne could see she was a little perturbed at the news. A part of her wanted to believe it was because Liz was worried, or would miss her support, but experience told her Liz was only thinking of losing access to Anne's car, the occasional meals Anne made, and the other domestic comforts that Liz took as her due but would never lift a finger to help supply.

"I don't consider myself a martyr, and I'm not doing this to be hurtful, but I want to live my life more independently, that's all. You'll both be fine without me. I'll still live here in town or nearby, I'll still be working at the festival; this isn't an estrangement, it's just going to be . . . different."

Her father exhaled deeply. "Well, I can't say I'm not disappointed, Anne. I didn't think an Elliot would abandon ship this way—your mother certainly would have never—And for what? To be alone?"

Little as she cared for her father's judgment or approbation, Anne still felt the lash of his words across her heart, but her resolve held. *My mother would not have wanted this for me. I don't want this for me. That's sufficient.*

When Anne didn't answer, her father shoved back the cinnamon buns. "Well, best of luck to you, then. I hope this experiment works out for you, but I doubt it." And he left the dining room.

Anne looked to Liz, waiting for her reaction. Liz was gently testing the dryness of her nails, and deeming them satisfactorily hardened, she reached over to take a cinnamon bun.

"Okay, well, I don't see what the big deal is, if you're, like, just living down the street. By the way, that tall, auburn-haired guy I've been seeing in town, didn't you used to date him? Like, years ago?"

Anne jolted a little at the change in topic and the sudden mention of Ben, but she replied calmly, "Yes, I did. I brought him home to meet everyone around the time I finished grad school. We had a terrible breakup."

Anne waited; would this be the moment Liz showed a flicker of sisterly interest? No one but Mom had ever cared about that relationship and its end, but if Liz couldn't be interested in estates or lawyers, or reliving family memories at the Pumpkin Festival, was a sour romance the kind of gossipy thing she would care about?

No, not likely.

"Huh," Liz replied, tearing off a bite-sized piece of the bun and popping it in her mouth, careful not to brush her lipstick. "He looks super serious all the time." And with that Liz was gone.

It went exactly as Anne expected. It hurt, but it was done. And she was free.

Twenty-Two

Anne spent much of her time over the next few days look-ing at properties online and starting to pack up her things. She didn't expect to find her new place quickly, espe-cially as the holiday season approached, but she wanted to be ready to go when the time came.

And, of course, there was the dinner with Anthony.

Anthony picked her up at exactly five after seven, which Anne conceded was perfect—while still on time, it meant she had those extra five minutes that are usually found wanting right before a dinner date. She had a feeling he knew that.

Not that this was a *date*, she conceded. He'd picked her up, yes, and he held open her car door, yes, but he was toeing the line between personal and professional admirably, keeping the chat light and touching on other areas of his business and her town while they drove over. He was in a dark shirt and suit, but no tie, and he'd left his collar open. He looked sleek.

Anne herself had tried to look professional, but a slightly softer version. She felt a dress would have sent the wrong message—what exactly the message was she wanted to send was unclear even to herself, so perhaps the goal was ambiguity—and so had worn a pair of black cigarette pants with a kitten-heeled boot, and a luxurious red cashmere sweater with a wide boat neckline that exposed her collarbones and the top of her back. But then at the last minute—those critical five extra minutes he'd left her—she added a red lipstick to match, so . . . maybe it was a date.

They went to the Queen's Landing Hotel for dinner. Like the Pillar and Post, where they had held the town hall, the Queen's Landing was a luxurious hotel, and dining venue, but it had the advantage of not only being a little farther off the main strip, but also hugging the picturesque harbor. The curving floor-to-ceiling windows of the dining room, lounge, and adjoining outdoor stone terrace overlooked a courtyard of boats, now docked for the winter, and the lake beyond, dappled dark and glassy in the autumn evening.

"Anne, how lovely to see you," the maître d', Oksana, said, kissing both her cheeks in the European style.

"You really do know everyone in town," Anthony said wryly to Anne, and then to the maître d' he added, "I have a reservation, Harbringer, for two."

"Yes, the table will be ready in just a few minutes," Oksana replied, "if you'd like to wait at the bar in the lounge and have a drink? A server will collect you shortly."

When Anthony turned to help Anne out of her long wool dress coat, Oksana appraised him with a quick up and down and then gave Anne a wink and a grin, which Anne took to be congratulatory.

———————

Seated at the bar, Anthony soon found out Anne's teetotal status.

"Really? In a town crawling with wineries and vineyards and wine tastings, you . . . don't drink?" He sounded more surprised than incredulous or disappointed, which had sometimes been Anne's experience when relating this fact to men who wanted to wine and dine her.

"I just don't enjoy the sensation of being befuddled, however slight, and honestly I'm so overexposed to the industry, at some point I just lost interest."

"Don't you have to talk vintages and labels for work functions?"

"I've never met someone knowledgeable about wines who wasn't happy to share their knowledge. I smile and nod and let them keep talking. And for functions we have an event planner who consults a sommelier and then approaches the appropriate labels and local vineyards," Anne said, as the bartender placed both a lime soda and a scotch in front of them. Anne picked up her nonalcoholic drink with a smile and a shrug.

Anthony leaned in and smiled back. "You . . . are a very clever woman, and a little bit sneaky. I like it."

At that moment someone passing behind them bumped Anne's barstool.

"Sorry, excuse me . . . Oh, Anne, hi!"

It was Sabrina and, following just behind her . . . Ben.

The bottom fell out of Anne's stomach, and for the space of a moment, just a moment, every scrap of composure deserted her; she felt herself staring dumbly at them both.

With a Herculean effort she pulled herself back into focus.

"Sabrina, how nice to see you." The strain in her voice was barely audible, thank god, and then feeling compelled to do the thing properly and introduce all parties, she added, "This is Anthony. Anthony, this is Sabrina and Wentworth. Sabrina is an actress with the Elysium Festival."

Anne was self-conscious about calling him "Wentworth," but calling him "Ben" seemed somehow too intimate, too casual, too exposing in this moment. She hadn't called him Ben to his face since his reappearance in her life. He was standing there like an immovable statue, rigid and silent, as off-putting as he had been when they chatted at the Fairchilds' patio dinner. Anne frantically rewound their last encounters. Hadn't their rapport been softening lately? Why the change?

"An actress, that's very exciting," Anthony was saying to Sabrina with polite interest. "What part do you play?"

"Oh, I'm everybody's understudy right now, but I'm in the running for Juliet next season."

"Wow, a starring role. Best of luck to you on getting it."

Ben eyed Anthony as he spoke, though his face remained impassive. Anthony returned the look but with something more friendly, which was explained when he exclaimed in the next moment—

"Don't I know you? You look familiar." Anthony paused a moment and then snapped his fingers in recognition. "You were at that conference a few years ago, something to do with infrastructure funding and development. It was hosted by that investment bank that lost their shirt over that Cayman Islands deal."

"Yes, Wesley, right?"

"Anthony," said Anthony, and he shook hands with Ben. They looked like they were both gripping rather tightly. "I think it was a mutual acquaintance that introduced us at the cocktail party afterward, Edward Rosen."

"Yes," Ben agreed succinctly.

Not to be deterred by these monosyllabic answers, Anthony pressed on. "How is Rosen doing? Still out in Vancouver, right? He must be nearly head of the law department now. Have you seen him lately?"

"Yes, I visited him and his wife, Jane, last year," Ben said, but no more information was forthcoming and Anthony tactfully filled the silence.

"Well, that's great. I always liked Rosen."

"Really? Because he said you're a tricky bastard."

There was a split second where everyone froze, and then Anthony burst into laughter. Ben's deadpan expression didn't flicker.

"Well, Rosen always speaks his mind. Wasn't he thrown out of his own firm a couple of years ago? Guess that trait gets him into trouble sometimes. Ah, but he's a good man," Anthony said with his usual easy manner. "Not surprised he doesn't think too highly of me. He's the cleverest man I've ever met. I don't think he has much patience for mortal men like me with our ordinary IQs."

Ben didn't answer, and in a desperate attempt to politely smooth the conversation, Anne turned to Sabrina and complimented her dress.

"Thanks!" Sabrina said, and gave a little twirl to let the full skirt of her purple dress flare out. She looked like a Disney princess. It even had bows on the sleeves. Anne was grateful for her own mild makeover; she didn't feel frumpy and spinsterish by comparison. Actually, in her red lipstick and sweater and modern haircut, Anne felt cool and sophisticated. It was a nice change.

"Hey, why don't we all have dinner together?" Sabrina said, oblivious to Anne's internalized horror at the prospect. "Like a double date! Or, like, a triple date." Because at that moment—before Anne could even decide if she wanted to contest the fact that she and Anthony were on a date—the Fairchilds arrived to join their nephew and Sabrina, spotting their cluster at the bar.

"Were we so slow that you found replacements?" the colonel said. He was clearly joking, but he regarded the group with a slight frown, his eyes flicking from his stony-faced nephew to the relaxed Anthony and then casting an inquiring look at Anne.

His wife was less circumspect, rooting in her purse for something, and she distractedly echoed Sabrina's idea, that it would be lovely for them all to have dinner together. She looked up just long enough to see Oksana passing by and immediately inquired if their reservation could be altered, and—*please say no, please say the restaurant is too busy*—miraculously a larger table had apparently just opened up.

With that, there was no polite way to stop it, and Anne followed everyone to the table for six with the sense of a prisoner going to the gallows.

*W*ho did I piss off in a past life? Anne wondered. *I mean, really.*

A slight warm pressure told her that Anthony's hand was on the small of her back, and Anne was distinctly aware that

Ben and Sabrina were following right behind them and this contact would be fully in their sight. *Not that it matters, right?*

Anthony pulled out Anne's chair for her, and as she sat he removed his hand from the back of her seat and lightly grazed her skin at the base of her neck, exposed by her shorter haircut and the boatneck collar line of her sweater. It was a soft touch, perhaps accidental, yet it lingered and felt rather intimate.

Anne looked up, slightly startled, straight into Ben's eyes. He was in the act of pulling out Sabrina's own chair across the table but was looking at Anne and had clearly clocked everything.

They locked eyes for a moment, and though Anne couldn't read his expression, the intensity was such that she felt the back of her knees start to sweat.

Sabrina addressed some slight remark to Ben, he looked down and away, and the moment was broken.

"Anne?"

Anthony was talking to her.

"Sorry, what was that?"

A waiter had approached as they'd gotten settled—Ben and Sabrina directly across from Anne and Anthony, the colonel and Jenny each sitting at the ends of the rectangular table— and was taking drink orders. Anne realized she'd left her lime soda back at the bar.

"Would you like to see our specialty cocktail menu for the evening?" the waiter asked, seeing how she hadn't touched the wine menu.

"She doesn't drink," Anthony said, only Ben said it at the same time.

The waiter looked taken aback at the chorus.

"I'm fine, thank you," Anne said to him, recovering quickly, "but could I please get another lime soda?"

"I didn't know you don't drink, Anne. Didn't your family once own a winery?" Sabrina asked. "I'd like a cosmopolitan," she said to the waiter. She turned to the group and gave a little laugh. "I always wanted to order cosmopolitans when I was a teenager because I thought it was so cool they were always having them on *Sex and the City*. So now I always order a cosmo."

"Surely you weren't old enough to be watching *Sex and the City* when it was on TV?" Anthony asked.

Sabrina laughed again. "No, but I have my mother's box sets. I found this vintage DVD player at a thrift shop to stream them . . . or I guess I mean *play* them."

Ben cleared his throat, and Anne realized belatedly that Anthony's callout of his date's young age had embarrassed him.

But it's not a huge age gap. He's thirty-four, she's twenty-four; that's reasonable. Then again, I'm thirty-two and the fact that she just called a DVD player vintage is definitely making me feel a hundred.

"So how long are you in town for, Ben?" Anthony asked in a friendly manner. "A young firm like yours, those first few years can be critical, must be hard to pull yourself away from it."

"I'm here as long as I want to be. Toronto isn't an onerous commute."

A couple of hours wasn't quite the easy commute he made it out to be. Were his open-ended plans and downplaying a return to the city because of his relationship with Sabrina?

Ben took a swallow of his beer and regarded Anthony levelly. "Why are you in town? They won't allow a big developer building skyscrapers here; wouldn't want you to waste your time."

Anthony gave a wry smile. "I'm hardly a big developer; we're still getting our feet wet. We have a few big projects under way in nearby cities like Hamilton and Mississauga, the standard cookie-cutter condo towers." He waved his hand, self-deprecating. "But if we could get a project going in Niagara-on-the-Lake—well, that would be the holy grail in our portfolio, so I'm focusing my attention here. If we get to do this, we need to do it right. And don't worry about me bringing the skyscrapers—I'd never get a single cement mixer past Anne. She's the guardian angel of this town, and don't I know it."

"'Angel' is really pushing it," Anne said dryly, unsure if she wanted to blush or roll her eyes.

"You have impeccable taste and high standards," Anthony insisted, draping an arm around the back of her chair, and then quietly—but not so quietly the rest of the table couldn't hear—he added, "And I'm aiming to clear that high bar."

She was wretchedly aware of everyone's eyes on her. The words could still be open to a professional interpretation, but his body language was making it clear he had a secondary interest. Was her red lipstick confirming for everyone that the interest was invited, reciprocated? Why couldn't she just have been the type of woman who wore red lipstick all the time so that it was unremarkable?

"So, as the guardian of the town and our de facto town host, what's best to eat here, Anne? What should we order?"

Thank god for the colonel.

His interruption helped segue the pregnant moment into something more mundane, as everyone turned to their menu, and Anne gave them a quick rundown of what the chef was best known for.

"Anything with seafood will be amazing, and there's quite a few different dishes from the east coast, but I would recommend the Prince Edward Island mussels, followed by the Nova Scotia lobster with the mascarpone cream sauce."

The colonel, Jenny, and Ben all took her suggestion, while Anthony requested the linguine. Sabrina ordered a starter salad and another cosmo.

From there the talk turned to more neutral topics. Jenny started telling them all about their latest ups and downs with starting up the winery, and Anthony was very interested in how they came to acquire the property and what their plans for it were.

"And you're only selling off the one parcel of land? It's such a big property for a retirement project; you could sell a few more of the outlying fields, enjoy a tidy profit, and have the whole thing scaled down to something much more manageable."

"My uncle has been running air force units and missions for decades. He can handle the full winery. And they have me. We'll manage fine," Ben cut in, with the longest response he'd offered this entire evening. "And if you're looking to scoop up land from them, we're not selling off any more of it, only the field for Anne, for her festival."

The field for Anne, for her festival. It had been a business transaction that he had treated with the utmost suspicion. Now he made it sound like a gift, just for her, because it was her.

Anthony held up his hands in silent surrender, with a self-deprecating smile, while Anne stared down at her plate, wondering if she was hearing things correctly or just imagining them.

"That reminds me, I have to warn you, Anne, the field

might come part and parcel with a fowl feature," Jenny said with a teasing tone.

"What?" Anne asked, and then groaned in the next moment as the penny dropped. The colonel and Jenny both burst into good-natured laughter. Even Ben chuckled.

"A fowl feature?" Sabrina asked.

"Double-Oh-Goose, as Emmie calls him. The goose that likes to dive-bomb the theater and that destroyed the Pumpkin Festival. He's a one-goose wrecking ball. Professor Davis is convinced he needs protecting, but that bird will outlast us all," Anne explained. "Why is he in your field? I thought he made a permanent setup in our man-made pond in the theater grounds. Half my landscaping crew was out there with pool skimmers trying to move him."

"Pool skimmers?" Ben asked.

"We got inventive."

He chuckled at her reply, and it felt as intimate as Anthony's hand brushing her skin earlier.

"You never met a problem you couldn't solve. Maybe you've met your match in Double-Oh-Goose," he said teasingly, and then Anne did blush. For a moment, just a moment, they'd slipped back into something that felt like their old rapport, with his admiring, gentle teasing for her hyperorganized ways. Had it been intentional on his part, or just muscle memory?

This time it was Anthony's eyes she could feel on her, questioning.

"Well, I'm not sure if he's permanently moved or just expanding his real estate, but that goose has been in the field, honking up a storm, three out of seven days last week," Jenny said.

"Since he seems to be a festival goose, maybe he senses that the field is now part of Elysium," Anthony joked.

The topic lapsed as dessert was served—vanilla crème brûlée with Chantilly cream and maple biscotti—and when conversation resumed, they were discussing the ups and downs of the economy and the latest federal election.

Sabrina had demurred at the feature dessert and ordered a slice—"just a teeny tiny one," she'd implored the waiter; "I'm being sooo bad," she added with a giggle, to which no one responded—of chocolate cake with peanut caramel sauce. Tired of a conversation she was unable to participate in, she busied herself with seductively licking sauce off her fork. Anne couldn't help but notice that Ben—for whom this performance was clearly intended—was refusing to notice.

She followed up her performance by trying to playfully feed him a forkful of cake, as he was arguing against the combined forces of Jenny and Anne about the merits of stimulus efforts.

"I'm allergic to peanuts, remember?" he said, jerking his head away from the incoming fork, and resumed his argument.

Feeling it was rude to exclude members of the table, and feeling alarmed when Anthony entered the conversational fray and the friendly debate with Ben slanted aggressive, Anne worked to steer the topic back to something neutral and asked Jenny if she and the colonel were at all interested in hiking, since they were determined to sample all the delights Niagara-on-the-Lake had to offer.

Self-consciousness about the last hike she had been on, how Ben had wrapped his arm around her waist, made her fall silent again.

Anthony took over, for which Anne was grateful, but that gratitude was short-lived as he volleyed a series of topics Ben's way that made her squirm.

"So, Ben, will you be enjoying the sailing next summer, now that you've got family out here?"

"I don't sail."

"That's a shame; they have a beautiful harbor here." He gestured out the window. "I've got my own boat stored there for now. What about polo, do you play at all?"

"No."

"What about skiing?"

"No."

"Spend any time at the National Club when you're in Toronto? I've bumped into Rosen there a few times . . ."

"I'm not a member."

Anne cleared her throat loudly to make some slight observation about her dessert. It was inane, but it did the trick and Anthony recalibrated and steered the conversation back to Kellynch and the plans for the joint project with the festival. In fact, he asked so many questions—where they might put the band shell, the seats, how much would be collapsed in the colder months, how much of the structures would stay—that Jenny quickly offered for everyone to join them for brunch and a tour of the winery in a few days.

"Come and see this field you want to buy—kick the tires a bit!" Colonel Fairchild chuckled, and Anthony had warmly accepted the invitation for both himself and Anne, before Anne could swallow the bite of biscotti she'd just taken and decline. Sabrina enthusiastically echoed her participation in the plan—Ben said nothing—and Anne was left dumbfounded to realize she was somehow entrapped in yet another social encounter like this one.

The interminable dinner finally ended as she was still contemplating excuses to bail on the plan, only snapping out of it as she watched Ben hold Sabrina's coat for her with a smile.

O n the car ride home Anthony hummed along with the softly playing radio, occasionally remarking on the beauty of her town at night, lit up in all its twinkly glory.

"The Fairchilds seem like nice folk. I like them," he remarked at last. "You don't mind that our evening was detoured, do you?"

Yes, that was a fucking disaster. "Not at all. As you say, they're really lovely and warm people."

Anne tried one last escape hatch. "Although if you want to bail on the brunch and tour invitation, I'd be very happy to get us out of it . . ." *Us?* she questioned herself. *It's been one sort-of date.* But the couples dinner and the joint invitation seemed to have somehow accelerated the situation.

"No, I'd really like to see the property, actually. I hear it's spectacular. I'm not sure they have the business acumen for what they're planning," he continued mildly, "although I suppose with the outdoor venue at least, you'll be the brains behind the operation."

"Hardly the brains. It was Naomi, our marketing director, who came up with the idea originally. And I think the Fairchilds will surprise you, and besides they have their nephew to help them."

"That Wentworth guy, have you known him long?"

"We were at the same university, but I haven't seen him in years, not until the Fairchilds bought Kellynch in September."

"Ah, that explains it," Anthony said with a chuckle.

"Explains what?"

"The vibe I was getting from him. He clearly had a crush on you back in university, and you didn't even know it."

"I don't . . . I don't think you've got that right."

"Oh, trust me," Anthony said with a laugh, "I know his type, and I know yours. You probably had any number of suitors, and you were too focused on your studies to clock them. It's the same way you've been so focused on the town and town council that you've totally misinterpreted my shameless flirting with you. He probably just loomed near you, all silent and surly, and hoped you'd notice him."

Unbidden came that first memory of Ben, reaching down a book for her unasked at the campus bookstore, a coffee stain on his flannel button-down and a warm smile on his face. He opened with one of his terrible jokes, Anne gave him a polite pity laugh, which he called her on, and then suddenly they were chatting, flying really, through topics, ideas, favorite films, books, their interests, and worries about the grueling school year ahead.

Anne had asked him, months later, what had made him approach her, or was it simply to helpfully reach her book.

"No, I saw you wandering up and down the aisle for a few minutes, trying to find all your books. You had a notebook in your hand, and I could see all the titles written down were color-coded with prices and notations listed next to them. You had this little frown, and you were concentrating so intensely. Someone had left their bag on the ground, and you just kept gracefully stepping over it without ever taking your

eyes off the shelves. Like nothing was going to break your focus to find those books. I thought it was cute. Then we got
talking, and I was a goner. You were so awesome." No one had
ever thought Anne—responsible, organized, polite Anne—was
awesome before.

It wasn't a meet-cute, or a spectacular kismet encounter. It
was just a bookstore and a boy with a smile. And it had suited
her fine.

And it had been effortless, suddenly finding herself in sync
with this stranger, like they'd fallen into step together, and
nothing marred that synchronicity until she stumbled away
from him in fear of their potential future.

Her reminiscences had spun out the rest of the car ride,
and soon Anthony was holding open her door for her
and helping her out with a hand on her arm.

He lingered for a moment and then asked if she wanted to
go for a little walk before calling it a night. He gestured down
the street; a ten-minute walk would take them to a small park
abutting the lake.

Happy to shake off her tension from dinner, Anne agreed.

The park was one she had frequented many times, but a
scene at night is always a very different thing. The grassy
knoll was dark and velvety, and on it gleamed the large white
gazebo that looked toward the little bit of rocky beach, shel-
tered by trees. A nearly full moon painted the foam of the
waves silver and let the copper of the leaves flash as they shivered in the wind.

Anne shivered along with them as they stood at the gazebo's wooden rail, and Anthony produced a pair of gloves from

his pocket, which he wordlessly slipped onto her hands. He pulled her a little closer and shifted around to block the wind with his back. It was nice, to be taken care of this way. Vidya was right about the lack of care of her in life.

"I admire you, you know," Anthony said quietly, his voice a pleasant low baritone against the hushed noise of the water. "I know what it is to be shrouded in family legacy, always trying to measure up to your parent. I feel like we have that in common. It's part of why I left the family company and started my own, and why I'm going far afield with projects like the one I hope to do here, to make my own mark. But you've managed it better. People talk about your mother, and then they talk about you with equal respect. You didn't go flailing at the world like I did; you figured it out. I'm almost jealous—you've got business acumen and talent in heaps. And you look beautiful while you're at it."

It wasn't the most romantic compliment she ever received, but it wasn't a false, generic bit of flattery either. It was understated and exactly about her. It felt more real than most interactions she'd had with men who weren't Ben.

He leaned in slowly to broadcast his intent, giving her a chance to pull away. Anne had a split second of indecision—was she really going to proceed with this? Mixing business with pleasure? Sealing the deal that this had been a date, not just a friendly dinner, albeit a date with four other people along for most of it, and was she really moving on? If Ben had introduced Sabrina to the Fairchilds, if they were all out for dinner together, surely that meant they were serious and progressing in their relationship. So why had Ben seemed slightly annoyed at Sabrina's remarks? Why had he taken such an aversion to Anthony? Surely . . . it couldn't be, not jealousy over Anne.

Or was it just a ghost of a feeling, an instinctive reaction to seeing someone with your ex, even if you didn't want that ex anymore?

The fact alone that Ben featured so heavily in her decision about whether she would let Anthony kiss her was what finally determined it. Ben was with someone else. She had passed on any number of nice, attractive men because they hadn't measured up to Ben. How long was she going to self-sabotage using that excuse? Anthony was handsome, courteous, and interesting; she was attracted to him physically; and he had just enough mystery to him that she might want to figure him out as a person.

She let the kiss happen.

Twenty-Three

The weather was ominous on the day she was meant to have brunch at Kellynch. An early frost on the ground that morning was a sharp warning crack that the golden autumn would soon fade away. The sun had struggled to project a few weak beams and then seemed to give up entirely, and a biting wind blew on and off.

Anne was unclear how much of this brunch was meant to be indoors, versus how much time they would spend standing in the empty field, so she dressed warmly.

Anthony had untimely come down with a stomach bug and called to cancel that morning.

"I'm really sorry, Anne, I hate to miss it, but I was in Niagara Falls meeting a business contact, and we had this sushi that must have been off . . ."

Anne had reassured him it was fine. And it was fine. Really. But like hell was she going alone.

She called Naomi.

It's really a business brunch; we're going to tour our venue, she reasoned to herself.

"It's a field . . . It's a pile of dirt and grass, right?" Naomi said, her tone flat. "Like, there isn't actually an outdoor theater pitch there yet, right? Why the hell are you even bothering? This is a waste of your time."

In the end she took Emmie as a buffer.

"What the hell am I doing?" Anne said aloud to herself in the car as she drove to pick up Emmie.

This is not freaking Jane Austen, where you have to socialize with the same group of people, no matter how awkward. This is modern times. Just fucking opt out!

But she kept driving.

The Fairchilds greeted her as warmly as they had the evening at the restaurant. They were sorry to hear about Anthony's illness but were delighted that she had brought Emmie. They seemed to have taken a particular shine to Emmie, which pleased Anne—not everyone appreciated her unique assistant.

"And then Double-Oh-Goose pooped, and the understudy cried, and . . ."

And Emmie had a way of filling up the conversation that was rather useful.

They were seated in the kitchen, the same room where Ben had stared her down on the night of the patio dinner. That night it had been filled with the tension and clutter of hosting a large gathering, but today, while outside the winds and gray skies pushed against the large windows facing the fields, the kitchen was bright and cheery. The round wood table was groaning with plates of hot scrambled eggs, bacon, buttered croissants, ham-and-spinach quiche, and maple Danish, and an old-fashioned red kettle was whistling merrily on the stove, while the Fairchilds were laughing uproariously at Emmie's story.

It was immensely cozy. It was Kellynch the way it was meant to be.

"Are your nephew and Sabrina not joining us?" Anne asked during a pause in the conversation, when the suspense became too much. *Please say no.*

The Fairchilds gave each other a quick look, a couple's private language. Anne couldn't interpret it.

"Yes, Ben's joining us. Sabrina came to visit about an hour ago and they went out on the grounds for a bit. I'm not sure if she's staying for brunch."

"Oh, that's too bad," Anne said politely.

"I don't think we'll be seeing much more of her . . ." the colonel started to say before he was shushed by his wife. "What?" he said in an aside to her. "Is it a secret that it's not going well? Wouldn't be surprised if they were ending it right now . . ."

But Mrs. Fairchild began to speak loudly and obviously about the vegetable garden she planned to start in the spring.

Anne desperately wanted more information—Ben and Sabrina were breaking up? Who was breaking up with whom? They'd seemed smitten at the Pumpkin Festival; sure, they'd been a *little* out of sync at the dinner, but Sabrina had clearly still been besotted with Ben, and Ben had brought her out to spend time with his pseudo-parents, so was it *Ben* who was ending it? And why?

With great restraint, she smiled and listened to Jenny go

on about different types of peas, without giving in to the urge to shake her until the older woman gave up the information she wanted or let her husband keep spilling his thoughts. Anne had to remind herself forcibly that she was exceptionally fond of Jenny under normal circumstances.

A half hour went by. Emmie was on her third helping of Danish, Anne was on her second coffee and feeling jittery, and the conversation had moved from the perils of growing peas to decorative garden trellises.

Colonel Fairchild finally looked at the clock and frowned. "They've been gone for nearly two hours. Ben said he would definitely join us."

"Just text him," his wife suggested.

The colonel did just that but frowned at the response he got. "Thinks he'll be a bit longer. Y'know what?" He turned to Emmie and Anne. "He and Sabrina were heading for the north quadrant where the field is—why don't you and Emmie head out there? You can look at the field and drag him back. The missus and I will tidy up the breakfast, and when you return we can all have a chat about where you want to put that big stage of yours and so forth."

Anne could think of nothing she'd like less than interrupting Ben and Sabrina either having a romantic windswept stroll or having a messy breakup. But Emmie had jumped to her feet already and Anne didn't want to gainsay her hosts by forcing them all to stay seated or forcing two seniors out into the biting wind, and so she acquiesced.

Anne would swear that she knew the Kellynch Winery like the back of her hand, but the truth was the surrounding property had once been *massive*. Even as her father shut down fields and sold off parcels of land, it remained extensive, so there were acres she had only a glancing memory of, from walking through them from time to time as a child.

They were walking for about twenty minutes, a brisk pace helping to keep them warm, before they spotted the fencing that indicated they were approximately in the right place.

"From here to a road where the new highway turnoff is going in," she said proudly to Emmie.

"Looks smaller on a map. It's pretty huge," her assistant said with a grin. "But we're gonna need a helluva lawn mower." She stared at places where the grass was waist-high.

"Oh, we'll have to clear the field, but if it's just weeds and rocks and some shrubby leftover vineyard trees, I'm sure— they're not hard to pull up—it won't take long . . ."

"There they are!" Emmie interjected, and pointed some yards away.

Ben's height made him easy to spot, as did Sabrina's flaming hair. They were facing each other, Ben speaking earnestly; Sabrina had her back turned to them.

It was awkward to interrupt, but Emmie cheerfully trotted up to them, ignoring their surprise, with salutations and a brief explanation of the brunch they'd missed and the mission they'd been sent on.

"Oh, uh, great," Ben responded, passing a hand through his hair. His eyes flicked to Anne and then settled on a distant point on the horizon. Sabrina's cheeks were flushed, but it didn't look like a happy in-love glow. There was an awkward pause, four people standing in a field. Emmie finally clocked the awkwardness and looked to Anne for direction.

"Well . . . I think this is the property, then?" Anne prompted, gesturing around. "Starting at the fencing?"

"This is where it starts," Ben confirmed, nodding eagerly,

seemingly grateful for the conversation starter. He began walking farther into the field, gesturing, with Emmie and Anne following and a suddenly sulking Sabrina trailing along behind. "And then to the road, which is farther—let's keep going in that direction; there's something I want to show you—your plans anticipated using the Kellynch Winery parking, but I think there might be room for an overflow lot . . ."

"We wouldn't want to divert people passing through by the winery itself, though . . ."

They stomped through the overgrown brush, heading toward the road, discussing the details, Ben helpful and willing to talk over ideas as if it truly was a joint project now. But the conversation was frequently interrupted by non sequiturs from Sabrina, who—declining Ben's offer to return to the house and warm up if she was cold—insisted on accompanying them.

"Look, Ben, a cardinal!" she called out, pointing to the vivid red bird perching on a bramble. "Isn't it beautiful?"

"Cool," he replied, without much enthusiasm.

"God, I feel so hungover; all those cosmopolitans when I was out with the girls last night!" she exclaimed laughingly another time, as they climbed over a stile, holding out her hands to Ben for assistance. He seemed to stifle a sigh but dutifully helped her surmount the obstacle. Safely on the other side, she clung to him, batting her eyelashes and smiling up at him winningly. Ben gently unwound her arms from around his neck and resumed walking.

Had Colonel Fairchild hit on the truth? Did Anne and Emmie interrupt a breakup? Or merely a lover's tiff? Anne shook her head. The other night Anthony had kissed her and now just a few days later she was calculating the probable single status of another man. A man who had showed no interest in resuming their relationship. She should be grateful that they were interacting so easily now and leave it at that. *It was only one date and one kiss*, a sly part of her brain protested. *That's hardly a commitment to Anthony.*

As if he could hear her thoughts, Ben asked if Anthony had come to Kellynch that morning with her.

"No, he's under the weather this morning, ate something bad while he was out with a business associate," Anne replied.

"Really?" Emmie said. "I thought I saw him in town this morning talking to Naomi."

"Naomi?" Anne asked, genuinely confused. "I don't think he knows Naomi; he's only met you and Vidya."

Emmie shrugged, and Anne was suddenly self-conscious of having said too much—did she sound like they were an item and she should know his schedule? What impression did Ben have from the dinner that night, without having seen the kiss that concluded it?

They trudged a little farther before Ben pulled the party up short. "This is the part I'm concerned about, that I wanted to show you," he said. A massive expanse of something lay before them . . . *Is that a marsh?* Anne peered closer.

It looked like a pond at first, pools of water covering the ground, but in some places it seemed quite shallow and filmy, littered with all manner of natural debris.

"Is it a bog?" Emmie asked, confused.

"I'm not sure what it is," Ben replied. "I don't know anything about farming or wetland environments, but this field hasn't been used in a decade—could it just be accumulated rainwater? A broken underground pipe? There are a lot of sprinkler systems around here . . ."

"I guess it's a mystery!" Sabrina said gaily, clearly unable to fathom the desire to stand in the cold for another minute to contemplate this phenomenon. "Ben, why don't we take everyone back to the house for some yummy pastries?"

"We're not finished here, but I already said you should go back to the house if you want to," he replied, not unkindly, but with a neutral tone that spoke volumes.

Sabrina's expression turned to hurt, but the predominant emotion flickering across her pretty face was frustration. Her smiling and innocent flirtations, which Ben had clearly found charming and enrapturing back when they first met, were now having no effect, and she had no other resources in her arsenal with which to entice him back. But she wasn't giving up just yet.

While discussion with Ben and Emmie resumed as to what had caused the water before them, Anne saw from the corner of her eye Sabrina skip over to where the water started. A series of large rocks and a rotted, half-submerged log made a sort of inadvertent foot path into a deep swell of the marshy area. Sickly green weeds floated at the surface, giving it that strange mirage-like feel of solid ground that moved and rippled.

Sabrina lightly leapt onto the first rock and, foot over foot like a tightrope walker, traversed the rotted log. The rocks were farther apart here, and she had to jump to make it onto the highest rock, her stance precarious on the pitted surface, her effort to balance stretching out her arms in a perfect ballerina's pose.

She did look lovely, Anne thought wistfully, with her moonshine skin and red hair whipped up by the wind, shining brightly against the gray-and-green backdrop, although Anne wondered worriedly if balancing up there was quite safe.

But Ben, at whom this was all aimed, was still determinedly discussing acreage with Emmie.

"Ben! Come be my Romeo—I need to practice my Juliet and I could do the balcony scene from here!" Sabrina called across the yards of distance between them, striking another pose. "Wherefore art thou, Romeo? Deny thy father and refuse thy game . . ."

"Refuse thy *name*," Emmie hollered back, breaking off her own conversation. "Romeo doesn't have any *game*; if he did, maybe he could have gotten Rosaline and not ended up dead."

"We should just let you write the program for next season, Emmie," Anne teased.

The corner of Ben's mouth kicked up in a smile and he chuckled. Anne felt a quiet thrill at having made him laugh.

"BEN!" Sabrina shouted.

He smothered another sigh and obediently turned to observe her, and the lingering smile dropped off his face. Sabrina was now pirouetting atop the largest rock.

"Sabrina, get down from there! It's not safe."

"It's perfectly safe." She laughed. "It's my stage before the real stage is built."

"You'll slip and fall!"

Silently Anne added the worry that if she did fall, that opaque weed-covered water could be hiding any number of smaller, sharper rocks or old thorny grapevines that would cushion the landing poorly.

"Ben, c'mon . . ." Sabrina was still smiling, still laughing, delighted to have finally succeeded in wresting his attention away from talk of business.

"Sabrina, I'm serious. Get down from there before you get

hurt." He started to move toward her, and Anne and Emmie followed.

Sabrina's smile turned sour at the stern look on Ben's face. Her lower lip trembled a little, but she tried to rally. "C'mon, Mr. Play It Safe! What happened to spontaneity and being a little wild?" Her voice slipped into a plaintive tone. "I thought you liked that I was spontaneous and fun." She leapt back to the first rock, her body making a graceful arc in the air.

Closer to the scene, it became visible that the surface of the stones was slick and wet from the morning's melted frost. Sabrina's thin cotton sneakers provided little traction. She landed with too much force, her leading foot slid across the surface with an audible squeak, and with a terrible look of fear on her face and a cry, she fell into the murky water below.

The water was not, as Anne had feared, very deep, perhaps no more than two feet, as parts of Sabrina's body remained visible while the rest of her was submerged. She was lying facedown, red hair floating on the surface, tangling with the weeds. Not a Juliet after all, but an Ophelia.

Anne had taken off running the second Sabrina had cried out, barely aware that Ben and Emmie had frozen for precious seconds before following suit.

Sabrina was not moving in the shallow pool. She must have hit her head, and Anne put on a burst of speed, thinking of terrible stories of unconscious boaters who drowned in half an inch of water.

Ben's long legs caught up to her, just as Anne reached the water first and plunged in.

Icy cold greeted her with a shock, saturating her clothes and stinging her skin. She stumbled and struggled through the weeds and the muck, soaking herself. Ben pushed past her, stronger and taller, able to wade through faster and reach Sabrina first, lifting her prone torso up. Her lips were tinged lightly blue. There was a bloody gash on her forehead.

"I'm calling 911!" Emmie shouted.

Anne worked to untangle the young woman's legs from the weeds, so that Ben could lift her fully into his arms and stride back to the shore, where Emmie waited, cell phone pressed to her ear as she relayed the situation to an operator.

Gently laid on the grass, Sabrina hadn't so much as fluttered an eyelash. Anne pressed an ear to the too-still chest and passed a hand over her mouth. No breath.

"Compressions," Ben barked.

She adjusted the body into the correct position, and he immediately set to work.

"Ambulance is coming," Emmie said.

"Emmie, run back to the house, let the Fairchilds know what's happened, and then bring the paramedics here when they arrive," Anne directed, and Emmie took off like a shot, running back to the main buildings, cell phone still in hand.

Ben had just finished his first set of compressions and mouth-to-mouth when Sabrina jerked, her eyes flying open. Together they flipped her onto her side, where she convulsed for a moment and then vomited a rush of the fetid-looking water that had nearly claimed her.

"It's okay," Anne said, supporting Sabrina's head while she gasped in air noisily, "it's okay. Can you hear me?" Sabrina's light blue eyes were dazed, but at the question, they locked on to Anne's face like a lifeline. She nodded.

"Do you know who I am?"

Sabrina nodded again, mouth still open and gasping, but she managed to rasp out, "Anne."

"Okay, that's good. An ambulance is coming. You've banged your head and swallowed some water, but you're going to be fine. Just take it easy and breathe." She touched a gentle hand to the gash on Sabrina's forehead. It was messy but seemed shallow. Emmie had worn a scarf that morning and it was lying on the grass a few feet away, dropped and forgotten in the panic. Ben saw Anne's eyes turn toward it, and with wordless communication leapt up and retrieved it for her; she folded it over and pressed it to the wound.

After a few moments Sabrina's labored breathing started to come a little more evenly, and with the return to awareness came the belated fear and shock of what had happened to her. She began to cry, choking on the sobs that she didn't quite have enough air for yet. She also started to shiver.

Anne made low shushing noises and murmured soothing nonsense, stroked the wet red hair back from the pale face, and tried to calm the younger woman, coaxing her to just breathe.

"We should get her to the house, get her warm and wait for the ambulance there," Ben said decisively, but his eyes were on Anne with a strange expression.

"Yes," Anne agreed, and stood back so he could lift Sabrina back into his arms, bridal style. The walk across the fields was long, but Ben showed no signs of strain from the extra burden. Sabrina rested meekly against his chest, crying quietly now, and Anne followed, trying to keep up with Ben's rapid pace. The sodden, freezing state of her clothing should have made her teeth chatter like it had on her disastrous hike in the rain, but her blood was still pumping hard with adrenaline.

Colonel Fairchild came jogging across the lawn as soon as they were within a few yards of the house. Without a word he reached for the injured woman and with the efficiency and expertise of a military man checked her pulse, her pupils, and the gash on her head, and then stepped back with a relieved nod that clearly meant she would be all right, because a sliver of tension suddenly drained from the rigid line of Ben's shoulders.

"Ambulance is just pulling into the driveway. Your aunt's gone out to meet them," the colonel said. "Bring her through the house."

Anne trailed behind the trio as they traversed the long hallway out to the part of the driveway that kissed the front of the house, right before it began its curve around the smaller buildings and the patio where Ben and Sabrina had first met the night of the dinner party.

Emmie and Jenny were standing speaking worriedly with an older paramedic, while his younger partner finished setting up the stretcher that had been unloaded from the back of the parked ambulance.

"She's awake and responsive," Colonel Fairchild told the group. Ben laid her down gently, and one of the men moved to immediately cover the patient with a warming blanket and affix an oxygen mask.

"Head injury, concern of hypothermia—she was submerged for less than two minutes—one round of CPR but she brought up the water and mostly cleared her lungs, I think," Ben recited to the professionals.

"Okay, we'll take it from here," the older one responded. "They'll most likely keep her overnight for observation and tests. Who's accompanying her? You can ride in the back."

Ben took a deep breath but Jenny spoke first. "I'll go—you're soaked through. And she may prefer to have a woman with her."

"Okay," Ben agreed. "Sabrina has a roommate; they share an apartment on Fell Street. I don't have her contact information, but if we could get ahold of her, she could bring a change of clothes to the hospital, and someone should let her know Sabrina's not coming home tonight."

"We have . . ." Anne tried to speak but a croak emerged instead. She cleared her throat and tried again. "The festival has Sabrina's emergency contact information. We'll have it on computer somewhere in HR. It'll have her roommate's number and her parents' information. They're a province away but they'll still want to know. I can go to the office and—"

"You're soaked as well. Emmie can go," the colonel said firmly. "She can take our car, since you drove her here—c'mon, Emmie, let's see if you're big enough to drive the jeep."

In a flurry of movement, the party on the drive dispersed, moving with the grim awareness that comes with near misses. Sabrina, Jenny, and the paramedics loaded into the vehicle and sped back down the hill, while the colonel and Emmie disappeared around the side of the house to where the Fairchilds' jeep was habitually parked.

Anne stood listlessly, without a task, watching from Kellynch's high vantage point as the ambulance smoothly joined the highway at the bottom of the hill and disappeared from sight.

Sabrina would be all right.

The adrenaline finally ebbed away and exhaustion immediately rolled in. Her mind felt sluggish and slow; blearily she knew that was a bad sign, that the cold was finally penetrating her system. Though the water had been shallow, the effort of the rescue had thoroughly soaked her, and the chilly wind whipping across the fields was now compounding the effect.

Clothes . . . I should probably change my clothes? She was now shivering violently, swooning a little on the spot.

Two large warm hands landed on her shoulders and forcefully steered her back into the house. The momentum moving her along didn't stop until they reached a ground-floor bedroom with an en suite that had once been Liz's—she always complained the bathroom was too small, but the ground-floor level let her sneak out with minimum chance of getting caught, Anne vaguely remembered.

Ben had clearly been using it for both sleep and work—a bed and dresser were shoved to a corner of the room, while a massive IKEA-style desk took center space, with a closed laptop and many tidy piles of documents covering its surface. A large printout with bar charts was tacked to the wall, projecting financial earnings for something for the next three quarters. Beside it, held together with a bull clip and hanging from a thumbtack, was a stack of miscellaneous bits of paper—was that a cookie wrapper in there?—scrawled over with notes in blue ink.

In other circumstances Anne might be fascinated to have another glimpse of Ben the businessman at work. In other circumstances she might be mortified and self-conscious to the point of paralysis to find herself alone in his bedroom with him. But the cold-numbed version of Anne's brain registered none of this, only cried out in silent protest when the warmth on her shoulders and at her back moved away.

Ben moved around her to the dresser, where he pulled out a drawer so violently it nearly slid free of its structure. He yanked out a dark, faded fleece hoodie, a pair of black sweat-pants, and thick lumpy socks.

Yes, that makes sense, Anne thought. *He got wet too.*

Except his next step was to steer her and the clothes into the small en suite, with a firm hand on her back, and then begin stripping off her cashmere sweater to the long-sleeved T-shirt she wore underneath.

"Whoa, what . . . ?!" Anne finally woke from her fugue state a little.

He tossed the sodden garment onto the bottom of the tub, where it landed with a wet splat. It was probably going to be impossible to clean the mud out of it.

"You've been soaked and freezing for over half an hour now," he said gruffly. "You're already spacing out. You'll be needing an ambulance yourself if we don't get you out of those clothes and warmed up right the fuck now."

He reached for the hem of her shirt, the warmth of his fingers burning where they brushed the icy skin of her stomach. Anne jerked away, adrenaline pumping hard again, flooding her mind with awareness. He was standing so close in the tiny bathroom, their chests were nearly brushing. He was breathing hard, too, glaring as if this was all her fault.

"I can do it myself," Anne said, voice trembling.

"Can you?" he asked, and to her burning embarrassment she realized his skepticism was justified. Her numbed fingers could barely fumble the fly on her jeans. Extending her arms seemed impossible with her muscles stiff and contracted, her shoulders hunched up against the shudders that racked her.

He waited for her response. Unspoken was the fact that he had seen it all before.

Anne gave a tiny jerky nod.

The shirt was yanked over her head and tossed into the tub. The jeans soon followed, with Anne resting one shaking hand on Ben's shoulder for balance as he crouched to peel off her socks and shoes. She could feel the muscles of his back working under her hand as his arms moved. She would have dearly liked a shower, both for the warmth and to rid herself of the squelchy feeling of mud, but she knew that hot showers were dangerous when a person was this cold and could send the body into shock.

When her bra and panties were all that was left, Ben reached for the stack of dry clothes from the dresser and pulled the hoodie down over her head. Though Anne was not a short woman, it still reached down to mid-thigh; it was obviously Ben's. The fleece was warm and soft and dry and instantly gave a modicum of room-temperature relief.

He made a vague gesture and Anne understood that with the hoodie acting as a modesty barrier, she could remove her undergarments. The panties easily slid down her legs, and Ben dropped them into the tub while very studiously not looking at the garment, then helped her step into the sweatpants, Anne staring hard at the ceiling at the feeling of his hand sliding up the outside of her thigh. The bra proved more of a challenge—fingers still too numb for the hooks—so Ben deftly unclasped it, arms around her, reaching under the back of the sweatshirt, a pantomime of a lover's embrace, and then stepped back to let Anne fumble it off and out from the under the hem. He'd always been handy with bras, she thought with a touch of hysteria. The lumpy socks came next, floppy and oversized on her feet, but thick and padded.

I must look ridiculous. The overlong hoodie, the sweatpants rolled up several times at the ankle, the socks puddling at the ankles and feet, but Ben didn't laugh. He still looked angry . . . and wet.

"You need to change too," Anne said, "even if you're more impervious to the cold, you'll be feeling it too."

"I will in a minute," he said, rubbing her fingers between his own to restore circulation. He really did look like he would start shivering soon himself.

"No, not in a minute, now," Anne insisted.

"I said in a minute," he barked, and Anne reared back, pulling her hands out of reach. Ben had never lost his temper with her before. Even in those few disagreements they'd had as a couple, he'd never snapped or shouted. It was only with other people that Anne had seen him lose it, and on those rare occasions his fury was the quiet kind that preceded drastic actions, but never explosive or angry words.

But then he'd just seen his girlfriend—*was she still his girlfriend?*—carried off in an ambulance, so perhaps there was a first time for everything.

"Sabrina is going to be okay," Anne said, aiming for a soothing tone, which was somewhat diminished by her current wobbly state. "Both your uncle and the paramedic thought so. The hospital in town may be small, but it's full of wonderful doctors. You'll be able to go and see her tomorrow."

Now it was Ben's turn to rear back, looking at Anne like she had started speaking in tongues.

"I know that."

"Okay, then why . . ."

"For fuck's sake, Anne, I'm worrying about you!" he shouted.

"Oh. I'm . . . I'm okay," Anne said hesitantly, though she was still far from a normal body temperature.

"Yes, very okay, sliding into hypothermia right there in

the driveway while everyone rushed around," he said, eyes blazing. "Why are you always the last person to be taken care of? You, who takes care of everybody!"

Anne was stunned.

Ben clenched his jaw like he immediately regretted the outburst, cheeks going red. He swiftly left the bathroom, conversation clearly over, and Anne could see him back in the bedroom stripping off his own clothes and rifling through his drawers for dry ones.

She sat down shakily on the edge of the tub, unable to look away. He'd left the door open, he must know he was in plain sight, but that didn't stop him from removing everything, including his briefs, before pulling on a sweater, sweatpants, and lumpy socks like her own. Anne's heart was definitely beating faster, suddenly becoming a little more effective at returning heat to her body.

He returned to the bathroom, face impassive, no hint of what he might have been thinking giving her that show, before he helped her stand back up on her shaky legs and led her out to the living room.

The Fairchilds' living room furniture was plush and large—no wonder, the colonel and Ben were both tall men—and she curled into a corner of a comfy couch, pulling a throw blanket over herself. It was crocheted and more decorative than warming.

Ben disappeared immediately into the kitchen, and Anne heard him put on the kettle before disappearing into another room and returning with an armful of flannel blankets. These he shook out and placed over Anne. His expression was back to something calmer.

"I apologize. How you live your life is none of my business," he said, a little formally, but sincere.

"It's all right," Anne said softly, unsure what had just happened. "I'm . . . I'm always going to try and help people, but looking after myself is something I'm working on. And you can get in line behind my friend Vidya because she's had plenty to say on the same topic lately," Anne quipped, and was relieved to see Ben crack a smile.

"Is that so?"

She looked down at the flannel in her lap, picking at a loose thread. "I've been . . . reevaluating some aspects of my life. Some of the responsibilities that I need to let go of."

"I've been doing some reevaluating myself," he said quietly, "thinking about the things I let go of that I should have fought to hold on to."

Anne looked up sharply, breathless, wondering if it was in any way possible that he'd meant that the way it sounded, or god help her, was he referring to something mundane like holding on to his last car or the last croissant at the breakfast table . . .

Ben was looking back at her levelly.

The sharp whistle of the kettle broke the moment, jostling them both, and Ben took off for the kitchen again.

In the next moment Anne heard the warm tones of the colonel, explaining that after a fifteen-minute refresher tutorial on how to drive stick, Emmie had safely driven off in the jeep.

"She'll call the hospital and relay the information to Jenny and she'll call the roommate, too, once she gets to the office," he was saying as the two men came back to the living room together. Whatever the moment had been, it was lost.

Ben had two mugs in hand, fragrant with hot chocolate. "You need the sugar and the warm-up," was all he said.

"You all right, Anne?" the colonel asked with genuine concern. "That must have been harrowing to witness."

Anne told him she was fine and took a big sip of her hot chocolate, feeling instantly better as it started to warm her from the inside out.

Ben was crouched down in front of the living room fireplace, and in a few moments he had a crackling blaze going.

Despite the stress of the last few hours and a desperate desire to know if Ben would have said more, the fatigue, the lulling heat seeping deliciously back into her, and the bittersweet comfort of smelling Ben on the clothes shrouding her lured Anne into a deep sleep, buried in flannel blankets, and listening to the low tones of Ben and his uncle discuss last night's hockey game.

There was no further chance for hidden meanings or heated looks. When Anne woke she was feeling well enough to drive herself home. There, she finally got the longed-for shower to wash the lingering muck out of her hair. She put Ben's clothes in the laundry bag, telling herself she would wash and return them and not give in to the temptation to wear them again and breathe in their familiar warmth.

Twenty-Four

It sometimes happens that when something shocking occurs abruptly, disrupting the ordinary flow of things, and then just as abruptly resolves, the memory takes on an unreal, dreamlike quality. After a long sleep and a substantial breakfast, Anne felt restored from the exertion and horror of the brunch accident, but the memory had taken on just that strange mirage haze. She had visceral flashes of what had happened—the horror of realizing Sabrina was falling, the bite of the icy water, the warmth of the hot chocolate Ben put in her hands, and the even more scalding heat of his hands on her—but the rest felt jumbled and illusory. Was she remembering correctly how distant and polite Ben was with Sabrina? Had he really snapped at Anne in worry—worry for *her*—and undressed her? And then undressed in front of her?

None of it made sense, sitting under the banal fluorescent lighting of her office reviewing the latest ticket sales, going about her ordinary day. Or rather it did make sense, but in a way that terrified Anne. Ben was a good man, unable to see someone suffering without helping, without acting the protector, and throwing himself bodily at the problem. It was an essential part of him, along with his love of corny jokes and his sometimes taciturn nature. His rescue of her on the hiking trail, helping out at the Pumpkin Festival disaster, even his interference quelling the town hall and wrangling her father, made sense from that perspective. Anne told herself firmly he would have done the same for anyone.

And in theory, helping a woman undress when she was in shock and unable to function wasn't *such* a stretch of the imagination . . . except—and here was where she distrusted her memory. Had the scene in the bathroom really felt so charged? If she had been anyone in distress, would he really have shouted and lost his temper? Would he have stripped down in front of her, made himself so physically vulnerable and open to her gaze, if she was just anyone?

Despite his ability to chat on any number of inconsequential topics, like that day in the bookstore when they first met, Anne knew that stronger emotions often made him go nearly silent. He felt deeply but was rarely loquacious about it, which sometimes used to frustrate her. It took ages to draw him out sometimes, monosyllabic answers disguising the books' worth of feelings and thoughts inside his head. But his actions gave away the game, and over time she'd learned to interpret a sentence or a look or a deed, and know what he meant.

But what he meant by his outburst and actions that day . . .

The narrative it presented was too fantastical to be believed, too fantastical to hope for—that Ben still had some ember, some lingering flicker of feeling and attraction and care for Anne Elliot, who had broken his heart eight years ago, was impossible. Wasn't it? She couldn't let her interpretation wander down that garden path lest there be nothing but devastation at the end of it. He'd softened toward her, sure, perhaps he even forgave her after seeing how the shadow of her parents had colored her decision about their relationship. Maybe he now had kinder, warmer remembrances of their shared past. But that didn't mean he was interested in picking up where they left off.

Eight years! Anne reminded herself. *Eight years!* That was a long time to fall out of practice in reading Ben Wentworth. That was a long time to be estranged and think you still knew a person. That was a long time to try to revive something that had been dead and buried in their twenties. Eight years of silence and hurt stood between them.

There was no gaining any kind of perspective on the situation; it was all confusion.

Further muddying the waters were the attentions of Anthony, who, though still feeling under the weather, took it upon himself to keep up the courtship via an onslaught of texts and the delivery of an ostentatious bouquet of flowers to her home.

Liz had eyed the roses beadily. Apparently, she'd finally met the handsome stranger in town, bumping into him at a coffee shop a day before Anne's dinner date. According to the barista who made Anne's coffee in the morning, Liz had been in full flirt mode, delighted to discover Anthony was rich, owned a boat, conducted himself with class, and filled out his sweater in exemplary form. Really, he was exactly Liz's type, and Anne was a little flattered that he hadn't swapped his attentions to the more beautiful sister—it had happened with suitors before.

But Anthony seemed keen on Anne, and, flattered or not, with the image of Ben's burning eyes staring into hers, and the broad expanse of Ben's shoulders before they disappeared into a shirt standing vividly in her mind, she couldn't seem to resurrect any of the attraction she had felt for Anthony. She should let him know there wasn't going to be another date . . . right?

Am I going to self-sabotage another romance for the ghost of Ben, again? Anne thought morosely, tapping out a halfhearted reply to Anthony's latest text.

Her phone buzzed with an incoming phone call, startling her into nearly dropping it. It was Ben's number flashing across the screen—why was he calling her? He usually went through Emmie.

"Anne Elliot speaking," she answered, just in case it wasn't really him.

But it was.

"Hi, it's Ben," his deep voice smoothed across the phone line.

"Hi," she repeated, idiotically.

"Do you have a minute?"

"Yes, I have . . . yes." Anne shook herself, remembering what was important. "How is Sabrina doing?" she asked, frantically trying to remember if Choi had mentioned when Sabrina was coming back to work.

"Oh yeah, she's good, she was discharged the other day," he said. Anne waited—had he picked her up from the hospital? was he staying with her while she recuperated? had they rekindled their romance in response to the near-death experience?—but no more information was forthcoming.

"So, I was thinking," Ben continued, after the pause became nearly unbearable. "We never really figured out where all that water came from, and if it's permanent and going to affect our plans or what. I've hired a surveyor to come take a look and give us an opinion."

So caught up in all that had happened that day, Anne had completely forgotten the very professional reason she had been in that field in the first place, and the very concerning fact that what looked like a swamp was taking up a third of her build site. Surely it was just a bit of shallow water or heavy rainfall from that thunderstorm that caught her and Ben on the trail.

"That's a good idea, and of course the festival will pay for half of the fee," Anne replied, snapping back into focus.

"Yeah, that's . . . I mean, there's no need. But I thought you might like to come out to Kellynch and meet with her; we can both hear her report directly and ask her any questions, once she's finished doing her investigation."

"Thank you, that's very considerate," Anne replied, sincerely grateful.

"Great." Ben sounded relieved. "How does tomorrow afternoon work? Can you get some time away from the office?"

They agreed on the time and hung up.

Okay, now she was confused about Ben, cooling on Anthony, and worried for her very expensive project.

Her phone blipped with another text from Anthony.

Anne groaned. Maybe she should go find a muffin.

The next afternoon when Anne pulled into Kellynch Winery, the sun was shiningly brightly, as if the stormy day of the accident was forgotten altogether. Threads of black branches were beginning to be visible through the thinning red leaves of the trees, like piping on a stained-glass window, and waving patches of goldenrod bowed in the gentle breeze.

There was no answer at the front door—well, she was a bit early—but Anne had seen a little bit of commotion out back behind the barn when she had come up the long drive, and so abandoning the house she walked around until she was past the patio and facing the smaller outbuildings.

"Hello?" she called, approaching a pair of freshly painted sliding barn doors. They slid open and Ben was suddenly silhouetted in the entrance, nearly toppling into her.

"Anne, hi—Hi." Ben's face was open and startled. He shoved his hands in his pockets and then pulled them out again, like he wasn't sure what to do with his limbs, and then scratched the back of his neck awkwardly.

The awkwardness, instead of his usual controlled exterior, was a new development.

As was his appearance.

Gone was the slick, sharply cut suit and immaculate hairstyle; gone was the weekend-warrior casual of high-end athletic wear and even higher-end sunglasses he'd worn on the hike.

The Ben before her was a different creature altogether. He was in a pair of well-worn jeans, a little faded, a little frayed at the knee and pocket, and soft looking, topped with a dark green Henley over a T-shirt. More surprising still was the few days' worth of stubble on his face and uncombed hair.

Ex-boyfriends shouldn't be allowed to wear Henleys. That's just not fair.

Anne tried her best to conquer her unpreparedness for this

sight, compose herself, and not admire the sight of him looking like any farmhand female fantasy come to life.

It was a lot for one woman to handle in the space of fifteen seconds, even for one as self-possessed as Anne Elliot.

She was about to beat a tactical retreat—make her apologies for being early, pretend she left something in her car—when Ben threw out an arm as if to stop her half motion to turn away, and then immediately retracted his arm again self-consciously.

"I'm sorry I'm . . ."

"I was running a bit . . ."

They spoke at the same time and abandoned their sentences at the same time, leaving nothing but dead air.

What is happening right now?

"The surveyor." Ben stopped and then started again. "She's out in the field. I thought she'd be finished by the time you arrived . . ."

"Yes, sorry, I got here a bit early—"

"No, that's fine," he hastily cut in, and then fell silent again.

"Um . . ." Anne said intelligently.

He looked down and scuffed the dirt a bit, clearing a cobblestone underfoot. "I . . . I could take you out to meet her, to the field, but I don't know if you want to go back there, so soon after . . ."

Sabrina's accident, Anne silently finished.

Anne hesitated. Was it just politeness—did he want her to demur?

"I don't mind going back, but I wouldn't want to take up your time . . ."

"Nah, not a problem at all, and we don't have to walk; I have the UTV already out and ready to go . . ." He held out his arm again, wide of actually touching her, but firmly ushering her toward the grassy path that led behind the barn to where the larger equipment was kept. There a utility terrain vehicle sat waiting, its flatbed empty.

"Um . . . okay. Thank you."

Without much recourse she fell into step beside him and they walked in total silence. She had the appropriate footwear for once, to climb into the open-frame vehicle, having worn Chelsea boots and wide-leg pants for this visit, but without a word Ben lifted her by the waist and placed her in the passenger seat, just as he had the night he gave her a ride home in the jeep.

"Thank . . . you," Anne said, and he gave a jerky nod before walking around to climb into the driver's seat.

Out of her peripheral vision Anne clocked again his newly unshaven and uncombed abandon. It was still a far cry from the long hair and beard of Ben at twenty-six, but nor was it so severe as the man he had shown her since he came to town. Something a little softer, but more grown-up. She liked it. Like the Henley, it seemed grossly unfair.

They drove in complete silence for several minutes before Anne recalled the oblique mention of Sabrina and remembered that he'd barely given her any information over the phone.

"How is Sabrina doing, really?" she asked.

He gave her a funny look before focusing on his driving again. "She's good. I hear she's good."

He hasn't seen her?

"She's planning to move home to Newfoundland," he added.

Anne was sure her expression must have shown her surprise. "Why? She was so keen on working with the festival."

"I think . . . she was pretty shaken from the accident, but really things haven't been going well for her here lately. She didn't think that director was really going to cast her as Juliet after all, and it was going to be another season of being the understudy . . ."

Damn it, Choi, just be direct with people, Anne silently cursed, knowing that was probably the reason behind the director's silence on the topic of Sabrina.

"And," Ben continued, "we ended things."

Anne worked valiantly to tamp down the spike of elation that shot through her. She just about managed in level tones a cursory response of "I'm sorry, I hope it was an amicable split."

Ben gave a shrug. "It was on my part. I mean, I went to visit her in the hospital and everything, but, uh, she wasn't so happy about it—the breakup I mean. When you and Emmie joined us after the brunch, it was still pretty fresh."

"Still pretty fresh" was the polite way of putting it, Anne realized. The colonel had been right, Ben had been breaking up with Sabrina that morning, and based on her antics on the walk and subsequent disaster, Sabrina had been refusing to accept the state of affairs.

"Sounds like being at home with her friends and family will be a good thing for her right now. I'll send her an email and let her know she's always welcome back at Elysium if she wants," Anne said, making a mental note to do just that. "She may not thank me for it, but there's no shame in being an understudy."

Ben had a bit of a twisted smile on his face.

"What?" Anne asked, suddenly worrying that perhaps the breakup had been hasty, and this news of Sabrina's departure was affecting him after all. Perhaps that hospital visit had been emotional and reconciliatory and . . .

"Nothing," he replied. "It's just that's really kind of you, and she wasn't always . . ." He broke off, and Anne realized the rest of the sentence was "she wasn't always kind about you."

Those hurtful things Sabrina had said in the corn maze that she wasn't supposed to know.

But Sabrina had been flying high back then, her career and personal life seeming to soar, flush with confidence it was all happening for her effortlessly: a leading role as Juliet and a handsome Toronto businessman on her arm. Now she was going home with neither, to lick her wounds and start all over again. Anne remembered her vision of Ben and Sabrina's future at the Pumpkin Festival and felt sure Sabrina had been picturing the same. She felt a surge of empathy for the younger woman, remembering what that defeated feeling was like.

In response to Ben's unspoken admission, rather than admit what she'd overheard in the corn maze, she only lightly replied, "I know what some people say about me; I can take a good guess at what Sabrina thought. But no, I wouldn't hold it against her, because . . . well, it's just natural, isn't it? When you're fresh out of school and everything is so bright, it's easy to think that it's a given that you'll 'have it all,' and you judge those people ahead of you who don't have it all, like they must be at fault or something. But then you have your first couple of real setbacks and you find out life's a lot harder than you thought, that there are fewer amazing partners and more asshole bosses around each corner, and that the wins are rarer and further between. You get a little less judgmental and a little more realistic. I don't blame Sabrina for what she thought, but

I suspect she'll have a different outlook now. Anyway"—she gulped, a little embarrassed to have said so much—"honestly, I wish her well."

Ben's smile looked bittersweet now. "So, you knew she didn't like you back on the day of the brunch, and still you were kind. You were stroking her hair and being so caring and gentle with her."

"She was injured," Anne protested.

"Yes, but a lot of people wouldn't have . . ." He simply shook his head. "I thought I must have exaggerated that part of you in my memories, that endless capacity for compassion."

Anne didn't know what to say to that—did he dwell on memories of her the way she did on him? frequently enough that he doubted himself?—and she was saved an immediate reply by the vehicle going over a particularly big bump that made her busy herself with holding on, but she could feel her face blushing bright red.

She wanted to ask more, hear more. What else did he think about her? What else was he comparing of the Anne of now and the Anne of eight years ago, and finding alike or different? Had he darkened his memories with anger after their breakup, and was he now looking at them with fresh sunlight?

But whether through design or by accident, his last remark had brought them to the section of the field that housed the bog, where a capable-looking woman in wellies was packing up a variety of equipment and called out a greeting.

Ben parked and gave Anne a hand down, while addressing the woman with his usual pithy directness.

"What's the verdict?"

"You have a resident duck," she said with a bemused grin

and pointed to where Double-Oh-Goose was happily pad-dling about.

"Him we know about," Anne said. "What about the field? I'm Anne, by the way."

"Dr. Sheltin," she said, shaking hands. The woman's face became serious and professional. "This actually is a bog, al-beit a small one. The high rainfall has currently elevated the water levels, but that doesn't mean it will dry up and disap-pear, even in the dead of summer. There's a strange topography here. I can't figure it out—there are these very deep furrows, I'd say at least four feet deep, too deep for farming, and the growth overtop of them has trapped the groundwater, and over time the result has been this." She waved her arm at the aquatic feature. "There might have once been topsoil con-cealing the furrows that kept it from becoming a bog before and now it's eroded, but honestly sometimes nature just does as she pleases."

Anne's stomach sunk at the news, and she could see Ben's mind turning over this information as a frown deepened on his face. "Can it be removed? Is the field usable?"

"Oh, it's not deep," the woman reassured them, before her next words punctured that reassurance. "But you're definitely looking at a job to remove it. You'll need to drain the water and fill it all in—it will probably take about fifty K."

Anne put a hand up to her mouth, feeling sick. Fifty thou-sand to make it usable. Fifty thousand that was not budgeted for in all her and Paul's careful calculations. Paul had warned her about the debt and the interest rate they were carrying just to buy the property; they couldn't float another fifty thousand! Never mind the time delay it would cause before the field could be a venue turning a profit. Why, oh why, hadn't she gotten a surveyor out here in the first place? Why hadn't she at least viewed it in person, earlier in the process?

Because she was distracted by her own turmoil, that's why, and she'd made a critical professional oversight as a result. Neither Naomi nor the colonel, Ben, or Jenny had questioned that the field would be fine and usable, but Anne knew that ultimately the success of this project rested on her.

Ben was running a hand through his hair agitatedly and asking further questions, but Anne struggled to focus on what was being said.

Oh god, I'll be fired.

The trip back to the house was a blur. Dr. Sheltin and her gear were rattling around in the flatbed, and Ben was driving with tight knuckles and a fierce frown. Anne didn't register the scenery whizzing by; she was desperately trying to think of a way to fix the massive hole just blown through her plans.

Back at the house Dr. Sheltin shook both their hands, promised to email them a full report, and took off down the long driveway in a dusty SUV.

"I'll need to go into the office. I have to call Paul and the board of directors," Anne said distractedly, already making mental notes of everything that needed doing, but Ben put a hand on her arm, stopping her path to her own car, pulling her around to face him.

"Wait, just wait. This doesn't have to be a disaster."

"How?! It already *is* a disaster. Elysium can't afford that work."

"I can," he said firmly, and then corrected himself. "We can."

"No, no," Anne said quickly, "I would never ask the colonel and Jenny to pick up this bill. This was the buyer's responsibility, not the sellers', and I know that they didn't have any idea . . ."

"Not my aunt and uncle. I meant we, as in my firm. We can easily put up the money for the drainage work."

Anne stared at him, gobsmacked. His ducked his head, dark navy eyes boring into hers, serious and determined.

"*Ben*," Anne said with wondering disbelief, and then startled a little when she realized it was the first time she hadn't called him "Wentworth" since he came to town. He took a half step closer, but Anne shook her head, trying to focus, and he stopped. "I can't tell you how much I appreciate that, really, but I also can't let you do it. That's not fair to you or your business partners. You can't just bail us out."

"Who said anything about bailing? I was talking about an investment. That's what my firm does; we invest in businesses we think will be a success, and I *know* this will be a success. I've already reviewed all the plans, remember? And you're running it—how could it not be?"

"I think my catastrophic failure to realize there's a bog on the property would be a pretty big dent in anyone's belief in my competency," Anne said, feeling watery-eyed.

"Shit happens," he said prosaically, and Anne had to laugh, albeit weakly, at the return of Ben's shrug-and-move-on philosophy. He used to say that all the time when she was fretting about responsibilities and essay deadlines.

"I mean it," Ben said. "Sometimes life throws you a curveball, and you gotta adjust. Isn't that what you were just saying on the ride over? You need another investor to cover costs; let me invest."

Anne mulled it over. It would be a genuine business arrangement. It would go a long way toward solving her problems. The board would still have questions and be pissed, there would still be delays, and Ben's firm would need recompense for the investment, but it would be much farther down the line, once they were up and running and could afford it. Any bank would be a lot less patient.

It would keep the project and her career from ruin.

But still she wavered. How many times was she going to let him help her? *Don't*, she wanted to say. *Don't help me if you don't want me. Don't help me if you don't mean it, not in the way I want you to mean it.*

"C'mon, Annie. We can fix this."

Annie. He hadn't called her that since . . .

Anne's phone rang in her jacket pocket, and to buy herself time she fumbled to retrieve it. Anthony's name and face flashed across the screen. She hit decline and shoved it back in her pocket, but not before Ben saw it. *Shit.*

He straightened up and half turned away, his demeanor suddenly professional and brisk, like he'd been the night of the Kellynch dinner when they'd first met again.

"Of course, I have personal reasons for wanting the project to go well—my aunt and uncle may not be financially exposed like Elysium, but they've sunk a lot of time and effort into this joint venture, and they're very excited about it. I want it to be a success for them."

"Of course," Anne said softly, dizzy with the sudden change, although his reasoning made perfect sense. Hadn't Jenny told her this idea of building a community and busy project for the colonel was Ben's idea? Of course he would want to ensure it took off, and Anne also owed it to them to do everything she could to make it happen. But the sudden mood swing . . .

It was too much to take in right now; there was only one decision she could make in this moment.

"I accept your offer, provided your business partners agree. Thank you, Ben."

He nodded, but his expression was distant and cool.

"I'll message them this afternoon. Hold off telling the board for a day, and bring them the drainage problem when you already have the solution ready to go."

A nne drove home feeling a sense of having gone to the edge of a cliff before stepping back onto solid turf.

It wasn't just the near disaster of the field. It was Ben, Ben's wild swing from beseeching and tender and intimate straight back into clinical and detached, ascribing all his motivation to helping his relatives and none to saving her. But her heart whispered that he *had* been thinking at least partially of her.

Only for Anne, for Anne's festival, he had said that night at the disastrous three-way dinner date. It must be that damned phone call, the sight of the other man flashing across her phone screen at the most inopportune moment.

Jealousy—jealousy of Anthony was the only explanation Anne could logically see for this about-face, and while it gave her wild hope it also made her despair. How could she undo the damage? How could she regain that moment, tangled as it was with yet another business deal with Ben?

Half a dozen times she was tempted to drive back up the hill and demand answers from him, tell him how she felt, that Anthony faded to obscurity next to him. But, really, how would that go down?

Hey, I know I broke your heart eight years ago, and you've ex-

pressed absolutely no interest in me since meeting again, except for this bread-crumb trail of evidence, which seems like it's super obvious but might be entirely made-up in my head, and you just broke up with your girlfriend who nearly died, and you think I'm seeing this other guy, but—spoiler alert—I'm not, and by the way do you want to give our relationship another go?

Anne nearly banged her head into the steering wheel trying to imagine it.

Twenty-Five

Crap. You couldn't turn it around? Find a subtle way to . . ."

"To what?" she asked Vidya.

"I don't know. Encourage him!"

"How?"

"Well, clearly he likes to take your clothes off . . ." Vidya waggled her eyebrows suggestively. "Or you could take his clothes off. I'm all for equality."

Anne groaned and laughed at the same time, which produced a very strange noise, and that set Vidya laughing as well. "Well, I don't know what to tell you, Anne. You're usually the master of subtle social maneuvers."

"This is different," Anne said with frustration. "I can't be wrong, I just can't. I couldn't take seeing the 'no' on his face. And to be fair I was more than a little distracted at the end of the conversation by the giant freaking swamp sinkhole in my future outdoor theater." After a pause, she admitted, "And I may have also been distracted by the fact that he was wearing a Henley."

"Mmm, yeah, that would do it," Vidya murmured. She returned to the fine stitching she was doing on a bundle of cream-colored velvet laid across her workstation.

Anne watched her work in silence for a little while, soothed by the peaceful in-and-out motions of the needle. There were a thousand things she needed to do back in her own office, but she just wanted to hide here with Vidya for a little while.

"So have his business partners agreed, then?" Vidya finally asked as she tied off her thread and snipped the end.

"Yes, they did." There had been a very professional email from his firm—very professional and very cold.

"And what did the board say?"

Anne winced, thinking back to the painful two-hour-long meeting that had taken place that morning. It was always difficult to predict how the board might react to unexpected developments. They were generally so torpid, so loath to pay attention to the more intricate workings of the business, that Anne found it difficult to convey the idea that draining a field was something of concern they should know about. The price tag of approximately fifty thousand dollars did finally make them sit up, and then Anne was forced to start at the beginning and run through the story again.

Ben's advice was good—it helped that she had a solution at the ready, before they were too outraged by the problem, but though they accepted her plan to move forward, it was clear they were not best pleased. Miraculously it had been Paul standing at her shoulder in solidarity and support, saving his "I told you so" for the privacy of her office. Naomi had taken a few personal days and was nowhere to be found.

"All right, so things are shaky, but okay career-wise," Vidya summed up. "So, focus on your personal life. When do you see Ben again?"

"No idea," Anne said miserably. "I called the colonel and Jenny to let them know about the St. Patrick's Day party at the Harp . . ."

"So that the invitation would be indirectly passed to him, well done," Vidya said.

"Yes, but they mentioned he's gone to back to Toronto for a few days and they don't know if he'll be back in time."

"So did he go back because he's shut down on you or go back just because he had business to take care of, like getting your investment, which could also be proof that he's totally into you?"

"Well, that's the million-dollar question, isn't it?" Anne replied.

"No, the million-dollar question is why our town is having a St. Patrick's Day party in November," Vidya said. "And isn't this our second St. Patrick's Day party this year?"

"Jason owns the Harp. It's the only Irish pub in town, so whenever he feels like having a blowout party, it's St. Patrick's Day, according to him," Anne explained.

"Well, I won't fault the logic of a man who likes to throw parties. Now, I think," Vidya said, snapping the last thread on the bundle of fabric in her hands, "this is finished. And just in time for the not–St. Patrick's Day party."

She shook out the creamy velvet and held it up. It was a dress, beautifully designed as only Vidya could do, knee-length and long sleeved, perfect for winter, cut close to the body, the rich velvet overlapping itself so that a simple sheath shape looked like the petals of a just barely opened winter rosebud. It was trimmed with thin lengths of the cream-and-wildflower fabric Anne had gifted her, just peeking out of the carefully arranged folds of the dress.

"Vidya, that's stunning," Anne said with fervent admiration.

"Good," Vidya said, "because it's for you."

Anne gaped at her. "I can't accept that. That fabric was a gift." But even as she said it her hands were reaching to feel the soft delicacy of the dress. It looked like it would fit perfectly.

"Relax, I only used a bit of that fabric. The rest was stuff I had lying around. I was originally going to use black velvet for the piping, for contrast, but it was looking too much like an Oreo, so the Liberty wildflowers tana lawn was the perfect solution."

"You went to all this trouble . . ." Anne said incredulously.

"Well, actually," Vidya said, and for the first time in the history of Vidya she looked a little bashful. "One of the boutiques in town—y'know the one run by Allison McClare? We got to chatting a little while ago and turns out she loves my costume designs; she wanted to know if I'd ever consider creating a few original designs for her shop. I told her I don't really do street clothes, I do stage clothes, but then, well . . ." She shrugged. "I always hear you talking to Emmie about her career and what other kinds of projects she'd like to explore, and I started thinking about myself and . . ." She shrugged again, like it was no big deal, but Anne could see that it was.

"Vidya, that's fantastic!" Anne exclaimed.

"Yeah?" Vidya said hopefully.

"Of course! You'd be amazing at that. If you're designing things like this, women will be fighting each other to buy your clothes. I can't believe you're just giving me this one. We should put it in Allison's shop and I can buy it, your first customer."

"Nah, this was just a prototype; it's yours, Anne. But if you insist on paying me back—since we're working on this reciprocal friendship thing—then the only payment I will accept is that you wear it to the St. Patrick's Day party and show off what a fab designer I am."

"Deal," Anne said firmly, and when Vidya pulled her into a bear hug, she didn't question it all. She enthusiastically hugged her right back.

Twenty-Six

The Harp was an Irish pub, a sprawling two-story building with a gleaming black pillared facade with burgundy signage, down the street from the main-stage theater and Anne's office. Unlike many seemingly Irish pubs in the area, this one was the real deal. The original owner had come over from Derry, Northern Ireland, in the early 2000s and set about painstakingly re-creating his beloved local pub from home, shipping over the chairs and wall hangings and perfecting his menu. The result was a gorgeous, glowing wood-paneled interior, with frosted glass panels between booths, wrought-iron fixtures, a burnt-looking fireplace, plank-hewn tables constantly groaning under generous steaming plates of soda bread and thick stews and bread puddings. It was divided into one long dining room, and a larger taproom with a bar and smaller seating rounds; the upstairs had a couple of rooms for rent for overnight stays. The whole effect was that of the rough but ornate comfort of another century, a pub sailors after a long stretch away might have come home to, on the cold and dreary shores of the Irish Sea.

On any given Friday night there would be fiddlers with stomping feet or cheering, singalong pub songs, or melancholic sea shanties.

Tonight, the 1993 hit "What Is Love (Baby Don't Hurt Me)" was playing loudly instead, which was . . . disconcerting. And definitely not on theme.

The party was packed. The flickering of the dimmed lights and the fire in the fireplace danced over the moving bodies as people circulated, chatted, and shouted to be heard over the din. Anne had arrived late—wearing Vidya's fabulous dress as promised, which fit her like a glove—and had to wend her way into the swirling press of bodies; the larger barroom area had been semicleared to make a dance floor, and in the corner a table had been set up with a temporary sound system, controlling the wireless speakers throughout the pub. It was presided over by a morose-looking young man whom Anne recognized as the trigger-happy soldier who had helped Emmie with the disastrous Double-Oh-Goose plan at the Pumpkin Festival.

Peter, that's his name. She started to make her way over to him to fix the situation when she was intercepted by Emmie, whose expression was somewhere between annoyed and distraught.

"Ohmigod, Anne, I'm dying, this is so embarrassing. We went on like *two* dates, okay, maybe like three, because we did spend a lot of time together at Pumpkin Fest, but this is, like, the worst." She had a wineglass in hand—clearly not her first drink of the night—and it sloshed over the side as she gestured.

"So, step one, keep the wineglass still," Anne said, steadying Emmie's hand. "Step two is giving me context. Dates with who?"

Emmie looked guiltily over her shoulder at Peter.

"Ah, I see," said Anne, putting it together. "So, I take it you're the reason for the heartbreak music selection."

"I told him yesterday morning I wasn't feeling it. He sent me a mix playlist to express his feelings on that. Just be glad tonight it's Haddaway he's playing and not his favorite selection of Nine Inch Nails. Anne," she said very seriously, "he listens to a *lot* of Nine Inch Nails." And with that ominous pronouncement she disappeared again, no doubt back to the bar to top up her wineglass.

Anne scored a few Irish egg rolls from a platter of nibbles being circulated by one of the stressed-looking waiters and said a small note of gratitude that for once this was a town event in which she had no responsibilities but to enjoy herself. She snacked on the surprisingly delicious combination of cabbage, beef, and mustard and said hi to the locals, as she tried to make her own way to the bar, from which Emmie had disappeared again.

"That's a fabulous dress, Anne!" Oksana called to her.

"Thanks! It's all Vidya's talent."

Oksana stepped closer and lowered her voice. "By the way, I hate to mention it, but your father was at the Queen's Landing last night, and there's a little matter of an unpaid—"

"Oksana," Anne said, stopping the other woman midsentence, "I'm not going to play my father's keeper anymore. That arrangement is over. If he's drunk, disorderly, or in debt, or if my sister Liz has parked her car on your front lawn, you'll have to take that up with them. I love my family, and I'm very sorry for the disruption they cause, but I won't be held responsible for it."

Oksana eyed her levelly for a moment, but then she patted Anne on the shoulder, simply said, "Good for you," and turned around to say hi to someone else.

God, I should have done that years ago.

Anne sidestepped a raucous group from the farmers' association and helped herself to another tray full of coconut-coated shrimp.

"Anne, I've got a few ideas how we can make next year's Pumpkin Festival safer—" Councilor Singh started.

"And I'd love to hear those ideas, but not tonight. Maybe another time, Singh."

Another few steps, and there was an old acquaintance from the annual fundraiser for the fire hall, for a quick hello and a handshake, before pivoting again and . . . straight into Councilor Rait.

"Anne, I want to address these very serious rumors I've been hearing that you have been fraternizing with that building developer we met with."

"We meet with so many developers, you'll have to be more specific," Anne said, deliberately obtuse—Councilor Rait had blocked her from the bite-sized sticky toffee pudding tray, and now it was being whisked away.

"You know which developer I'm talking about! The ridiculously handsome one."

"If I am fraternizing with ridiculously handsome men, should this conversation not be congratulatory?" *Unprofessional,* she chided herself, but it was worth it to see the woman's face go red.

"I do not need to explain to you how fraught relations between the town and a developer can be—"

"Rait, please." Anne held up a hand to stop the tirade she knew was coming. "This is my personal time. When I went out to dinner with Anthony Harbringer—where other people were in attendance, I might add—it was my personal time. I'd ask that you respect my boundaries here."

"That is very irresponsible to . . ."

Two more steps and Anne had at last gained the bar. Through the pass-through of the bar into an adjacent dining room, she could just make out Anthony's dark hair, his head tipped down in conversation with an irate-looking Naomi.

Huh, guess they do know each other.

Oh well, time for fortification and then to let him know there wouldn't be any more dinner dates or kisses. And hope he wasn't also a fan of breakup playlists with Nine Inch Nails.

"Anne Maria Elliot, you told me you don't drink," Vidya said with playful accusation. She'd sidled up to the bar and was eyeing the fragrant copper mug that had just been placed in Anne's hands.

"I don't drink, except for this one drink. When it's cold out, and the annual Harp party is in full swing, I make an exception only for hot buttered rum."

"That sounds disgusting. Butter?"

"It's amazing. This drink has been around since the 1650s, and it was originally used to warm people up. It's dark rum, cinnamon, and allspice and I don't know what else. It's sweet, try some."

Vidya obligingly took a taste while she eyed Anne's outfit. "That dress looks amazing on you. Damn but I'm good! I even impress myself sometimes."

Anne laughed. "Thank you, it fits like a dream and I love it."

"I'm not sure tonight was the night to wear it after all," Vidya said cryptically.

"Why not?"

"Because as it turns out, both your magnificent ex and your hunky sailor are in attendance tonight and have been looking for you, asking me when you'd arrive, and I think seeing you in that dress might incite a riot. It's about to be an Anne-a-thon in here."

"Oh god," Anne said, and expelled a deep breath. She tried to get things straight in her head. She needed to tell Anthony she wasn't interested—assuming *he* was still interested, because maybe he was looking for her to tell her he'd changed his mind and the bad sushi was just an excuse—but then why the flowers and constant texts? And she needed to talk to Ben and hopefully resume that conversation that had been interrupted—assuming *he* was interested, and that she hadn't wildly misinterpreted his changing behavior toward her, in which case her tentative unfurling of hope was about to be strangled on the vine.

It was a lot to cope with in a packed, dark party, the swirl of bodies all around her.

"Oh, and one last thing," Vidya said, helping herself to another long pull on Anne's drink. "Professor Davis is looking for you as well. That's probably going to be the least fun of the three men, so I'd save him for last. Catch you later—there's a farmhand over there I'm going to try and take home."

She'd left Anne no more than a mouthful at the bottom of her mug, which was probably for the best, the slight buzz of the alcohol feeling a little more potent as her blood coursed through her faster at all the possibilities of how tonight might unfold.

The song playing across the loudspeakers came to an end. After a pause, the opening bars of "What Is Love" started all over again. The whole room groaned.

"The one drink that can tempt Anne Elliot. I've never seen it in action before."

Whether by accident or design, Ben had already found her.

A signal to the bartender brought him a rich, frothy Guinness. Ben was wearing dark, smart jeans and a navy-blue cable-knit sweater that looked thick and soft and matched his eyes—a middle ground between old Ben and new Ben. She liked it. He smelled deliciously like cold fall air, wood fire, and rich beer.

"What?" Anne asked, dazed by his sudden appearance. She wanted to burrow in that sweater stretched across his broad chest.

"Hot buttered rum, right?" He gestured to the mug in front of her. "Your one drink."

"That's an . . . amazing memory," she said somewhat breathlessly.

He shrugged. "I remember the important things." Before Anne could fully accept the implication of that—herself and her silly details, what drink she had, if ever, was one of his important things, important memories—he went on: "By the way, is there a reason that the DJ is playing 'What Is Love' on a loop, or is that a quirk of the town's musical taste?" Ben asked with a curious smile.

"No, not a town thing." Anne laughed, recovering her equilibrium a bit. "It would seem that Emmie's been a bit of a heartbreaker, and our volunteer DJ was star-crossed by her, to his detriment. This is how he is expressing his pain, so now we can all be in pain with him."

Ben looked over Anne's head at the DJ stall, where Peter was still a sorry, slumped-looking sight.

"Poor bastard," Ben said with feeling.

"I know, but I'm sure he'll bounce back," Anne replied. "Just a bit of puppy love."

"Maybe," Ben said thoughtfully. "I hope he does, if only because he has appalling taste in music. But your Emmie is an amazing young woman, and when it's an amazing woman that's slipped away from you, well . . ." He'd leaned closer as he spoke—so close that his deep voice was low but audible, even over the blare of the awful music—until Anne felt like all that was in her field of vision was his blue eyes, serious and intent. "We move on as best we can, but no, we don't bounce back. Not really."

The dazed feeling was back, heat licking through her system that was entirely due to his proximity and her resurging hope, and nothing to do with the warmth of the rum drink pooling in her system.

"For the LOVE OF GOD!!" came a booming voice, and both Anne and Ben jumped back from each other. "Can somebody do something about this GODDAMNED MUSIC?!" Farmer O'Clannery was having none of it, as Peter restarted "What Is Love" for the fourth—no, fifth, time that evening.

"Anne!" Someone—the event organizer? Anne couldn't remember her name just now—put a hand on her arm and started to lever her toward the sound system. "Anne, I know you're off the clock tonight, but I really need your help. That boy's not likely to stop until someone forcibly wrests the equipment away from him, and if you could just talk to him . . ."

Anne tried to halt the sudden progress across the room, to dig in her heels and turn back, but she'd already been swept halfway across the pub, and away from Ben.

She sighed and tried not to let her heart sink, hoping she would be able to speak with him again before the evening was out.

Convincing Peter that everyone, himself included, would benefit from a change in music was not easy, but eventually three large looming fiddlers impatiently tapping their bows and waiting to set up their microphones convinced the young man that better solace would be found in the back kitchen with a plate of fries.

"She's just really cool, y'know?" he said miserably, drowning the contents of his plate with even more ketchup. "And pretty, and just really, really cool. And weird. But mostly cool."

"That's a very . . . uh, eloquent description of Emmie," Anne said, trying to be comforting, "but there are lots of other, um, very cool girls out there, Peter, and I'm sure you'll find one that will reciprocate your feelings."

Leaving Peter to his breakup fries, she pushed through the swinging kitchen doors back out into the dining room again. The fiddlers were in full swing and the makeshift dance floor was filled with people twirling wildly, alone or with partners, a rhythmic stamp of feet and clap of hands accompanying the frantic music of the bows, a centuries-old sort of music that made Anne's heart beat in time with it.

"Anne, I really must speak to you on an important matter." It was Professor Davis, not in one of his reenactment costumes for once, but in a rather nice blue suit and tie.

"Hello, Professor, you clean up very nicely in twenty-first-century gear," she said by way of greeting.

He looked down at himself with a moue of distaste. "A belt does not give a man the same comfort about the security of his pants as buttonhole suspenders do."

"I'll take your word for it," Anne replied. "Now, what can I do for you?"

"As you know, I have been observing Double-Oh-Goose at the Fairchilds' property and spending quite a lot of time in his natural habitat . . ."

The song came to a close and Professor Davis was temporarily drowned out by the crowd clapping and cheering. When the applause quieted down, the fiddlers changed tack entirely and began to play a slow, haunting ballad.

"As I was saying . . ." Professor Davis began again, but this time he was interrupted by the tall form of Ben Wentworth.

"Sorry to interrupt," he said, although Anne couldn't have been less sorry about the interruption, "but would you like to dance? It's a nice song."

People around them seemed to agree, as many broke off into pairings, shuffling closer to one another and beginning a slow, romantic sway.

"Yes, yes, I'd love to," Anne said immediately, trying to blink at a normal speed. "I'm sorry, Professor Davis, but let's chat about this later."

It took only a few steps to place them on the dance floor. Once there, Anne tentatively took his proffered hand and reached up with her other hand to rest it lightly on his shoulder. He wrapped an arm around her waist and she fought desperately not to immediately cozy in and lay her head on his shoulder. It was all so achingly familiar, being with him like this.

A distraction, she needed a distraction.

"I understood from the colonel you were in Toronto and were going to miss tonight?" she asked.

Ben nodded. "Yeah, I was there for a few days. I thought I was going to stay longer, but I drove back this afternoon. I stopped by your office—Emmie said you were out to lunch." *He came to see me?* "I dropped off some paperwork for you, the outline for the investment."

A professional visit, then.

"Oh, that's right, the folder Emmie left on my desk. I saw it when I came back, thank you."

Ben gave her a searing look, an expectant one, but Anne couldn't think of what response he was looking for. She'd glanced at the outline; everything seemed in order with what had been discussed.

There was an awkward silence.

"Are the colonel and Jenny not here tonight?" Anne asked, to fill the dead air.

"Hockey game on tonight; they're glued to the TV at home," he replied, and Anne laughed. Ben relaxed fractionally at her laughter. She could feel his shoulder sink just a little, the muscles under her hand releasing from their tight knot, but his expression was still oddly curious.

The dim lighting and warm glow of the room, the bittersweet strains of the fiddlers, the creak of the old wooden floorboards under their gently shifting feet, Ben filling her field of vision—Anne felt hypnotized and lulled, and it was with effort she registered Ben's next remark.

"Are the fiddlers the music for the night, or is that young guy coming back on again?"

"I think Peter saw the wisdom of packing in his DJ career." Anne smiled.

"Good, I was bracing to hear 'What Is Love' in December at the holiday concerts, and in February at the Ice Wine Festival." He said it with a warm and affectionate smile, like he was charmed by the town's eccentricities, instead of that aloof bemusement he'd expressed when he'd first heard about the Pumpkin Festival.

"Are you . . . are you planning to stay through the winter?" Anne asked, with a fast-beating heart.

She paused to give a polite smile of greeting over his shoulder to Farmer O'Clannery, who had waved at her. Ben was silent until she made eye contact with him again, his expression suddenly serious. "Would I be welcome to stay that long?"

Is he asking me . . . ?

"I'm sure your aunt and uncle would be thrilled," Anne hedged, equivocating in her nervousness.

Ben frowned, and Anne's heart leapt at the confirmation that it wasn't the answer he wanted.

"I know I'm always welcome at Kellynch," Ben said slowly. "But that's not what I asked. Would I be welcome here, in town, and on the hiking paths, and at the festivals . . . where you are?"

It could have meant any number of things. It could have meant a considerate ex ensuring they were respecting boundaries. It could have meant an overture to a kind of friendship after their earlier rocky collisions. But although it might be foolish and although it might be vain, Anne felt frantic hope burning through her like wildfire, leaving scorched earth where these more reasonable alternatives should take up space. It had to mean—it just *had* to—that he was considering looking her way again. That he was considering whether or not there might be something of the past still between them, that his heart was more than just softened toward her, as she had thought back at the field. It was all she could do to keep dancing normally, to not throw herself fully into his arms and tell him she was as madly in love with him today as she had been eight years ago.

"Yes," Anne said, barely above a whisper. "You . . . I'd like it very much if you stayed."

His frown cleared. "Good, that's . . . that's good." He leaned a little closer.

"Mind if I cut in?" It was Anthony, and Anne could have screamed.

"I do mind, actually . . ."

"I'd like to finish this dance with . . ."

Ben and Anne spoke at the same time, declining Anthony's request, the latter with much more polite a tone than the former, but at that moment the final refrain of the song came to a close, and the lead fiddler announced into the microphone they'd be taking a short break, jarring the dreamy mood of the room. The spell was broken; Ben and Anne took a small step back from each other. Just enough for the other man to deftly step into the small space left between them.

"Great, that was getting on my nerves," Anthony said. "Strings really need to be part of an orchestra; anything more than a solo just starts to grate. And now we can hear ourselves talk, and I do need to talk to Anne."

He had taken her arm and was tugging her away, the push of the crowd heading from the dance floor to the bar helping him along. "Anne, there are some things about my business prospects I really need to tell you, and I want you to hear it from me before someone else tries to give you the wrong idea . . ."

"Anthony, excuse me, but I was still in conversation with

Ben, and . . ." She dug in her heels and tried to turn back to where Ben was standing, rigid and immovable, his eyes tracking Anthony's proprietary hand on Anne's arm.

Farmer O'Clannery's broad frame pushed between them, and in that split section of distraction Ben disappeared again, melted back into the dark outline of bodies.

Tears welled up in her eyes. This couldn't be happening; they'd been so close to actually—

"Anne, I know we've only known each other a short time, but I feel really connected to you—"

"Anthony, I said I wasn't finished with—"

"Mr. Harbringer!" Councilor Rait was accosting them, a stern look on her face. "I need to know if you'll be making a secondary proposal and if I need to reconvene the council. We're starting to approach the holiday season and . . ."

Anne took advantage of Rait's overbearing envelopment of Anthony with her list of demands and darted away. She owed Anthony a conversation, to decline openly anything further between them, but she couldn't lose another second and risk Ben getting the wrong impression, again.

She saw the door to the pub open and close, a brief flush of cool fresh air sliding into the over-warm room. Was that him? Was he leaving?

Anne rushed after the thought, pushing through the door and onto the street, the sound and warmth of the pub immediately falling away. She frantically looked up and down the sidewalk. Maybe the parking lot?

"Lost someone?"

It was Naomi, standing just a few steps away from the door Anne had just burst through, about to run past her without seeing her. She had her shoulders hunched against the cold, dragging on a cigarette, looking less like a happy partygoer under the twinkly lights that adorned the front of the pub and more like a backlit, chain-smoking villain. Her outfit and softly waved hair were immaculate as always, but her brisk demeanor seemed to have . . . crumpled. She had a bitter, contemplative look on her face as she regarded the stone urns of chrysanthemums decorating the entranceway, their red petals dyed so deep by the moonlight as to appear almost bloody.

"Look at these. Fall floral arrangements." She glared at them like they'd committed an offense.

"Uh, they're nice?" Anne said hesitantly, unsure where this was going.

Naomi snorted and rolled her eyes, like Anne was a class A idiot. "Really. Nice. You can't go two steps in this town without seasonally appropriate floral arrangements, and wreaths, and these goddamned fairy lights, and that stupid goddamned clock tower going off every single hour. We have phones; we know what time it is! What era are we in, the 1950s?" She took another deep pull on her cigarette, the tip flaring red in the shadowy gloom, the smell starting to overpower the scent of the hated chrysanthemums.

"Okay, Naomi, what's going on? What's wrong?" Anne said gently.

Naomi rolled her eyes again and stubbed out the end of her cigarette underfoot before immediately lighting up another one. "My boyfriend broke up with me."

"Oh," Anne said. "I'm really sorry." *Maybe that's what the days off work were about.* "I didn't know you were seeing anyone."

"Yeah, I was. But not anymore. Turns out he wants to see you."

Anne blinked, confused, and for one wild moment her

thoughts swung to Ben, but no, he had been seeing Sabrina, who had gone home now and . . . oh. It clicked.

"Anthony," Anne said, trying not to show her surprise. "You've been dating Anthony Harbringer?"

"Clever girl." Naomi smirked.

"I'm sorry, I honestly didn't know," Anne said, "or I wouldn't have accepted his dinner invitation. This probably doesn't help, but I'm genuinely not interested in pursuing anything with him."

"Didn't fuck him, then?"

Anne involuntarily took a step back, unused to this level of crassness. Naomi had always been direct, aggressive, sharp, and a little rude, but never vicious like this.

"No, I didn't sleep with him."

"Really? Because he definitely wants to fuck you. In fact, he already has, professionally speaking."

"What?" Anne said, bewildered.

At that moment a burst of music made both women turn, the pub doors momentarily opening and Anthony spilling out, Emmie hot on his heels.

"Anne! I've been looking for you. Let's go back inside." Anthony had a false smile of confidence on his face, and he slid an arm around her waist, immediately applying pressure to move her toward the door and back inside. He gave a warning look to Naomi, who stared bitterly back at him.

"No, and I'd like you to take your hands off me," Anne said firmly, pulling away. His charming smile, instead of making him look handsome like usual, was giving her chills. She straightened her shoulders and stood firm, snapping on some of her professional persona like a shield. "Now, I'm a little tired of being out of the loop here, so one of you is going to drop this cryptic shit and tell me what's going on. Emmie, why are you here?"

Emmie raised her hands in innocence. "I know nothing, but I sensed drama. Came to see it."

Naomi flicked her second cigarette to the ground and sauntered closer.

"Yes, let's tell her, Anthony. Tell her about her precious Elysium field project."

Anthony sighed and tilted his head back, looking up at the night sky like this was really all quite fatiguing and beneath him. "I don't know why you're making a scene, Naomi. I've told you the job is still yours."

Anne felt her stomach drop. This was more than a breakup; something bigger was at play here.

"Thanks so much," Naomi sneered nastily.

"What's this about?" Ben was walking toward them, coming from the direction of the parking lot, his long strides eating up the ground quickly, a cell phone in his hand.

Emmie raised her own cell phone in explanation to the group. "Naomi mentioned the field project. I texted him to come, thought it might be important."

"I was about to drive home," Ben clarified.

"Oh good, the hero is here." Naomi laughed. "Well, you're a little late to save the day, although points for trying, buddy. Your little last-minute investment nearly did the trick."

Ben blinked at her in confusion.

She looked around and seemed gratified to have everyone's attention on her. "Well, here's a little drama you can mount on your stage that will never be built. Harbringer Developments is buying that field from the Elysium Festival. The board of directors will be signing off on it this week."

"What?" Anne and Emmie said at the same time.

"No, that's not possible," Anne continued. "We've secured the investment to drain the field and make this work."

"Doesn't matter, you're still in debt for a property that won't be profitable until all that extra work is done; that's a long time to wait," Naomi countered. "Harbringer's offer is gener-ous, very generous—why would the board approve us staying in debt when they could make an amazing profit now? And please, Anne, don't act surprised—you know the board won't give a shit what they build on that spot—it could be a sixty-floor concrete condo building, a prison, a shopping mall, or an eyesore parking lot."

"I don't understand," Anne said, turning to Anthony. "You approached the town council; you said you wanted to build something with and for the community."

"That was plan B. Plan A was the field," he said, without an inch of embarrassment.

"How could plan A be the field? You didn't know *we'd* buy the field and go into debt . . . Oh." Anne took a step back and put a hand to her head, feeling like her brain was splintering as the last few months replayed in her head in a different light. She'd been so distracted by Ben's return, so caught up in her own anguish. *Idiot.*

Naomi had brought the idea of an outdoor venue to her. Naomi had done the research and insisted the Kellynch field was ideal and no other would do. Naomi had downplayed and dissuaded her from visiting the field until the transaction had been pushed through. And then Naomi had become mysteri-ously absent on the project. Under the warm, twinkling lights, and the faint strains of fiddle music emanating from the warm, glowing pub, Anne felt chilled down to her bones.

"Harbringer Developments wanted land, but no one in the community would sell to them, including the Fairchilds," Anne said. She looked to Ben for confirmation and found his eyes already on her, their navy-blue color a stormy swirl. He was clearly putting together the pieces as well.

He gave a brief nod. "My aunt and uncle were approached with an offer when they first bought the winery, but they turned it down and didn't think anything more of it. They didn't want the money and they knew how the town felt about big developers. The only reason they were interested in Elysium's offer was because of the nature of the project." His expression became stony-faced, which Anne knew, because she knew Ben, meant he was only just keeping his temper at these revelations in check. She appreciated his restraint. She really needed to get to the bottom of this before she let him possibly punch Anthony.

"So, Naomi, working on the inside of Elysium," Anne said, putting it all together, "would get us to buy the field without letting us know it needed expensive work before it could be usable, and the Fairchilds luckily didn't know it either when they sold to us."

Ben gave another terse nod and Anne had a moment's relief that the Fairchilds were completely innocent in this.

"And then," she continued, feeling a bit like Miss Marple, revealing all in a drawing room mystery, except it wasn't the least bit cozy or quaint. "Then Elysium wouldn't be able to afford the work, and we'd be forced to sell it ASAP to get it off our books. When Harbringer Developments offered to buy it from the Fairchilds they said no, but when Harbringer Developments offered to buy it from Elysium, we'd have no choice but to say yes."

"Fuck," swore Emmie, making them all jump. She turned to Naomi. "How long have you been a dirty rotten traitor?"

For once, Anne wasn't going to correct her language.

"Anthony and I met in Toronto last year; we've been together ever since," Naomi said. "We put the plan together months ago. And it was a pretty solid plan," Naomi said. "Until the last-minute investment nearly saved it, so I went over Anne's head to the board. I figured they would still jump at getting rid of the debt."

"All this for a guy?" Anne asked. "*This* guy? Really?"

For the first time Anthony showed some emotion, with a flicker of annoyance.

Naomi scoffed. "And a job offer. Once the deal was finished, I would have a job at Harbringer Developments as chief marketing officer back in Toronto."

Anne remembered Naomi's bitter scowl from the start of this encounter—her miserable words about her boyfriend dumping her—and knew the relationship must have had at least equal weight in her mind with the job offer. She felt a flicker of pity for the other woman, despite her anger and horror at the scheme she had participated in. But it was a very brief flicker.

"And all for what?" Naomi continued. "So that when we're almost at the finish line, he can call me up and dump me because, oh gee, it turns out he *actually* likes Anne." Naomi drew out her cell phone and waved it at them. Anne could just make out a final text message from Anthony that said Job is still yours if you want it. No hard feelings.

Naomi turned to Anne with a venomous expression on her face. "He thought he could just pretend, like, oh no, Elysium needs help, he'd buy the field and you'd be grateful to him for taking if off your hands, and you'd understand it was just business when he built something awful." She turned to Anthony. "You're such a dick, you think you're *that* pretty? Think you're *that* good in bed you could just screw her out of caring about an ugly concrete block in her precious town? You think I didn't fake a few when we were together?"

"Oh snap!" said Emmie. If it weren't for the impending professional disaster, Anne was pretty sure Emmie would be having the time of her life witnessing this.

"Shut up," hissed Naomi. She turned back to Anthony. "Well, joke's on you. Your wonderful Anne here was just telling me all about how she doesn't want you. Guess the only way you'll get to fuck her over is professionally."

"Darling Naomi," Anthony replied to her calmly, "you really are such a tremendous bitch."

"Hey, Lord and Lady Macbeth, we're not interested in this evil lovers' quarrel. When will the board approve the sale?" Ben cut in, his voice tense.

"Oh, fuck off, Wentworth, like we don't know why you're here," Anthony snapped, finally showing some temper. "Hoping if you throw enough money at the problem Anne will be ready to slum it and look your way?"

It took Ben two large strides to reach Anthony, but he'd saved time by pulling back his arm on the way, so that the punch arrived at the same time he did.

Anthony went down like a ton of bricks, and Naomi and Emmie both shrieked in surprise and alarm, while Anne stood, frozen, though she had known Ben's temper with this man had long ago exceeded its limit.

Anthony was back on his feet a split second later, swearing and spitting blood, all cool detachment gone, and he leapt at the taller man, clipping Ben on the jaw with a wildly aimed punch, before Ben did some complicated move, hooking one of Anthony's feet out from beneath him, and dropped him again with remarkable efficiency.

Coming from a military family really did have its benefits, Anne supposed.

"Stop, stop, stop!" It was Professor Davis running wildly toward them from across the street, Paul hot on his heels. They crossed the empty road and came to a jumbled stop where the group had congregated outside the pub. Anthony was groggily trying to gain his feet again. Professor Davis doubled over for a second to catch his breath.

Paul took in the scene in front of him. "Personal insurance does not usually cover assault," he observed mildly, though he seemed in no hurry to intervene on Anthony's behalf.

"Anne," Davis panted, "I've been trying to talk to you all night, and then I gave up and left and decided to talk to you tomorrow morning, but after what Paul has told me, this really can't wait!"

"Yes, I'm very sorry," Anne said, "but we've got a situation here . . ."

Anthony had finally regained his feet again and looked like he was contemplating the wisdom of going at Ben again, while Ben stood, feet planted, calmly waiting for him to charge. Welcoming it.

"All right, young brigadiers, that's enough, stand down," said Davis, using his reenactment voice and inserting himself bravely between the two men. Anne grabbed Emmie's arm and pulled her out of the way as well, lest she be injured trying to get a ringside position on the fight.

"Anne," said Paul, while the young men glared at each other

and Professor Davis postured, "an offer went to the board this afternoon to relieve the Elysium Festival of the Kellynch field for a substantial sum. I noticed you were left off the communication, and I don't think I'm being paranoid that this was deliberate."

"You weren't, and I know," Anne replied.

"There's been a plot afoot," Davis added, "like when General Hull's forces feigned that they were coming from Detroit to attack . . ."

"For fuck's sake, they know! Enough with this cartoon town!" Naomi said, though she seemed to be distracted by her enjoyment of Anthony's bloodied nose.

"Right, well, Paul did some forensic accounting," Davis continued, casting an admiring glance back at the other man, "and he told me what he feared, and I have to tell you, Anne, the board absolutely, positively cannot sell that field to a developer. I mean they can, but the developer can't use more than a third of it."

"What the hell do you mean?" Anthony interjected, pinching his nose and putting his head back, his shirtfront streaked with blood.

Emmie not-so-subtly snapped a picture with her phone, probably hoping to include it in the company newsletter.

"As you may know, Double-Oh-Goose has taken up residence in that field," Paul carried on. "Davis has been, with the kind permission of the Fairchilds, observing him in this natural habitat."

"And while I was squatting in my hip waders for the sixth straight hour—he really is the most fascinating bird," said Davis, "I found these."

He held out his palm with a dramatic flourish and everyone

leaned closer to peer at the objects. They were odd, slightly lumpen shapes of metal, and very old and dirty looking.

"Bullets!" exclaimed Emmie.

"Not bullets, musket balls. Bullets as we know them wouldn't have been used until . . ." Davis started, with all his usual markings of gearing up for a great lecture, but he took stock of the scene again—a bleeding Anthony, a bruised Wentworth, a sulking Naomi, and Anne and Emmie's expectant faces— and for once restrained himself.

"They're musket balls. According to my research there's reason to believe that an army encampment in the 1800s once pitched camp on that sight. The earth is furrowed in keeping with remnants of man-made trenches—that's why it's filled with water so badly. That site is of historical significance."

There was a pause as that sunk in, and then . . .

"It's a couple of lumps of metal!" shouted Anthony. "This whole town is riddled with historical leftovers everywhere! I went into a café for an ice cream and they spent thirty minutes telling me about the centuries-old ghost that messes with their refrigeration, and they're not a fucking designated site! They're charging for runny ice cream! You can't take my site and just designate it!"

"Oh, but we can," Anne said, mind spinning at the whiplash turn of events. "I think you'll find it's part of the bylaws the town council passed last year. Anything designated by the historical society—that's Professor Davis—is protected until he deems otherwise. You won't be able to sink a single spade in it until he says so."

"Could take years," Emmie piped in. "He's very thorough."

"If I can't build on it, neither can you," Anthony reminded them.

"But we're not building a condo building or a parking lot like you planned. We just want to put up a stage and have people sit on blankets. I think we'll be able to clear a corner of the field for that, and the money from Wentworth's investment can keep us afloat until then," Anne said.

"Plus the historical society has its own dedicated budget," Davis added. "By all rights we should share in the expense of the draining, and we'd be very happy to give historical tours of the ongoing work and split the profits until we finish, at which point the field would be fully yours."

Every polite, reasonable word that Davis uttered fueled the growing fury on Anthony's face. None of tonight's unraveling had rattled him—not the exposure, Naomi's barbs, or even Ben's punches—like the disintegration of his carefully laid plans.

Had she ever thought him handsome? She'd never seen such an ugly expression as the one on his livid, snarling face.

"Really, Mr. Harbringer," said Anne lightly, "I don't think you're a very good businessman. You've shown a serious lack of due diligence here. I think you'll want to withdraw your offer to the board. You may also want to get out of town quick, because while we don't tar and feather people anymore, for you this town might make an exception."

Emmie gave a fist pump beside her. Ben laughed.

Anthony glared, but ever the strategist, he made one last play. "I really did like you, Anne, and I think—"

"And you really did lie to me, and I think you need to leave before Ben breaks your jaw," she replied. With one last look of furious disdain, he turned and limped off.

"And you, Naomi," she said, addressing the remaining villain, "you might want to take him up on that job offer because you're fired. And if you ever come after my town again, musket balls and floral arrangements coming at you will be the least of your worries."

"I hate this place anyway," Naomi said succinctly, pulling out yet another cigarette and disappearing into the night.

Anne blew out a big breath, feeling giddy with such a tumultuous evening. Emmie was outright laughing with glee, and through her laughter she posed the last question of the evening to Professor Davis. "How did you and Paul even end up swapping notes on this, to put it all together?"

"Well," Professor Davis said a little bashfully, and he reached over and took Paul's hand. "We've been seeing each other since that day in the gardens, when they tried to capture the goose."

"That's wonderful," Anne said with enthusiasm, focusing on the bright spot of them finding each other, and ignoring the slight concern of how Paul's paranoia and Professor Davis's militant attention to detail were going to combine in a way that would probably spell trouble for her down the line.

"Anne," said Paul, very seriously, and she jumped guiltily like he could read her thoughts, "what are you doing standing here congratulating us? You need to inform the board of these developments immediately. They cannot be allowed to progress even one step further on this sale."

"It's, like, midnight . . ." Emmie pointed out, but Paul was right. Who knew what early morning would bring, or if Anthony, knowing his plans were exposed, would make any further attempts?

"Tell them now," Ben said firmly, and Anne trusted his judgment, just as she had trusted his advice on presenting the investment to the board. The office was only a ten-minute walk away, and she needed the board contacts and that document on the bylaws to attach to the email . . .

"Anne, what the hell is going on out here?" It was the event organizer who had co-opted Anne into dealing with Peter earlier in the evening. "Apparently there's a fistfight? And people smoking? You can't smoke within five feet of the doors; there's a sign right there about it. Do I need to call security? Are there damages . . . ?" She was picking up steam, and Anne could see she was about to be sucked in, delayed from her all-important mission.

"Anne, go do what you have to do. I've got this," Ben said, and firmly inserted himself in front of the irate woman. "There was an altercation this evening, but security isn't needed," he began in his most confident and soothing tone. "I'm sure Professor Davis here, who witnessed it, will vouch for us . . ."

Paul was suddenly stepping forward as well, blocking Anne from view. He gave her a gentle shove. "Get to the office, send the email, end this battle, and defeat the enemy," he hissed, and, good god, Professor Davis was already having an influence on him.

Anne took off down the street, grateful for her flat, knee-high suede boots, which let her trot as quickly as possible, and the brilliant design of Vidya's dress, which encompassed panels of extra fabric that didn't shorten her stride, all the while trying to ignore the lingering regret that she couldn't stay and talk to Ben, to try to get back to where they were earlier in the evening, before all the drama.

She arrived breathless and sweaty, barreling into the dark theater, past the lobby, pushing through the heavy double doors

that separated the office suites from the rest of the building, and all but collapsed into her desk chair. She spent the
next thirty minutes furiously drafting her email, attaching
the new bylaws, and adding details of Professor Davis's find,
along with the perfidy of Naomi and Harbringer Developments. She doubted the board would read it all, but she tried
to encapsulate the vital details in big bolded font with bullet
points at the top.

She hit send and breathed out, sitting back in her chair.

The office was silent and dark around her. Okay, so this
part of tonight's denouement was anticlimactic.

A stack of papers lying on the desk caught her eye. The
outline for Ben's firm's investment. Her mind went back to
the dance, his intense stare and then confused look when she'd
mentioned reading it. What was that about? She picked up
the sheaf of papers and shuffled through it; nothing appeared
out of the ordinary. He could have emailed this . . . unless he
was looking for a reason to visit? Another missed opportunity, then.

With a sigh Anne flipped them over to leave them facedown on her desk and then sighed again when they slipped
from her fingers and fluttered to the surface in disarray.

She suddenly drew in a deep breath. For there, on the back
of the sheets, was his handwriting in blue ink. It looked just
like the notes he used to leave, the love messages, to-do lists,
and random "don't forgets" written on whatever piece of paper was nearest, be it a napkin, receipt, or torn piece of notebook paper. He must have been planning to talk to her when
he came to drop off the folder, and in her absence he grabbed
one of these papers and started to write.

Anne, it started, direct and to the point.

I've messed things up and I don't know how to fix it. When I first came to town, I acted like our past was nothing, because I wanted to pretend it was, but that was a lie. Every detail of being with you was Technicolor in my brain. It never faded. You broke my heart eight years ago, but broken or whole, it's yours. It's always been yours. I love you, with all my stupid broken heart. I know it was a long time ago. I know we were young. I know that . . .

And here something was scratched out.

. . . even though I've spent the last eight years trying to prove that your fears about me were wrong, I know that I still didn't handle the breakup well and that probably counts against me. I count that against me. I was an ass back then, and I've been an ass now. But I think . . . I like to believe that, for a while there, when we were together, we made each other so happy—didn't we? I know I was happy, and I thought I was good at making you happy too. And if there was the smallest sliver of a chance that you would let me try again, try to make you happy, I would just . . . my whole future would be you, it would be us. You are the loveliest, loveliest thing. The most wonderful, complicated, true, warm, kick-ass woman I have ever met. I loved you then and I love you now. My love is to-the-bone deep, Anne. And it will never leave me.

It covered two page backs before ending abruptly, the last line dashed out like maybe he was running out of time, or Emmie was coming through the door.

Ben, her Ben—and she had proof right here in her hands

that he *was* her Ben—had given this written outpouring of feelings? Had articulated those depths that she so often had to prize out of him in the past?

Anne felt lit up like she'd swallowed the sun, sheer boundless joy radiating through her every atom, her heart pounding like she'd run a mile.

Ben loved her, had never stopped loving her. He wanted her, they could start again, have each other, and threaded through her joy ran a thin vein of relief. No more separations. Because this would be it this time, she just knew it, and for the rest of their time on this earth, she could reach out a hand, and Ben would be there to take it, warm, strong, steadfast, loving her, caring for her, and seeing her in a way only he ever did.

Anne realized she was crying, wet smears of tears on her cheeks as she stood alone in her darkened office, clutching this sheaf of papers like it contained the answers to the universe. But how long had she been standing there, overcome? Where was Ben? She had to find Ben. How long had these papers waited on her desk? He hadn't said anything about them when they danced. He'd given her such a look when Anthony interrupted. Did he think it was too late? But surely after this evening, after Anthony's insidious plot was revealed and his lights punched out . . .

It didn't matter, the how and when didn't matter; she had to get to Ben, tell him as fervently as she could that she felt the same, now, tonight, before he assumed rejection or doubted or did something stupid like take off back to Toronto. She would chase him down, of course, if that was the case, but the delay would be agony. He disappeared for eight years last time; another two hours would be unbearable.

So where would he be? She tried his cell phone several times, but there was no answer. Should she drive straight to Kellynch? Wait, the Harp—maybe someone at the Harp saw him leave or talked to him in the aftermath of the fight (most likely Emmie) and would have a clue.

She no sooner had the thought than she took off running for the second time that night. She flew through the corridors of the building, past the lobby, and burst through the double doors out into the street. Double-Oh-Goose was nestled in a nearby potted shrub and he squawked and beat his wings, feathers flying at the unexpected nighttime interruption, as Anne tore past him in a whirling commotion.

"I'm sorry! Sorry, Double-Oh-Goose!" she cried nonsensically, never stopping for a moment. "But I have to find Ben!"

The blazing bright lights and thumping music from earlier had disappeared, and the Harp was quiet and dimmed—dimmed but not fully darkened! The party might be over but there were surely a few people still inside.

Anne pulled open the heavy doors and stumbled inside, panting from her run. She scanned the dining room, so much easier to do now that it was near empty. Only one or two staff members remained, unstacking the chairs and tables that had been cleared to create a dance floor and setting them back up for tomorrow's dining customers, before disappearing into the back kitchen.

Disappointment crashed through her, but not for long; she would just have to make the drive to Kellynch and hope that . . .

Anne spun back around to head out the door, and in doing so caught site of the bar on her left. It was mostly dark, like the rest of the pub, and the rows of scotches and whiskeys and ales on the wood shelves shimmered in the gloom like the banked embers of a dying fire.

And there, sitting on a stool with his elbows propped up on the bar and his head in his hands and his hair sticking up in a thousand directions, was Ben. His back was to her, the navy cable-knit sweater stretched across his long, lean form was dirty and crumpled from the fight. The knuckles on one hand were purpling with a bruise. A glass of whiskey sat near his elbow, the contents barely touched. His entire posture spoke of fatigue and defeat.

Anne had never seen such a lovely, lovely sight.

With quiet footsteps she approached and with a shaking hand tugged on his arm.

"Ben."

At the sound of Anne's voice his head lifted up slowly, and he half swiveled to face her, his eyes wide with surprise.

There were no words for what she had to say, nothing that could counter that beautiful scrawled letter or answer the disbelieving question on his face. So she simply stepped into his space, raised up on her toes, and kissed him.

And then kissed him again and again, because it felt familiar and good and right. Her hands reached up to cradle his face, end-of-day stubble rough against her palms.

And Ben, Ben who had sat there frozen, finally snapped out of his shocked state and returned her kiss so forcefully it nearly pushed Anne a step back, but not for long, because his long arms wrapped around and pulled her closer, closer, until she was stepping up to stand on the lower rungs of the stool to reach him better, balancing precariously but perfectly safe because there was no way Ben would let her fall.

She slid her hands into that chestnut-colored hair she loved so much; she slid her hands over his shoulders, across his chest, over his biceps; she couldn't seem to stop touching him. Ben's hands were entirely focused on keeping her as close to him as possible, with the fingers of his right hand threaded through her hair and the palm gently cradling her head, angling her closer for his kiss, and his left arm wrapped firmly around her waist, fingers splayed across her back, gently pushing, securing her body to his.

When they finally paused for a moment, neither pulled away, just rested with foreheads touching, and a laugh tumbled out of Ben, an expression of pure joy and relief.

"Yes, then?" he asked.

"Yes. Definitely, definitely yes," Anne replied, and then laughed herself as he tried to kiss her with his smile still stretched wide in a grin.

He wrapped both arms around her and hugged her so tight she could barely breathe, but she only returned the hug with the same ferocity, her arms around his shoulders. He buried his face in the side of her neck and just breathed there for a moment.

"I love you," Anne whispered against his temple, and he shuddered in her arms.

"Thank god," he rasped. "Because I had no fucking clue what I was going to do with myself if it was goodbye again."

"The plan so far was to sit at the bar?" Anne asked, teasingly.

"The plan was to get myself blackout drunk," he said, pulling back just enough to gesture to the still nearly full whiskey glass on the bar. "I even rented a room upstairs so I wouldn't have to try to get home, but it turns out I don't really enjoy drinking myself into oblivion."

"Good. I'd have been very annoyed to have to wait until

morning when you were sobered up," Anne said decisively, and Ben kissed her again, which turned into several long minutes of kissing before Anne pulled back to ask another question. "But what were you thinking, that I'd read your letter and was ignoring it? I only just found it now when I went to email the board."

He nuzzled his face into the soft velvet covering her shoulder and sighed. "I don't know, I wasn't being logical. At the beginning of the party I felt sure you hadn't read it yet, but then . . . maybe you were stalling to find a way to let me down gently or something, maybe you'd already chosen that Harbringer asshole over me, and then after the whole debacle tonight, either you'd be heartbroken over him or you really wouldn't have time for me."

"I was seeing him, just briefly," said Anne, wanting to start this new relationship with complete honesty. "But he never held a candle to you . . ."

"I don't care," Ben said firmly. "I don't care what happened before, I've got you now. That's all I want."

"And I've got you," Anne replied quietly.

Ben lifted his head from where it had been hiding on her shoulder, a shadow on his face. "Do you care about my nonsense with Sabrina?"

Anne stroked his hair back from his forehead to soothe him while she thought about her answer; she shouldn't care, it was over now and he'd been free and single then, but Vidya's question lingered in her mind—if you wanted an Anne Elliot, why did you then go for a Sabrina, or vice versa?

"I don't care about it, really . . ." Anne started, but Ben was immediately talking again, explaining himself in a way he never used to do before. She would have to get used to this new easily sharing Ben.

"I genuinely thought I liked her at first. When I saw you for the first time again, at that patio dinner, I swore up and down to myself that I was over you." He laughed darkly. "Sabrina was so impressed with me, and knowing you were always out of my league stung so badly, it was easy to go for her and soothe my ego. I was just so . . . it was like I was twenty-six again, losing the best thing in my life. Only now I'd been festering on it for eight years."

Anne felt her eyes fill with tears at this honest admission of the heartbreak she had caused him, but Ben was plowing on, like he needed to tell her everything and get it off his chest.

"That was the tough part about it—I told myself it was all rose-colored glasses on my memories of being with you. But you kept proving, over and over again, that everything I remembered being wonderful about you was true. When the Pumpkin Festival disaster happened, when the tent collapsed, I wanted to help you, make sure you were safe. I felt that old tug—Anne Elliot in action, always the one to take care of others, and I always wanted to be the one to take care of you. Instead, I threw myself further into the relationship with Sabrina, like a shield against you. I didn't realize that's what I was doing, I know that's not fair to her, but it was instinctive. I wanted her to protect me from the temptation of you."

Although Anne believed every word of his letter, it was something else to hear directly from his lips what a siren-call hold she had on him. It was near unbelievable to her, that overlooked Anne Elliot could rivet this incredible man's affections and keep them for eight years.

"I don't care about Sabrina," Anne said honestly. "I really don't. And you're not the only one who's made messes—I'm sorry I hurt us both, all those years ago. I'm sorry I let other people get in my head and I'm sorry I didn't have faith in you, but I am so proud of who you are, and so in love with you." She held his gaze so he'd know she meant it, and then suddenly they were kissing again, their combined weight and motions making the spindly wood barstool creak ominously.

"Fuck, Annie, I've missed you," Ben breathed. "I love you so much." He kissed her cheek, her ear, her collarbone, his hands getting more insistent as they traversed her back, her waist, her hips, her neck. It was like he couldn't stop touching her, reassuring himself she was there, and Anne felt the same, digging her fingers into his rumpled sweater to feel his muscles and tendons and warmth underneath.

"Hey, you two, it's after hours but this is still a public place. Get a room!" one of the waiters called out. At some point they'd returned from the kitchen to the dining room and were standing with hands on hips, looking disgusted.

"He's got a room!" Anne shot back, forgetting all her diplomacy and propriety, forgetting her standing in the town, forgetting her politeness, forgetting that she was half climbing a man in a restaurant and the waiter had a fair point. Nothing mattered more than Ben.

But Ben was chuckling, his chest rumbling under her hands.

"Then use it!" one waiter said, before throwing up his hands and going back to his tasks.

Ben stood up from his seat, setting Anne's feet back gently on the floor though he kept her pressed against him. He kissed the top of her head and wrapped an arm around her shoulders. "Do you want me to drive you home?"

Anne looked up into his navy eyes, seeing the genuine question. Going home would be the sensible thing to do, the safe thing to do. They could talk again in the morning, perhaps go to breakfast, chat more about their feelings and mis-understandings, take it slow. Yes, that would be very sensible and smart.

Anne hated the thought of it.

"What I want," she enunciated clearly to Ben, summoning all her courage though her cheeks were blushing bright red, "is for you to take me upstairs to your room and show me how much you missed me. Repeatedly."

His eyes flashed, turning a darker hue, and before Anne knew it, she'd been thrown over his shoulder in a fireman's hold, and they were headed for the staircase that led to the pub's hotel rooms.

"Don't tell Vidya, but that dress is going to be on the floor in less than thirty seconds," Ben said, and Anne wriggled in delight.

She watched from her upside-down position, the heavy wooden stairs and banisters moving beneath her, until they were in a small hallway of doors. Ben approached one, and dipping a hand into his pocket to retrieve a key in a way that made his shoulder muscles ripple wonderfully where they were pressed against Anne's stomach, he unlocked the door and let them in.

If she expected any hesitation, any awkwardness to their situation, there was none. Ben was on her like a sailor just returned home from a long voyage at sea, hands demanding and covetous, trying to touch every inch of her at once, and Anne was no less greedy. As promised her dress was instantly on the floor, and his navy sweater and dark, smart jeans immediately followed, the fly button pinging off and rolling across the floorboards in their haste.

Then they were stumbling toward the bed, their sounds

noisy and desperate. In all their time together before, sometimes passionate, sometimes tender, Anne couldn't remember
them ever being so frantic for each other.

"Eight fucking years," Ben groaned as he dragged his mouth
down her body.

"I know," Anne gasped, arching into his touch, pressing
against his strength, delighted when he pressed back, letting
her feel more of him, always wanting more.

The window panes rattled a little in their wooden frame
with the harsh winds outside, and a cold draft blew across the
room, but it meant nothing to the busy occupants in the bed;
the long length of Ben covered her like a weighted blanket,
and Anne felt nothing but overwhelming pleasure and heat.

It was after round two—or was it round three?—that they
finally caught their breath and began to talk again.

Lounging in the rumpled bed, lying on Ben's chest, Anne
took in the room—small but cozy, decorated in soft greens
and yellows. At some point Ben had turned on the small
shaded lamps on either size of the bed, giving everything a
gentle glow.

"So, when did you really stop hating me?" Anne asked.
She wanted to know everything, every thought that had gone
through his head since he arrived with his inscrutable expres-
sions, when she could only guess at what he was thinking and
feeling.

Ben sighed and scrubbed a hand through his hair, looking
at the ceiling. His other stroked gently up and down her back.

"I didn't *hate* you, not really, but when did I stop being
pissed and hurt and unfair to you? I don't know, a lot of things

triggered it. That evening at the Prince of Wales with your father was a big piece. It made me realize there were things in your background that put our breakup in a different light. Hearing that your mother had died. And dating Sabrina, actually." He chuckled. "That certainly helped. I mean, she was a sweet girl, but for the first time I felt some empathy for what it must have been like for you, being with me, always assuming everything would work out magically. She never once practiced her lines, though that director kept telling her the Juliet part was on the line."

Poor Sabrina, Anne thought.

"Anyway," Ben continued, "once I stopped being an idiot, I realized I was as in love with you now as I was back then. I should have pursued you the second fate threw me in your path again, and I was so mad at myself that I spent all that time instead pushing you away and getting involved with Sabrina. I was trying to figure out how to fix it all when that Harbringer asshole came on the scene."

"So you *were* jealous of him, that night of the triple date!"

Ben huffed, but when Anne prodded him in the ribs he admitted that was pretty much the case. He rolled to his side, taking her with him so that they were eye to eye, and playfully wedged her hands between them so she couldn't keep poking him.

"What did you think of me, seeing me again?" he asked curiously. "I knew you felt awkward . . ."

"Awkward, embarrassed, self-conscious, jealous, and desperately wanting to throw myself into your arms," Anne recited, summing it all up as concisely as possible.

"Really?" Ben said, pulling her even closer. Anne tried not to wriggle, want for him already rising within her again, but she also wanted to finish this conversation. "You mean that night if I'd said, 'Hey, I know it's been eight years but want to try again,' you would have said yes?"

Anne nodded emphatically and Ben's face settled into unhappy lines. "Then I really could have saved us all this trouble and misery."

"Ben," Anne soothed, tracing her fingers over his brow and mouth, trying to relax his unhappy expression. "We can't go in circles of should have done, could have done. Maybe I shouldn't have let my fears get the better of me and broken up with you, but it gave us a both an opportunity to grow up and figure our lives out. Maybe you should have talked to me on that first night, but we were both embarrassed and overwhelmed and needed to work through things. So maybe, really, this is everything working out for the best."

He nodded and relaxed back into the pillows again. "The breakup was a kick in the head, but it got a fire under my ass to prove myself," he conceded, "and I'm glad of that, that I have something to show for myself. I might not have liked how I turned out otherwise."

"One more question," Anne said, but at that moment Ben's stomach gave a loud grumble between them and sent her into fits of laughter.

"I've been working up an appetite!" he defended himself. "C'mon, then." With a groan he rolled off the mattress to his feet, and Anne was treated to that wonderful familiar view until he slipped his boxers and a T-shirt back on.

"Where are you going? It's"—she craned her head to look at the bedside clock—"past two in the morning. Everything is closed."

"We are literally sleeping in a pub. There's a kitchen right downstairs, and I'm going to raid it."

"We can't do that!" Anne protested, but Ben had already pulled her out of bed and slipped his sweater over her head. Like the sweatshirt he'd dressed her in after the accident at Kellynch, the sweater went nearly down to her knees and covered her respectably like a dress.

"I'll tell them when I check out and they can put it on my bill. Let's go."

Anne let herself be pulled along. Although she loved the mature and responsible Ben, it was nice that his irrepressible devil-may-care attitude was still in there as well.

Hand in hand, they crept quietly down the stairs and into the empty dining room. The double pair of swinging doors led them to the kitchen, where industrial-sized fridges, stoves, and counters lined the perimeter of the room. A rough wood-topped island with three high stools stood in the center.

Ben began opening each of the fridges, poking his head in before moving on to the next one.

Anne sat at the island and indulged herself in admiring his tall, graceful form as he moved about.

"Aha!" he exclaimed in triumph, pulling back from the last fridge with a covered plate in hand. He caught Anne's gaze and blushed and grinned, ducking his head at her open appraisal. "Leftovers from the party," he explained, uncovering the plate and placing it between them.

It turned out Anne really was hungry, and so they both helped themselves to the plate in companionable silence. Ben got up at one point and found a half-empty bottle of apple cider and poured them both a glass.

Half-dressed in a darkened pub kitchen, eating leftover canapés and warm, flat cider, with Ben's dark navy eyes on her and a smile on his face, she thought she'd never enjoyed a meal more.

"So, you had one more question," Ben prompted her, and she had to cast her mind back to remember what it was.

"Right. I sent you an email once, after we'd broken up but years ago. You never answered it."

Ben nodded, looking down at the plate.

"I wanted to. I went to answer it half a dozen times. I had vague fantasies that you wanted me back. But then I googled you, and this photo came up from a local paper. It was at some gala at the theater, I think. You looked gorgeous, and you were on this guy's arm and I just . . . It suddenly occurred to me how monumentally egotistical it was, thinking you might still want me. For all I knew you were engaged and contacting me as a courtesy to let me know. I didn't want to hear it. And I never googled you again."

Anne thought back to galas she'd attended. Back when her mother was still trying to supply her with "appropriate" dates, there had been one or two that lasted awhile and acted as a plus one.

"I pictured you having this charmed life," Ben admitted quietly, "all these perfect guys from perfect families swanning around you, taking you for weekend getaways in New York and rides on their yachts, and charming your parents, who would approve of them completely. It was agony. Meanwhile I was sweating away on Bay Street, falling asleep at my desk most nights, trying to just hammer out a career for myself, a good one that would show you that . . . Well. I never pictured that you were sweating it out over your career just like me, or that you'd lose a family member, or be treated badly. I never thought you might be lonely like me, or missing me."

"I was all of those things," Anne said quietly, and Ben leaned across the island and kissed her softly in response.

"What will the colonel and Jenny think?" Anne murmured when they pulled apart.

Ben's face instantly slid into a smile. "They'll be absolutely delighted. They practically want to adopt you. And they want me to settle down. This will be Christmas come early for them. They might be a bit overbearing at first . . . You do like them, don't you?"

"I adore them, they're lovely," Anne reassured him, and his smile only grew.

They tidied up their impromptu meal and crept back up the stairs.

"Will your father and sister have a problem with me?" Ben asked as they entered their room. *Will it be like last time? Will you be persuaded to give me up again?* was unspoken in the air.

"I don't listen to outside opinions anymore. I've grown up these past eight years, too, you know, and I trust in my own judgment now. They're my family, I love them, but I don't give a flying fuck what they think," she said, with all the ferocity she could muster, and saw the relief on his face.

"Anne Elliot swearing," he teased. "Must be an eclipse." And he tackled her down to the bed again.

Twenty-Seven

Anne woke at her usual early hour the next morning, deliciously warm and deliciously sore in all the best ways, Ben snoring softly in her ear. She went back to sleep.

At around eleven they were finally up and out the door. Getting dressed had been a prolonged process as every time Anne tried to put a garment on, Ben peeled it right off of her again, with kisses effectively weakening her objections, but finally they were both fully clothed. Vidya's masterpiece dress was rather wrinkled, and definitely had that walk-of-shame vibe to it, so Ben drove them the short distance to Anne's office, where she kept a pair of yoga pants, sneakers, and a sweater stashed in her gym bag. While she was changing Ben read out loud the emails on her desktop.

"'As it has come to the board's attention that Mr. Anthony

Harbringer of Harbringer Developments was engaging in fraudulent business practices, we have declined his offer of purchase with the strongest possible reprobation . . . '"

"Meaning they know this whole debacle will be town gossip, and they want to look righteous and innocent, instead of greedy and outmaneuvered by a goose and an old battlefield," Anne interjected, stripping off her dress.

Ben snorted in response before continuing. "'Therefore, the amended plan for the outdoor theater in partnership with Kellynch Winery, the Niagara-on-the-Lake Historical Society, and with an investment from Wentworth, Callahan and Liu, will move forward.'"

"A few more partners than we originally planned, but I guess it takes a village." Anne laughed.

Ben swiveled around in her desk chair to face her and gave a wolf whistle as she pulled her yoga pants on. Then he frowned. "Why is this email written like they're informing *you* what happened? Weren't you the one telling them?"

Anne rolled her eyes and ducked her head into her sweater. "Now that the historical society is involved, they'll have to involve more people, so they will have cc'd the entire town council."

Ben swiveled back around to check the email and confirmed that was the case. "So, you're not going to get credit for anything."

"Don't care," Anne said genuinely. "The project's going ahead and we'll have our brand-new theater. Eyes on the prize, Wentworth." She bent over to tie her laces.

"My eyes *are* on the prize," he growled, eyeing her form.

"What else is in my inbox?" She laughed.

He swiveled around again. "An email from Emmie. One line. 'We should name it Goose Theatre.'"

Anne and Ben both burst into laughter.

B en insisted on driving them to Kellynch afterward, stating that he, too, needed a change of clothes, and that the colonel and Jenny would wonder at him staying out all night, despite him sending a text. Anne had no desire to go to her own home, and though she might have chosen to announce their relationship to Ben's aunt and uncle while she wasn't freshly sexed up and wearing semiclean gym clothes, it was perhaps better to get everything out in the open now. Gossip traveled fast in this town (she could already hear Vidya shrieking in her head with excitement, and made a mental note to call her as soon as possible), and anyone outside the Harp this morning would have seen her leave with Ben. She wasn't downplaying what they were to each other for another minute.

On the way Anne asked about Ben's Toronto office and condo. Two hours' distance, either by car or by train, wasn't far, but he'd be expected to return eventually, right? Ben took one hand off the steering wheel to reach for her hand.

"We'll make it work. Most people downtown are hybrid after the pandemic anyway. I do have to travel sometimes, but the rest of the time I can alternate between time in the office and working remote. You forget I'm my own boss, and I'm very easy on myself as an employee."

Anne laughed at his corny joke—she'd missed those—but had to clarify, "You don't mind spending the majority of your time here in Niagara? It's hardly downtown Toronto."

Ben shrugged. "You're here, my aunt and uncle are here.

It's a beautiful place, and it's your home." He looked over at her worriedly. "Why? Am I crowding you? Do you need space or to go slower?"

"No to space, and no to going slow," Anne reassured him, as they rounded the long driveway to Kellynch.

"Good. Because I want to be where you are, and I'm pretty sure this town can't do without you. They might tar and feather me along with Harbringer if I tried to take you away. Although . . ." he said thoughtfully, "it would be nice to leave *occasionally*. When was the last time you took a vacation?"

"I can't even remember," Anne said truthfully. Suddenly nothing sounded better than a few weeks away with Ben and no responsibilities. She could love the town and still take time for herself.

They pulled around to the back of the house just as the colonel stepped out onto the patio bundled up in what her father would have called an "old-man cardigan," a steaming cup of coffee in hand.

He appraised them as they got out of the car, uncharacteristically silent. As they stepped onto the patio, Ben reached back and took Anne's hand in his.

The colonel's shoulders instantly relaxed, and he rolled his eyes at them. "Thank god, finally!"

"What?" Ben squawked, his voice going up an octave. "What do you mean *finally*?"

"Jenny!" the colonel hollered, sticking his head through the open back door into the house. "They're together!"

"Finally!" they heard her faintly call back. The colonel chuckled and closed the door again.

"What do you mean *finally*?" Ben demanded once more.

"You finally put it back together. Your aunt and I had a bet going when you'd figure things out. I said early spring. She has less faith in you; she said late summer."

"You knew? This whole time you knew?" Anne asked.

"Not the whole time, but by the time we went to that town hall, yeah." He smiled pityingly at them both. "The only thing more obvious than two people looking at each other is two people determined *not* to look at each other. Even if I hadn't remembered about Ben's old university girlfriend, the one who lived in Niagara, I'm pretty sure I would've figured it out that you two had a history that was itching to make itself present."

"Why didn't you say something?" Ben grumbled.

"Interfere with you? Mr. Proud, Stubborn, and Silent? If I'd said anything you would have doubled down on whatever nonsense you had in your head. Had to let you work it out yourselves. Both of you being so clever with your negotiations and your business talk, drawing out this whole purchase process"—he scoffed—"missing the forest for the trees." He shook his head at them. "Young people. Now, c'mon inside, you're late for breakfast but we'll turn it into brunch."

Ben walked into the house, but the colonel tapped Anne's arm and drew her aside for a moment.

"It didn't take you until town hall to figure it out, did it?" she said.

"Smart girl," replied the colonel. "No, I had my suspicions before then. Town hall is when Jenny figured it out and we pooled our observations."

"When did you know, then?" Anne asked.

He turned to her with a twinkle in his eyes, eyes so much like Ben's. "When you fainted the night we met." He winked at her surprised expression. "I'm a military man, Anne. I'm trained to observe. When you came round, you called me

'Colonel.' I hadn't given you my rank yet or told you I was military. How did you know I was a colonel? I hadn't forgotten Ben's ex-girlfriend lived in Niagara, the one he was so devastated about, though he would hardly admit it. He never did share information easily."

"He's getting a lot better at it," Anne said truthfully, thinking about his letter and how much they had discussed last night and this morning.

"Glad to hear it," said the colonel.

"You're . . . happy that we're together, right?" Anne asked. The colonel had seemed happy—happy and relieved—but it occurred to Anne that having broken Ben's heart once before, it was possible she was out here for the shovel talk.

The colonel grinned at her nervous expression. "Yes, I'm very happy for you both. I'm not holding the past against you, if that's what you're worried about. When Ben told me you'd broken up, I knew I was only getting one side of the story— and that side told from all the distortion of someone in pain."

He sighed and leaned against the patio railing. "We did our best to give Ben some kind of a home, but he grew up with a whole lot of time alone, and rootless. Now that I've met you, I can see you had a whole lot of the opposite, didn't you? Too many roots with a stranglehold on you. Ben couldn't see where you were coming from. I imagine you couldn't see where he was coming from either."

"I did," Anne said, "but only after we'd broken up. Afterward, I understood what I had done."

"What you did to each other, sweetheart," he gently corrected her. "I imagine it was just as much of a shock to you how completely he disappeared from your life. This town and your family, the annual traditions—how long has that damn

Pumpkin Festival been going on now?—things don't get up and leave and never look back. Ben couldn't understand why you needed a planned future, and you couldn't understand why he just wanted to grab you and run. I guess what I'm trying to say is, if you want the advice of an old man—both of you, try not to hold on to your pasts this time, just hold on to each other. You'll be all right." He gave her a one-armed hug, paternal and comforting. "Now, come inside and eat some damn bacon."

They stepped into the warmth and light of the kitchen, where Jenny was buttering up toast at the stove and Ben was setting the table. He came over and gave Anne a firm kiss, large hands cupping her face, both of them smiling, until the sound of the kettle whistling broke them apart.

It wasn't how Anne would have pictured it at twenty-four, being at Kellynch, happy and in love with Ben. But then nothing was much like she pictured the future would be, eight years ago. Those dreams had faded, and then at some point she'd forgotten to picture a future for herself at all.

However, as she sat at the table, being served hot coffee and eggs, telling the colonel and Jenny about the party last night, how the theater project would change going forward, listening to them laugh about Emmie's woebegone suitor, and feeling Ben's arm firmly around the back of her chair, the present seemed full and good and happy, and the future was a shimmering, tantalizing thing again.

Epilogue

A year and a bit later

And now we'll close out the afternoon with 'Jingle Bell Rock'! Everybody can sing along!"

The loudspeakers in their protective winter coverings vibrated with the opening notes of the familiar holiday tune, as families, snug in their winter gear and holding disposable festive cups of hot chocolate, belted along.

Goose Theatre—Anne still couldn't believe they'd gone with that name—had had its first successful run this past autumn, exactly one year since they started the project. The bog had been drained and Professor Davis and his volunteer crew had been joyfully excavating for some time now. They never seemed to turn up more than musket balls or the occasional shoe buckle, but they were thrilled, and the family-friendly programming of Goose Theatre meant there were always lots of kids who loved to climb down into the old trenches with Professor Davis and hear tales about the wars. The intention was to close the theater in November, but the unseasonably dry spell through early December had persuaded them to keep it open a little longer and hold some holiday singalongs, along with a few food booths serving hot chocolate, hot apple cider, and gingerbread cookies.

Anne looked around at the small but packed area, the joyful looks on the faces of the audience, and felt pride. Who would have thought that something that caused such strife a year ago would turn out so well?

"Anne! I didn't know you were coming today." It was Professor Davis, dressed in a historically accurate nineteenth-century Santa costume, a smile on his face and a shiny new wedding band from his August wedding to Paul on his finger.

"I wasn't planning to," Anne replied, "but I couldn't resist. It's the last performance until we shut down for the holidays, and then we won't see Goose Theatre again until the spring."

"You and Ben planning to go traveling again, take advantage of the offseason?" he asked. "Paul says January is the worst time to travel; he has statistics on it."

"I bet he does," Anne replied. "And yes, we'll be traveling, just haven't decided where we're going yet."

Ben had made good on the promise he'd given her the morning after their reunion, to whisk her away on vacation. They'd both taken time off work and spent August hiking in New Zealand, as far away from both Toronto and Niagara as they could get. It was several glorious weeks of breathtaking scenery, cozy pubs and inns, and some nights just spent under the stars, with Ben's old, patched camping tent and a shared sleeping bag their only accommodations. They'd come home in time to prep for the opening of Goose Theatre, with wonderful memories from that trip.

"Speaking of traveling, I'd better get going. I've got dinner to prep." She bade goodbye to Professor Davis and headed to her car, where she immediately turned the heater on full blast. There might not be snow yet, but it was still freezing cold. She checked her phone and saw a message from Ben, confirming he'd arrived home from Toronto and was Officially off work for the holidays! ☺ XOXO. Grinning, Anne pulled out of the parking lot.

That real estate agent Anne had contacted, back when she first made plans to move out of her family's King Street house, had gotten a much bigger commission than she'd expected. Anne and Ben had quickly decided to move in together, and rather than the little two-bedroom condo she'd been tasked to find, instead a beautiful Tudor-style cottage—just down the road from Kellynch—was their joint purchase. Ben kept a small studio in the city for times he needed to be near the office, and Anne, flexing her new freedom, quickly began to enjoy unexpectedly joining him for a few days at a time in Toronto. But mostly they loved their new home and spent the majority of their time in it.

When Anne pulled into the driveway, she saw Ben's SUV already parked in the garage, and what looked like half of what must be a truly monstrous fir tree sticking its top out a back window.

What the . . . ?

"Ben?" Anne called, stepping in the front door. The house was warm and smelled like cloves and cinnamon. He must have already started cooking.

"Kitchen!" he called back.

Anne dropped her bags and heavy down coat and went to find him whistling merrily to himself as he prepped vegetables on the counter.

"Sweetheart," she started playfully, hugging him around his middle. "Why is there a giant Christmas tree sticking out of your car?"

"That seems self-explanatory," he replied, kissing her hello. "It's Christmas in a few days; we said we needed a tree. I know we both got busy with work, so I stopped to get one on the way home. We can't have dinner guests in December and no tree."

"Yes, that would be truly faulty logic," Anne agreed, laughing. "But why is it so tall?"

"It's not that tall," Ben said, his brow doing that adorable furrow.

"And for people who are not six feet and over?" Anne asked, reaching up to smooth that furrow away, and he laughed. Though Anne wasn't a short woman, it had taken a few weeks of living together, putting up bookshelves in the living room, hanging pots and pans in the kitchen and a mirror in the bathroom, before she discovered that tall men had a natural tendency to arrange their living spaces at their own eye level and for their own height, sometimes forgetting the limitations of their smaller companions. It was now an ongoing joke between them.

"The tree might be a bit tall," he conceded. "I'll tell Uncle Grant to bring one of his saws with him tonight. I'll lop off a few inches."

"Six inches," Anne amended, and then pulled him down for another kiss, because he'd been gone since yesterday morning and she had already been missing him.

"When do the guests arrive?" he asked after several minutes of kissing, and by his wandering hands Anne knew what he was hoping they'd have time for.

"Not for several hours, but I insist we get the food into the oven before you seduce me. Dinner prep is on a schedule."

"Yes, ma'am," he said huskily, and with one last lingering kiss, he returned to his task.

It would be their first Christmas together in their new home, and it filled Anne with inordinate joy to see Ben, working away with his sleeves rolled up on his green sweater, completely at ease in their kitchen, chatting about inconsequential domestic things with her, like dinner guests and Christmas trees, their whole future together deliciously and unhurriedly unfurling at their feet, winter holidays, vacation plans, grocery lists, and squabbles over who used the last of the toothpaste. It made her deliriously happy.

"What?" Ben asked curiously, noting Anne's sappy expression. His hands were occupied with the food, and Anne took advantage to pull him down by the shoulders and kiss him again, laughing as he twisted comically to keep his hands away from her pristine white sweater while still reaching her lips.

"Nothing," she replied, "I'm just really happy."

He grinned, pride and accomplishment on his face like he'd achieved something miraculous. No matter how often she told him she was happy, he always responded that way.

"You're mangling that charcuterie board. Let me take over," Anne said, trying to break the moment before he really did drag her to bed. He hip checked her and muttered something that sounded suspiciously like "bossy" under his breath, but acquiesced with a laugh.

"So who's coming tonight again?" he asked, as Anne rolled up her sleeves and he washed his hands in the sink.

"Your aunt and uncle, obviously, Davis and Paul, Vidya, Emmie is coming, and I don't know where she and Peter are at with their on-off thing, but if they're currently *on* then he'll be here too." She'd extended an invitation to her father and Liz, but as expected, both declined, too busy with other engagements. Anne would have liked to think that her family had learned from her departure, had changed, or taken better care of their affairs now that there was no Anne to curtail them, but that would be a false hope. Liz and her father carried on as they had always done, with only the interference of Pereskin Jr. to keep them from depleting their resources to the point of bankruptcy. It didn't make them any wiser or more self-aware; it only meant that her father was now permanently banned from a growing number of drinking establishments in Niagara and Liz had had her driving license suspended for a second time. It hurt Anne's heart sometimes, but she wouldn't look back.

"Why don't we put on some Christmas music," she said, to shake it off. Ben kissed her shoulder and nuzzled her ear, no doubt knowing what dark cloud had passed through her mind. Only when she relaxed back into him, peaceful and happy again, did he move away.

"My phone is dead. Can I use yours for music?"

"Sure," Anne called, "it's in my bag at the front door."

There were several long moments of silence, but instead of the faint refrain of Christmas music, it was Ben's voice she heard as he returned to the kitchen.

"Annie, what's this?"

Her iPhone was in his hand, the music app open, and there at the top was "Anne's heartbreak and perspective playlist." She'd called it up the other day, wanting to hear "Mine" again. The song meant something different to her now, something good.

"Oh, that's . . . uh . . ." Anne blushed and ducked her head.

"What?" Ben asked, bemused. "'Anne's heartbreak' . . . something you want to tell me?"

"Back over a year ago, when I found out you were going to be in town, I told Vidya about . . . well, about us. She decided I hadn't properly processed the breakup and that I needed emotional coaching via Taylor Swift songs. They're in a specific order and everything. And I'd like to mock her for it and say it didn't do anything for me, but . . . well, some of it was kinda prescient."

Ben gave a rueful smile, and now it was his turn to blush. "What?" Anne asked.

He gave a one-shouldered shrug like he wouldn't answer but then admitted, "Years ago, the first girl I went on a date with . . . after you, well, I told her a little about you, that I'd just had a breakup. She told me I clearly wasn't ready to date yet, and the next day sent me a link to a Taylor Swift song." His shoulders were practically up around his ears with embarrassment.

"Which one?" Anne asked with genuine curiosity.

"I think it was called 'Clean'? Yeah, I think the message was meant to be that I should contact her once I had you out of my system."

"Did you contact her again?"

"No. To be honest, I listened to the song and it just pissed me off because I told myself I had cleaned you out of my system and she was dead wrong." He paused and then admitted, "She was one hundred percent on the mark."

Anne laughed gently. "So you're still not *clean* of me?"

He smiled to see her smile, and then bent down for a kiss. "I never was, Anne Elliot, not for a second."

ACKNOWLEDGMENTS

The town of Niagara-on-the-Lake has always been a magical place, and it was a delight to make it the setting of my second novel, and thus have many excuses to visit and drink tea at the Prince of Wales Hotel. Also please note that while many real locations have been used, certain elements and all of the characters are fictional—for example the board of directors at the Shaw Theatre Festival—upon which the Elysium Theatre Festival is based—are probably actually wonderful people (though I've never met them) and not at all like the board of directors in this book.

With deep gratitude to my agent, Melissa—I can't believe my absolute luck that a blind query led me to signing with you.

With thanks to Kate Seaver—your rock-star editing prowess continues to teach me so much about writing; thanks to the entire Berkley team—Kristin Cipolla, Jessica Plummer, Amanda Maurer, and all the others—for your ongoing support, enthusiasm, and professional expertise.

Thanks to my sister for playing the '07 *Persuasion* film in our home ad nauseum.

And finally with full reverence to Jane Austen, for the obvious reasons.

Once Persuaded, Twice Shy

A Modern Reimagining of Persuasion

MELODIE EDWARDS

READERS GUIDE

DISCUSSION QUESTIONS

1. Jane Austen's final novel, *Persuasion* (1817), is essentially a story of two people yearning across an imagined barrier of hurt from their past. Getting them to acknowledge their regret, forgive, and relaunch their romantic love is the journey of the story. Do you know people who've reconnected with long-lost loves through social media or reunions and felt those past sparks? Or does your mind wander back to a high school or college sweetheart and wonder, *Why did we split?*

2. A small historic town like Niagara-on-the-Lake has its own culture. You might want to look up the wonderful artworks of Trisha Romance, who visited as an art student and made a career of painting the beautiful buildings and houses. Life there is lived in the present, with an ever-constant view of celebrating and preserving the military and pioneer past. How does this setting reinforce the themes for a modern reimagining of *Persuasion*?

3. Anne is highly educated and well raised and comes from an influential (in some ways privileged) family, and yet she

has matured into what many would call a "workhorse" in that she serves and prioritizes others while her own needs are ignored or suppressed. What "workhorse" people have you observed, or does the description fit you? What drives this behavior? Is it fear; excess energy; a need for praise; an arrogance of superior competence; a mangled self-worth? What is driving Anne?

4. Embarrassment. We all remember embarrassing moments that are riveted into our memories. Anne is also upended and loses her very practiced professional calm and competence when she and Ben are repeatedly tossed into close proximity by awkward social or business circumstances. For Anne it is particularly difficult to remain professional, but does Ben seem similarly affected by these encounters? What stance does he take and how does it change as the novel progresses?

5. What did you think of the comedic antics of Double-Oh-Goose as another means of testing Anne's composure, particularly at the Pumpkin Festival? What inner motivation do Ben's actions reveal during the chaos of this event, while on his hot date with Sabrina?

6. Vidya and Emmie share an earnest desire to help and support Anne. Why do they miss the mark? And why does Anne resist?

7. What prompts Anne to finally turn the focus on herself when prepping to hike the gorge? Is this the best approach to reviving her former self?

8. Anthony and Ben have much in common in terms of their professional presentation, but their personal conduct hints at differences. In the restaurant dinner scene, there is some competitive posturing. What do you learn about the character and the values of each man? How are they different?

9. Realizations and self-reflection glimmer slowly for Ben over the novel, but what prompts Ben's epiphany about being dumped by Anne eight years ago? Was her mother justified to be concerned about Ben as a life partner, or was she projecting too much, based on her own romantic choice? Most of us have given relationship advice, willingly or reluctantly, at some point. How did your advice pan out?

10. We always know that Anne yearns for Ben and has regrets, but at what point specifically did you feel sure Ben gains the confidence to try for Anne again? Can you track back through their scenes to see the pattern of his distant but stalwart offers of service and care?

11. Anne and Ben are on solid footing by the end of the novel, and probably always were, so did the eight years apart serve a useful purpose? For Ben? For Anne? Or was it all precious lost time, unnecessary yearning? How can people be romantically risk averse? How do they construct barriers and obstacles with feelings such as personal pride or fear of humiliation, rejection, or failure?

Author photo by Dahlia Katz

Melodie Edwards is the author of *Jane & Edward*. She has a BA from the University of Toronto and a master's degree from McMaster University and Syracuse University (2023), studied comedy writing at the Second City Training Centre, and works in communications.

VISIT MELODIE EDWARDS ONLINE

MelodieEdwards.com
Melodie_Edward
MelodieWritesEdwards

Ready to find
your next great read?

Let us help.

Visit prh.com/nextread